I0739149

Spiderworld

A story from the mind of
Orlando Oversight

Richard Bunning

Spiderworld
Richard Bunning

Ebook ISBN: 978-0-9942192-3-7
Paperback: ISBN: 978-0-9942192-4-4

Published by AIA Publishing
Available to order from most book shops and Internet book retailers throughout the Earth.

Line edited by Tahlia Newland
Proofread by Harmony Kent

Cover design by Velvet Wings Design

In memory of:
Boris
Charlotte
Shelob
Ungoliant
Arachne
Aragog
Mosag
Atlach-Nacha
And other famous arachnids.

Contents

PROLOGUE

I am Orlando Oversight, time-lord, space historian and
adventurer. This book was 'dictated' by me whilst I was in
what, probability theory dictates, is still an unmodified
time-worm of the Annun Universe. It is in this familiar
quantum dimension that God created at least three highly
successful and intelligent sentient species. These are the
bipedal Homo sapiens, the octopedal Aranian ungolian,
and the decapedal Cheetan trogaff. All three of these
creatures are of crucial importance in the history of the
'Milky Way'. The most profound difference to the sentient
qualities of these species is that the first is gonochoristic
while the latter two species are hermaphroditic. The latter
two are respectfully given the genderless third person
pronoun ze. The English 'it' is hardly appropriate to such
advanced sentient beings, neither is 'he' really suitable as a
gender neutral. Personally, I would no more call all humans
it, or even he for that matter. Irrelevant to the story, though
not to me, is the fact that I, Orlando, was born of male
gender. I originally heralded from the planet Gallifrey,

which used to be near the centre of what was then identified as the Kasterborous Constellation.

I no longer have a physical form. This makes it necessary for me to choose corporeal creatures as my 'actors'; my enablers of physical action. So in order for this book to come into being, I needed a scribe capable of taking down my dictation. The easily manipulated mind I selected as my medium was that contained by the body of Richard Bunning. He lived on planet Earth a short while before the dictated events in this book actually happened. That's right, before! And unless there is ever a most extraordinarily unlikely and precise reversal in time between the period of writing and the events dictated, then this will always remain true.

As a time-lord I can influence some minds, and virtually control others. In so doing I am able to make a physical mark in the material Multiverse, just as I would if I still had a physical form. My 'container of soul' disintegrated many eons ago, as measured in relation to timelines of this book, so that my tiny original quotient of physical stardust is long dispersed. Some time-lords learn the 'skill' of temporarily taking over other life-forms, by literally entering their shells. This then gives these time travellers a physical presence. I, Orlando, am disgusted by that zombic practice, as are a majority of others like me with which I am acquainted.

Humans that practice meditations and mind relaxing techniques are easy to manipulate, especially during their trance states. Writers, accustomed to falling into detached states of mind, make easy 'mediums'. I will leave it to you to decide whether to accept the idea that physical beings can be manipulated by external thought; by an un-measurable other presence. At the extremes, some beings can embrace mystical, external, influences that have no evident logic whatsoever, and some can accept nothing unless demonstrated by empirical experiment even when such experimentation is impossible to conduct.

I require this book to make a real impact on the future as it presently is set to be and as is dictated here. That doesn't mean it has to have an impact on you. Sufficient readers will inevitably take on enough of the message from this or other sources. The 'minds' that are required to absorb such stories are few in number. Few will always be plenty as, when carefully mediated, very few individuals are needed to act as a catalyst in re-spinning future outcomes. It is the quality of minds that matters. Ideas will be implanted sufficiently deeply and widely to ensure that enough strong individuals act appropriately. These individuals will ensure the right outcomes in the future present. Readers of fantasy may not believe in dragons, but those readers would be better prepared for a meeting with such creatures than those that never read. Just the suggestion that this or that might be fashioned can be preparation enough.

The most advanced of sentient creatures are quite unable to recognise when they are being directed unless there is a quantifiable outside stimulus; this is true even of time-lords. No being can really be sure that it ever exercises 'free will'. To the author, this book is uniquely his speculative fiction. Humm! See the logical contradiction. This being that I, a seemingly likely figment of imagination as far as most physical creatures are concerned, am to Richard merely a device of his plot, whilst I, myself, am sure that I exist as the progenitor of his written thoughts. I can no more prove to you that Richard isn't exercising free will, than he could prove that he is. There is a sort of tautological coincidence of opposite logics. As the two simply can't be reconciled, any excess of speculation may only cause stress. In order to 'enjoy this book', you must either accept my words or else decide that for the sake of progress you will humour me. You must exercise what we all understand as free will, whether it truly exists for you or not.

Time-lords now 'beyond' a physical form were 'flesh and blood' creatures before Creation freed us from the illusion that there is such a thing as incorruptible sequential time, and before we learnt to see beyond the dimension that contained our original physical lives. To enable this book, I 'exist' as an un-measurable presence in the writer's consciousness, as though I was a part of him. I am an 'independence of thought' and 'thought' is all I now am. Or else one might say, I'm only soul; I quite happily settle for that religiously charged word.

As I said earlier, some of us choose to temporarily 'inhabit' borrowed physical frames, but we can only time travel in a 'disembodied form'. Physics simply doesn't allow biological creatures to travel at will anywhere in time, even in manufactured 'time and relative dimension in space' machines. Actually, a **TARDIS** is truly a mythological device and probably always will be and always was. I can only be a time-lord because I don't exist as matter. Like the apparent fabric of time in which I travel, I can have no physical mass when I'm travelling. Accepting the idea that without physical force I've had Richard write a factual account of what is as yet to happen will be unbelievable, ridiculous even, to many mortals. I can't help that.

How does a mortal being go about being 'upgraded' to time-lord? The simple answer is that almost certainly one can't plan and dictate the process. Only Creation can give cause to such things. I believe that the honour was granted to me by the 'Almighty' simply because I was one of the last sentient survivors from a dying star system, part of an already biologically extinct race. I have never been truly aware of the Almighty, but merely of a voice of Creation, a voice that came to me in the bleak wilderness of my decaying planet. I had no choice but to listen as I 'died', before being 'reborn' with merely my soul.

I have a few more pedantic points that I can't resist mentioning ahead of the story. For example, how can one alter any being's expectation of the future without risking eventually affecting any number of other players' fortunes? On a micro scale one can't. But, actually, the cosmos is very resilient, possibly even resistant to rogue time-lords. At a macro level the cosmos won't be damaged one iota by the creatures in this story. The Multiverse is like an infinitely large sponge, absorbing all motion and constantly balancing one action against another.

Through my words, Richard—as a dictating machine—has a profound influence on the Cosmos. But apart from this, his life was almost entirely inconsequential. What is just one in a sea of millions writing science 'fiction'?

Anyway, that's enough introspection. The important point is that I posted these words to Richard's mind from the future, enabling him to know the following story before it happened. None of the events portrayed in this book took place until some period outside of Richard's life.

Time-lords are responsible for maintaining the balance of the cosmos, which like any mechanism needs occasional tweaking. We must ensure that diversity isn't threatened, by preventing any group of beings from becoming over dominant in any universe. An Aranian invasion of Earth was tolerated because balance required the future of man to be set on a different course.

Nothing is ever totally predictable. Perhaps the course of 'The Aranian Invasion of Earth' was highly likely from the outset, but I certainly didn't predict its full impact correctly. The nations of mankind were expected to stand together to defeat a common enemy. They didn't. Hindsight tells me that the fourth 'Yellowstone' explosion, though far smaller than any of the previous ones in this series of catastrophic seismic events, hit human civilisation harder than I realised. The explosion happened only an Earth century before The Aranian Slave Trade started in earnest. The planet-wide devastation had weakened the cohesive elements between human populations to such a degree that a united response didn't prove possible.

As a consequence, it became clear that I needed to implant information about the future, which specifically prepared a percentage of humans to cope with becoming a subservient species. Humans had been dominant creatures in their environment for so long that considerable psychological help was needed in order for them to cope with their new inferiority. Thus I chose this period, this now, in which to dictate this book. As events subsequently unfold, this history should help sufficient of Earth's humans gain the wherewithal to make progress as a species despite the trauma of 'invasion by spiders'.

Humans are too useful to The Annun Universe to be lost as an independent species. Thus, I strove to allow them to regain a measure of control over their destiny. To make that future possible, I acted through several characters in the story almost as strongly as I did through Richard Bunning.

What, you might ask, would happen if the actual characters in this book ever read about themselves and their own futures? Could that be enough to change time? Theoretically yes, but this would be infinitesimally unlikely. If someone close to this story, or mentioned in it, did read their future before it happened they would probably file away any subsequent 'déjà vu' as 'magic', or religious insight, or as what has become self-fulfilling prophecy. Even seeing prediction unfold, they would be extremely unlikely to change anything that would actually impact on their still further futures. We do little that is really uncharacteristic or illogical in any present moment. Nevertheless, we follow our expectations, and I must do what I can to avoid any clumsiness that might lead an individual to read their future before it becomes the present. Our precise memories are short. Though certainly, to read one's future and then watch it unfold precisely, might risk psychological stability.

Why was it necessary to allow another sentient species to make adjustments to human destiny?

Simply put, humans had grown so environmentally irresponsible that they had become a danger to their own survival and even to the existence of their home planet, and this hadn't changed significantly even after the setback to civilisation caused by the exploding Yellowstone Cauldron. Destroying a planet before its natural end is exactly the sort of event that badly disrupts cosmic stability. As often in such cases of intervention, I needed to accept that this universe required their decimation while I did just sufficient to guard against the annihilation of this irresponsible but potentially valuable species.

I decided to help this useful terraforming creature reach other areas of the Annun Universe that would eventually benefit from their colonisation. One could say that our intention was to allow the drastic depopulation of one large 'zoo' of humans, and open a series of distantly spread small zoos instead. Those humans that avoided the slavers were reduced to the developmental level of hunter gatherers, so temporarily decreasing to near zero their impact on Planet Earth.

Time-Lords shouldn't ever be in the business of wiping out advanced life-forms, but simply of culling when necessary. On balance, the development of sentience benefits from the preservation of all advanced species.

Why was this book written before its events took place? For the same reason as a lot of other what were then called 'speculative fictions' were introduced; namely, to plant expectations, warnings, into the human consciousness.

Why weren't 'ideas' introduced more forcefully and just immediately prior to their emerging need, when such mental preparation was more urgent? Because it was only briefly that man had the industrial capacity to spread ideas efficiently across his globe. Information technologies of the early twenty-first century ensured that enough copies of this and other histories were created well before the eruption of Yellowstone, so instilling subtle but deep 'expectations' into the human psyche.

Suitable, usually relatively unknown authors with enough desire for fame that they would publish any story, however farfetched, were easy to find. I, Orlando, through this book and others, laid some of the foundations of psychological preparation. Science 'fictions' would, not for the first time, help humans come to terms with their inevitable path.

1

UNGOLIANTIS

On a bright clear day, a Salvius Seven slave-ship breaks through the kármán layer and enters the atmosphere of the planet Ungoliantis. The eyes of the spider-like pilot of the spacecraft look down on zis home planet. The creature sees a view not very different from the one that greets visitors to Earth. Humans shouldn't be surprised. This planet in the Lush Star System supports oxygen breathing life-forms that were created out of an almost identical primordial soup. God may even have cast life on Earth and Ungoliantis from the same saucepan, ladling out biological rain across the planets' surfaces.

The bowl-shaped craft descends ever nearer to the ground, leaving the shapes of seas and continents behind in the narrowing horizons observed by the pilot's stalked eyes. Its view is now a vista of rugged mountains and broad undulating plains—then, as we drop ever lower, it becomes one of farmlands, forests and rivers. Soon we see towns and cities, then finally the ever approaching buildings of just one city, Cirithia.

The spacecraft hovers for a time, waiting for a landing spot at the Nuzkarflux Spaceport. We look through Aranian eyes onto a world some 1,600 petametres distant from Earth. The Salvius Seven has endured three Earth-years and four months of travel at a speed averaging very close to fifteen thousand million metres per second, having departed from the Aranian controlled

Kennedy Space Station. This may seem fast to the first generation of human readers of this book, but it is only fifty times the speed of light. Fighter spacecraft, built by civilisations on two of the Lush planets, can travel at twice this speed for short periods of time. However, even travelling at fifty times this speed, it takes 2000 Earth-years to cross our Milky Way Galaxy from one edge of its nebular disc to the other.

The less than busy co-pilot of the Salvius looks down into The Forest of Doonlau, as the craft slowly levels off a couple of hundred metres above the ground. Zis eyes are drawn towards one of the most familiar sights of competitive life, the chase between hunter and intended victim, the struggle to survive.

***

I, Orlando, now draw you away from the eight-legged co-pilot's view. I release you to soar like a bird away from the craft and now to hover over this natural drama. Your voyeuristic eyes take in one particular wretched struggle on this particular planetary body, within our Orion-Cygnus spiral arm of the Milky Way.

***

An Aranian hunter has already been trailing a human for an hour, and with the greater speed that the eight-legged hunter can sustain, it will very soon catch up with its quarry. Aranian have a higher top speed as well, so once they're close the chase is usually all but over.

The human sprints through the undergrowth following his pre-planned defensive line, praying that his strength-sapped muscles can keep him going for a few more vital minutes. The spider-like hunter pauses, looking into the water of a little stream running at an angle from the left across zis path. Ze sniffs to ascertain the direction of zis quarry. The creature's scent floats above the damp ground down zis side of the stream.

For a brief moment time seems to freeze, and then, we are inside the hunter's mind.

Hmm. Intelligent enough to avoid running straight across. Arrh yes! Here it paddled into the meandering flow. Would the stinking creature wade downstream, so roughly maintaining its direction, or go upstream,

10

attempting to outwit me? It would go upstream … or is there a double bluff? No, this is an intelligent yeng that recognises that I'm more so. Triple bluff. It will have indeed gone upstream, away from the possible sanctuary of the Tristian Marshes.

The hunter scuttles along the edge of the stream, peering at the ground, then stops and sniffs again.

Either wetbugs or that yeng has recently disturbed the sediment. It's the yeng, I know it. I'll go up the other bank until I smell its stink leave the water. Arrh! I smell it already. Just here it climbed out and headed back in its accustomed direction. It will be running fast now, not caring about making a noise. What can be heard above the bellow of that cursed spacecraft's engines hovering above me, anyway? Hassh, the yeng won't hear me either … Haagh, I do believe the craft is moving away at last.

I intend to make a feast of this crafty yeng, not just a gobbled dinner. This time I will resist consuming more than an appetiser of sweet offal.

As always at this stage of the hunt, the Aranian, while following zis prey at a brisk pace, imagined preparing zis quarry, skewering it on a spit and starting a fire. Ze reminds zimself not to rush the preparation, but carefully puncture every part of its flesh. If ze's as overeager as last time, then ze'll again fail to inject enough saliva to tenderise the tissues. The chase always results in flesh full of stress hormones, souring and toughening meat. Aranians are creatures that prefer meat 'sweetened' through being well hung for at least one low-light. When the meat is suitably ripe, a nice, slow, foil-covered roasting keeps it succulent. Older yeng are usually stewed, but judging by its speed over the ground, this one is still in its prime. Of course, any yeng is considered to taste especially good on the back of an enjoyable hunt.

Oh! How easy it is to get carried away by the smell of a fresh kill. I could so easily 'yeng-out', stuffing my face, failing to patiently wait to savour well tenderised, quality meats. As last time, I would end up leaving much of it to rot or be eaten by foulter and suvaran.

To make the very best of my good fortune, I should take the carcass home where I can cure meats to perfection.

Wait, wait, patience has its reward; wait until this yeng is ripe. For now, just enjoy its warm guts. What sweet anticipation. I love the scent of

***

The Aranian hunter looks incredibly similar to an Earth-spider; however, ze is thirty times bigger and five hundred times heavier than Theraphosa blondi, the Goliath Bird-eating Spider, of what mankind calls South America. My scaling is based on the decimal counting system. This raises another point, because Aranian use octinal units, which give corresponding multiplication factors of thirty-six and seven hundred and sixty-four. The reason spiders count in this way seems obvious enough, for why would primitive octopods have ever started numbering things in tens? They have four digits on the end of each of their eight limbs and ten of absolutely nothing.

Differences in counting are not difficult to translate, but it's not so easy to write language that differs so vastly from our own. Here, I'll sometimes give you a rough phonetic spelling of the Aranian word and sometimes a translation. The word for 'human' in Aranian, for example, sounds like yeng, but I translate the Aranian word for the Earth as the Waterball. The Aranian name for the Earth sounds something like Timartaeafok. That seems to me to be an overly ugly word for regular use.

The Aranian call their two suns, or lushs, Solush and Ralush. These words, and countless others, trigger one to think about linguistic connections with human languages, at least some of which must surely be generated by something greater than random chance.

To understand how such linguistic connections came about, one has to think like a time-lord rather than like a mortal sentient being. They understand that creatures in distant parts of this universe have all sorts of metaphysical and physical connections that stretch back through the eons to before any recorded histories.

The physical connections are obvious enough if one accepts the physics of independent strands of time, where time-worms occasionally cross each other's paths, or even double back on themselves. These movements have the dual effect of splitting or cutting and displacing segments of logically progressing time. The deeper connections between widely dispersed creatures that may not have passed through the same spaces in time are far harder to explain.

I believe that distant places, and possibly even different universes, are metaphysically connected, binding every corner of 'Space' together irrespective of the activities of time-worms. This metaphysical connectivity allows time-lords to move between different physical strands, worms, of time. I decide to move through universes and, hence, I move. My wanderings through 'time' are generated by similarly shallow subliminal thoughts as those required by organic creatures to move limbs. I don't truly understand the mechanism of my movement any better than do simple creatures such as the hunter and zis desperate prey.

***

The spider charges on, rapidly eating up the ground between zim and the fleeing man. This eight-legged 'monster' maintains a steady speed of about twenty kilometres an hour, despite the fact that zis two front limbs support a gun. The weapon is the size and weight of an average man's leg—at least fifteen kilograms—an inconsequential weight to an Aranian. Across its back ze wears a series of panniers stuffed with hunting equipment, which are tied to straps around zis three middle 'hip' joints. The main body of the spider is over two metres long, and when ze stands on zis hind legs ze towers over a tall man.

Jack arrives, panting, at the site of a pit he dug months ago in anticipation of just such a threat. He swiftly lifts the far corner of the timber and dirt cover, and slips underneath. He crouches in the void's centre, and lifts a long, strong stake so that it points up between the timbers of the roof. The spider crashes through the undergrowth, charging ever closer. Jack says a quick prayer, begging the hunter to come directly over his trap. A patch of sharp brambles causes the spider to be partially distracted as ze stretches over onto what ze assumes to be firm ground beyond. The trap is sprung.

The roof above Jack sags, and he drives the spear point up into the underbelly of the spider. A flood of stinking black blood cascades down, spurting while he drives and twists the spear further into the spider's guts. The monster squeals like a tortured 'earth-pig' and thrashes its legs down through the timber. The roof sags further, then half collapses, and the wooden spear shaft flings Jack into the hard soil wall. The spider gives an almighty groan as zis impalement continues. Zis own weight adds to that of the roof driving the stake the rest of the way through zis abdomen. After one long wheezed exhale and the stink and whistle of escaping gas, the creature appears to have died.

Jack leans back against the side of the pit, trembling and fighting for breath. The creature's oxygen starved muscles relax and zis gun tumbles down into the pit, coming to rest at Jack's feet. He stares up, shocked, at what he's achieved, wondering how such a powerful creature died so quickly, once impaled. Is the creature faking death, awaiting a final pounce when Jack's guard drops? To be sure that he's won the day, Jack pulls free his machete then climbs up the heaped debris and slashes it across the creature's exposed throat. He is greeted with no movement other than a further deluge of black blood.

Before clambering out, Jack lifts the gun, and points it into the spider's belly. He pulls and pulls on the trigger whilst systematically studying every detail of its visible mechanisms, yet fails to make it fire. Eventually, he flings the gun down in frustration, deciding that, as far as he is concerned, it is nothing but scrap metal.

2

BOKLUNG AND HOSK

You already know a little about the dominant species of Ungoliantis, the Aranians, or spiders as the yeng know them. Boklung is an important Aranian, the owner of several businesses with operations in general agriculture, horticulture and specialist yeng breeding. Hosk is of a different species. Ze is a ten-limbed creature that vaguely resembles a giant Earth woodlouse. Ze certainly has more of a likeness to an Aranian than ze has a yeng, even if only for having closer to the same number of appendages.

***

Boklung is in the dining room of zis home talking to the Cheetan Ambassador to the city-state of Cirithia, Huigark Hosk. Boklung likes to mix business and pleasure, believing that entertaining at home is a good way of extending one's business influence.

"I will start by telling you a little about my day, and see where my story leads us, if that is okay with you, Huigark."

Hosk tilts zis head. "Go ahead, my hearing is attuned."

"Usually, I buy bulk shipments of yeng straight from the shippers, but I do enjoy visiting the regular livestock market. As much as anything, I go to meet old friends. While there, I was talked into purchasing a very good looking bitch yeng. They are easier to handle than even the male castrates, being less aggressive and less likely to stray. I also prefer the shape of them, usually more pleasantly rounded, perhaps even in some very subtle way, more like us. It's strange that these creatures have two biological forms, and only one can give birth; but that is the case amongst all higher Waterball species. Clearly this is a less robust reproductive system than seems sensible. When any of their species are down to a single sex, even though there might still be multiple individuals, they are already biologically extinct."

Hosk nods while Boklung continues. "My purchase was on the spur of the moment, a whimsical choice based on nothing more than the creature's beautiful conformation. But what I really need is a top breeding male, as I am still striving to replace the one that called itself Jack. It escaped into the bush some time ago. I had to report the fact to the authorities because the loss of a breeding male is a notifiable offence. Did you know that we have such exacting laws, Ambassador?"

The Cheetan shakes zis head. "You have so many rules governing your world, Boklung. I have not yet found the time to try to understand ones so obscure. We rely much more heavily on the single word, obey."

Hosk prepares for a new flood of words from Boklung. Zis long body collapses onto the floor, ten rigid legs twisting out sideways, and zis body muscles relax, causing a degree of spreading of zis considerable girth.

"The powers that be prefer to avoid the possibility of yeng reproducing in the wild. So they threatened to take away my Breeder's Licence. I was not prepared to see that happen; and luckily a quick word with my cousin and your acquaintance, in our government, Afric Nadarchis, sorted my little problem out. I have a huge investment in my programme, and couldn't risk losing the income it generates. There is nothing quite so tiresome as dealing with state apparatchiks, and I pity the entrepreneur that lacks the contacts to get around them. Unfortunately, I can't so easily deal with the potentially more serious legal aspects of the case, but at least I'm able to run my business without any really detrimental effects in the meantime."

Hosk fixes Boklung with a penetrating, almost mesmerising stare. Ze looks settled, as if for a long sleep-inducing lecture. Hosk is well aware from past meetings that Boklung is fond of hearing zimself speak.

"Anyway Ambassador, I've been thinking about the particular consequences of your planet's plans to start properly administered yeng breeding programmes. I think there is perfect sense in you doing so. Not surprisingly, there's some resistance to the prospect of aiding your growing independence from our slave trade. After all, our economy has benefited hugely from the steady export of yeng into Trogaffin. Times change though, and nowadays we see far greater benefit in more balanced trade relations. Let's be honest, it exercises minds when you threaten to limit your exports of rare-earths if we don't better share our economic resources in return. I am sure we can work out a deal that is to our personal, our mutual, benefit as well as that of both planets."

"Grace, come here ..." Boklung calls to the female yeng who stands quietly at the side of the room, naked apart from a wrap of woven material around her hips. "I need a massage, and I'm sure my guest does. Get that organised."

"Yes, Zir, and some snacks if you wish?"

"Yes, yes. Hurry along now." Boklung waves a forelimb as a signal of dismissal and Grace scurries away.

"Splendid idea, Boklung. My favourite use of yeng; well, apart from as a roast, you understand. Kaaagh! But not just now, as I really haven't long. I'll save my massage for the hotel this low-light. The masseurs there are well trained in the therapeutic arts."

"Just me then, Grace!" Boklung shouts after the yeng. "Yes, Ambassador, it takes a lot to beat a good rub-down, especially of the under parts. Hggaaah. Anyway, back to business. I'll have some breeding guidebooks modified and translated. Naturally, I'll offer expert consultation on a long-term basis. Our personal businesses should grow exponentially, as we guide our respective governments. We must be particularly careful to make private arrangements to ensure that, even if interplanetary trade catastrophically fails, neither of us is left short of funds."

"You rub my legs and I will rub yours, Boklung. I am sure we see eyes to eyes on this."

Boklung opens wide zis two rows of breathing spiracles that run the length of zis body, and takes a huge contented breath. "I take it that we have a deal. Shake limbs on it ..."

The creatures grasp a pair of each other's 'legs' and grunt.

"Now that we have agreed to cover our backsides," Boklung continues, "let me talk a bit more openly about my private interests and concerns. As I have said, certain officials are pursuing legal sanctions against me for failing to secure a breeding buck. The probability is high that the creature in question has perished. Whatever its fate, I absolutely don't agree that an extra tribe or two of breeding wild yeng is undesirable. Hunting them, which incidentally keeps their population down very efficiently, is the best sport bar none. Their natural cunning makes them such an entertaining quarry. I must take you hunting sometime soon, Ambassador."

Hosk's eyes light up. "I will indeed look forward to that. There's nothing I enjoy more than blood sports. If only the thinner atmosphere of my planet did not prevent us using them as quarry. Imagine how dull the chase would be with their lungs collapsing before they had crawled more than a short kilometre.

"I'll enjoy reading all the information you are able to provide about pedigree yeng breeding programmes, and I am very excited about working with you. Anyway, much as I like listening, I must be getting along. Thank you very much for your usual hospitality ... until next time, quite possibly as soon as tomorrow? Take care my friend, and I extend my forelimbs to our mutual prosperity."

After the Cheetan's departure, Boklung ruminates while awaiting zis masseuse.

It's been a tough day. I'm glad to see the back of the Cheetan. It's not easy to trust that species. Things were so much more straightforward when we were enemies, pure and simple. However, our civilisations have moved on, and I pray that physical conflicts between our species really are a thing of the past. If we continue our long history of intermittent warfare, eventually one or both of our planets will likely be destroyed. The development of mutually needed trade is our protection. It will make our previously isolated infrastructures more interdependent, and so will make conflicts less aggressive and more eagerly solved.

I think that Hosk will go along with everything, even if only out of self-interest. However, I must strive to secure a deal that ze can't worm zis way out of if the figures start to seem less favourable to zim. Despite my positive thoughts, I trust some of my yeng slaves more than I do my 'friend' Huigark Hosk. And look how badly trusting slaves can turn out. I'm sure that both our species will always put our own planets' vital needs way before the strongest of inter-planetary relationships, but I must do all I can within threatening our friendship to tie zim in to our deals.

Is it worth my while trying to keep some influence over slaves once they are traded away? Since trust comes easier on the back of good intelligence, my gut feeling, coupled with my desire to keep control, says yes. Hggh ... But how to achieve it? Keep the relatives of exported yeng hostage to their continuing obedience? Yes; to refine that, I could export mainly breeding females that already have offspring. As in nearly all higher species, the bond between an adult and its young is strong. Holding their families under a constant threat of termination would be one way to secure cooperation, but at what a cost in a deep hatred that might eventually come back to haunt me. What is more, could I ever carry out such a dastardly threat? I think not. I'm a sentimental old fool in many ways. One should never make a threat that one isn't prepared to keep. Drowning yeng babies in a tub isn't my hippotion, even if I don't have to watch.

Boklung, rather unusually for an Aranian, is very much a believer in the rights of all species, especially other intelligent sentient creatures. That may seem to be contradicted by zis love for hunting yeng, but these things are relative. Few sentients are all light or all dark. Ze certainly isn't one for seeing animals in pain and tortured in death, but rather preferring to see a quick and clean kill.

Keeping an eye on exported yeng will only be really beneficial if I can find a way of collecting information from them unbeknown to the Cheetan. However, since we'll have exported them into a harder life, the yeng may well do all they can to avoid our officials. So how do I get hold of the data unless I persuade them that it is their interest to fully cooperate?

Any practice that attempts to threaten the yeng, when they'll be so distant, would be ridiculously short-sighted. Even if I felt comfortable doing so, threatening their youngsters would make them resent us even more than they already do. No, if this is going to work at all then the yeng must see some true benefit. We may gain far more by encouraging them to feel that we are concerned about their welfare, despite the fact that we have sold them to 'savage' Cheetan. I should consider lending a few of my valuable trustees into the export shipments. That makes less than obvious economic sense, but a great deal of political.

The trustees can be manipulated with the promise of freedoms when, and if, I get them back. I certainly hope they would be returned. The Cheetan will gain from having a few experienced slaves to teach skills to the general stock. The yeng need to be able to demonstrate to sceptical Cheetan that they are good for far more than just being eaten, and well trained yeng will help with that.

I know what I could do! I could have them re-chipped with partitioned memory that contains a relatively small secret read-only store of data that my agents on Trogaffin can download, whilst the vast majority of the data would be made readable to the Cheetan. The easy access to the bulk of the storage should then help mask the relatively small area of secret capacity. Obviously, I can't hope to discreetly read such chip devices across even that planet's minimum distance from Ungoliantis, of three hundred thousand kilometres, and through two atmospheres. There really is no alternative to having our local agents read the information and then pass it back through diplomatic channels.

First, Hosk has to be convinced that I need to receive data to help me support zis enterprise. Yes, shifting a lot of detailed routine information will provide plenty of cover for the secret data flow. I will point out how very much shared information will help our business partnership.

The benefits of knowledge gained would be great enough that the risks of discovery would be worthwhile. Even this tiny little industrial espionage may help us maintain our dominance in the trade. Not to mention that there may be vital lessons to learn about management from afar, as we dispatch yeng out to explore space in the new Arcraft. We need to learn everything we can about controlling yeng that are remote from Ungoliantis.

All livestock on Ungoliantis is 'chipped' with electronic tags and data recording devices. In fact, tagging is common practice on both planets, and not just of livestock but of the 'ruling species' as well.

Escaped 'wild' yeng—the favoured quarry of the hunts—are particularly good sport as they almost always learn how to override their tags, and so put an end to our electronic tracking. Officials deny that hunt supporters feed information to the 'wild' yeng about how to supress their tags, although such clearly happens. At times, alliances of convenience between animal lovers and hunt enthusiasts have been formed in order to distribute chip scanners to the feral yeng. Once the yeng have found the chips, they can often be 'surgically' removed. Perhaps butchery would describe the process better. With no electronic tags to follow straight to the escapee, traditional stalking skills are kept vital.

Recently, some wild populations have learnt how to deactivate chips in a way that avoids crude and often life-threatening surgery. The Aranians don't actually have proof as to how this is being done, although they have their suspicions. Basically, the yeng risk death by electrocution in order to fry the devices.

Boklung believes that yeng perform best if they are free to make day-to-day decisions, but ze is torn between bowing to established opinion that yeng need to be completely subjugated in all situations and zis more liberal ideas.

Boklung yawns, or rather exhales in the way that Aranians do, as ze reflects on the issue. Airs escape from tiny orifices along the length of zis thorax and abdomen.

What can I expect of yeng if they are treated more like equals? Will they just take any given freedom as more room in which to attack us? I pray not. Anyway, I don't have to decide this minute. Now, it is time for a well-earned intoxicant and bed.

"Grace, bring me my evening hippotion and prepare my bath."

3

JACK. PUGWASH. FREEDOM

Jack sits in the mouth of the cave that has become his adopted home. He peers out through the rain along the valley running from the foot of the steep scree slope below him.

Lying next to him, a suvaran dozes contently, absorbing what it can of the relative weak warmth of the cold season's suns. Jack found the only living creature that he presently has any sort of sentient connection with at the foot of the scree slopes below his cave. This lizard-like animal, though more akin to a leggy Komodo dragon with a stunted tail than to any canine, behaves as though it's a dog. In size and weight it isn't much different to an Earth Alsatian. Jack calls his pet suvaran, Pugwash.

Suvaran can respond to their names and even seem to have a vague understanding of a range of words, in much the same way as bright earthbound dogs do. Jack is convinced that Pugwash understands far more than just the tone of his voice and a few odd sounds. In reality, the apparent conceptual 'understanding' is almost certainly more to do with a high level of emotional empathy, than with any true linguistic comprehension.

Jack's original discovery of Pugwash was initiated by a very distressed squeal, which caused him to explore into the shadows of an overhanging rock wall. He discovered this frightened young creature trying to nestle into its recently dead 'mother'. Being a human born to the Earth, Jack made an initial assumption that the dead 'lizardesque' creature was female, but, in reality, all native fauna on Ungoliantis is hermaphroditic.

The young animal's vulnerability, grief and fear, bonded with human loneliness, empathy and compassion. The bond between Jack and this suvaran soon grew to be as strong as that between any human hunter and his faithful four-legged companion.

Jack idly pets the animal as he mumbles a prayer, thanking God for his freedom. He doesn't worship in any ritualised way, just quietly acknowledges the Creator for allowing him to escape the tight clutches of the spiders. A nominally Anglican upbringing gave Jack some vague concept of God as the Creator and possibly even as the guardian of Mankind. Always much less than pious, Jack has become even more doubtful of the Almighty's particular interest in humanity, as He has seemingly been rather lax in the role of human protector. Unsurprisingly then, soon after arrival, Jack expanded his philosophical thoughts beyond the man made in God's image precept of that Anglican Church.

When pushed to rationalise the full measure of his religious self, Jack now considers it likely that God loves spiders rather more than He loves humans. The idea of a special arrangement between mankind and the Almighty seems just too ridiculously illogical. How, he asks himself, could God allow the pillaging of the Earth, and man's enslavement, unless spiders are at least equally chosen ones and possibly even built in God's own image?

As a slave to the generally religious Aranian and having lost any comfort in the little he remembers from his Sunday School teacher, Jack looks increasingly to the faith of the dominant species and their version of the single God, Sinanna. The symbol of 'God' is represented in some way on or in every building in Cirithia as eight lines radiating from an elongated octagonal shape. Piety comes as automatically to most Aranian as breathing, and fortunately without most of the divisive cultural baggage added by the tribes of Mankind. The worship of

Sinanna varies little from one city-state to another or between any population groups within those states.

As already implied, Jack's search for strong enough values to help him survive has encouraged him to absorb rather than reject Aranian religious philosophy. His new faith usually holds to the notion that neither man nor spider has any inkling of God's likeness at all. But like a steadily increasing number of humans, when under true pressure, Jack finds it easiest to look to Sinanna as the supreme and hopefully benevolent Creator of the Multiverse. If God is normally depicted with eight legs, then so be it.

***

If I, Orlando, weren't a time-lord living beyond the physical Multiverse, but part of an enslaved race, I would be calling to any version of God I could conjure. Can any higher sentient species live without some concept of God, some reason for existence? I cannot answer that, as though I have travelled so very long and so very far, I have never found an intelligent sentient species that doesn't believe in a higher force. Sometimes such creatures simply see one of their own as being a god, but they are the minority. To be quite frank, we cosmic time travellers are really no nearer to understanding where or what God is than is any other intelligence. All we know is that the 'Multiverse' is just too interconnected, too mathematically consistent, too stable, too beautiful, to be the work of any unruly committee or atomic chance.

***

Survival has at times been a very close run thing, but Jack has somehow always found the good fortune needed to support his cunning. Now, as free of worries as he can be, Jack is reflecting on the large quotient of luck that has enabled him to remain sexually 'entire' and on his not unconnected urge to find company. On the day the slaver carrying Jack landed on Ungoliantis, all the male prisoners were lined up and told to strip off what remained of their ragged clothing, before being forced to walk through a heavily chlorinated shower. After this, the

24

spiders had forced them to line up in rows, and extremely eager arachnids had 'surgically' bitten off their gonads. The creatures had even made a game of it. This competition had caused a good deal of agitated excitement amongst the spiders, and some individuals seemed to be betting on the outcome.

At the time, Jack assumed that male gonads were a much sought-after delicacy. He only later learned that this was a recently introduced ritual amongst young spider soldiers, aimed at gauging their toughness. Most spiders actually consider the organs to taste revolting.

The number of men that one spider could castrate in a short time seemed to be the favoured game. Some males died from loss of blood, septic shock, or simply, Jack suspected, out of blind fear. The Homo-sapiens couldn't know what body parts might become the focus of any next game, and like a terrified flock of sheep, some seemed able to simply will their lives away.

The spiders ensured that most of the castrates survived by providing rudimentary trauma medicine. Being an economically valuable asset, the game was only allowed to take a relatively small number of lives. Jack assumed that the few who remained entire were selected by some sort of standard of conformation, not that the details mattered to him other than that they made him very lucky. On that day, it was perhaps only one in a hundred that avoided castration.

Cloud suddenly covers the suns, and rain lashes deep into the mouth of the cave, driving Jack and the still-sleepy suvaran back. Jack pulls his treasured waterproof sheet, a huge variegated blue and green leaf, over his shoulders, and reminisces.

He remembers a time, or possibly many, when he ran from the playground of his Elementary School on the Isle of Wight into the dry of the noisy classroom. He remembers the faces of the children, if not their names. Mostly he remembers one playground game, the object of which was to see who was best at removing the wings from crane flies and then encouraging them to race away from flicking fingers—on their six, not eight, legs. Now he wonders if such monstrous games are played by all higher beings. This thought draws his focus back onto the most powerful creatures he has ever met, the spiders.

Without dark night it is hard to record the progress of 'time'. Each revolution of the planet has a period which is generally hotter, when the largest sun is directly overhead, and a corresponding time when the suns are both low in the sky. The very gloomiest, dullest light occurs when one sun sinks below the horizon and the other only casts long shadows. The relative positions of the suns mark the major divisions of the Ungolian day, and only very rarely does any part of the planet experience true darkness. When the blackness of space does impose itself, however briefly and rarely, then the Aranian seem to scurry towards whatever artificial light they can. They seem genuinely fearful of it.

Jack tries to chalk days on his cave wall, but often feels that he either forgets, or sometimes marks too many strokes. It's hard to measure such long days, which for humans have to be split into periods of sleep and periods of activity, often called retreats and shifts. Jack attempts to keep the regime he had as a slave, with its six retreats of sleep and six periods of activity in every daily planetary rotation.

He has had to unlearn a great deal. Living in a world ordered with a mathematical system that counts from one to seven then ten, with no eight or nine, is just one tiny example. Jack makes full use of his hands to count in eights, just as he does to count in tens. Humans use their natural abacus by including their thumbs for decimal numbers and excluding them when counting in Aranian numbers.

Jack has been alone for longer than he cares to remember. He talks to himself and to Pugwash, reassuring himself that he's alive by the sound of his own voice. Part of his on-going dialogue has branched out into naming the objects and landscapes around him. Once alone in the wilds, it quickly became apparent to Jack that he had difficulty analysing things without naming them first. Objects, even living creatures, just don't seem so real, so solid and memorable, until they are properly labelled with a name. In Jack's mind, without being a something, anything less impressive than overwhelming hardly seemed to have any long-term conscious existence.

***

I take you away, for a moment, from Jack and the words vital to the story so that I may indulge my own obsessional thoughts. Humans are so much more than biological machines dedicated to species survival. Like a few of God's high creatures, man is naturally curious about everything, whether or not it impacts directly on survival. He is a creature that tries to make rational assessments about all that surrounds him. He is a truly intelligent being, rather than a biological robot that simply accumulates and orders required information. Even if Homo-sapiens has no genuine free will he has something that masquerades very well as it. There is the general conviction that rational choices can be made, and that even actions with absolutely no supporting logic can be deliberately selected.

Human thought has a quality just as profound and just as defining of individuals as is seen in the mental activity of any creature I've ever come across. Survival demands emotional, existential and intuitive intelligence, not just the logic of picking best 'numbers'. One can even speculate that mankind's very survival required the emergence of lateral and unpredictable thinking as a way for balancing other starkly obvious deficiencies.

The 'naked ape' isn't exactly well designed for even a vast majority of Earth's climate zones, let alone for survival in the cosmos. Aranian as well, although able to withstand a marginally greater range of conditions, are similarly warm-blooded creatures sensitive to tiny changes in the environment.

How does an animal, a dodark for example, manage to think about its world without giving each object a name? Perhaps for a dodark a particular smell is a name, a signature, a way of ordering thoughts. Yes, that works. For a screebur, clever compared to a dodark, naming might be a mix of sound and smell, and for a bird of prey, vision must be of greatest importance in tagging memories. For man and Aranian a particular visual image signs for an object, but any sign may have been influenced by any, or all, of the other senses.

***

The rain recedes and Jack returns outdoors. He finds a grassy spot and rolls onto his back to observe the wispy clouds that scurry across the pale sky in the wake of the storm. Compared to where he lived on Earth, he rarely sees flying creatures. Little except bugs and massive turvult enjoy the freedom of the air. He can't even recall seeing any feathers on this planet except ones that belong to chickens. These birds, imported early on with the humans, are now extensively and intensively farmed, as on Earth. Jack remembers England, where the songs of a hundred different birds almost defined the dawn.

Jack calls the sweep of territory visible from the rim of his cave, Freedom Valley. On the far side, he can see the lights of the city of Cirithia and the constant air-traffic in and out of the Nuzkarflux Spaceport. From his viewpoint the city seems to nestle in the shade of the rugged hills he knows as the Alps, but, in fact, a flat hinterland stretches some twenty kilometres beyond the city before the land starts to rise steeply.

Now Jack, as he is accustomed to do, reflects on all that has befallen him since he was taken from the Earth. A date claws at his mind: the twenty-seventh of May, his mother's birthday, and the day he saw her for the last time. The spiders' huge ships arrived from space the following dawn, having already swept away what little was left of both the local militia and the British Royal Air Force. The spiders then decimated the Isle of Wight, one of the last areas of the Earth to have, up to then, avoided their 'harvesting'.

The raiders hadn't had it all their own way that warm Whitsuntide, however; Churchill fighters from the distant and well hidden Pershore base on the British mainland had managed to temporarily cripple one of the slave ships, sending it crashing into the silent Queen Helen Docks in Southampton. The short air battle came to its inevitable end when the gravity wrenches of the spider fleet flattened the three engaging Churchills. These planes, popularly known as Faith, Hope, and Charity, were the last vestige of the British air defences, and some of the last fighter aircraft on Earth.

Two of the three pilots died as the gravity wrenches yanked the fighters into final nose dives. The undamaged slavers landed and set about their work, which didn't end until nearly every man, woman and child on the island were either herded into massive cargo holds or had been killed.

Jack often remembers being driven up the ramp into the bowels of the huge slave ship that was to transport him to the spiders' world. The event was so overwhelming that he tends to remember it as the death of a previous life.

***

I yet again interrupt, in order to be Orlando rather than simply the narrator. I need to give you a little mathematics, just so that you get some idea of how different time scales are on Ungoliantis.

One Ungolian cycle, or year, is sixteen years of earth-time, or the equivalent of twenty Earth-years by Aran counting. By this reckoning, Jack has been on the planet for fifteen Earth-years. Just short of a single Ungolian planetary year.

Humans live as comparatively long to an Aranian, as a gerbil, or a very old queen bee, does to humans. I expect that most Earth dwelling humans will consider this to be a very sobering fact. It is believed that both mankind and Aranian perceive themselves as living for similar periods of time. In other words five Ungolian years feels like eighty Earth-years to a man, and one thousand two hundred Earth-years feel like roughly eighty years to an Aranian. Why has this idea become established in both species' thinking? There may be a factual basis to this, or it may be sentient illusion. God only knows. Is one human year seven to a dog?

$$4$$

UNDERSTANDING DEVELOPS

Boklung awakes, stretches, and grunts as ze rises from the bedding cushions on which ze has spent zis night.

Haggh! Another day has arrived so quickly, and Councillor Hosk has predictably sent a message asking permission to visit. At least I've got enough time for a quick read-through of yeng husbandry documents. It is vital to check that I don't unwittingly give zim information the Council might consider to be sensitive, even though in reality this stuff is all commercially available. Politicians have strange ideas. I can't afford to upset them by being seen as the one to give advantage away. Hggh, especially as I know I'm going to risk being seriously deceptive later.

Boklung much prefers big-picture thinking to exacting details while knowing the latter is important. The scientific and technical papers dull zim so much that even though it is early in the day ze is constantly losing concentration in tangential trains of thought. Zis head jerks from time to time, as ze lurches back into more alert states and then out again into day dreams. For now ze is focussed on zis reading.

'Yeng, like all developed creatures, are the product of a long history of natural selection. Yeng and Aranian are almost equally, if differentially, advanced species whose survival has depended on the ingenuity of efficient brains. Both our species have become expert at manipulating environments to fit our needs. Though we Aranian are, by most significant criteria, more intelligent creatures, it is fair to say that the cleverest yeng are at least as cunning as many of our average wits. How much our superiority is solely down to having lives that are so much longer is not in any scientific way quantifiable.'

Yes, intelligence is certainly a mixed blessing, especially when yeng escape to live independently. However much I enjoy the chase, I wouldn't want to see the wild population growing so large that regular hunting failed to control numbers. As it is, we have to continually talk down the environmentalists' fears, some of which I admit I have some sympathy for. I can't deny the view of the anti-hunting organisations that clever competition for scarce resources could cause the decline, even extinction, of many of our native species.

But the fear mongers go out of their way to ignore the success of hunting. It really has prevented yeng becoming a real threat to our planet's natural diversity. Hunting provides good natural food, a lot of rural employment, not to mention a great deal of enjoyment. The fact that wild game provides far more healthy meats than our intensive farms shouldn't be overlooked either. Wild yeng provide lean meat, free of antibiotics, growth promoters, fungicides, drugs and disinfecting agents necessary to modern intensive farming.

Actually, gross unforeseen problems with exotic introductions, both accidental and planned, have proved to be surprisingly uncommon. One planned introduction that had really unfortunate consequences was the release of the zyfose from the planet Asgormia. Ironically, they were introduced to control the then tiny wild population of yeng. At first the policy worked as intended, because the zyfose craved yeng meat. That was until the crafty yeng introduced the zyfose to the easily acquired meat of dodarks. Now the dodark is comparatively rare in some areas, and to make matters worse, the yeng have had

some success in persuading the zyfose to hunt Aranian. Boklung
reads on.

> 'The Waterball from which the yeng come has a
> surface that is only about one-third dry land. The yeng
> live on that comparatively small solid surface, as do all
> the creatures we have traditionally imported from there.
> A lot of scientists say we should also be exploiting its
> seas, and in all probability this will eventually happen.
> It is a fantastically diverse planet, even richer in fauna
> and flora than our own. In all the cycles that our trading
> ships have been exploring space, we have never found
> any other planets so well-stocked with such a wide
> range of life-forms. The biological diversity of the
> Waterball is something to behold, despite
> overexploitation by yeng having so badly degraded
> their home environment. We can only marvel at what
> an incredible biosphere of living organisms once
> covered that planet's surface.'

*If only someone could build a time-machine, it would be great to
visit the Waterball before the yeng trashed it. Theoretically, space-time
physics creates time loops, but we are nowhere near developing technologies
that would allow us to go back and forwards within the time spectrum.*
The Aranian Holy Book of Eruvatar states that there are
beings that can lord it over time, acting as guardians of Sinanna's
Multiverse. The book says that true disciples can communicate
on a telepathic level with these super beings. Sinanna, is the
Aranian name of the one true God. Through 'The Good Book'
Sinanna instructs readers to understand that these guardian lords
are the 'dirtbugs' that patrol the Cosmic Garden. Boklung hasn't
paid homage at a city shrine for a long time, but ze'll never forget
zis childhood indoctrination. Though Boklung no longer accepts
chapter and verse on Sinanna's time-lords, as constant watchers
over Creation, ze would never dismiss the key foundations of zis

religion either. Boklung's head jerks zim awake. Ze reads a little more.

> 'In recent times, the reduction in the human population, as a result of our trade, has allowed the partial reinvigoration of some other Waterball species. The slave-trade is generally seen as being environmentally beneficial to the Waterball.'

Yes, this pamphlet is suitably light on detail, making it safe material to give to the Ambassador. I don't suppose it contains a single fact or idea that Cheetan aren't fully aware of, while allowing me to be seen as cooperative.

Waterball is a fascinating place. One day we should properly colonise it; that is, once we have given the natural rhythms of the planet a chance to mend nature.

The specimens in our zoos of the tiny octopedal creatures that resemble Aranian are amazing. The yeng generic name for these tiny octopedal creatures is spider, so we need not guess as to why yeng use that same name for us. And, thinking about other strange connections between our two worlds, that expert who spoke on native yeng behaviour and communication recently said that forebears long ago named our brightest star Delta Octantis. How weird is that numeric connection? Perhaps there's a God message tangled in this fact.

I can't put this down to any sort of mathematical fluke, that's for sure, and it does reinforce our belief that Sinanna created the Multiverse, and everything in it. Certainly, it's another of the many tiny observations and anecdotes that support cosmological unity. Added together, they give a measure of religious credibility, though we may always be far short of anything approaching empirical evidence.

That yeng would stumble upon a name for Solush with such a strong resonance without there being real connectivity seems 'astronomically' unlikely. The yeng couldn't possibly have known about the existence of Ungoliantis, other than as a distant planetary speck about which they knew next to nothing, unless, of course, sentient paths had already crossed each other in some physical or spiritual way.

I, Orlando, must inject a note. More profound than the apparent linguistic connections between Ungoliantis and the Earth, for me at least, is the amount of 'religious' doctrine that revolves around the existence of time-lords. Fascinating stuff; though I am not so sure that I like the idea of being merely a cosmic dirtbug! Possibly such filthy sounding little creatures are as important to Creation as I am, but I do prefer to think of myself as having a somewhat higher status.

The Aranian Civilisation certainly has some reasonably accurate ideas about what we time-lords do, though they are less attuned when it comes to knowing what we are. For one, they regard us as preternatural entities. Actually, that is hardly surprising as we are almost always invisible to them, with the very obvious exception of those renegade time-lords who invade and then use other creatures' physical bodies.

Many humans are equally aware that we more advanced beings could or do exist—calling us angels, devils, space aliens, or sometimes even simply ghosts or spectral beings. In truth, Aranian, Cheetan, and indeed humans do get occasional glimpses of us even when we don't inhabit borrowed carcasses. However, like other intelligent creatures, they are often mortified with fear when they manage to see through the imprisoning walls of their carefully constructed visual 'realities'. These species mix up the ephemeral visions they have had of us with their religious beliefs about their local versions of God. Many of their older scriptures actually contain a hodgepodge of vaguely reported sightings of other dimensional beings. Mostly us, I assume! Anyway, I waffle, let me return you to the mind of Boklung.

I have often thought about the tiny spiders of the Waterball. They have eight legs that not only make them very mobile and athletic, but they also have a few common characteristics that I'm happy we don't share. The biggest difference, apart from their tiny size and total lack of intelligence, is their ability to produce 'web' filaments. These fibres are manufactured from glands in these creatures' rear-ends, a quite revolting idea. Another big difference is that they are not as dexterous as we are. This is almost entirely a consequence of them lacking articulated backbones. But despite this ergonomic encumbrance they are nearly always extremely agile. These tiny octopods seem to rely entirely on simplistic pre-programmed 'instinctive' behaviours. Perhaps in evolution's due course some of these tiny copycats of our form can grow into large and intelligent tool users, but they are millions of cycles back down any such evolutionary trail ... Which reminds me, evolution still demands that I exercise. Anyway, I'll be drifting off if I don't do something.

Boklung wraps a towel around zis neck and climbs onto zis treadmill. Once ze is going ze sets the interactive screen to a landscape across which ze is a moving hunter. Ze speeds up zis movement to catch up with the running yeng. Soon growing tired, ze switches the scene to a tranquil stroll through a quiet garden with rich herbaceous borders and relaxing occupants. Zis mind drifts back to thoughts about the yeng species.

It is tempting to think that we should intervene to advance the progress of these octamerous familiars. But quite probably it would be dangerous to play at being God, in case our meddling allowed the 'evolution' of something dangerous, or worse, superior, to ourselves. What an excellent rationale for leaving 'creation' to our Creator. Of course, the upsides of intervention in evolution can be so massive that we are often happy to take the consequential risks. Our development of yeng is proof enough. But the gradual improvement of farm breeding-lines is very different from intervention to produce a species so similar to us that we could potentially be replaced. Recent engineering breeds yeng that are less our intellectual equals rather than more so. We are rightly wary of making robots too intelligent, and likewise we should be equally circumspect with biological machines ... This walking machine is puffing me out. No wonder, the programme has had me walking up a ruddy great mountain. When did that happen? "Huggg, huggg."

Boklung is soon able to concentrate on little else except zis increasingly tiring exercise regime. As usual it is zis intention to remain fit for hunting specifically rather than overall concerns for zis general health that keep zim going. Ze is nevertheless overjoyed when the levelling of the treadmill lets zim know that ze has reached the top of the simulated climb. Ze stops the machine and heads for the shower room. On the way, ze passes a glass-fronted cabinet in which ze keeps a couple of tarantulas, and watches for a moment as a dirtbug draws close enough to be grabbed.

Boklung finishes zis ablutions and sprawls on the cushions with reading matter. Ze stares across the room at a figurine of Sinanna standing on a corner pedestal. The icon, made of white marble, is carved to stand tall on two hind limbs. Each other limb holds up a symbolic icon of faith. The forelimbs hold up the twin suns, while in the next limbs down are smaller balls, symbolising the two principle planets of Lush, and down again the limbs hold out symbolic representations of the two 'special' sentient species. The one in the right 'arm' shows eight 'spokes' and the left has ten. While Bolklung recovers, the statue sets off a tangential train of thought.

In the future, could a representation of yeng be carved somewhere on the plinth? Perhaps the hind limbs of Sinanna could be standing on a yeng, which is gazing up in awe of the Almighty. Then, will there need to be our ten-legged familiars running around the base? Not to mention some Waterball species with Cheetan's twelve legs? Lobster is a name I recall.

[Please note that Boklung is using zis species' octinal counting system, so making eight ten and ten twelve.]

There's absolutely no genetic connection between us, yet one can't help but speculate. But if we did discover a biological link, could we psychologically cope with the idea that we weren't so uniquely special to Sinanna? Could we accept as certain fact that we are just one of many life-forms built using similar 'manufacturing templates'? Biologists say Cheetans and Aranians are genetically connected by some very distant ancestor, but that was only discovered a couple of generations ago. So who knows what mysterious truths wait to be uncovered?

Perhaps the little Earth spiders could be hung below the statue's legs, as though dangling on their 'strings'. Amazing filaments, how they create those incredibly complicated prey-catching nets. To think that they're built strand by thin strand into the lattices that entrap their victims. I pity the prey, so often completely wrapped and stored for later consumption.

Clever how they use the filaments for rapid movement across space, using these webs of 'rope' to form 'bridges' between solid surfaces. I wonder which use of the strings evolved first?

We can only have nightmares, or in some perverted cases perhaps fantasies, about excreting such strangely useful material. I imagine it would be very draining to produce these sometimes extraordinarily long fibres. Ugh! Luckily, for the sake of these little familiars, these silky threads are spun from special glands, not as secretions from their anuses—no creature would wish to have anything so closely to do with their fundamental excretions!

***

I think it relevant to tell you that Boklung's curiosity about natural science has led to zim being academically interested in a rather grotesque breeding programme, in which the embryos of humans have been split in such a way as to create conjoined twins. Ze finds the science so interesting that this to some degree submerges zis strong hatred of cruelty. Boklung's attitude is not an unfamiliar one. Scientists of many sentient species are able to find justification for all sorts of frivolous experiments, however little they do for the advancement of science. As often as not, these experiments only ever serve the interests of the disturbed, perverted and socially deviant.

These conjoined beings have eight limbs, thus the obvious attraction of this particular project to Aranian. Of course, they also have a surplus of many other parts and organs. The double anus has proved to be of little concern as normally the two digestive systems develop the same rhythm, and the surplus head is removed at a foetal stage. These creatures are ostensibly being developed as mere pets. Those with political oversight are watching to make sure that the experiments don't allow the development of a truly powerful octopedal humanoid. However scientifically and morally dubious such experimentation is, the Aranians are certainly not the only sentient creatures to have followed such 'uncivilised' pursuits.

It is reasonable to expect that these creatures will only ever be bred in laboratory conditions, as the female human isn't designed to give birth to eight-legged babies. Boklung is personally reassured by this perceived positive, as like most Aranian, ze finds the idea of producing 'babies' straight from internal wombs extremely distasteful. Viviparous birth is seen as so evolutionarily strange that it reinforces many Aranians' belief that mankind is a primitive creature. Of course, Boklung being the relatively sensitive soul that ze is, sees the avoidance of excessive suffering through unnatural birthing as crucially important in itself.

Aranian scientists are actually baffled as to why humans aren't designed to give birth to externally gestated eggs. The common view is that they have evolved in this manner in order to keep the egg better protected during its relatively long gestation, even though this is only achieved by putting the far more valuable, mature, breeding female at much greater risk. Aranian and Cheetan believe that a vast majority of life-forms in the known universe are born oviparously. In terms of numbers, that is actually the case even on Waterball. It's just that nearly all that particular planet's large creatures produce by live excretion. Boklung is very relieved that zis species doesn't have to suffer such biological indignity; just the idea of young being born as relatively large and already independently moving creatures from between the legs makes zim exhale shivered vapours from zis spiracles.

***

Ding, ding.

Ah! The doorbell, Huigark Hosk has arrived ...

"Ambassador, do come in."

"It is so kind of you to see me again so soon and at even shorter notice," Hosk says as ze manoeuvres zis way out the door on just five legs. "I will not take up more of your time than I find absolutely necessary. If I may scratch your brains, I would like your opinion as to how I should get across the advantages of

38

developing our own yeng farming beyond the production of meat."

"Haag. Not a problem. Come in and make yourself comfortable … Grace, hippotion! … Where would you like me to start?"

The Cheetan settles onto a long cushion on a low lounging board. "We have a real battle on our limbs to win the argument for any continued use of yeng in production and service industries. Have you got any strong arguments that might help me convince my superiors that biological yeng are really more useful than mechanical robots? Our planned trade is likely to be short-lived if our Monarch keeps pushing zis current agenda. Ze is keen on the further development of robots to replace yeng in all 'slave' systems, rare though they are on our planet. Ze is only really thinking of long-term use of the species to provide meat, as is more or less the case to date."

Boklung's tongue wiggles in zis mouth, preparing to speak, but Hosk continues without a pause.

"I am all for doing business with you, Boklung, but you must recognise that I am under political pressure from home. Any help with formulating a strong case for diverse yeng development will be greatly appreciated. I am facing conservative economic forces that have their powerbases in heavy industry and the military-industrial complex. These powerful groups push the case for industrial power built on robotic 'muscle', and consider the further development of robotics to be a mark of true civilisation. While other less focused groups, representing the numerical majority, prefer to live and work among other living creatures. Inevitably, the powerful military and business elites more often catch the ear of the Royal Household. I know we need both, technological and biological solutions, but convincing our First Family that this is the case is proving to be far from easy."

Once again the Cheetan continues without a break, leaving no space for Boklung to reply.

"Some Aranian are saying that we are giving away our natural resources far too cheaply in exchange for yeng breeding technologies we don't actually need. So, Boklung, we supporters of diverse yeng trade have our work cut out. Royal whim fluctuates like the wind, but suddenly my hopes seem to be pinned on loosening leaves."

Boklung's reply bursts out before Hosk can take breath. "It is certainly a fact that even here it is becoming increasingly common to use robots for simplistic tasks. This process is on-going, even here on Ungoliantis, especially since replacement stocks from the Waterball have grown increasingly scarce. This reverses the historical imperative, which saw yeng as a cheap and flexible replacement for our then expensive machine technologies. Let's face it, we were using microprocessor run labouring machines for a very long time before we discovered the advantages of the then extremely plentiful and flexible yeng.

"It is undeniable that robots have certain advantages, the greatest being that at least the basic designs do exactly as commanded, and work without tiring. Indeed, they are so efficient that it can be highly dangerous to give robots anything approaching the brains to make value judgments. But it is just exactly towards building artificial intelligence that robotics naturally progresses in the absence of yeng. Yeng can be used in situations where an independence of thought is needed, far more safely than robots can. They also have mental flexibilities that it is almost impossible to design. Robots aren't built to have freedom of choice, and that is the way things should stay. Yeng are dangerous enough, with all their vulnerabilities, but imagine how much more dangerous an army of truly intelligent 'bots could be.

"Biological weaknesses make yeng easy to control, if and when they start acting too independently. Robots given the means to make independent decisions are potentially a far more dangerous proposition. Independent thinking robots could 'discover' how to build and develop technologies for themselves. If robots ever learnt how to 'reproduce' themselves and learnt how to gain their independence from us, then our civilization might well face annihilation."

Grace enters with the requested drinks on a tray.

"… Thank you, Grace, and another cushion for my friend; you really are most thoughtful."

She smiles, places the tray on the low table and shifts a cushion from an unused board to behind the Cheetan.

"Hggh! Just what I needed," Hosk says. "The lounging boards are hard on my old frame. As you say, Boklung, yeng can think for themselves."

Boklung nods. "But what dangers when robots can? Look at what happened on the yengs' original home, the planet they call Mars. Well, so says the Great Book of Eruvatar. Scholars are now certain that the Negalares of scriptures is indeed 'Mars'. The Book says that robotic machines destroyed all biological life. During the height of the Negalares-Yeng Civilisation, scientists, greedy for superior soldiers, gave their robot machines real intelligence. These cyborgs, built with a mix of biological wet-brain and non-living electronic technology, dry-brain, weren't the servants for very long. First, the cyborgs turned on their yeng builders, and destroyed them. Then they purged themselves of all their biological parts. Finally, perhaps fortunately, the robots turned on each other, as vital rare metals became scarce.

"Imagine how dangerous that robotic species would have been if its armies had cooperated to look more aggressively for resources beyond their 'Sun System'. When the war eventually ended, Negalares was left as a virtually abandoned desert, and the creatures that survived on Waterball were left with nothing but memories of the civilisation they had recently enjoyed. Hggh … How about Grace serves our drinks, Ambassador, before I talk myself into dry salt crystals?"

"Yes, yes. I'm more than ready. You can certainly talk, my friend, and for rather longer than I naturally listen. What you say is so important that I need to concentrate. Have you any chilled yeng blood, perfect if flavoured with some spindlefix seeds, perchance?"

Boklung gestured to zis yeng servant who stood just out of sight behind the door. "Grace, prepare us both redfix and bring a plate of biscuits. … Now, where was I? Hgg yes! We

Aranian are fortunate in being inclined to fight less fiercely amongst ourselves than are the yeng. Our strongest biological programming generally leans towards self-sacrifice for the good of our species, while yeng is towards individual survival. At best, they only care deeply for others in their close communities. Perhaps it was that selfishness 'inherited' by the robots through yeng wet-brain material that saved the Galaxy from their destructive armies. Their cooperation might have meant our annihilation."

"Surely, not. Your race is superior in every way. As is ours."

Boklung's mouth opens slightly into something that, though it only faintly resembles it, serves the same function for Aranians as a smile does for yeng. "Indeed, but some think that Aranians are not psychologically equipped to cope with permanent dispatch into lonely space, whereas yeng don't seem to have that problem."

"Humpf. That is a small thing. For all our races' blunders neither of us has come close to destroying our own planet. That is the utmost foolishness."

"I agree, but the mutual destruction of robot 'clans' described so vividly in the Holy Eruvator stands as a warning to all, Ungoliants and Trogaffinians alike. We see only too well how easy it is for a 'civilisation' to implode.

"Our mythologies and ancient scriptures are full of stories about the Negalarites, the yeng ancients, the murderous bipedal hordes that briefly visited us in 'winged chariots'. We were the backward species then. Of course, it is partly these ancient legends that led us to voyage beyond our star system, following the ancient flight paths described in Eruvator scriptures. We were fortunate to find Waterball inhabited by relatively weak, and still highly fracticidal, yeng, rather than a new breed of the savage Negalarites.

"Those on Trogaffin, keen on developing robots further, should be reminded of yeng history, Huigark. Artificial intelligence is a threat to biological species. The yeng species came within a whisker of being destroyed by their own robotic technologies, and even though they survived, their civilisation had, by then, been set back ten thousand Waterball cycles. We would all do well to remember that. We may believe that we are now a superior species to yeng, but we would be fools to assume we could resist truly intelligent, self-developing, self-multiplying machines any better than they could."

"These are excellent points," Hosk says. "I shall put them forward most strongly."

"Also, to be flippant, the idea of using machines to do one's chores is just not as appealing as making use of sentient beings. There's a strong preference here for keeping yeng, especially amongst those that like animals in general. They sometimes work indifferently, but they are better at finding ways of adapting to nouvelle situations. And they certainly satisfy our personal need to have soft creatures to share our lives. When they fail they are very easily recycled as food. But then, of course, machines can always be recycled as well, if less tastily! ... Hggaahhh."

"Khggh, khggh!" The Cheetan's mouth rounded to allow a 'laugh'. "I strongly believe that for the sake of both our planets, we have to get on together, and one of the best ways of facilitating that is through mutually beneficial trade. My problem is making sure that key members of our Royal Family's government see more benefit from cooperation than from warfare.

"It is not always easy to make the case for peace, but the more we trade and cooperate the harder it is for the warmongers to get the upper hand. A shared interest in yeng is a part of that, just as is our exporting of the rare metals needed in industry ..."

Grace returns to top up cups, breaking the Cheetan's attention. Hosk habitually sees yeng as potential sex toys first and as servants second. The yeng and Aranian notice a sudden waft of hormonal odour from the Cheetan flesh.

"What about that massage you offered me yesterday, Boklung, is there any chance? I am slightly less strapped for time."

"An excellent idea! My muscles are actually quite stiff; the effect of rather too much exercise earlier. Grace, two masseurs, if you will be so good as to arrange that?"

Grace curtsies and leaves without delay. Boklung turns back to Hosk. "We are in accord, Huigark. Likewise, I am only too eager to do all I can to keep our planets on friendly terms. We must fully recognise that over-development of artificial intelligence threatens not just our civilisations, but potentially our planets and even our galaxy and all the biological species in it. Sentient prospects may not be so lucky in the future as they were when the robots battered each other to extinction on Negalares. Come, we will wander over to the relaxation suite."

The Aranian and Cheetan move to the adjoining room, where they lower their bodies across well-padded boards and let their limbs flop over the sides. The 'beds' are free of structure across the mid-sections over which the creatures place their more fundamental regions. Boklung never ceases talking.

"Many of the most telling arguments in favour of the yeng trade are centred on issues affecting our very survival. But all reasoning needs pursuit. I really enjoy training yeng, especially teaching them enough language to respond quickly to our needs. I would rather spend my life surrounded by flesh and blood yeng than cold metal machines. As you have already mentioned, even the majority of ordinary Cheetan feel the same. Talking of needs of the flesh, come, come, yeng. Get set up. I hope you have brought plenty of oil."

Two yeng, both castrates, enter and prepare to massage from underneath the tables. The masseurs squat and kneel in discomfort whilst working the leathery flesh above them. They knead and pummel with the false keenness expected of slaves. Whilst the yeng work, Boklung carries on talking business.

"Naturally enough, there are other problems with yeng that the pamphlet hasn't mentioned, such as the arguments that the robot supporters constantly bring up. As an example, the long wait of at least five hundred low-lights for them to be mature enough to be of any economic use. To compound that problem, the birthing yeng is less able to work while she is required to nurture. I am quite content to put up with these inconveniencies, especially as watching them develop is actually quite entertaining. The way I would tackle the argument, is not by trying to say that robots are inferior tools, they certainly aren't, but rather by emphasising that each has its benefits. Make the case on the grounds of diversifying possibilities, not exclusion."

Hosk nods zis fleshy head. "That is an excellent point. This is not really a mathematical conundrum. I need to think more like an Aranian. Trying to deny weaknesses and claim the same functionality is a tenuous approach. Anyway, whatever else may be true, I know that out of robot and yeng I would prefer the latter to do my daily grooming. I would never choose a machine, no matter how many vibrating and massaging attachments it had. When exhausted, I find nothing better than having a yeng or two massaging my limbs, not to mention using them to stimulate the nether regions! Actually, I think the exotic usage of yeng gives us hope of getting enough royals on our side. There are plenty of particularly perverted minds amongst our hereditary rulers. Hhaaah! Your body politic, elected by popular mandate, makes ours look very, um, 'primitive'. I may be a loyal Cheetan, but I am far from being a sycophantic supporter of rule by hereditary monarchs … Haaagh. I am getting quite excited. Rub my hole a little harder, yeng."

A good deal of slapping from the yeng, and groans from the tables, accompany the conversation.

Boklung continues, "I certainly believe that the acquisition of the right to rule simply because one is the progeny of a prestigious dynasty is ridiculous. Even the yeng came to the conclusion that power through birth-right is illogical. But you have to deal with the governance you have, Huigark, and appealing to the particular private 'interests' of royals is for you a likely worthwhile tactic."

"If only our rulers could at least be made to prove their capacity to lead, instead of being established even when often inbred imbeciles." Hosk's eyes suddenly bulge in their sockets and the iris's constrict and dilate in rapid succession.

Boklung shakes zis head. "My yeng are good, aren't they, but haagh … I feel quite dizzy. There is something quite unnerving to Aranian about your expressive Cheetan eyes."

"Sorry, I forgot where I was for a moment. Quite carried away by my own deviant thoughts. Pray continue. And don't stare, my good zir, you don't have to look deep into my orbs when you speak."

"Yes, well, changing the subject, breeding them has been a hobby of mine for as long as I can remember. Yeng I mean, not royals, Hgaag. I have a breeding-house in the grounds of The Gardens, which I manage for the benefit of the whole city. Basically, I aim to produce strong and psychologically calm yeng. Would you like to take a look?"

"Yes, very much so. Anytime now that I feel fully relieved."

"Let's go and get some fresh air, then … that is if you've finished your drink?" Boklung rises.

"Yes indeed. Lead on, by all means. If you could just towel me down first, yeng, then I will be right along."

5

LOOKING OUTWARDS

Only one other human had crossed Jack's path since he escaped. A lurking, cannibalistic creature for which few would ever have much compassion had been stalking Jack, hungry for his flesh. No doubt the spiders, as they do occasionally, had persuaded this insane human into craving meats cut from his own kind, then released him to seek out escapees that the hunt fails to find. The minds of such creatures are forever damaged by a cocktail of drugs injected into the meats that the spiders feed them. When such a creature attacked, half-invisible in the fading light, Jack was ready.

After realising he was being followed, Jack had waited, tense, for what seemed like hours until he sensed that an attack was being launched. He'd fought the urge to run, and struggled to hide his awareness from his pursuer. Fleeing may have been a solution of the moment, but that would only have delayed a meeting, if not for Jack then for some other poor victim.

Fear itself can behave like a physical presence; can appear as solid matter, lingering both within us and outside us. Many can get a sudden 'sixth sense' that quivers their very souls—a feeling appearing as if from nowhere, which says that evil is afoot. Sometimes those people feel as though they have stepped into an area of psychologically chilling ground that touches them like a spectral frost. Jack shivered as he felt the evil closing from

47

behind, prickling his scalp, chilling his spine. Without turning, without even a minute check to his stride, Jack prepared.

Are you one of those that have ever felt your soul screaming, warning of a stalking killer? Such telepathic instinct is a primordial defence vital to prey species. This is a sense that many humans lose when accustomed to an existence in which they are easily the masters of their environment.

Jack has never lost his childhood ability to be attuned to the stink of evil, which is just as well, for in this moment Pugwash, an animal always sensitive to lurking danger, was not yet his companion. Jack felt as though his blood would freeze, but his nerve held. He was ready for this creation of the spiders, this ghoul.

The once-human sprung from the shadows. Instantly, Jack planted the butt of his spear in the dirt and turned its point towards his previous step. The spear flexed, and a shudder ran up Jack's right arm before he had properly sized up the already dying creature. The weight and momentum of this hollow-eyed devil forced Jack to his knees. The long-shaft spear buried deeper and deeper in flesh, and then ripped out near its spine. Forced down further onto his haunches, shaking from the shock, Jack watched the skewered creature drop its club and twitch its last. As the cannibal expired, gurgled soft words drifted from its lips: "Con la grazia di Dio!" Dead now, still the monster slid down the shaft, until Jack flexed his left shoulder and tipped the impaled creature away from him. It fell on its side with a thump.

Incidents like this attack had helped make Jack timid of venturing too far from known territory. However dangerous his present locality felt, the distant unknowns seemed still more risky. That, and the shelter and relative safety of his cave, had proved attractive enough to keep Jack settled. Lingering so long with the distant view of the familiar city had, at least, given him time to learn much about survival and the hunting techniques of the spiders. Now he could move about so quietly, so secretively, that at times even his shadow seemed to struggle to find him.

Jack knows that despite his growing cunning, his hard-earned freedom isn't a good long-term bet unless he is prepared to move further into the wilds. Being so close to the city, whatever the benefits of his cave, the future has him marked as disembowelled quarry.

Lack of action hasn't meant a lack of planning. Jack has spent a lot of time contemplating striking out in various directions, but he sees no advantage in moving further from this city's hunters if that only means venturing further into the familiar hunting grounds of another population's killers. Jack is inclined to the idea that the safest direction might be back past Cirithia into what he calls the Alps. The snow-capped mountains seem to promise safety from spiders, if not from the weather. Greater wilderness would make life safer for Pugwash as well. Naturally though, whenever the attractive qualities of any route come to mind they are quickly followed by exotic fears. Terrors of the unknown, of strange evil monsters, fill his dreams. Possibly, going back to the streets he knows, and hiding in the derelict shadows and deep sewers of 'Spiderdom' is as safe as any option. Out in the wilds he faces all the hazards of nature, including, he is sure, many he doesn't know. Possibly, other free-living humans are the gravest danger of all, skilled intelligent hunters, full of cunning, possibly cannibalistic and determined to keep other human competition for resources at bay.

Most days, the city provides the strongest magnet, if only Jack could think of a way to keep Pugwash with him and yet safe. Both human and spider are predators that any suvaran must fear. The species has long been reared for meat by the Aranian, playing the same historic role that the pig has for so many humans. Knowing that one day he might have to abandon his pet, Jack spends much time trying to teach Pugwash the skills of survival that pure instinct hasn't instilled.

Jack has taught zim to hunt moving into the wind, so keeping zis odour from the prey's nostrils. He has encouraged attack at the moment quarry turns away, or drops its head to eat. His pet has learned to spot the weaker creature in a herd, to take any large beast by attacking its vulnerable flanks and when expediency demands, the abandonment of a carcass as stronger scavengers circle. But he cannot teach Pugwash independence, the confidence to survive alone, and most importantly, enough true fear of man.

It isn't just the constant danger of living so close to a spider population that demands Jack move; increasingly he craves real company, companionship, and the strength and security granted by a tribe. On any day the hunt might find him, alone and so an easy dinner. Often he hears the sound of spiders crashing through the undergrowth, shooting at everything that moves. They come in lines and ranks with flanking columns driving game down Freedom Valley with packs of screebur. When that happens, Jack retreats far into his cave and hides amongst the boulders and damp, slippery moulds that mark avalanches fallen from the crumbling roof. The nagawad serpents, which the hunters fear, make these deep places a little more secure from the advance of spiders. It must, though, be inevitable that one day a hunter will follow its sense of smell deeper into the cave and discover him. Up until now they have never ventured much further than the first lofty vaults, quite possibly smelling quarry, but judiciously deciding to look for easier targets.

Jack has survived the venom of the nagawad, in the process noting that the bite has a far more lethal effect on most Ungolian creatures than on humans. This seems logical enough, for why would nature have developed venom to intentionally kill an unknown species except by fluke. In fact, not only has Jack come to survive the venom, he occasionally welcomes it. The hallucinogenic qualities of the bite have become Jack's most effective weapon against paralysing terrors, a natural antidote to stress. Swirling, vivid splashes of kaleidoscopic colour and unnatural sounds that seem to bounce differently off every object are enough to give real, if temporary, relief from life's terrors. The bite itself is not so pleasant, being reminiscent of a very painful, misplaced, medical needle. That this pain is extremely off-putting is probably just as well, as Jack suspects that the drug is addictive. He fears a permanent physiological coshing of his cunning.

The presence of the nagawad's mind-blowing venom is, even when considered in isolation, becoming a good enough reason for moving away. Jack's belief that what is a temporary hallucinogen to him will easily kill Pugwash reinforces his reasoning. One particular nagawad has become almost a second pet; it certainly seems to seek Jack out. In return for providing the snake's favourite lunch of firebugs, he has taught this one to always place its bite on the same part of his thigh. A site less endowed with shallow nerve endings than most flesh. Collecting firebugs entails smoking them out of decaying wood, by taking care not to let the timber get too rapidly hot or engulfed in flame. He named the hissing nagawad Poppy, and Pugwash and Poppy have learnt to let each other be.

These 'snakes' look much like earthbound ones but behave differently. Nagawad, just like suvaran, seem to be able to distinguish between man's expressive vocal tones and even hidden feelings, and to respond to them selectively. Sensing anger, frustration, joy, even affection, surely indicates a familiarity with that emotion. Jack finds the idea of having a mutually affectionate relationship with a snake as totally weird, not that that has stopped him. And compared to the many strange things on Ungoliantis, a snake sensitive to emotion doesn't really seem so totally extraordinary.

Jack's need for human company is working on his consciousness on several levels. Though driven to distraction by his lack of female company, the overriding reason for seeking others is that one alone is no real match for a spider. Only by operating in packs has man a reasonable chance of prevailing. The fact that Jack has slain a hunter without the help of others might not be as unique as David's defeat of Goliath, but it certainly isn't a common event either.

A high degree of equality exists between spider and man when one considers wit and pure cunning, though in every other way the contest is one-sided. Speed, agility, strength, weaponry, organisation, and pure size are all factors in the spiders' favour. When standing on just their hindmost legs, an adult spider measures three metres tall, and yet they can conceal themselves by laying nearly as flat as a human can. They climb vertical walls, unless they are as smooth as glass, their guns can accurately kill over a distance of five hundred metres, and they can physically throw a full-grown human at least twenty meters.

Unlike humans, the Aranian seldom physically fight each other, and their warfare is usually more akin to the struggle between rutting stags than to any attempted annihilation of an opponent; though, as with the clash of such antlered deer, sometimes fatalities occur. Nevertheless, different populations of spiders have historically quarrelled and occasionally fought each other, and still do, and that gives many escaped slaves a chance of maintaining a flimsy independence. Using the dynamics of the relationship between various populations of spiders, the few independent tribes of humans are sometimes able to find relatively safe territorial niches. These 'de facto' demilitarised zones and disputed, ungoverned slithers of land between the semi-autonomous city-states provide the only real sanctuaries from systematic hunting. Jack has, in the past, heard many rumours about these safer areas, though he has absolutely no idea where any might lie.

As warfare between Aranian is always more of a game of strategy than a bloody feud, the disputed areas tend to be left abandoned rather than be continuously under the marching feet of one state or the other. At present, the city-state of Cirithia and its neighbour Hostagrifonta are technically in a state of war. Cirithia is recognised by all as the most powerful state, so the Hostagrian are unlikely to take their posturing far. The seat of the Federal Department for Interplanetary Relations and the Headquarters of the greater part of the Ungol Space fleet are situated there. What Cirithia says, usually goes.

***

Jack was born in a little village not far from the edge of what the English have long called the New Forest. Well, it was new in 1079, when William the Conqueror claimed it. By the time slave-ships took the fifteen-year-old Jack from his later adopted home on the Isle of Wight, there was little left of trees or man on the mainland of southern England. Now Jack's home territory is in a sea of trees, if not one that earth-dwellers would recognise as familiar. Some of the massive plants look a bit like exotic conifers, some like giant ferns and bamboos, and some look like nothing on Earth at all except perhaps great lumps of green-coloured polystyrene foam. If one is interested to understand how different such a basically similar biology can be, then imagine the Earth with all the plants that are tiny having grown huge, and vice versa. The image will not, of course, be Ungolian, but it will give an idea of the profundity of the differences new arrivals to the planet have to come to terms with.

Clearly, the human population doesn't face the risk of extinction on Ungoliantis, as it is too valuable a commodity, like the pig on Earth. Small populations of humans may be able to survive completely independently of the Aranian, but only in tenuously held niches and in constant peril—just as wild pigs have clung onto a fragile and marginalised existence on Earth, while at the same time the survival of the domesticated species is guaranteed by the farming of its flesh.

Wild breeding populations of humans will always have difficulty remaining hidden. The long development of the baby into an adult human makes the application of a quiet and secretive existence very challenging. So very often, screaming babies or the straying play of noisy children have revealed human communities to the hunters. Humans are generally poor at discreet, shadowy existence. The need of the human digestion system to cook many otherwise unsuitable but vital foods doesn't help either. Rising twirls of smoke often give camps away.

Independent existence has to be hand to mouth, basic and semi-nomadic. Though possible to survive like this, it is almost impossible to prosper. On Earth, pockets of Neanderthal primates survived alongside the physically weaker but more cunning Homo-sapiens for thousands of years. They rarely had a long enough reprieve from danger to build anything close to real culture; nevertheless, these isolated populations of 'ogres' hung on tenaciously. Possibly they survived in pockets of isolated territory into the twenty-first Christian Century. If

Almas, Sasquatch, Yeti, or whatever other 'Neanderthal' tags the humans of that century called them, had survived until the remaining pockets of 'civilisation' were exploited as slaves then they might have come down from the harshest zones and recolonised the whole Earth. Unfortunately for them, the two hundred years that saw the human population explode from two to ten thousand million individuals, also forced the last of these creatures into extinction.

***

Jack engages in one of his regular monologues with Pugwash, the most attentive of audiences. "It's time I connected with other escapees. Living alone is getting me down. I'm afraid I'll forget how to talk to humans if things go on like this. At least I had company as a slave. What would have become of me if I hadn't taken my chance to escape? I was fortunate to be given work in the Spakron Gardens with its relative freedoms. Most 'bucks' are lucky to ever get out of chains.

"And Borstave, the head-gardener, taught me some of the things that have helped me survive, just as I've taught you, Pugwash. Borstave's demands helped distil my desire to escape. Ze wasn't a particularly harsh task master by spider standards, but ze didn't let up on us either."

Jack pats Pugwash's head, "I must treat you well, my friend. You would enjoy The Gardens; so full of colour, exotic plants and smells and drabbets to chase. Well, you would if I could save you from becoming some spider's dinner. The Gardens run right to the very fringes of the farmlands, and from there, it's just a short hop into the wilds."

Later, Jack lies on his tree-litter mattress, staring into the roof of the cave, and goes over his vague plans. Pugwash nestles close to get some warmth. The rain has chilled the air despite the best efforts of the suns to break up the cloud. Jack remembers incidents from the past as he absent-mindedly strokes Pugwash's belly.

It's weird that the native animals are all hermaphrodites, and that it's one of the last words I learnt on Earth. Sex education in biology was one of the few interesting subjects we had, and I remember being fascinated by Miss Margo Jones's explanation.' Jack smiles at the fond memory of his biology teacher. 'Most of the boys had a crush on her, but I doubt that the others' interest was quite as 'shape-shifting' as mine."

Jack hears a twig snap on the slope behind him: a noise associated with the movement of heavy game, or even something more dangerous. He listens, waiting to hear another irregular sound that would force a decision to investigate. But all is quiet. Pugwash seems unconcerned, so Jack lets his mind settle.

I've been hiding here far too long. Chances are I'll get caught eventually. Moving further from Cirithia makes sense. I don't think I could face joining a group of escapees living like rats in the city, right under the noses of the spiders. That kind of existence might be sustainable, but it's hardly tolerable. Freedom, but at such cost! Slavery isn't so bad when working for a good boss like Boklung. Compared with that, the street vermin's life is a poor deal.

Searching the wilds for another group could take forever. After all, I've been free for a long time without seeing another human; well, except that cannibal I killed and glimpses of short-lived quarry released by the hunts. I could try and build my own tribe by helping quarry escape, but I've never seen an opportunity to do that yet.

Whatever I do, I need better ways of defending myself. My spear is conspicuous and cumbersome when I get close enough for it to have any real advantage, and the bow I made, though powerful, isn't accurate enough to trust shooting at anything dangerous. The only weapon that would really give me power is one of the spiders' own guns—if I can find one that I can fire. Someone might be able to find a way of hacking the codes. Some chance! We could if my old mate Crofty was here; he could've hacked Whitehall. Hell, man, how many millions of miles away is Newport? I wonder if he's still alive. I'll never know.

Jack places his hands behind his head and sighs.

We can never defeat the spiders. Though maybe we could try for some sort of alliance with a few members from discontented fringe groups. But what could we offer to make an alliance attractive to dissident spiders? Actually, I rather doubt that there are many such creatures anyway. I've never even seen a disgruntled-looking spider, let alone a revolutionary.

Would I have settled for slavery, played the game, if I'd never tasted freedom on Earth? Probably! That's another weakness, isn't it? The lack of incentive to fight. Those born here can hardly miss what they've never had. They've never smelt freedom, and what's more, if it was thrust upon them they'd likely fear it. Fewer and fewer are arriving from Earth now, that's even fewer people with independent pasts.

Would I enslave the spiders if circumstances were reversed? We're many things, but we're no better than them. Actually, we're far worse, slaughtering our own on the thinnest pretences.

If I could be like Spartacus, the greatest warrior that ever escaped bondage! Well, I can dream. If and when I enter the city I'll tell anyone who asks that I'm Spartacus. The Roman Empire crumbled before him for a couple years before he was captured and crucified. I don't want to go the way he did; we all die though, don't we? Unless my generation gains freedom, possibly the last of the once free, then what hope has mankind of ever again being independent?

I wonder how much the spiders know about what we really think. They see more of us praying to their God—even I do it. But do they know that for many of us their God is really only ours hidden behind Sinanna's idol? Both deities must be manifestations of the same One God. Do they know we've retained so much of our culture, hidden in our whispered words? Some of them must do! They probably have a mass of documentary material, taken along with us, from the Earth. Where would they store artefacts from Earth? I wonder. Perhaps one day our ancestors will visit an Aranian museum to rediscover their own past.

Perhaps, we're actually cleverer than the spiders, when we're allowed to be. Maybe they only defeat us because the chance of time has them further down the technological path. Things could have been very different.

What do I miss most from Earth? Funnily enough, it's books more than electrical gadgets. I miss a really good chat with mates and having a proper dentist. Though Boklung has allowed the setting up of a dental practice, and given what help a dentine-free species can give with equipment. In many ways it would be good to be back in Cirithia, and not just to get my teeth seen to.

Talk about the lack of 'gadgets'! I own two long spears with fire-hardened tips, my inaccurate and currently broken bow, a heavy staff, half a dozen good fire-flints, and a strip of leather I 'cured' myself, which I tie around like a skirt to stop my manhood bouncing over much. Hell, I wear a skirt. Imagine walking downtown in Newport like that. Not that it matters here, only newly-arrived slaves have any strong feelings of modesty.

So I have a 'skirt', then I've the machete I took from the farmlands, and the knife from the spider I killed—a small hunting knife to zim, but a heavy military blade to me. There's the wooden-soled sandals I made, and, um, what else? A lump of granite-like stone I use to keep my knife sharp, another lump of rock with a natural hollow that I ground out to make a bowl, and a spider's water carrier.

Sometimes differences are hard to understand ... Funny how they hardly use the wheel. I've only ever seen them on things like hospital trolleys and meat carts. They don't realise that they've accidentally invented the pneumatic inner-tube with their circular water bladder. Their spacecraft technology is amazing, and yet in many ways they're no more technologically advanced than we are, or at least were, on Earth. We should've been able to fight them off. For sure, we'll never escape servitude unless we find a way of killing them at least as easily as they can kill us, but direct combat will never be the answer. They're just too strong.

I spent about three and a half Earth-years in the hold of that spaceship according to the old guy's antique wind-up watch. We never did work out why the others all malfunctioned, but Bill Bailey's watch ticked on regardless. Eight hundred and fifty earth-days Bill counted while we travelled at God only knows what speed. Bill and his beloved Einstein were probably right about time passing differently for us than for those we left behind. Thanks, Bill, for teaching me about time, gravity and space, though I doubt I'll ever be able to make use of the information. Whatever; that's all irrelevant for now, time is time, and how I experience it is all that actually matters.

I guess humans are lucky the Spiders haven't tried to settle on Earth. But I wonder why not. It seems like a logical development. Maybe it would cost them too much to maintain a colony so far away. Or maybe they can't tolerate something on the Earth. What could it be, and could it be introduced here? When they arrive on earth they shut down the electricity as soon as they can. But no, that's just to weaken us. They use electricity with abandon.

They've been raiding our planet for over a century; the idea of colonising it must have cropped up. Surely, they could survive on Earth if they chose to. Of course, in Aranian terms, they've been harvesting Earth for only a very short time. Colonisation might just be tomorrow's story. Or perhaps they just get homesick easily?

Or maybe I'm looking at things from the wrong perspective. Something on this planet might be needed to keep them alive. Something in the air, maybe? A particular chemical or something? No, a race clever enough to cross space would easily deal with a few ingredient shortages. I've probably got it already; the poor diddums are just insecure away from home.

6

YENG BREEDING

Boklung and Hosk stroll through The Gardens, heading in the direction of the breeding houses. They pass small paddocks in which groups of yeng walk in circles while pushing the spokes of large horizontally fixed wheels geared to work heavy pumps. The pumps lift subterranean water, which is then channelled to irrigate horticultural crops.

Despite the dullness and drizzle, both creatures walk with a light step, evidence of their good mood as they embrace the fresh winter air. They stop outside a pavilion with three walls, set behind a high wire fence topped with barbed wire. Looking out of place, two nearly fully-clothed albino yeng are playing Chess under the shade of a three-sided pavilion.

"You must try the yeng game Chess some time," Boklung says to Hosk. "It's so simple and yet so intriguingly complex. This game alone is ample evidence of strong yeng intellect and culture. In it, one royal lineage fights another, which must surely be of particular interest to any Cheetan."

Hosk peers at the board and nods. "Perhaps, I shall look into it some time."

"If yeng were a longer lived species," Boklung continues, "so having more time to develop individual intellectual skills, I'm sure we would have found it harder to defeat them. And I don't mean at chess, Hggah. As it is, they hardly live long enough to breed and fully develop their young. Well, that is a bit of an exaggeration, but they certainly lose a lot of potential from being born so very short of time."

"How do you produce such unusually white ones?" Hosk asks.

"Creative yeng breeding, Ambassador. I'm fascinated by the diversity of characteristics that can be produced this way, and though getting pure whites is difficult, I have developed this breeding line of albinos which I sell to gamers. They like to use white and black yeng for easy recognition of divisions."

"The pink eyes are most exotic."

"Yes, and very pretty, I think. Choosing characteristics suited to different functions and then breeding for them, is becoming an ever more important part of yeng farming. As well as studying the science of yeng reproduction and body conformation, breeders are getting better at judging stock for behavioural characteristics through records and evaluations of physical mannerisms.

"Of course, as a breeder with wider interests than commercial farming, I take great care to maintain biological diversity. The last thing I want is to end up with inferior Type-Two creatures."

"Type-Two?"

"Yes, the Genscieu Institute developed the Type-Two as a dull-witted creature for repetitive, robot-like tasks. They are increasingly used in mining, and on factory production lines. The Type-Two still seems to throw up some intelligent offspring, but individuals are statistically far more likely to be simple-minded. They are particularly used in work places from which escape is unavoidably easy for intelligent creatures."

"This seems like a sensible move."

Boklung's eyestalks contract a little and zis voice takes on a slightly terse tone. "Personally, I have never had much trouble with the standard creature; they seem to settle so long as they are fed, kept warm, and not excessively worked. I prefer to maintain some intelligence in my stock. Once given a task, they require less direction if they can use their own initiative to solve any problems that may arise."

"Oh, yes. I see your point. I jumped on an obvious thought without really thinking things through. And this 'creative breeding' of yours, that must take many generations."

"It used to, but increasingly, genetic selection is done at little cost 'in vitro' using stored embryos. The female is then surgically implanted. That means producers can develop variant stock without long breeding programmes. So now we have ever less real need to farm experimental lines of livestock, although this is still normal industrial practice. I can't imagine abandoning traditional breeding programmes, but that is just me. Test-tubes might be fine for crude screening, but artificial insemination and egg implanting aren't my idea of farming."

Hosk crosses zis eyes and appears to be in deep thought. "I am trying to picture what you're saying. Correct me if I am wrong, these laboratory fertilised eggs are put back to be gestated inside the female?"

"Well, yes! Yeng don't pop out of eggshells already capable of independent living. Unlike our kind, born developed enough to be placed immediately into nursery schools, yeng are born so immature that they are still totally dependent on their parent. To get to an equally advanced point of release into the big wide world, we would have to create artificial yeng 'shells' that new-born could be placed into to develop further. I'm not even sure that that would be possible."

Hosk regards the chess-playing albinos again. "Do different colours ever have different flavours?"

"No, all yeng taste the same no matter what their colour. Unusual characteristics of form are sought for meat quality, fertility, and performance in the arena. For food, a marbling of fat through the muscle is desirable, without the animal losing good muscle definition.

"Traditionally, the castrates have tended to go too much to fat, but with care and the use of high protein diets we have greatly improved eating quality. Of course, there are inherent dangers in making them stronger. With this in mind, a friend of mine has been breeding ones with longer, and thicker noses. This makes them suitable for ringing, so that they can be controlled better on a tether. This also has the effect of making them look more like Ungolian creatures; rather less shockingly exotic. Unfortunately, the nose ring is relatively easily ripped free, destroying the nasal tissue, but while they last they give a very good measure of control."

"In the arena—a favourite pastime of mine—" Hosk says, "those that do best are strong, fast, and agile."

"Yes, and generally leaner than stock bred for meat."

There's a sudden cheer from an albino. It seems that one of the players has won the game.

"Whichever of you is the winner," Boklung says, "I would like a game sometime. Grace will call on you when I am free."

"The variety is fascinating," Hosk says as they wander on, "everything from jet black to pearly white. Your race, Boklung, while being less varied, does carry many subtle tones. But look, by comparison, at my grey dull skin, common to all Cheetan unless we are actually very sick."

"Yes." Boklung and the Cheetan wander on. "Colour diversity is certainly a feature of the yeng species. To get pure white colouration isn't easy, and there are several tricks that one can use to disguise a poor product. We can, for instance, irradiate all dark hair follicles and keep the creature out of the sun. The albinos you just saw are only allowed out of the shade when conditions are dull. All light colours are difficult, seemingly always based on recessive genes and, as you know, too much inbreeding makes creatures weak."

Hosk grunts. "Inbreeding seems to be a universal problem, from royalty so scared of outsiders that they literally breed their young from coupling individuals who are too genetically close, to farmers and breeders who over select for certain characteristics!"

"Indeed! I introduce stronger blood into close albino lines from time to time, so as to get the genetic input from more robust physiologies. Albinos can be physiologically weak because their scarcity makes genetic diversity hard to achieve. And of course, they need exercise, which is why we pump water with physical labour rather than machine power."

They watch a group leave one of the wheels and another group replace them. "Of course, we Cheetan see colours differently, as you probably know. We see a wider range, including into the ultra-violet, but can't distinguish the subtleties in the range of hues that Aranian can. Anyway, very interesting though this all is, with time being so limited perhaps we should focus on less esoteric details? Economics, perhaps?"

"Yes of course, I get quite carried away. Hggh ... okay, I stand reprimanded. But let us sit on this bench awhile." Ze waves a limb towards a wide wooden bench, which has a panoramic view of The Gardens.

Boklung sits and Hosk joins zim, easing zis bulbous body onto the platform while Boklung continues.

"Yeng breeding programmes are becoming ever more economical as the shortage of supply from the Waterball raises the price of imports. Of course, the scarcity we now suffer is largely self-inflicted. The result of unsustainable harvesting methods, and the high levels of mortality tolerated during shipment. Another reason for the shortage of imported stock is that over the cycles, the remaining earth-bound yeng have got better at avoiding capture. So even while selling technical knowhow to you, we are having to learn more about breeding the creatures for ourselves."

"What are the biggest challenges, would you say?" Hosk asks as ze stretches under the warming suns.

"One of the hardest to control is infanticide. The yeng, especially if harshly treated, are inclined to kill their babies rather than see them brought up as slaves. Then we have the popularity of meats from immature carcasses, the very young solely female gland-fed young fetch a good economic return for yeng farmers.

"As we all know, the best quality meat comes from young stock, but farming their young is not a practice yeng accept at all well. This one issue is dangerous enough that when sparked can lead to whole units rioting. To minimise the spreading of subversion amongst yeng populations, we only fatten young stock for food inside sealed commercial units. No 'outside' yeng is allowed anywhere near these specially isolated populations. Most yeng are probably fully aware of the existence of these factory farms, but self-interest and their own immediate concerns are so dominant that we hear surprisingly few rebellious comments raised by their existence. These factories are normally hidden in the countryside behind razor-wire and gun turrets. Just in case!"

"That sounds most sensible."

"Yeng can be more easily pushed to accept the slaughter of the elderly than of their young. So we have learned to regularly go without young flesh, except when supplied from the specialist farms."

Hosk looks a little concerned about such dietary constraint, but Boklung simply continues without a break.

"Eating quality is improved by processing and making sure the older meat is well-hung. Young meats from the sealed units are saved for special feasts. As well as the legal production of juvenile carcasses, there's always a Black Market, but the Zanin Guard do everything they can to supress the trade. I strongly advise that if Cheetan insist on the availability of young meat that you produce it all from units separate by distance from the working populations."

Hosk belches. "KKkggggghhhgg. Pardon me."

"I hope you don't mind me waffling on like this, Ambassador, but everything I say is adding at least tangentially to the information you will need if our business partnership is to flourish."

"You cannot tell me too much, my friend, please go on. I am fascinated. I belch only from the comfort of this bench and the thought of sweet young yeng flesh, not through boredom."

"Perhaps we should walk on, then. The breeding houses are just up here." Ze indicates a further row of large industrial buildings.

Hosk heaves zimself off the bench and waddles on with Boklung beside zim, moderating zis pace for the slower Cheetan.

"I hope the walk has stopped your rumbling stomach." Boklung says.

"Wonderful, yes, and your gardens have so many powerful fragrances!"

"Indeed! Hgggrh! Look through the windows of this breeding house. I believe that the bucks have just been released into the unit. Yeng are most fertile at around a thousand days, one Ungolian cycle, when well fed and exercised. Male and female pairs are best isolated at around twenty degrees of heat, using our 'hundred-scale' between the solid and gas states of water."

A couple of yeng lie on a sofa engaged in an intense game of foreplay. At least the buck is. The female does seem to be accommodating, or at least tolerating, his advances, but makes none of her own. It appears that the buck is determined on his course whatever the wishes of his current interest and that she is only too aware of that fact.

Boklung doesn't pause to really look, or even to take much of a breath. Zis words seem to flow on effortlessly as though strung together. "The courting rituals leading to fertilisation makes for a very interesting spectacle, especially when the female behaves less than enthusiastically. It amazes me how badly many stud males treat the females. The base interests of the stud often seem to overwhelm any vestige of human affection."

The female wriggles off the couch and tries to escape the buck's advances, but he tackles her and pins her down by holding her wrists against the floor. She struggles ineffectually and with little enthusiasm. He pushes her legs apart with his knees and thrusts himself inside.

"The psychology of the birthing yeng seems to be designed to accept moderate levels of physical domination by the stud," Boklung says, "but some males are seen to use whatever force is required to inseminate any female. These over-aggressive bucks are not as beneficial to farm output as one may first assume, as this behaviour seems to lead to much higher tendencies amongst the female yeng to abort the fertilized egg, or to later commit infanticide. This buck is only moderately aggressive compared to the worst, which I generally cull."

The two creatures watch as the sexual encounter draws to an insistent and rapid conclusion. Perhaps a little conscious of the excessiveness of zis voyeuristic rather than scientific interest, Hosk makes a rather distracting and disconnected comment.

"The whole building looks very clean and smartly appointed. You certainly treat yeng with far more care than is our custom on Trogaffin."

"And better than most yeng are treated on this planet, Hiugark … The best quality servants seem to be born to females that are allowed to form close bonds with the stud, at least for the duration of the offspring's infancy. The female produces by live birth at between forty and fifty days … Um! What have I missed? For now, even I am running out of steam. Anyway, I will make sure you have notes on all that comes to mind. Note that I like to give paired yeng time together for more than just sexual intercourse, thus the comfy layout of these particular quarters."

"How do you select the bucks?" Hosk asks, zis eyes still on the couple now sprawled, panting, on the floor.

"With tests of speed and strength, and by conformation. Once a buck is selected for breeding, he should be isolated from other entire specimens. The females can be jealous enough of their time with the bucks, without the complication of having competing males in the same pens." Boklung takes a couple of steps, waits for Hosk to follow, then they walk on together. "Only one in fifty male yeng is needed for breeding programmes. Profitability of the whole business relies on the economic use made of the vast excess of males, all of which are best castrated.

"There isn't much demand for males in the largest commercial sector, domestic service. Females are greatly preferred for this work. However, in agriculture, heavy industry and as hunt quarry, the demand for strong males partially offsets their lack of favour as servants. A large proportion of the male castrates go straight to fattening units.

"Routine castration can mean there being temporary shortages of breeding bucks, but one good buck is more than sufficient to keep a herd of fifty females breeding at maximum speed."

They stop outside another window, observing the females that have stopped activity to watch them pass. Many are clearly well on in pregnancy. They sit on chairs or lounge on the floor, chatting quietly.

"Female breeding stock are best kept lean, but never bony," Boklung continues. "They can be quickly fattened when their breeding days are over using hormone injections if they don't cooperate towards live weight gain. That, as you may imagine, is not infrequently. The fastest rates of fattening are achieved with the use of drugs that push the creatures into a state of constant, ravenous hunger.

"As for the males, most go straight to fattening units, though some of the muscular-looking castrates are sent to the Gantri along with enough children and females to give variety to the sport. Selection varies with the relative prices of meat and abundance of fighters."

"Your talk is all most useful," Hosk says.

Boklung's eyestalks straighten at the praise. "I am happy to make myself available to talk directly to your opinion leaders if you or they seek it. An occasional trip to Trogaffin would make for pleasant changes of scene."

Hosk glances at the timepiece strapped around one of zis limbs. "That is generous of you! But now, unfortunately, I must rush. I have an interview with one of our satellite news programmes. The topic is the possible replacement of some of the Royal Fleet Fighter Squadrons. The Monarch needs to raise taxes to pay for any new craft. The old ones are disarmed and sold on to privateers, but that only covers a fifth of the capital cost of replacement. The hope is that I can find a better market for demilitarised, used craft here."

"Of course. Don't let me keep you."

"I thank you for giving me yet more of your time, Boklung. I am pleased that our plans seem so well matched.

Perhaps I will see you tonight at the Gantri Amphitheatre. The excitement of the combats is another very good reason for breeding yeng. Anyway, for now you must excuse me."

"Of course! As regards the entertainments, unfortunately I won't make it, as I am overwhelmed with work. As it happens, it isn't in my nature to attend very often. I much prefer the sporting chance of the hunt to the savage cruelty of the Gantri. Enjoy the spectacle, my friend, and I will see you soon."

Hosk waddles off and Boklung strolls to one of zis favourite seats beneath a blue-flowering pretorienza tree. Ze takes a deep breath, relishing this time of cycle where the days slowly warm without the doubling heat of two high summer suns. From zis vantage spot, ze can enjoy the early flowering plants and watch yeng engaged in gardening. However, ze is preoccupied with the details of zis conversations with Huigark Hosk.

I must remember to remind Councillor Hosk to double check all maths between our numerical system and their base plus two counting systems. Not that ze is going to forget as such, but accidents do happen. The fact that both Cheetan and yeng use the same strange system makes me wonder what is most common across all civilisations. Is there actually some deep underlying mathematical reason for the popularity of decimal base, as I believe they call it? If there is, it is lost on me.

It might be a good idea to put in all figures using both numeric bases, so that we can be sure of avoiding confusion.

Boklung draws some of the Aranian advisory literature on yeng farming from the yeng-hide satchel strung on a belt around zis abdomen.

***

The Aranian reaching into zis satchel raises an obvious detail. This is that neither Cheetan nor Aranian use clothing of any kind unless it is used as protection against specific hazards, or as a device to demonstrate important status. The skin of both species is much more protective than is mankind's. From a practical point of view this resilience is probably just as well, because any techniques

**used to enable the clothing of creatures with so many legs
would seemingly be extremely complex!**

***

Boklung angles zis papers, so as to benefit from the
shade, and starts reading from the top corner ze'd previously
turned down.

> 'Long before we started importing yeng from
> Waterball, large numbers of alien creatures were
> already being used to meet the demands of the sporting
> arenas. The first yeng were imported exclusively for
> this entertainment. It was only subsequently that we
> discovered that they are uniquely useful as slave-
> workers.
>
> 'Gladiators', as the mostly male yeng fighters call
> themselves, are matched to fight to the death purely for
> our amusement. Before the development of the service
> industry and, latterly, breeding programmes, most
> females were used purely for meat along with the
> castrates. Initially, harvesting from Waterball was so
> easy that setting up breeding farms was considered to
> be uneconomic.
>
> Of course, the meat of even the gladiatorial males isn't
> wasted nowadays, tainted by stress hormones though it
> is. Only meats that may have toxic loads are burnt, such
> as those from battles involving wertutututua. Those
> cadavers go straight to the city's incinerators. Most of
> the meat from arenas ends up being fed back to other
> species of livestock.
>
> The largest quantities of buck meat are ground-down
> into drabbet chow. Drabbets, for some reason, seem to
> particularly relish the strong taste of the human
> androgen hormones. So, as one might expect, drabbet

are particularly keen on yeng gonads. The drabbets, of course, go for consumption in our best kitchens and restaurants, as they have a much preferred texture and taste to all but those yeng meats from young solely female gland-fed stock. A lot of yeng go to feeding the vast herds of pigs—creatures that originally came from Waterball.

Nowadays, arena fights between yeng of the birthing gender are becoming ever more popular. They may not be as physically strong, but what makes any fighting exciting is the struggle between equals. Barren females are often so used, as are those with bad conformation. Narrow-hipped females, which have more trouble dropping their young, and those that produce less succulent meat, are nowadays often marked for the arena. As a general rule of conformation, the thinly haunched adult females go to the arena, and the heavy ones are worked, sent for breeding, or if tending to excess fat, are dispatched at low live weight gains to the butchers.

The economics of farming are straight forward enough. A well-muscled stud that produces offspring with good conformation, crossed with good breeding females, makes for a healthy profit. Females that are too fat or thin are hard to impregnate, and also produce lower rates of live birth. Calm females with wide hips produce healthy young with the least trouble. As should be obvious, the less intelligent stock is easier to handle and far less likely to repeatedly escape. A good breeder that is generally docile always attracts a premium price. For this reason, intelligence and fight cunning tend to be slowly bred out of good fatstock herds. Whilst we had plenty of imports, this diversity of intelligence was little more than an interesting fact. However, it is inevitable that in the future we will go much further in developing different races for the meat trade, and for work or entertainment. Already, we have seen the development of the Type-Two.'

Hargh, when it comes to the hunt, the more intelligent they are the better the sport. Yes, the hunt ... it's been a very long day. Time has come for a bit of leisure!

1

THE HUNT MEET

The bugles sound across the Bluur Valley and the low rolling hills of Rapawaira. A group of yeng have been released from the set, in Yengcover Wood. They are a quarry that has been especially bred or later selected for hunting; being lean, with plenty of the sprinter's fast-twitch muscle and natural cunning, which all makes for challenging sport. However, as this is a training hunt, the group should have all been partially incapacitated with drugs. Inevitably the overseers, wishing to have good sport, use as little chemical coshing as is deemed necessary to provide a sop to the demands of local officials. However, today the hunters are particularly inexperienced, so heavier drugging of the quarry was thought necessary.

The hunts are often in conflict with the government, due to their very different interests in yeng breeding. If certain nervous governors had their way, all yeng would be Type-Two, thus reducing even what weak potential exists for them to threaten the established inter-species hierarchy. On the one side, those that value the breeding of intelligent quarry argue for chemical coshing when necessary. They maintain that whenever less cunning is required that stock can easily be dumbed down by using feed laced with certain heavy metals and pharmacological products, whilst the underlying genetic potential is preserved. The argument is also made that yeng genetic inheritance has proved to be complicated, especially when trying to select for level of intelligence. This makes producing consistently low intelligence specimens through breeding nearly impossible anyway. While on the other side, it is easy to make the case that anything that reduces yeng intelligence and independence of spirit would make Aranian society more secure, and that Type-Two breeding programmes clearly lowers the likelihood of dangerous behaviour.

As the Chief of the Rapawaira Hunt, it is Boklung's duty to regularly help with instruction. The truly feral yeng, like Jack, are often very dangerous. However, the reared creatures, when suddenly released, aren't normally able to do anything more threatening than throwing a few stones. Almost invariably, they have little idea as to how to best cooperate as a group. This particular collection of yeng has half a dozen imported slaves amongst the farmed ranks, part of a group brought in to add some particular genetic characteristic or another to the 'herd'. This half dozen were then later rejected for breeding. However, the hunt is unaware that they have been sold anything but ignorant Ungol born stock. Amongst the imports are two sisters.

Boklung arrives too late to witness the release of the quarry, so it is the horde of juvenile and over-eager-looking Aranian that draw zis attention. Ze has almost lost interest before the chase has even begun. Boklung takes a quick swig of the inebriating cocktail that is invariably on offer before the chase, and then turns to wave off the scouts and their packs of hunting screebur. These four-legged creatures look not so unlike hairless Waterball hyenas.

The screebur are soon hot on the scent of the yeng runners. The quarry has been given a good start, not that that usually makes much difference. As is usually the case, the scent-lines indicate that the yeng at first stuck close together, but over time, individuals and small groups had peeled away. The screebur pack similarly splinters. It isn't long before the first yeng is in sight—a limping female that is almost immediately dragged to the ground by two screebur, one with teeth deep in her buttocks and the other ripping out her throat. A moment later the yeng is already just a twitching lump of raw meat surrounded by a tearing, whining pack.

Another female looks on from nearby, all but submerged in the filthy wallow of a herd of recently stampeded dodarks. Athalie looks on in horror as her elder sister is ripped apart, and almost screams as a screebur turns with Annah's scalp hanging from its jaws. Another animal, half hearing Athalie's whimper, turns and stands still, staring in her direction until finally dropping its head and re-joining the feast. Annah has sacrificed herself, having first deliberately skirted the wallow with Athalie, then by moving away alone, drawing the pursuit onto her. Athalie, terrified of being discovered, sinks even lower in the mud until, with head tipped back, nothing is exposed to even the sharpest eyes except the almost closed lips of her mouth. She senses rather than sees screebur and spiders skirting the edge of the wallow.

Lying as still as shallow, panicked ventilation will allow, she'll not dare stagger from the mud and slowly clearing, chilling water for a couple of Earth hours. Though she feels the pain of tiny mudfish biting at her toes and then everywhere else, she hardly moves. Fear motivates the endurance that survival demands. Few can ever exercise such fortitude until valued life is threatened with being extinguished.

The hunt moves on, and one by one the hunted succumb. Most are quickly dispatched, overwhelmed by the pack, and occasionally a few yeng hold them at bay only to be hacked down by the spiders. The body count is taken several times, with an average disparity of one, but then the carnage was so severe at the start that no one is quite sure about how to effectively quantify the remains. Some make a half-hearted attempt to retrace movements, to look for a possible missing yeng, but the issue is soon dismissed. Boklung signs the hunting card—thirty released, thirty killed, and the Aranian retire to celebrate their success.

Athalie, now cold, aching, flesh nibbled raw, crawls out of the wallow. The caked on mud cracks and flakes off as she struggles to her knees. A slow visual traverse of her surroundings reveals nothing moving, so she slowly straightens and, rubbing her arms, hobbles off, directly away from the city and towards nearby hills.

Tears roll down her face; she feels the throb of a growing headache, and every movement hurts her patches of mudfish skinned flesh. Panic slowly subsides, replaced by a terrible feeling of loss and guilt. After all, she has only survived because of Annah's brave self-sacrifice.

Later, Athalie is so hungry that, despite all she has been through, she finds herself scanning the surroundings for anything edible. Illness has prevented her eating for a week. Little does she know that this enforced starvation has guarded her naturally sharp mind, her cunning, and that maybe this has a lot to do with her having survived the day. She is strong and fortunate to be from a hunt-breeding programme that produces yeng known for their physical fitness.

By low-light she has eaten some berries that have settled in her belly without causing her to vomit. Later, as the vegetation thickens and the ground slopes steeply into the hills, she finds a babbling stream. Finally, exhausted, she falls to her knees and prays for her brave sister as she slips slowly away into a nightmare-tortured sleep.

8

BUSINESS MATTERS

Boklung and Hosk meet in the bar of The Bugle, where they enjoy the local refreshments and eat snacks of desiccated, salted bugs. As is usually the way when Aranian and Cheetan meet, the Aranian is doing most of the talking.

"I am proud to be the Chief of our local hunt. We meet once every five full-lights throughout the cycle. A good chase does wonders for taking my mind off work. Today I was just out with the youngsters after doped releases. Meets like this are nothing like as exciting as hunting feral yeng, but I have a responsibility to pass on my skills to the young."

"From what I hear, I'm surprised that feral yeng are tolerated at all," Hosk says.

"They often aren't, but a balance is kept between the wishes of the hunts for fresh stock, and the demands of those for who even a small number of wild yeng are an unacceptable danger. Yes, wild colonies do need to be well managed lest they become a real security threat. Let me read directly from a recent government pamphlet, noting that I don't ascribe to all it says." Boklung picks up the brochure ze'd checked off as being suitable for Cheetan consumption and reads aloud:

"'Wild yeng can harbour and spread disease to our domestic stock. There's also the possibility that physical contact between the populations may enable the spreading of seditious ideas. From the security angle, it is only beneficial that resupply from their home planet is no longer sustainable, as it is always the first generation imports that are the greatest cause of trouble. They provide the individuals most likely to have the wherewithal to rebel. The imports quite naturally come with all sorts of independent views and skills, and always with a new disease load' ..."

Boklung looks up, distracted by a young and spritely Aranian entering the bar. Zis four eyestalks swivel together to follow the newcomer's progress. Suddenly ze looks very damp around the breathing holes on zis thorax. "Good full-light, dear Lebl."

"And the best to you, Cingwin, lovely to see you," the youngster replies.

"I'm afraid I'm rather busy, my special, but perhaps I could call you later. May I introduce you to the Cheetan Ambassador to our city, Huigark Hosk."

"Charmed to meet you, Ambassador; I'll not disturb your business. Yes, please call, Cingwin."

Lebl saunters off to the other end of the bar and into the company of a group of half-intoxicated young individuals.

Boklung, looking extremely flustered, chokes out, "Excuse me! I'll just have a sip of water."

"Take your time. What a charming creature."

"Yes indeed! Lebl is a very particular friend of mine. Hgghg. Excuse me ... Anyway, the buck that I lost was a recent import and too cunning for words. The chances that it has survived may be small, but rather worryingly I heard a report that a murdered hunter was found in the bush. Apparently, this very experienced tracker was outwitted by a yeng. It killed by leading the scout over a pit trap. I have a gut feeling that the killer was Jack, my own escaped property. God forbid."

"Will others suspect that your animal was the killer? That could be difficult."

"Quite possibly, but I certainly won't mention my fears to anyone but close friends."

"And I shall say nothing."

"Thank you. Nowadays we have ways of building in safety systems in case yeng turn violent or threaten to escape. For example, we can implant chips that if not regularly recharged disintegrate and cause the death of the animal, or ones that can be exploded, or ones that are designed to allow longer distance tracking. These control systems are rarely employed at present, but have the potential to allow us to take minimal risks while retaining a good deal of versatility in the species. Breeding Type-Twos is totally unnecessary. It is, after all, the very fact yeng are so versatile that makes it hard to see us running a modern economy without them. I don't believe we can afford to lose any diversity. Our very survival may depend on having a good supply of variously useful yeng. Hgg ..." Boklung's voice quietens. "Particularly in the case of the Arcraft project."

Hosk's eyes sparkle with interest.

Boklung observes zim closely. "I assume that you have already gathered intelligence on our space plans. Am I correct in that assumption?"

"Well, yes, I cannot deny that we know about the Arcraft project."

"At the moment, my government is building spacecraft to send out on long distance missions. We intend running these ships with breeding colonies of yeng used alongside robots."

"Yeng? Ah. Do you mind if I take a few notes? It is reasonable to assume that we have interpreted some gathered Arcraft data inaccurately."

"Go ahead. There needn't be any pretence of secrecy; well, at least not at this stage."

Hosk takes an electronic writing tablet from a satchel around zis neck.

"Now then, what in particular would you like to know?" Boklung asks zis eager friend.

"I would be delighted to hear all you feel able to tell me."

Boklung nods, reminds zimself to be careful not to expose anything the Cheetan shouldn't know, then begins zis explanation: "Each self-sustaining Arcraft will carry possibly three hundred yeng, six hundred ambulatory robots, and another couple of hundred fixed location 'bots. I intend that there be no Aranian on-board: for whom would we send on such a tough, likely suicidal, mission? Hggh ... the missions will be one way. We could conscript, but that is hardly a way to build a crew to be trusted. So it is probably best to just load Aranian eggs. Though that is my real intention, it is presently a long way from being a seriously considered or even generally known proposition." Boklung pauses for a moment and observes Hosk writing on zis tablet. "Perhaps, on second thoughts, if you don't mind, you could memorise rather than physically record these more sensitive words."

"Of course." Hosk erases a note and clicks the pen back into the device and Boklung continues.

"Our eggs will be in secret compartments in the craft. At least some would have it that these be programmed to hatch unbeknown to the yeng, sometime after a successful landing. That idea is ridiculous of course, though at present I'm rather forced to go through the pretence of planning for such an event.

"There's this widely-held view that we can somehow engineer systems so robustly that they will enable new-born Aranian aided by the robots to seamlessly regain control from independently acting yeng. The concept is that the robots will have all the information and chemical controls at their disposal needed to quickly help the new hatchings regain their status as dominant species. According to these plans, the first generation will be nurtured through infancy by suitably programmed robots. I see glaring flaws in what is at best a ridiculously unrealistic expectation. That the yeng, having been more or less their own masters for so long, would just bow down to Aranians is ludicrous."

Hosk nods and looks like ze may have planned to say something, but Boklung continues without a pause.

"Of course, the complete maintenance of our domination through all stages of the project was the psychological starting point for most of those that have thought the project through. This thinking is all based on the false premise that the expedition need never be dependent on yeng. Personally, I see the yeng having to be left to lord it over all, from the moment of take-off and until the long awaited arrival of a second Arcraft into the already established colony."

The Cheetan's eyes glisten with moisture and then spasm into a characteristic hypnotic swivel as ze fails to hide zis shock.

"You understand that this part of our conversation is in confidence, Huigark," Boklung says, "between you, me and Sinanna."

"Of course. I am flattered that you trust me, my friend."

"Yes. Well, to continue; I am convinced that practicality demands that our young will remain subservient to the yeng until a second ship arrives. It is quite stupid to assume that we can programme the 'bots' to maintain control throughout the process, and even more ridiculous to believe that they could simply snatch back command from the yeng at a later stage. The project will be dependent on yeng ingenuity. Most of our politicians' thinking is totally delusional."

Boklung becomes increasingly agitated as ze spouts zis monologue. This has led to zim speaking ever more stridently. Perhaps this is in part to try and kid zimself that ze has no fears in giving away so much of zis revolutionary thinking to a Cheetan. Or possibly ze is just so agitated that ze can't currently keep zis own counsel. Boklung knows ze has to trust at least a few key others if zis plans are going to have any chance, but as to whether one of those creatures should really be Hosk isn't immediately obvious. Whatever, zis secret is out of the bag, and there's no chance of retracting anything already said.

"I will do all that I can, authorised or not, to at very least water down government intentions. Aranian infancy is relatively short as a part of lifespan, but it is still far too long for such a naïve plan. The yeng would easily overcome any stupid attempt by our hatchlings to seize control, even if we could guarantee the most efficient of robot support.”

“I can see you have put a lot of thought into this, Boklung. It is very farsighted of you to allow for medium to long-term yeng dominance. I find that your simple logic is very compelling. I can assure you that I will guard your private views. Anyway, I’m not at all sure that anyone would believe me, a Cheetan, if I did report your uncommon agenda. My reportage would seem as outlandish as it surely did when the ancient astronomer Uccinipose Ulocinas first tried to convince the ‘Churches of Sinanna’ that the stars didn’t rotate about the planets. Your idea is certainly revolutionary.”

Saliva dribbles from Boklung’s mouth, and pungent gas flows into the air as ze continues. Boklung’s sensitivities about zis honesty are causing zim more than a mild fluster. “If I thought there was any way I could adhere to the wishes of the Council and give the Arcraft a reasonable chance, I would opt for it. I just don’t think that is possible. The Project is totally dependent on the yeng, and I wish others could recognise that. Progress demands that we are the subservient race during a short period of local history in a distant corner of space.

“The Arcraft won’t even have escape pods, saving on non-vital payload, so helping ensure the yeng can’t escape the broad destiny we choose for them. Once the craft has left our Lush System, its passengers will be truly doomed to never return. Any Aranian crew would go mad facing such a bleak future. Yeng are far better suited to guarding our ambitious plans than we are of doing it for ourselves.”

“So, you are totally serious about setting up colonies far away across the Galaxy that you are prepared for Aranian to be subservient to yeng to ensure success. That is either heroic loyalty to a plausible policy or subversive stupidity.”

“Haaagh. Do you see me as subversive?”

Boklung’s vehement tone makes the Cheetan recoil slightly. “Not at all. I simply meant that others may see it that way.”

“Which is why this conversation must remain private.”

"Of course."

"For me, it is simply the only way we will achieve our aims. The concept that the yeng and robots will build well-structured colonies out on other planets, for Aranian to emerge into or conquer later is totally robust. Yeng will do all the pioneering without risking Aranian lives. Problem solving will be enhanced considerably by the yeng's desire to survive. They will, however, be trapped into following our grand design; that is provided we build-in sufficiently subtle controls. That shouldn't be hard to achieve, as, actually, all our species require many of the same developmental solutions. Haaagh ... To be totally flippant, if let us say, for the sake of argument, that some of their homes are built a little on the small side for Lush species, we can easily raise a few roofs later. Food supply, water, power; these are crucial, not architectural detail.

"The Council will be allowed to continue to believe that the robots control the yeng at the moment of our brood's emergence. I have no hope of changing that view, so I can only draw suspicion on my plans by trying. Only the core team in the project will know that this is never going to be the case.

"Best reality will mean that when follow-up ships, manned by Aranian, arrive to take a firm grip on the new colony, these migrants will find an established population of young Aranian, but realistically still enslaved to yeng masters. This doesn't at all have to mean being mistreated. I don't personally treat slaves badly, and I have to believe that the descendants of the yeng I send won't do so either. Whatever happens, these Aranian won't be beasts of burden for long. Even if the worst happens, namely the hatchings have been supressed or never born, that wouldn't be the end of any new Aranian world. Despite my respect for the skills of yeng, I'm certain that we will always be quite superior enough as an invading force to put them back in their place."

"Absolutely. Were that not true, they wouldn't be here now."

"Indeed. The many Councillors holding out for sending Aranian on the initial flight, claim—with some justification—

that they could always find a crew. Yes, we could find enough Aranian prepared to volunteer to make that self-sacrifice, but in reality they'd never psychologically cope with a one-way ticket to what could be literally a doomed hell. It is one thing being brave sitting down here and quite another feeling the same a few billion kilometres out in space with, for example, a possibly untreatable virus killing off crew members, no new medicine, and an already sick doctor."

"You are a true visionary, Boklung; I am in awe. That you recognise the need to deceive your own race and that you are prepared to risk making your own subservient, is incredible. What is more, I can hardly believe that I so easily see the merit in your plan. I guess I should fear your colonial ambitions, and worry that your civilisation will steal a march on ours. But actually, I don't. Space is big enough for both of us, even though our shared system has often failed to be so. I have to admit that, at the present time, we Cheetan think that the idea of setting up distant colonies is over challenging ... We haven't considered any idea as clever as using yeng as pioneers."

"We have no need to hide our expansion plans from each other. As you say, however short of space we are in the Lush System, a shortage beyond is impossible. Anyway, it is quite certain that we will both achieve more if we can help each other deal with the massive challenges of permanently expanding into distant star systems. What really is different about us, other than your extra pair of legs? I am sure that the very different creatures we encounter will be challenging enough for even our combined resources."

"Indeed." The Cheetan thrusts another bug in zis mouth, and Boklung takes a sip of zis bright red drink before continuing.

"A bit of yeng history may amuse you. Their worst enemies throughout most of their history have been from competing colonies of their own kind. Neither of our species is immune to such behaviour, but we have never been able to generate the tribal hatred that yeng are capable of. Zoologists put this all down to their sexual dimorphism, which encourages aggressive competition for partners.

"Anyway, for a time, two opposing political blocks of yeng threatened to destroy not only themselves but their planet, by using a large quantity of nuclear fission weapons. Hggh ... This wasn't male against female creatures, though it might seem logical to assume that. Rather, yeng conflict grows out of the desire of the male to own and control as many assets, including females, as possible. This was dressed up as a war between differing philosophical systems, though really it is more easily understood as being driven by a combination of mutual fear and pure greed in two equally powerful geo-political empires.

"Yet a blink of an eye later, these still-competing blocks were united in their exploration of space. If those worst of enemies can cooperate to expand their horizons, I'm sure our two planets, living as we have in recent harmony, can co-operate to expand our separate empires."

"It always pays to work together, my friend, especially when the rewards of so doing can be so huge. Scarcity of resources is only ever a local phenomenon. And, as you say, how little is one pair of limbs between us when we both have to face creatures with any number from none to what, a hundred?"

"Haash! Yes, and then, of course, there's the pesky spherical mollash that seems to be able to grow any number of limbs, at will. Anyway, even though our social orders don't put a high value on individual lives, Aranian individuals certainly value themselves. We all consider ourselves far too precious and we're certainly too psychologically vulnerable when any great distance from home. So we are very fortunate to have a species that we can use to take risks on our behalf, especially in the frontiers of space."

"Yes, the yeng is certainly variously useful and I follow your thinking, Boklung. Using them as a pioneer corps is certainly logical. I wonder how much we could achieve with selective breeding. All sorts of commercial opportunities come to mind."

"Since I have been on your planet," Hosk explains, "I've become most interested in well-muscled males, which are so much better at the massaging of my nether regions. Hahgahahg!

I have their nails and teeth pulled as a matter of course, but what about saving on veterinary bills by breeding ones without these sharp irritants? Castrates fill the bill well enough, so I am not saying I go out looking for expensive bucks to satisfy my needs."

Boklung assumes that the drift away from seriousness in Hosks' words indicate a certain level of intoxication. Ze responds to the Cheetan by adding zis own note of flippancy. "Haash! That would make massage feel less, hggg, risky, but it is hardly economically feasible. To have any success we would have to do a lot of expensive genetic engineering. It is unlikely that natural breeding would be able to provide answers. Anyway, their real value is as workers and meat, not as toys! Breeding out teeth, for example, which are necessary for the creatures' ingestion of a natural, healthy diet, would be a rather short-sighted development. Can I guess why one would want a massaging tool free of teeth?"

The Cheetan's mouth comes as close to a yeng smile as they ever do, a sort of a widening and flattening of the orifice. "Haaaash, I am quite sure you can, Boklung. Our species' sexual passions differ little."

"And thinking about succulence rather than sucking, conformation is very much the buzz in yeng farming. Just thinking over some of the success we have had with our own breeding programmes makes me feel hungry. Perhaps I could treat you to a nice juicy castrate from my freezer. Well, not a whole one, not at this time of day, but a nice snack of yeng rump might go down a treat. What do you say to us adjourning to my residence? Some good food will help mollify our excessive consumption of happy juice."

"That sounds like a splendid idea, Boklung, and very generous of you. But first, to make such a snack worthwhile, let me get in another quick round of hippotion before we go. Harrhh, bartender ... Next time we must have a meal and liquid refreshments on my business account at the Port Hotel."

"Good idea, Huigark." Ze calls to the bartender. "And the same again for me! Hgg ... Not to embarrass you but, now that we are business associates and, may I say, friends, I hope you don't mind me calling you by your familiar name. I am very aware that I've already let the customary formality between our species slip."

"Not at all, this is your world. We Cheetan are certainly known for preserving our social distance. That trait seems to go with our stronger sense of hierarchy. There is some truth in the view, widely held here, that our society is over-heavily drilled. We don't tolerate the, hhuurrg, the freedom of expression that you Aranian display so readily. I am becoming increasingly well adjusted to your ways; nevertheless, your willingness to entertain a Cheetan, in your private house, when I turn up practically uninvited, is greatly appreciated. I still have some way to go to get used to the full spontaneity and flexibility of your social order. However, you have done a great deal to help me abandon much of my reticence about behaving in such an Aranian way."

"I really don't deserve all the credit for my lack of turgid formality. A not inconsiderable measure of influence has been provided by our strong hippotion."

"Well yes: that too! Haagh … Drinking together certainly helps overcome social barriers! Anyway, enough of that, likewise, may I feel at ease calling you Cingwin?"

"As the instigator, I'm certainly happy with less formality. Provided, that is, you don't play the 'sounds like' game in your language. I don't want to be known by your people as a fundamental excretion."

"Hgg! Do not worry. You will never be Singwn. We punish the mocking of given names with hard labour. That courtesy extends even to the names of friendly foreigners. Come to think of it, we punish most transgressions with hard labour. Haagh!"

"There's certainly more than a trifling amount of truth in those old generalisations we have about each other's society. I easily concede that point, and admit that our typically high degree of selfish individuality, especially when someone has to do the chores, has resulted in Aranian's natural inclination towards a heavy reliance on slaves. Yeng are the ideal creatures for doing the work we so despise. They grow our crops, clean our sewers, nurture the eggs of our off-spring, clean our houses, and keep us groomed and free from nits. Yeng are very versatile."

"Indeed. You don't need to convince me of their usefulness, especially in the area of grooming. Haagh!"

"But we do have long-standing and strict laws about how we treat them as meat providers. Such laws safeguard a balance between their rebellious tendencies and our needs, and yeng welfare is always on the political agenda. As I touched on earlier, we long ago took the pragmatic decision to respect certain standards of yeng welfare. It is illegal in our society to slaughter young stock that is still dependent on lactating females or formula feeds without a special farm license.

"Anyway, in my opinion, it is incumbent on higher beings to show due respect for all life. Mental torture of sentient creatures, which slaughtering the young in front of the parent stock is definitely a form of, falls below modern, civilised standards."

The skin above Hosk's eyes lifts. "Most Cheetan find the concept of effectively giving lowly animals any formal rights highly amusing. The general opinion is that the younger the meat the better its flavour, and the better it is for the consumer's health."

Boklung's face draws long with obvious concern, while zis eye-stems pull close together, suggesting determination to not be distracted. Perhaps Huigark is showing a glimpse of zis true self. "Let us set this issue aside for now. It would be politically expedient for The Cheetan Government to at least give a nod to the idea of respecting basic animal rights."

Hosk's eyes flick from one side to the other, perhaps considering how ze would raise such an idea.

"You should be doing all you can to mitigate against the cause of those opposed to selling breeding knowhow," Boklung continues. "Concerns about the treatment of yeng are taken very seriously by a small but strong and vociferous minority. We can't afford to ignore the animal rights activists. They could jeopardise all our trading plans. And, as it happens, I share very many of their concerns.

"Anyway, that's enough, drink up! It's time we adjourned to my residence if we are to give my yeng time to cook us a decent supper."

Hosk gives Boklung a hefty nudge. "Or, to be the decently cooked supper!"

***

Later, after eating, Boklung and Hosk settle down on comfy loungers. Boklung, as usual, is first to dive into conversation.

"So then, Huigark! What do you think of the look of the yeng that washed your mandibles? She goes by the name of Diane. Sired by a now deceased, but very good, white skin of mine, Tom Wilson, out of a black named Della. She has a very nice temperament and is an excellent cook."

On hearing her name, Diane drops onto one knee and lowers her head, as is the custom in domestic service. On rising, she backs away.

"I would rather be served by that soft creature than a robot any day. They make fine servants, Cingwin ... The earth-meat, 'cow' I believe you called it, was simply delicious. When you are next able to find the time to visit my world, I will be honoured to have you as my guest. As you know, I have an important final negotiation to make with your brood cousin, Governor Nadarchis as regards the status of the Finestorian Asteroid Cluster before I visit home. It has been a disputed territory for far too long. My government proposes a fair division of the area.

"If you don't mind, I will also put to zim a formalised version of our trade proposal whilst I am there. Here is a copy. Let me know if you think I have missed anything. In the long run it will pay to do everything by the book. Naturally, I will suggest, in the strongest possible terms, that you take charge of trade from this end. You understand that my full intention is to aid both of our private ambitions, Cingwin, not to circumvent you. We are firm friends and partners, and why indeed should we be restricted to only a single mutually beneficial partnership?

88

We must see beyond the narrow confines of our initial governmental projects."

"Quite! We must help ourselves, while of course, making sure we expedite our states' sponsored plans. I will draw up a detailed specimen private contract, based on your trade proposal. With you working as the most politically active partner, whilst I concentrate on the business end, we will be making best use of our individual talents.

"But whilst you're here, I would like to point out a few more things about the yeng business in general. You obviously know a lot of this, but so as to avoid unsound assumptions, I'll risk teaching you to hatch eggs. I'm sorry to go on so. I can assure you that I get as fed up with the sound of my voice as you must do. Nevertheless, I have a lot of information to impart, and in the shortest of time."

"Do not worry about it, Cingwin. I am here to learn, even if that means having some aspects over repeated. It is far better to be told something multiple times than not at all. What are ambassadors if not instruments for the absorption and distribution of information? Perhaps one of those quite delicious, what did you call them, redfix, yes that was it, would certainly help me keep up my concentration."

"A splendid idea! It's already late, so how about a fresh warm one. Diane, get Grace up here, so that you may bleed each other. You can have an extra rest period afterwards to help you recover."

The yeng is obviously used to such a request as she shows no particular concern as she scurries away to find Grace.

"Thank you for being tolerant of my monologues. Hgg … We let yeng sleep for a half of every light rotation in ten separate periods. They don't perform well otherwise. It is obvious why when one considers the short length of the Waterball day. We reckon that one of our cycles is roughly twenty for yeng, going by the length of their planet's day and their lifespan.

"Perhaps the most amazing thing about the planet Waterball is that it spins so very rapidly. Because it is a one star system, almost every point is in constantly changing light. In every four of our hours most locations on that planet move through a whole rotation of light and dark back to the starting point. Day length is actually more complicated than that though. Because the planet wobbles on its axis, these periods vary in their length depending on one's actual position on the planet and the time in the planetary cycle. Contrast that with our two planets that are bathed in very nearly constant, though variable, light from the two gas-ball suns in our cosmic circulation."

"Which explains the reason for the very short periods of productive work that yeng are physiologically suited to," Hosk says. "I sort of knew all that, but had never made the link. I am amazed at how much we need to learn about the species. I really cannot doubt that any business model for yeng production on Trogaffin will hugely benefit from our close partnership."

"I'm sure that you would manage on your own, but why go through the cycles of inevitable mishaps when we can help you avoid them. We have already made every mistake possible, so therefore you shouldn't need to."

"Indeed," Hosk says. "At what age do you slaughter them?"

"Ah yes, I was coming to that. Yeng die naturally at between three and five cycles, depending on how well they are looked after. A long span is six cycles, and very rarely they have been recorded as living for seven. We generally send slaves for slaughter at age four, which seems like a reasonable compromise between them having normal life spans and us having quality meat. The fat stock go for slaughter at the end of their first cycle. Of course, many die in infancy, but until a lot of effort has been put into training, one see's little real economic loss. This cost is further reduced if they are reasonably plump in relation to the amount of feed pumped into them at the time of death. The expense of early mortality is especially low if they are so young that all their feed came direct from the females' secretions. These young carcasses are, of course, not allowed to enter our food chain unless we are sure that their deaths were as a result of natural causes. Nowadays it is strictly forbidden to feed any species to its own kind. This is to reduce the risk of spreading species-specific diseases and disorders.

"Meat is the key to raising support for our venture on Trogaffin, I'm sure of that. Once that industry is better established, then we can make much more convincing arguments for expanding that production for wider use. So initially, we should be geared towards selecting for high fertility and fast live weight gain. I want them born and up to slaughter weight as quickly as possible.

"Hopefully those females selected for breeding can be carrying again shortly after. Your model of four cycles of use as labour before slaughter must be a long-term goal. If we do everything else right, without too many problems, then I'm sure that Cheetan interest in slave uses will steadily grow."

"I do understand, my friend. I appreciate that our planets are not the same. Of course, despite what I said earlier, even four cycles is only a marker post for us. Valuable trustees and skilled workers are treated very differently. They aren't slaughtered until they become totally compromised by age. I'm sure that over time, Cheetans accustomed to only seeing yeng in butchers' shops and on the plate will come to value them as the truly versatile creatures they are."

"We have many environmental factors that you don't share, Cingwin, such as our low oxygen level."

"You have to use sealed units anyway because of your low atmospheric pressure, so oxygen can easily be augmented. Experiments have shown that the performance of newly imported yeng is marginally improved when their environment is boosted with extra oxygen. A higher oxygen level better mirrors the atmosphere on Waterball. However, seeing as how rare imports are becoming, investment in the necessary equipment is no longer viable here. From where you start, Huigark, you are bound to think differently about that.

"Anyway, even imports soon seem to adapt if they aren't overworked early on. Our atmosphere is thirteen oktig oxygen compared with fifteen and a half on Waterball ... I remind myself once more to be careful not to confuse our octal counting system, and your decimal one. Where is my calculator?" Boklung looks around zis lower limbs, then extracts an electronic device from a satchel resting on the floor beside the lounger. "Arrh, yes, hgg."

Hosk doesn't wait for the Aranian to use zis device. "In decimal that is seventeen percent compared with twenty one. And whilst you are searching for numbers, Trogaffin's oxygen content is ten percent by our counting method and roughly six and a half oktig by yours. It is easy, Boklung, as for every hundred units with our counting you score one hundred and forty four. Like most of my species, I can do the calculation in my sleep. It always amazes me how poor most Aranian are at mental arithmetic."

Boklung puts zis device aside. "Well, we can't all be good at everything. You will obviously not have any trouble with my figures then."

"I am being flippant, my dear Boklung. We make mistakes as well. Both our nations have made tragic errors of calculation, especially when our two mathematical systems have been confused. Bridges that are not properly engineered for their loads, spacecraft put into dangerous orbits, huge errors of navigation. You will recall that fairly recently we lost a tourist vehicle when it crashed into your Mount Gnormicras, all on-board killed except, ironically, the navigator. Ze found the time to get into an escape capsule. We were very pleased your government returned the coward to be properly processed."

"Yes, a tragic incident! So, taking into consideration my mathematics, no guesses as to who should have primary responsibility for technical specifications in our joint ventures, Huigark. And we must share every detail of our business accounting, especially where it might be in our mutual interest to be, shall we say, creative in our choice of bookkeeping technique.

"I will do what I can to select and multiply livestock best suited to your planet. I even think that over time we have a good chance of engineering a yeng that is able to survive for greatly extended periods in your natural atmosphere. I know that some attempts have been made in that direction, but I suspect that our scientists were less than fully committed to such research as it offered Ungoliantis only marginal advantages. Pursuing such outcomes has suddenly become far more important to us now that we plan to use yeng in space. I have already set up a special breeding unit right here in The Gardens, which can be environmentally regulated. You may recall that we saw it in the distance when we passed my selective breeding houses; a brand new building with construction cranes still in position. Various areas can easily be set up with an atmosphere identical to that of your planet, Huigark."

"That would be very helpful."

"Our differing planetary requirements mirror to some degree a range of difficulties we will encounter in the space exploration project. Trogaffin models particularly well for space, as both environments require enclosed systems in which yeng are born, work and are eventually slaughtered.

"Our core business isn't going to be over hindered even if we can't produce a yeng that can work effectively outdoors on your planet. But wouldn't there be great commercial benefit to us if we could make a scientific breakthrough on that? If we were able produce a yeng that works efficiently in six oktig, even if only for relatively short work periods, then that would really be something. That might even raise the prospect of you using them as domestic servants, just as we do. That would certainly draw Cheetan thinking away from simple yeng for meat, robot for labour paradigms.

"Such an atmosphere-tolerant creature could be of huge benefit to both our races if and when we start sending out regular long distance missions of yeng to go where no Lushian has gone before."

"I'm very enthusiastic about trying to breed yeng to survive in our atmosphere. However unlikely total success might be, any improvement would help. On-going maintenance of sealed systems makes them a relatively expensive production method. It is not just pressurisation and gas exchange problems that these intensive units throw up. For example, there are all sorts of pollution problems resulting from the concentration of effluents produced by intensive systems. We have many constraints on waste disposal."

Boklung nods. "I will put extra resources into trials using partially deoxygenated air and artificially lowered gravities. I can start atmospherically challenging candidate yeng within days. I'll keep the fact that this work will be equally useful for our private ambitions as low profile as possible, so as to not attract unwelcomed political interest. There's no point drawing down the attention of those ready to find fault.

"As we all know, we have introduced other living things from Waterball. These include some feed crops and animals that suit yeng nutritional needs. Many of these have been fitted into our own diets, such as rat and chicken. We should do maximum-minimum gas and pressure tests on all these plants and animals as well."

Hosk manages to squeeze in a few words. "These are exciting days."

"I don't want to get carried away, but we should be thinking about other exotic trades that we may personally benefit from, and not just from the Waterball. So far, the only creatures from other star systems that have come even close to be anything like as useful as yeng themselves are from the Planet Cringlow. It, of course, provided us with the versatile gloot. Who would ever have believed that we could find a non-carbon based life-form that when chemically mixed with carbonates in varying quantities would provide us with such a range of versatile building materials? Though to be honest, I don't like the way this business causes so much suffering to the gloot."

"Hmph. I doubt that gloot suffer in the way that we understand the meaning of the word."

Boklung's eyestalks quiver. "They have a nervous system and react to stimulus just as we do."

"I suppose so, but such a lower life-form—"

Boklung charges on, obviously aggravated by Hosk's views, which are actually closer to most Aranians than are zis own. "Well, to my mind the comparative lack of concern for this life-form rather makes some of the environmentalists' demands about yeng welfare look ridiculous. They just don't dare risk the wide public anger that would ensue if they tried to condemn the exploitation of gloot. Because they are silicate life-forms and vital to the construction of our very comfy modern homes, we have quietly overlooked the fact that these creatures, primitive though they are, seem to feel pain. There are plenty of soft-minded Aranian that complain about the cruelty of blood sports and fight entertainment, but almost none that do about the agonies gloot suffer in the construction of our housing."

"Isn't the word 'agony' a little strong here?" Hosk says.

Boklung tilts zis head and observes zis 'friend' for a moment. Ze decides ze needs to calm down, so as not to be tempted to rise to the apparent bait. Ze measures zis reply.

"You know as well as I do that we have long shared the trade in gloot without, thankfully, ever coming to blows. After-all, we even have some cooperative ventures on Cringlow itself, don't we? Anyway, that is enough talk for now. I just want to point out that we should be looking together for exotic new opportunities. There must be any number of lucrative collaborations we could get into; it is just a matter of identifying them."

Hosk glances at the timepiece strapped to one of zis forelimbs.

Boklung notices. "What's the time? Haagg, I've been talking forever. I can call a transporter to take you back to your hotel."

"If it is all the same to you, and late though it is, I would like a little more time to talk, though I haven't got that long, as I have to prepare for a meeting with our new Trade Commissioner. I am amused that a hunting man would worry so about the suffering of a gloot, but you are a complex chap, Cingwin, that is for sure."

"Ah, but the short-lived and necessary pain inflicted by the hunter is not the same as the unnecessary pain caused in the construction business as the gloot is slowly desiccated. I abhor excessive cruelty to any life-form."

"Hghgh ... Let us leave that topic for now, as we know how different our views are. We have covered a lot of ground. You are a good teacher, Cingwin. I wonder if I might prevail on you to have a chat with Trade Commissioner Orflandis Hiygleest, sometime soon. Ze really is a bit like a 'yeng out of oxygen' here at the moment. I would love to get zim up to speed so that ze can take some of the routine issues off my limbs."

"I will be glad to find the time to talk to your new appointee."

"Thank you ... On another topic, perhaps I could privately purchase a small herd of yeng castrates from you? Believe it or not, I have a project for yeng that doesn't involve eating them. I have storage room for about twenty in the hold of my craft. Of course, that is twenty four in your mathematics. Ones straight off a meat farm, rather than more expensive trained creatures, will do fine."

"Of course; I'll be delighted to trade."

"I plan to use them in one of my mines. It has to be pumped with air as it is, so changing the pressure and gas composition should prove easy. I know from studying your mining industry that the biped configuration is reasonably well suited to working in narrow seams underground, provided they get rest periods to stretch tired muscles. I have duly noted that they work best if allowed to stand upright periodically. If we could arrange a trade, yeng to work my mine in return for some minerals that are hard to come by on Ungoliantis—I have Scandium and Godolinium aboard my craft now, purposely brought with the intention of a bit of private barter. The mine I need the yeng for has become unnecessarily dangerous to Cheetan, but is otherwise still commercially viable."

"See, Huigark, you are already coming to appreciate just how flexible yeng are. Why don't we take a transport out of the city and have a stroll around some industrial units that are very different to my business? I'll organise something for tomorrow. We use them a lot in mining, which is mostly open-cast rather than through shafts and tunnels. But we have experience of using them in narrow seams underground as well. Aranian are much more ergonomically suited to working underground, but the work isn't socially acceptable to us in these modern times. So, yes, yeng work our deep mines."

"Yes, I would enjoy that."

Boklung nods. "I want our two planets to become totally interdependent. I see our little private connectivities as being almost patriotic duty. The more our planets mutually benefit from cooperation the more we all benefit. It is high time we learned to live in permanent harmony and mutual prosperity. We have had enough capacity for mutually assured destruction for a long time. Perhaps it was only fear of annihilation that led us on our first tentative steps towards true cooperation. Whatever, for now that has been sufficient to persuade all sane commanders on both planets that trade not war is the only long-term solution. Let us ever keep things that way."

"I like that: trade as patriotic duty! On a personal level, we must set up an off-planet's financial holding company, to look after our mutual assets. It needs to be away from over-scrupulous oversight by tax officials in both jurisdictions. I suggest we set up a commercial bank on, shall we say, the satellite Sliefnam? I will send you a proposal. We can run it with a very small mixed species team, relying on static 'bots to run the machinery for our mutual deposit and investment accounts."

"Yes, that makes sense, Huigark. Gads, look at the time. Can I leave that with you? Sorry, I must go; I've a couple of jobs to do. I will give you a call at rising-light."

"Yes, quite right! Thank you, my friend. Have a restful retreat. As we are so far in this direction, I'll go back to the hotel via the Sclepatsouri Bridge. I'll see you tomorrow at rising-light."

***

Boklung needed to catch up on work details, but actually zis distraction is deeper than simple concerns about work. The question of whether ze's putting too much trust in the Cheetan again rose to the surface. Boklung has no intention of sleeping, until ze has got a nagging concern off zis mind.

As soon as the Cheetan is out of sight, Boklung heads up the hill towards zis private laboratories on the boundary of The Gardens. This area is furthest from the main road, so furthest from public view. Yet, as does everywhere in Spakron District, even that distant building feels to be under the looming shadows of the Gantri Amphitheatre's giant edifice.

Boklung is worried about the amount of information ze has given away. This feeling won't be eased again until zis suspicions have been properly exercised. The Cheetan Ambassador seems to be developing into a genuine friend, so all the more reason to check zim out. Certainly, the creature is behaving in an extraordinarily gracious manner for one of zis species. This has only been slightly spoilt by zis recent goading of Boklung.

A thousand cycles of on and off conflict between the planets, only recently ended by a mutual need for peace, guarantees that there is still ingrained wariness on both sides. So it isn't surprising that Boklung needs to know the wool isn't being pulled over zis eyes, or possibly over Hosk's by zis own kind. On arriving at the industrial laboratory, Boklung seeks out one of the centre's best electronics engineers.

"Pinardos, sorry to call so late, but I have a job for you. The Cheetan Hosk is visiting me at rising-light. Whilst ze is away from zis hotel room, I want you to go in and put a listening device on zis interplanetary phone. Is it technically possible to put in a device that will decay in an octad or so, leaving no trace; a devise that relays to a recorder in my office?"

"Consider the job done, Boss. I've a little chip that lasts for about six low-lights. It will run through a relay in the roof. I assume ze is in the Port Hotel."

"That's correct."

"These devices are very hard to spot, and if they are subject to the slightest disturbance the things simply disintegrate.

And the same sonic note will reduce the device to the finest of dust when it reaches a critical point in its energy reserves."

"Excellent."

Friends make the most dangerous of enemies. Now for some sleep. I really need to find my bed.

***

Boklung lies on zis sleeping pillows looking out across The Gardens as the light intensity slowly increases. Ze thinks about the wide implications of the death of an individual from Dancharis, slaughtered by its rebellious yeng. The Aranian was poisoned with arsenic-laced meats. Such attacks by yeng are rare, but they raise a good deal of speculation. Unsurprisingly, the fallout from this 'terrorist' activity can't possibly help Boklung sell the idea of sending highly independent yeng into space.

It's not the same as a hunter killed in the bush by wild colonies of yeng. That's just the way of things. But for such an attack to happen in the city, apparently orchestrated by house-slaves without any instigation from the outside, is most unusual. I wish I could stop this information from spreading amongst my yeng, but most of them get quite enough news for word of this atrocity to circulate, and plenty of them can read. The temptation to teach yeng to do ever more complex tasks has seduced me as much as any others into allowing complex language education. Only a fool would assume that news of this kind doesn't spread to all slave yeng.

We have much to fear from the emergence of rebellious intent, particularly amongst the domestic yeng. We must switch our concerned gaze from its ridiculous focus on the largely ignorant, and highly inconsequential, wild populations and concentrate on dealing with the far closer and more potentially dangerous problem of social subversion. If the wild population gets out of control, we can just spray the countryside with yengicides, but these chemicals also affect us if we are badly exposed to them, so we can hardly go around liberally spraying our own population centres.

On the face of things, it doesn't seem to be in the interest of those yeng that are in domestic service to risk losing their relatively less wretched positions. However, working in our homes is obviously not always as coveted an existence as we tend to assume. Though how much does simple logic play a part amongst impassioned yeng?

Boklung, along with the rest of the hunting lobby, constantly presses the point that rebellion from the yeng will rapidly reduce once masses of new stock aren't being constantly sourced from Waterball. The second generation of yeng are almost invariably calmer, less easily agitated animals. Of course, the breeding bucks will always be more of a problem, simply due to their natural hormone load. Even Boklung accepts that most of these entire male yeng need to be kept restrained, as ze has good cause to.

Despite the effect that the escape of Jack has had on zim, Boklung has continued to allow zis bucks a good measure of freedom. Ze believes that if managed sympathetically, yeng work far more efficiently. 'Happy livestock equals high profit', is one of zis mantras. Ze even encourages privacy and affection in bonding, something that few Aranian slave masters and probably no Cheetan ones would ever be likely to emulate. Boklung's breeding sheds are almost entirely free of the infanticide common in more brutally run ones.

If we allow yeng a measure of freedom, there'll always be unfortunate incidents. That creature Jack is a case in point. I should have kept him better restrained. However, he was clever enough to outwit me, pretending loyalty, and waiting his moment. I am embarrassed about being so deceived.

The slightest little problem can upset my plans. The political and psychological fallout from the 'Dancharis Killing' has come at a dreadful time. I don't need that legal case filling the papers every day. I need to speed things up considerably, especially in case we have any copycat incidents. I can't afford to see opinions on yeng management harden further, or else I'll have every yeng-related action I initiate scrutinised. I must attempt to bring forward the launch date, even if that means using a few more short legs and more of my personal savings. In theory, I could have a launch in only a couple of huis.

9

OSTERPHELIA

The Spakron Gardens' most senior female slave hears her name being called in the harshly rasping voice of Boss Boklung.

"Osterphelia, come here."

As always at this time of day, when she isn't carrying out an express instruction from Boklung, she is overseer in the greenhouses and keeping an eye on the smooth running of horticultural logistics. Osterphelia's relatives have been slaves for many generations. As a senior trustee, she is one of the highest status yeng in the city of Cirithia. She reluctantly heads for the doors.

"Ahrrrgg, there you are. Come, come, I have a job for you."

The two of them leave the potting-shed; Boklung leading Osterphelia out of possible earshot of all other creatures.

"This task is of the highest importance. You must hand over your usual duties for now. Things are not going as well for me politically as I would like, and one of the main reasons for this is the unfortunate, and very widely reported, disappearance of the buck, Jack. The loss of such potentially dangerous property hardly has the effect of making me look like a safe set of political limbs. I want him returned so that I can make my opponents eat their words. I am assigning you to the role of team leader with responsibility for bringing him in, alive if possible. I

102

don't mind what promises, threats, or force you use to get him, but get him you must. Use weapons, charm, guile, deceit, whatever, and up to an octate of trustees to help you. You will arm and brief what will be mostly your chosen team and head into the forest as soon as possible. I will select one or two. If you are successful you will be well rewarded. We assume that Jack cut out his chip, or else our hunters would have found him easily enough. Do what you wish with him, so long as he is returned. I hear that many females find him attractive! I'm sure you get my point. Hggh! As you know, I am not a vindictive creature, but I'm certainly demanding. I can assure you that it is in your best interests to bring him back."

Osterphelia nods, and Boklung walks away, leaving her thinking about the enormity of the task.

Well, yes, Boklung, I know what I'd like to do. If I could face the risk of a child then a bit fun with Jack would be high on my list ... But, though I hate to admit it, the truth is that my breeding years have passed, and it's a long time since I've had more than the feeble efforts of a castrate to enjoy. So I can well imagine a quick romp with him, *but I think survival rather than sex will be on my mind. I can't imagine him just giving himself up, not for my body anyway.*

God damn Boklung for reminding me how much I always craved a child, and God damn the emotional mess of deciding whether or not to birth a child into slavery—not that most have a choice. Cunning of Boklung to encourage me to bring in Jack alive. That sounds a tall order in anyone's book. I'll need every scrap of guile and good fortune just to find him, let alone bring him in. I must choose a female for my team that is young and attractive enough to tempt any buck. I haven't quite lost all my charms, but realistically
....

Osterphelia sighs and returns to the greenhouse where she sits on a bench near the door, supposedly to oversee the activities, but her mind is far from the scene before her.

On the face of it, this task is beyond difficult. Luckily, I— descended as I am from a long line of hunters—know a good deal more about survival outside the city than most think. Thanks to my mother for passing on the craft her father taught her. I doubt spiders know how much useful knowledge gets passed from generation to generation. Even so, I need to find a real tracker to see what I'm sure to miss.

I wish I'd been born to the Earth. The spiders would never have taken me. I'd love to squish a few of those tiny Earth spiders under my feet. That'd feel so liberating. Crushing ground-bugs is satisfying enough, but smashing itsy-bitsy little spiders would really be fun.

If only Boklung knew what I really thought of zis species. Ze certainly isn't a bad creature; there's no shortage of worse bosses. But, if I felt I could run with any chance of making a better life I wouldn't hesitate. If the whip was in my hands not many spiders would escape my wrath. Some people talk about a social order of the future with species equality. Not me! After being a slave all my life, while knowing so much about how we lived on Earth, I don't think I could find it in me to be so generous.

Do spiders think it's only a minority, like Jack, that aren't content to bow to the will of a superior species? I know they're aware of the rebelliousness of first generation slaves, but I doubt they know how well we preserve our history, our human values, our hatred and the concept of liberty. It's just as well they don't know the unrest hidden below the surface. If they did, we'd never have even the very limited freedoms that spiders like Boklung allow us.

Then again, I'm probably wrong. They might know everything, but fear us so little that they're content to let us talk-up our feeble plots. Perhaps they see our subversive chat as a simple way of letting 'yeng' relieve dangerously pent up frustrations. As things stand, they're easily our masters. So let them think us even weaker than we are.

I'm told that there are twice as many humans as Aranian on this planet. Then one day we, the downtrodden masses, the subservient species, are sure to upset the 'applecart'—a good analogy, I think, though I don't know exactly what an apple looks like. One day we'll build our own civilisation on Ungoliantis, one in which—if spiders are tolerated at all—they'll be the beasts of burden.

Or perhaps we can escape to elsewhere, and start again in another star system free of our multi-legged overseers. I wonder if it's true that Boklung is a key planner of an expedition to distant stars. It would explain why ze's started tests on us to see what environmental extremes we can tolerate. Any expeditionary force should require some slaves, and they'd look for them amongst trustees. If I do this job well, I might get a place.

Anyway, it's just as well Boklung doesn't know what I'm really thinking. If you did, you stinking spider, you'd never let me take a group into the forests. You might even be sending Jack a subversive ally that at last has the courage to act.

She sighs, knowing that she is unlikely to do other than she has been ordered.

I must select carefully. I need a good mix of skills and strengths, but above all else, I need bright individuals capable of making independent decisions. And they must be loyal to me. This won't be a walk through a flower garden. I'd love to choose mainly from the first generation, but that would make Boklung suspicions of my intentions. Ze might restrict who I choose, anyway.

Koolsverne should be one of the team. He's physically strong and knows bush craft—a bit of a maverick loner though. And there's Scunthorpe, gifted in many languages. He's good at holding people's attention and leading by example. I should try and recruit Peter Finch, too. He's old, but far from decrepit—first generation, true, but he's been around so long, and played the spiders' game so well, that they trust him. Stupid spiders! Finch is very good at finding practical solutions, and most importantly, secretly he hates the spiders as much as I do. But is he too old? I'll give him free choice to join me or not. Ideally, all those I choose should be volunteers.

If I do this job right then Boklung will trust me more. Maybe one day I might have gained enough freedom that I could sneak in and release a mass of trained gladiators. Then it might be possible to establish real independence, not one that's just a few individuals living a precarious life in the shadows of the forest. What if I could free the makings of an army?

First, Boklung must continue to believe ze can trust me. Yes, forget revolution for now, and I must be prepared to play Jack as a pawn in my ambitions. The more I'm seen as a supporter of spider rule the greater my chance of eventually finding space to break away. Sorry Jack! Though we both crave independence, mine may well depend on restricting yours. Which reminds me, which women can bait an irresistible trap?

10

CASTLEPOINT

I imagine that human readers are more than ready to hear something positive about mankind's future on the Earth. For that reason I've decided to include a bit of information grabbed from even further into the future than this book's main timeline. One dramatic, psychologically unsettling rather than substantive defeat for the Aranian, was to change everything. By this time strict quotas had been imposed on the slavers as conservation of such a valuable resource was deemed to be in the long-term interest of the Lush System sentients. Gathering was done by rotating the harvested area over five Ungolian years. In the year of this story, harvest was across south-east Asia and Australasia. The following piece is copied directly from a human manuscript written a couple of Earth centuries after this book's main story.

> 'The Battle of Castlepoint was instrumental in shifting the collective consciousness of the invaders. It proved to be the key to opening up a fundamental new debate amongst the Aranian leadership, which finally led them to abandon plans for a full-blown invasion of the Earth and eventually to even giving up their slave trade.

Although we only won this single tiny battle, its legacy was enough to give those Aranian campaigning against invasion a permanent majority. We might well owe our present civiĺisation to the Battle of Castlepoint. Within twenty years of this event, the increasingly irregular slave ships had simply stopped calling. So what real facts do we know about this battle?

On this seminal day, two massive slavers hovered over one of the then very last still properly governed stronghold in the world, New Zealand's Manawatu and Wairarapa provinces. Legend records that early on that day the massive space vehicles blotted out so much of the sky that they swept downtown Masterton into near darkness. Operations over the town were soon successfully completed. The slave holding pens, which had already been crowded from an earlier raid on Palmerston North, were now bulging. All that remained was for the slave-ships to lift off back into space and engage their warp drives.

The captain of one of the vast Slavius 19 ships chose not to rise vertically above the town, but rather to drift out towards the Pacific Ocean. Some human histories say ze was looking to destroy a military unit stationed near Whakataki that had fired field guns as the slavers had first approached. Some say that the slaver had problems with its engines, causing it to drift lower than intended towards the coast. The reason for its flight path hardly matters. What does, is that for whatever reason, a still-extended landing leg of the vast slaver caught the top of what was then known as Bird Island.

The local defence force, the very unit that had fired the earlier shells, were moving towards Castlepoint when they saw the craft drifting back almost over their heads. The NZ Defence Forces rapidly reset firing positions as the huge craft passed overhead. Then, only a moment later, the landing-leg caught the summit of Bird Island. The foot of the craft's massive leg dragged like an anchor on the inland slope of the hill. As the craft's flight stalled, its underbelly lifted and was almost immediately hit by repeated ordinance from the Defence Forces' ancient but still perfectly serviceable guns. The shells hardly dented the structure, but the push they provided along with the continuing propulsion of the ship's engines slowly flipped the whole structure, pivoting it over its grounded leg.

Desperate to get away, the pilots probably overpowered the craft's lift thrusters. Momentum now took control. The vast ship swung over onto its back, hastened in its ungainly movement by a further barrage of shells from the field-guns. The spacecraft's still-powered engines now drove it with unstoppable momentum onto the rocky sea cliffs and down into the ocean below. Upside down, with its lowest point in the sea and its bulk flat against the harsh rocks, the Slavius 19 was now little more than one massive pile of scrap metals.

The cargo of human prisoners escaped from the now ruptured hull. When the first bewildered spiders emerged they didn't stand a chance, as the rifles of the few defence force personnel and the bare hands of once-prisoners overwhelmed them. Disorientated, no doubt physically stressed and struggling with the psychology of suddenly being in a position of weakness, the spiders were hacked to pieces.

History tells us that the slaughter was ferocious as our ancestors took long-dreamed of revenge. Some of the spiders drowned, some died still trapped in the hull of smoke inhalation or from raging fires, but most had their legs smashed and their throats cut as they tried to flee. Any that broke the initial cordon were quickly hunted down. By the time the two fighters assigned to protect the slaver had switched off already engaged space flight engines, turned and come back to help their comrades, the people had melted away into the Wairarapa.

How had those individually weak humans won such a lopsided battle? The chance collision was important, but so was the invaders' arrogant conviction that they were so very superior. The fighter wing of the Ungolian convoy should never have been authorised to depart beyond the stratosphere ahead of the commercial slave-ships. As the ancient saying goes, 'pride precedes destruction and a haughty spirit precedes a fall'.

A high stone tower was subsequently built on the summit of Bird Island. The Tower of Mangu Toto still stands despite many major earth-tremors over the course of subsequent history. It is a powerful symbol of remembrance, and a poignant reminder of how fragile our dominion will always be. Very soon after the battle, Bird Island was given its now usual name of Spiderfall Hill.

A further thousand years on, Masterton has long been the largest city on Earth and Castlepoint is still dominated by Mangu Toto on the summit of Spiderfall Hill, the Earth's most famous landmark. Masterton is now one of the greatest space ports on the Orion spiral

of the Milky Way, with regular flights to the planets of
the ancient slavers and far beyond.'
(From *Secondary Level History Primer, Earth
Education Authority, 3756 AD*).

From what we have learned from the Aranian own
recorded history, it is difficult to overestimate the
psychological affect New Zealand's small victory had on
Ungoliantis. North Island New Zealand, and particularly
the Manawhatu and the Wairarapa, had been seen as one
of the few remaining really good sources of easily
harvestable humanity. This victory, coming at a time when
the Aranian had thought that any serious lingering
resistance was long broken, literally saved the dominion of
the Earth to mankind.

Having informed all readers, and in particular
having reassured humans living either before or during the
Aranian dominated centuries, that you do have a long
future on Earth, let me return you to this book's main
timeline.

11

BOKLUNG'S POWER GROWS

Nin Tarp, Chief Prosecutor for the Council of Cirithia sits with the other principle councillors on a dais in the large council room. Ze is 'dressed up' with all the pomp of zis position with a red cape and a sort of crown perched on zis head. Zis four eyestalks poke through and up above the crown. Boklung, not the sort to wear any status-giving attire, inwardly mocks this flagging of authority. Ze stands alone on another dais at the other side of the bleak and otherwise-unoccupied room. The city's coat of arms hangs on the wall above the Chief Prosecutor.

"Cingwin Boklung, you have been brought here to stand before this committee to face the full verdict pertaining to your conviction for negligence for allowing the escape of an entire male yeng. In normal times this conviction would have required us to at least temporarily revoke your yeng breeding licence. However, these are not normal times; unless perchance, we have just lost sight of what is normal! Nevertheless, you are fortunate to be of such distinguished and important standing, as otherwise we would not be able to justify the lenience, some may say even rewarding, course we now propose. We have been helped in our judgment by the commitment you have shown to recovering the buck. We are very pleased to hear that a task force has been assembled to ensure dead or alive recovery.

"In short, with the support of the Council, we have decided to appoint you, Boklung, as official head of the board of management for the 'Arcraft Project'. Responsibility is expected to hang particularly heavily on your back, with this being so much your own ridiculously ambitious scheme. Your failure, which many of your detractors see as inevitable, may well result in you receiving a long prison sentence and having all your assets seized by the State. We couldn't in all consciousness leave the failure of such an expensive project unpunished.

"My personal view is that you have got off far too lightly. If you fail the Council but somehow avoid prison, I will personally see that you are rewarded with governorship for life of one of the coldest outer planets."

Boklung replies, "I can promise you that the project will be a success. If it isn't, I will volunteer myself for your vital job in the wilderness."

Tarp's eyestalks contract slightly. "Your cynicism is noted. This has to be the most unusual case I have had to judge as Chief of Legal. In some ways it is difficult to see that you have received any punishment at all. But bearing the cost of using your own yeng on the Arcraft should be, at very least, an itch in your bank account. However, and particularly if you succeed to any degree, the crowd will only see the honour of prestigious leadership ... Never before has any Aranian been so honoured by being so 'severely' punished.

"The government takes a political risk by being seen to condone you getting away with it, so it is vital that you never forget the generosity shown despite your careless transgression. Mark my words, failure on your part will not lead to another effective promotion. This court is adjourned.

"Boklung, you are free to go, but first I wish you to be escorted to my chambers. The details of the verdict need some explaining. Guards, show Boklung the way and keep zim company there until I arrive."

Boklung follows the guards along a corridor to Nin Tarp's very large and expensively outfitted office. A few moments later, Ngu Clanten, Speaker of the House, and Admiral

Bagfung enter, accompanied by Nin Tarp. They sit while Boklung is left standing.

Clanten speaks. "In recent cycles we have all been alerted to just how concerned our environmentalists have become. Few of us now doubt that our growing population has unbalanced our planets natural rhythm. You Boklung, as one of those that have long pushed for us to move our space frontiers wider and as one of the Arcraft project's architects, are a natural and obvious leader. It seems to be vital to the long-term security of our species that we establish self-supporting colonies on other planets as soon as is feasible. Waterball may well be the site of one of these colonies, but I understand that this is not the target of Arcraft. Waterball is close, and relatively easy to colonise. Anyway, even though I'm hardly an expert in environmental sciences I do understand that the planet of the yeng is not currently suitable. After all, it is often reported to be in an even more dreadful condition than our own. Also, we hardly need to send yeng to Waterball, even if we should wish to build a colony there.

"If I understand correctly, Launch One is to have a far more ambitious goal than the colonisation of Waterball. The Admiralty can easily deal with that planet with the current fleet, isn't that so, Bagfung?"

Bagfung nods while Tarp continues talking.

"Whilst the Arcraft will sail out into distant space that our best equipped astronomers even struggle to map."

Boklung replies in zis best fawning voice. "That is quite correct, Councillor. I understand that I am being both punished and promoted. However incongruous the reasoning for me being chosen in light of my recent failing, I consider it an honour to make such a potentially vital contribution to our futures. Of course, I bow to the will of the Legislature, Prosecutor Tarp, fully accepting the conditions imposed on me. My extensive knowledge of both yeng management and husbandry means that I can add real value to the expedition in addition to providing leadership.

"I will immediately deputise my other activities so that Launch One has total priority. No one knows better than I the problems entailed in yeng management. The fact that a yeng buck deceived me only sharpens my awareness of their capabilities. I understand exactly why the escape of yeng bucks is so feared by Aranian civilisation. In light of my failing, I undertake to do all I can to ensure the success of our planned colonisation."

Tarp speaks: "Okay Boklung, I have heard enough from you for now. Whilst being fully responsible for the project, you will still be answerable to me and to Nga Clanten. Your day to day direct superior will, of course, be Admiral Bagfung, who I now invite to say a few words."

Bagfung takes a pace towards Boklung. Ze glares into Boklung's eyestalks. But as soon as Tarp turns away to gaze out of zis massive panoramic window, Bagfung squints at Boklung in the four-eyed way that only Aranian can. "I am happy to have the honorary job of supervising you, Boklung, because honorary will be all it needs be. And yes, Ngu, even I, old and enfeebled as I am, can organise the settlement of Waterball when and if required; comparatively speaking, a walk in the park—"

Tarp interrupts. "We will be greatly helped in justifying our policy of leniency towards you, Boklung, if the measures you have taken really lead to the recapture of your yeng, or proof of its death. If you can achieve that then Legal will no longer be required to supervise your activities quite so closely. For now, the Legal Committee must be given time to sign off on any substantive changes before they are applied. Please note that well, Admiral."

Bagfung interjects, "I particularly need things done without any unnecessary aggravations, as my responsibilities to the fleet will not be diminished despite the requirements of 'New Frontier', or as most of us know it, the Arcraft Project, so don't personally burden me with legal forms and procedures I won't understand, Prosecutor Tarp. After this meeting, Boklung, you are apparently required to see my adjunct engineer Pontu Prortung, who will discuss with you some of the technical aspects we require to be covered by your plans. It seems the officer is related to our esteemed Prosecutor ..."

"You are dismissed for now, Boklung," Tarp replies sharply. "And yes, Boklung, I have many legs on the ground, including those of that officer. I believe ze'll be waiting outside the door."

Tarp glares, all four eyes focused on the Admiral. Ze is clearly seething below zis legal robes. The Admiral looks totally unflustered. Boklung can't help but feel the animosity between the two creatures, filing away the information for possible future use. Ze nods to the assembled and turns to leave.

Outside, Prortung is indeed waiting. "Salutations Zir, I am honoured to meet you. May I say how glad I am that you have had the case against you effectively dismissed? I wish to add that I have great respect for you, and believe that you're the best possible Aranian to command such a far-sighted space project. Hggh ... I also know that most of the basic ideas were yours in the first place, despite the fact that the long-stalks in the Space Academy now claim so many of them ... I need to make that clear, Zir, that the Admiralty have little respect for the way that Legal has pilloried you for what is really a trivial misdemeanour, whatever we are forced to say in public. How dangerous are a few wild breeding bucks really going to be. The politicians have always overstated the dangers, searching for sure-fire excuse for the failures of particular social policies."

"Salutations," Boklung replies. "Shall we go and chat in the dining hall. I'm ready for a hippotion, to submerge the excremental dialogue of certain honourable and distinguished 'betters'. Lead on, if you will."

"An excellent idea! Can I order you something to eat to go with your drink, Zir?"

"Not for me, but feel free. We'll sit over there by the window. That should offer privacy enough for our conversations. Hggh. I know you are a lackey of Nin Tarp's." The officer, feeling the loathing in Boklung's words, sinks somewhat, almost seeming to melt into the ground.

With the now crestfallen Prortung gone, Boklung enjoys a moment to zimself. *Thank Sinanna that's all over. Now that I have got this case out of the way, I can resume doing more or less what I want. The project will go exactly my way, with all possible personal compensations for my required heavy expenditure built-in. Those political idiots aren't going to leave me out of pocket. The Admiral is clearly on my side, at least up to a point, and thanks to zim I have a measure of zis junior, Prortung. I will be careful with the information ze gleans to kiss up to Nin Tarp.*

Prortung returns with drinks and places them on the solid table before them.

"That was impressively quick, Prortung," Boklung says. "So, no more waffle, what's the bottom line on what those gaseous leaders have instructed you to say?"

"Let me just say that despite what you and my broodfather think, I've no wish to cause trouble, Zir. My first loyalty is to the Admiralty. Ze is the one being deceived, not the Admiral. However, the Prosecutor's office is behind what I'll say first. The Full Council has cautioned me to remind you that cost will be a number one consideration. They are very aware that individual launches will have little chance of success, especially when dispatched over the longer distances; so know that many are likely to be required. We are living in harsh economic times that push this project to quantity rather than quality. I know that the Council would settle far easier for a cheap failure than for a marginally successful overspend. But as far as the Admiralty and, in fact, the whole Space Academy is concerned, this project needs to succeed. We know only too well how fragile the whole biosphere has become."

Prortung takes a sip of zis drink, then continues. "To help the chances of this low budget operation, we believe that there's a need to be ready for a launch as soon as the suns are in lowest gravity alignment. This will allow for a maximum possible payload of material while keeping down energy costs. We know that this rather rushes things. Our engineers all agree with the assessment that tugs will be needed to help propel the craft away from our atmosphere. The next most favourable launch conditions are just over two huis from now. Is that at all feasible, Zir? I can make sure we have plenty of tugs allocated for then."

Boklung nods, while trying to weigh up whether to treat the officer like a political sneak, or a loyal ally. Ze decides to risk trusting zim. "Provided we are left to get on with it, Prortung, that timeline is just about feasible. If the following gets back to Tarp, I'll know the source. Do I need to spell out the consequences?"

Prortung shakes zis head, and Boklung continues: "I intend that the crew will be made up of at least three hundred yeng, eight hundred robots and as many unfertilized Aranian eggs as we feel we can store in good conditions aboard the craft. For your interest, my biology labs are also working on the idea of planting eggs in the tissue of yeng, so that they can be direct carriers of our destiny. This technology may be available in a few launch's time."

Prortung's eyestalks rise at this revelation.

"For all sorts of reasons," Boklung continues, "I prefer that the Aranian presence is kept down, hggh ... to as few as the councillors will allow. Check with me and the Admiral before you pass any information onto Tarp, and the moment I suspect you are doing anything else you will have to watch the shadows. Yes, that is a threat!"

Prortung nods, looking suitably subdued.

"As the time-served soldier I believe you to be Prortung, I assume you agree that Aranians are not psychologically up to the job of one way missions to hell. We both know many of those that'll give their lives in battle with hardly a thought will balk at the idea of submitting to the never ending deprivations of the sort of journey we plan for Arcraft."

"Indeed."

"To get full co-operation from the yeng, it is essential to hide from them the high risk of the expedition. They will be told, simply, that this is an exploratory trip designed to prove feasibility. We will say that they are to start a colony to which many Aranian colonists will be sent later. They must be allowed to feel a certain independence even from any Aranian travelling with them. The idea that a few Aranians could maintain control for so long is ludicrous anyway. So we must hope that the Council comes to accept that the yeng need to be given the incentives and power to make the project work. I believe such trust will make the yeng feel far less belligerent towards those few Aranian that we may be forced to send."

"Empowering yeng that way is risky," Prortung says.

Boklung takes a sip of zis drink before replying. "All the same, it seems expedient to make them feel that this is as close to a collaborative venture between equal species as we can. I believe that the chances of success are as low as one in an octate, whatever creatures are walking the decks. Successful or not, other similar flights are going to launch in the medium term."

"I see," Prortung says, "but these creatures have a capacity for fighting amongst themselves when not under our direct control. Indeed, their progress on Earth was continually checked and ultimately failed because of internecine warfare. They are a species that has few qualms about killing its own. Does that not concern you?"

Boklung nods. "I will minimise this risk by judicious selection of groups of yeng that appear to get on with each other. Though I'm put to great cost, I've the advantage of knowing my own slaves, so I can make a good show of choosing ones best suited for the job. Of course, we will have little control over subsequent generations of the crew. The yeng don't need to know that the expedition will take at least two of their lifetimes. In most cases it will be the original crew's grandchildren that have any chance of stepping onto solid ground."

"And yet the debate," Prortung says, "is very much about how many Aranian we should be sending, not about if they should be going at all. I think the Councillors are mad to believe that robots will be able to keep Aranian plans on course without our physical presence. I have seen plenty of robot units at war, and so know first limb their limitations. Hggh; how can I put this? Trust me, my loyalties are to the Admiralty, which has already come around to seeing things more your way. Actually, I'm no fool, Zir. I find it impossible to imagine, Zir, that a thinker of your quality hasn't already considered relying entirely on yeng as pioneers. That is where logic leads. My military training points only to the belief that no Aranians are psychologically suited to this mission. Haaarg! Zir, we heard very early on, unofficially, from idle chatter, from our spies that you see a need to rely on yeng. That information forced Space Command to really think things through as well ... Hggh ... Though, of course, we all have to respect the Council's wishes, don't we?"

Boklung replies, relieved that ze's hearing sympathetic noises from the space military. A weight seems to lift from zis mind, knowing that ze isn't completely alone.

"I'm a mere subject of the Council, just as you are, one that must appear to be in tune with the Council's expectations however ridiculous we believe them to be. We can assure the Council that we will try our damnedest to find suitably carefree individuals. I take it you won't be volunteering; I assume that you are one that enjoys a social life. Hhaaaggh! There's really no great likelihood of yeng subverting our colonial plans, because that would almost certainly mean them losing the opportunity to expand through space as well. But for now I have no choice other than to make provision to put living, breathing Aranian aboard, do I, Prortung?

"We all have to do what we are ordered to do. Please be sure to pass on my deep respects and extensive waffle to your political overseers, including Chief Prosecutor Tarp, and inform them that safety is guaranteed. Ensure them that all their concerns are respected and fully accounted for, blablablahhg."

"I will indeed, Zir. We seem to understand each other. I sense that you still have reservations about my loyalties, but remember, Zir, I'm military first and political second. I'll leave you in peace now, Zir, as I'm sure you are desperate for your own space. If I can give any assistance, don't hesitate to call." Prortung downs the rest of zis drink in one slurp, then stands, bids a final farewell and leaves.

Boklung sips zis drink and watches zim exit. *What a surprise that creature is! I wouldn't have trusted zim as far as I could kick a dodark, but now ... I'm sure that the Admiralty has its own agenda, differing from mine—but what a relief. One minute I feel Tarp squashing me from above and below, and in the next it seems that zis supposed support from the Admiralty is actually on my side. Whatever, Prortung has put my mind somewhat at ease. For now I will make every effort to make zim believe that I am a team player, though I'll do things my way with or without any military support.*

I have no intention of sending any Aranian older than an egg; whatever the demands of the Council or that bloody Legal Committee might be. I don't care if I embarrass Space Command in the process, either. The yeng will need to feel that they have a chance of not just surviving but of being free. It is only in that way that we will get the best out of them. And anyway, Aranian shouldn't be subjected to the inevitable level of stress that this expedition will entail. What a time I've had. I really think that Prortung was telling the truth, not bluffing me. Ze presently sees more to be gained through supporting Bagfung and even possibly me, than zis despicable broodfather.

For now, I'll go through the process of getting a crew of Aranian together, a crew that will accidentally never make the flight. I could choose some convicted felons that fancy the idea of being lost in space, when really they might be lost to some nice sunny but distant territory on Ungoliantis. Borstave has often indicated how easily ze can get in contact with the right sort of people. Another possibility would be choosing Aranian that I would happily waste. I've never committed murder yet, but if needs must. The future of our species comes first, and that isn't guaranteed by sending Aranian that are sure to be driven mad by living for so long in a tiny isolated metal world. The four huis round trip to Earth is enough to drive Aranian to the point of mutiny. Being dispatched on perhaps a fifteen cycle trip followed by declining into old age in some God forsaken wilderness will ensure insanity.

Boklung finishes zis drink, leaves the dining hall and walks towards the entrance to City Hall. A cold breeze blows across the front of the building as ze hurries towards a transporter.

"Spakron Gardens, as fast as."

"Certainly, Zir. I'll put the heater on; you look frozen."

"Thank you, I'll be much obliged."

"One of the coldest days I remember, this winter. I wouldn't put a yeng out in this." The transporter lurches into gear and hovers down the road.

The driver's throw-away line reminds Boklung of an obvious but previously unconsidered solution.

Cryogenic suspension could be the key to finding a compromise that even the Council will eventually accept. If I can get them to go that far, then they may eventually be persuaded that we don't need any ambulatory Aranian aboard. That is a realistic way of legally achieving my primary objective.

Whatever happens, I have to keep talking to the Speaker of the Council, Clanten, and zis motley crew of supporters; without them nothing can be achieved. They don't need to know that I'll do everything my way no matter what they decree. As for bloody Nin Tarp and zis Legal Committee, ze will come to a sticky end if ze tries to throw zis weight around anymore. At least I'm now certain that Bagfung is just playing up to Tarp. The Admiral appears to be at least reading the same book as I am, and we have mutual respect for each other. Ze did a very good job of making Tarp feel like the power ze likes to think ze is, without actually agreeing to anything crucial.

Boklung leans forward. "Driver, can we go via the Sclepatsouri Bridge so as to avoid all the carts and foot traffic on the Spakron Road? I am in a bit of a hurry."

"Certainly, Zir, though it will cost you a little more, because of the toll."

"That's fine."

***

Some low-lights later Boklung, Admiral Bagfung and Ngu Clanten sit around a restaurant platform, just outside the Spakron Gardens.

***

As you probably appreciate, a raised dais rather than a table at which humans happily sit is easier for spider-like creatures. The concept of properly sitting on a 'chair' isn't one that comes easily, let alone with any grace, to a multi-legged creature.

***

121

Boklung says: "I have instigated a lot of the processes and procedures that common sense dictates we will need to follow. I haven't had to be told that I need to select yeng that are robust enough to deal with marginally challenging atmospheric conditions. It is only logical that stronger than average tolerances to gravity and varying oxygen levels are worth selecting for. I have also worked on the obvious assumption that the expedition will require a higher proportion of intact males than in normal systems. Alternatively, I could have picked only females, and planned to rely on a large sperm bank. Actually, I have covered both options by including sperm-banks in the configuration. By good fortune, I was already engaged in working in many of these areas as a result of intended trade deals with the Cheetan."

"Yes," Bagfung says, "I support those initiatives. If our broods need to rely on yeng for survival with only the basic oversight that can be programmed into robots, then by extension we need the most robust slaves and breeding options available.

"The 'bots will be programmed to land the ship on whatever astral bodies the spacecraft reaches that has any remote chance of providing anything like suitable conditions. Obviously, in many cases, we will have to rely on robots making the initial landings and creating sufficiently suitable conditions for yeng and Aranian alike. The more flexible the yeng the better our options will be. Above all, we need intelligent yeng with an ability to make independent decisions. Yeng are good at lateral thinking, making 'new limbs from unconnected parts'. We have to be forward thinking and trusting enough to rely very heavily on their ingenuity to see the project through all inevitable crises."

Clanten clears zis throat. "I'm not really keen on having more than the usual ratio of entire males. They are just too unpredictable and dangerous. Also, we don't really need them for gene diversity, as most of the gene variability is expressed in the female chromosomes. At least that is what my scientific advisors tell me. It is time we ordered something to eat." Ze gestures to the yeng standing nearby. "Yeng, what is the dish of the day?"

"Yeng casserole, with sautéed greens and pickles, Zir."

"That'll do me, is that okay, comrades?"

The others nod enthusiastically.

"… Good. Three casseroles, a bottle of hippotion, water all around, and put it all on my business account."

"What you say is sensible, Honourable Speaker," Boklung says, "but there are other issues beyond the maintenance of a wide genetic pool. We may actually need aggressive male leadership. Their extra physical strength and their high degree of preparedness to take risks in combat are ingredients that we overlook at our peril. We need a range of different yeng qualities, including ones that we have previously been keen to breed out.

"There may also be all sorts of psychological reasons for having a more natural balance of yeng on this mission. The best quality yeng breeding units are made up of individuals in monogamous male-female relationships. I know that this is only seen in scientific labs, and never tolerated in commercial situations. However, this is natural yeng behaviour when they are left to their own devices. In the absence of Aranian to run the breeding programmes, a biological balance of males and females will be the next best thing."

"Ah," Clanten says, "but yeng are as unpredictable as robots are predictable."

"Yes, but if we can't predict responses then neither can any alien enemies that the mission may encounter. There are overwhelming reasons for giving yeng as much freedom as we can persuade the Council to accept. And while I am dismissing weak but popular options, the sending of castrates would be doubly stupid. They would hardly be a flexible use of valuable space. Anyway, we haven't much of a mature supply of well-trained castrates, have we? Nearly all breeders send them to meat processing as soon as they have put on bulk, rather than train them as slaves. Secondly, we would only be able to maintain castrates in the first generation. It should be obvious why! I really can't envisage the yeng simply allowing robots to emasculate their new-born, especially as there would be fewer young born anyway. The more male castrates as a proportion of yeng numbers, the lower the natural rate of replacement.

"We would have to integrate some sort of religious or medical 'reasoning' into yeng culture for them to accept such mutilation anyway, and such indoctrination isn't feasible in our planned timeline. Actually, I'm not sure that it would ever be feasible."

"Ah, I see your point," replies Clanten.

Boklung continues: "Of course, I risk bringing an over-heavy burden down on myself, by persuading you that we need a high proportion of breeding males. We have, after all, kept them scarce. I couldn't quickly buy in a hundred and fifty good breeding males even if I had the money, they just aren't available. When they are in surplus, the Gantri practically snaps limbs off to get hold of them. Whatever happens, their numbers will have to be made up in large part with immature new male stock."

"In that case, Boklung," Clanten says, "I propose a possibly achievable ratio of one buck to ten females, instead of the normal one to fifty. You being punished by the courts with the financial costs of providing yeng is one thing, but the cost of outbidding the Gantri for entire males is going to be astronomical. I'll see what I can do to give you access to an unaudited government revenue stream. Now that I have read up on everything you have planned and already achieved, Boklung, I am bound to say that Legal has treated you unjustly and harshly for what was after all only an unfortunate incident. Even if we could find sufficient adult breeding males, expecting you to pay the full cost would see you bankrupt!

"Great Sinanna, I found your punishment excessive enough even when the costs appeared to be well within your means. As far as I'm concerned you're a national treasure, not a rogue to be slapped down. I wish I could say the same of all those in senior government posts."

Three yeng arrive with plates of stew and lay them before the Aranians while Boklung responds enthusiastically. "Your idea on gender selection sounds to be a sensible compromise. I can work with that. I suggest we make policies more acceptable to the hardliners in Council by going through the motions of pursuing an aggressive electronic tagging system. We can say we are going to fix the first generation of yeng with a 'kill subject trigger' that we can instigate through air traffic control signalling from here. That would be sold as a last resort response should the bucks get so aggressive that they threaten the expedition. The robots would theoretically be coded to instigate a panic alarm that triggered a kill response under extreme circumstances. This is all really about smoke and mirrors, because if that was necessary the mission would have already effectively failed."

Clanten and the Admiral dig into their food while Boklung continues without a pause. "Even if such tagging is enforced for the original crew, as to the next generations of yeng, born free of our direct interference, such will be unfeasible. They aren't likely to accept tagging of their young any more than having their gonads cut off, unless the 'bots can assure them that the tagging is for their own benefit. Hggh … What possible reason would they ever be inclined to accept? Please understand that it will be totally impractical to instigate this tagging policy at all. Do either of you fundamentally disagree?"

The Admiral wipes a limb across zis mouth. "No, I agree with you. I understand that this policy may be politically required, but, how can I put it … it is sure to fail during implementation. As Aranian, we accept tagging as a rite of passage to adulthood, giving us the 'key' to the use of firearms and vehicles. But generations of yeng have been instilled with the knowledge that they are only tagged for controlling purposes. Why antagonise the yeng at all with such a futile process. Remember, they are all going to be in a tiny metal can, and then almost certainly in a space-restricted settlement for at least fifteen to twenty cycles. They are hardly going to stray far. As you say, Boklung, success of the mission will only be through yeng empowerment. But yes, I also agree that tagging needs to remain official policy, as a 'political sop' to the Council … Great food by the way, Ngu, thank you very much."

Boklung takes zis first taste of the yeng stew while Ngu Clanton replies with four eyes staring heavenwards, "I thank

Sinanna, the Almighty, for not creating us as a species capable of such mindless and self-defeating internecine behaviour as seen amongst yeng. It is bad enough that our city-states have seen the re-emergence of old tensions occasioned by diminishing resources. Especially at this time, we can no more afford war against our neighbouring cities than we can afford to outfit Arcraft to the standards an Aranian crew might be happy with. The on-going struggle with ruddy Hostagrifonta is more than we need at this time.

"However, surely tagging would actually continue to be beneficial. After all, it would give us sanction over dangerous individuals. I can see explosive tags as giving us a means of ensuring that the most suitable gang of yeng won any battle."

Boklung pauses in zis eating. Ze senses that a critical point in the project has just been reached. To be sure of some success with all zis plans ze knows that ze has to keep Clanten on zis side. The Speaker of the Council is the most powerful individual in Cirithia. Ze knows that in the next few minutes everything could blow up in zis face. How can ze get Clanten to at least come as far as the Admiralty has, to at least think about the unthinkable, empowering the yeng? Boklung decides that ze's just got to go for it, and hope that some guiding spirit is there to help give bite to zis words. Ze draws a big breath and prepares.

"Yes, Honourable Speaker, you are theoretically correct. However, how would we in practice monitor individuals to that degree of accuracy? The robots aren't capable of understanding really complex and often apparently illogical activities between maverick yeng individuals. The 'bots would as likely sanction the good as the bad. No, we really are better leaving yeng infighting to the yeng.

"Anyway, Zir, don't make the mistake of thinking we are so superior. We are hardly incapable of mindless aranicide. I feel that our Council both forgets hindsight and lacks foresight. In recent cycles we have always found peace with our neighbours after a very few military deaths; however, no guarantee can be found that this will continue when only the survival of the fittest seems likely. In an environment in which only the strongest have any chance of survival, we Aranian will fight each other just as viciously as would any other species. In truth, we are equally base animals. Could even we judge any situation accurately, let alone trusting the judgment of 'bots? And if Aranian were active crew, would it be acceptable to let an artificial intelligence decide any outcome?

"We are going to be so dependent on the yeng. We have to allow them to feel that they are, if not complete masters of their own destinies, at least not pawns. We even need to give them the perception that they are actually boss of the robots, or else they will find a way of destroying those machines. A sense of self-determination will give them the incentive to push towards a successful mission. Our whole strategy relies on the yeng fighting off all comers and any adverse physical conditions. Yeng are an intelligent enough species to feel that the future isn't fully pre-ordained and that they can better their circumstances. Even the worst treated of yeng slaves don't give up on life whilst they can believe that tomorrow may be better.

"They need a sense of hope in order to struggle hard to keep themselves alive, and in so doing inadvertently defend our yet-to-hatch colony. The balance between their freedom and our ultimate control is going to be difficult to accept even for me, but I really believe that the mission will fail unless the yeng believe that they are struggling to direct their own destiny. Explosive tags are useless in practice. But the Council will be reassured by their supposed presence, and they won't even comprehend their long-term obsolescence if we don't point that out. Just exactly how free the yeng will be has to remain our secret. A secret we keep even from the floor of your honourable Council, Zir. This mission fails if we don't have you with us in following whatever deceptions are necessary."

Admiral Bagfung licks zis lips. "I have certain reservations as well, Boklung. How can we be sure to give the hatching juvenile Aranian the chance to prosper amongst the independent-minded and aggressive yeng? Is there a way of ensuring that they, and not we, end up as slaves?"

Boklung, suddenly presented with the problem of keeping Bagfung onside as well, feels very uneasy with the way the conversation is going. Ze thinks to zimself that the whole project might fail in the here and now, in the restaurant. Ze decides on brutal honesty rather than sugaring zis reply.

"I am not at all sure that a new colony of juvenile Aranian could survive in the short to medium term in the absence of the skills of mature yeng. We need to assume that we will always be a superior race, that all else being equal we will always end up as supreme. This is where you really have got to rethink the square, Clanten … We have to leave some things to chance, and chance is best exploited by the intrinsically most powerful. We must trust that natural order will eventually ensure that Aranian and not yeng dominate any new society. We may have to accept, even with our natural superiority, the yeng having the kicking legs for quite some time. That may not change until the arrival of new ships of Aranian sent out to the new securely established colonies. We have trouble with the concept of sending Aranian on virtual suicide missions, but not on missions to outposts that contain all the ingredients for our prosperity. Our soldiers can defeat almost any number of yeng however well their resistance is organised. Remember that what really matters for our species is a long-term prosperity, even if that means medium-term hardship. Think of it as a long-term strategic retreat needed to regroup in order to win a terrible war, if that helps you rationalise away what I am asking of you.

"Whatever happens, we are almost certainly talking about perhaps as few as ten cycles of dependence on yeng after a landing, a couple of generations of that short-lived species. As soon as we have distant colonies to aim at, we will be sending full Aranian crews of our psychologically most robust offspring in our best engineered ships. This is a vital long-term plan, and we must not lose sight of that in the muddle of the interim."

"Tough talking," Bagfung says, "but you have me onside. One thing is for sure, Boklung, even yeng struggling to survive on a new planet are unlikely to be so pre-occupied with fighting each other that they would miss an early opportunity to squash a less than developed colony of Aranian, especially one that suddenly appeared as a threat. The more I think about what you say, Cingwin, the more I agree with you. Truthfully, the new colony may not survive with the yeng, and yet it is even less likely to survive without them. We have to just build in as much flexibility as possible, as you suggest, even being prepared to accept a period of slavery to yeng masters. The yeng will need to see an advantage to nurturing Aranian, just as we see one in nurturing yeng. We must be useful, as workers, as the strong labour needed to build cities in a new and almost certainly difficult environment. But whatever happens, our next spaceships will soon arrive. I can even see that if no eggs ever hatch, it won't be a disaster. Look how easily we dominated yeng on Waterball when we arrived suitably armed. We really need some brave, revolutionary, thinking.

"Anyway, I am formulating a bit of an idea, which may just increase the odds of early success. Perhaps we can fortify the natural direction of their 'spirituality'. We might keep the yeng on a lower dais if we can instil them with a version of our religious beliefs. Can we build for them a false culture, one that is based on the omnipresence of the Holy Spirit? May they be given 'scriptures' that look forward to a second coming, to the future birth of a God-chosen Aranian brood? What if these new-born Aranian were scripted to be the direct offspring of God, taught as equally the God of yeng and Aranian? Might we not indoctrinate the yeng to actually be the determined protectors of our infant descendants, born in the very image of Sinanna?"

Clanten interjects: "Genius, Bagfung! Can it be done? Can we give the yeng a brand new belief system that will actually be protective of Aranian? I should be putting you on a charge of sedition, Boklung; your ideas are so contrary, so anti-establishment. However, I just don't believe how much you two are turning my thinking on its head, and all within the course of one short period of our conversation. Holy Sinanna, should I be charging myself? Have I been drugged?"

"You flatter me, Zir," Boklung replies. "I use nothing but logic. I wouldn't be spouting such strong words if I didn't believe them. I need to put worst case before you. From that envisaged position we can start to think about ameliorating the affects of yeng independence. For one, the Admiral's vision is certainly theoretically possible. It will mean concentrated indoctrination. Second generation yeng, unaffected by Earth memories, will be far more susceptible. Yes, it is plausible. The myth can start from here and be reinforced during the voyage. As the yeng will have to breed on-board, probably through at least two generations, it should prove possible to reinforce new cultural traditions. Across the generations, our God could push away all their old myths. Many of them already see Sinanna as the one and the same God as their own: as the one true God."

Clanten almost bobs on the spot with excitement. Ze makes an instant decision. "Instigate a programme, Boklung. Make it State wide. I'll divert funds from somewhere. I think we can assume that at worst it will just not achieve anything useful. I can't see any negative side. Yes, giving them the Faith has to be a worthwhile pursuit. I will arrange for some of the yeng already worshipping Sinanna to be transferred to your works. I've the power to order such strategic transfers at State imposed prices. This shouldn't be yet another burden on your overstretched legs."

"Hggh!" Bagflung says. "On another topic, the ship will need regular maintenance as all craft do. The robots will be mainly responsible for this, as they are best suited to repetitive precision. Later, as systems decay, we will have to rely on yeng flexibility to patch solutions. In the end, the expedition's success may depend just as much on the quality of robots we commission as on our selecting suitable yeng, but neither can do the job we require without the other."

"Agreed!" Boklung nods enthusiastically. "And something to consider for the future, comrades! When it comes to hiding our eggs on-board, I may have the perfect long-term solution. My idea is that the yeng actually carry our brood inside a sort of parasitic worm, a parasite that bores into their internally gestated embryonic young. Developing inside the yeng body, our eggs will be safe, never exposed to the outside environment until a 'trigger code' causes their excretion. There will even be a period of safety if the yeng die out, as the new hatching can feed on yeng cadavers. Unfortunately, this is only a plan for future expeditions, as we haven't time to develop such complex technologies. We may not even want to, as such a start to new life would effectively make us into something different. Do we want to be born of larval parasites from between the limbs of yeng? However, this sort of science has great potential."

Ngu Clanten stops eating and turns a sickly yellow. "I'm not at all sure I am ready to accept the idea of us being born from yeng, whether cadavers or living, though I do believe certain Waterball familiars are born in this way from inside other dead creatures."

Boklung continues: "I can't say I disagree with your sentiment, Ngu. So let's leave such advanced science behind for the time being. Just note for the future that implanting our eggs in such a way that the yeng become protective carriers of our species is a possible solution. We already have some of the science to do this; at least we have modelled the technology in drabbets.

"Up until now, plans have entailed isolating the yeng into one section of the craft, but provided the eggs are well hidden in the actual construction materials then we can give yeng the run of the ship. This is sensible anyway. Imagine, for example, that the Arcraft came under threat from space pirates. To defend the craft the yeng would need full access. I propose that we inject the eggs as part of the fabrication of the ship. That way they will have nothing obvious to find. Integrating eggs in the construction materials, at least of internal partitions, is, I'm told, technologically feasible."

"Brilliant, Boklung," Clanten says, with a sudden new buzz of enthusiasm. "What resources does your lab need to build such panelling?"

"Nothing special, apart from being allowed to commandeer academics and technicians from other programmes and maintaining strong ties with my Cheetan comrades. I need to draw on their scientific community as well. I happen to know that the Cheetan have used this method to allow their eggs survival as ships pass through areas of high cosmic radiation. They colonised Tragoranashmeed in this way, before they had designed craft with low enough mass and high enough quality shielding. Instead of trying to shield the whole craft to a high enough standard, they made solid panels with eggs buried deep inside, and used the outer layers of the panels as radiation sponges.

"Another reason for a strong cooperation is that the Cheetan already keep yeng in conditions not unlike those we are going to need to establish on the Arcraft. As you know, on Trogaffin the yeng have to be kept in isolated buildings, which have sealed atmospheres. These self-contained units operate almost completely isolated from the planet's environment. And, of course, we are working with the Cheetan to improve their systems. The needs and experience of both planets complement each other."

Admiral Bagfung butts in. "For now, we have to acknowledge that the full Council simply won't accept the yeng having the freedom of the ship. We must do all we can to persuade them otherwise, while in the meantime being prepared to deceive them in order to make progress. That will have to do for this mission. However, we have to keep working on their thinking. They have to see the future as we do, before too many subversive tracks have been built. I would like us to push ahead with plans to use the yeng themselves as carriers, even if we only achieve that for much later launches. If we could develop that science, we may be able to get the Council to eventually accept a lot of the strategy we know they presently won't. We could have one group of animals assigned for the more dangerous tasks, and a better protected group could carry our eggs."

"That is easy, isn't it, Admiral?" Boklung says, after swallowing a quick bite. "The males are the better fighters and, anyway, tend towards protecting the females. So the simplest method might be to use their two forms. We use the females to nurture our broods, and increase the male population still further as the soldiers. Think of them as soldier yeng and brooder yeng.

After all, that isn't far different from what they are in their own primitive social orders. That gives me an idea, I will talk to my biologists about using the female's strange monthly cycle. We may be able to have the females excreting our eggs, along with their own fertile ones. What an interesting thought."

"We are going to need to keep the yeng fit," the Admiral chips in. "There are obvious military reasons for this, but other more direct ones as well. Yeng are less physiologically suited to low-gravity living, so to combat this they need a lot of physical conditioning. I suggest you enforce heavy and continuous training regimes. You will need equipment suitable for yeng physical conditioning on-board, even if this makes space for other things even more limited."

Boklung nods. "As well as getting suitable exercise equipment installed, some robots could be programmed as exercise technicians. Can I leave that job with you, Admiral?"

"Yes, certainly. As you know, the military often use robot instructors."

Clanten's eyestalks bob about with excitement. "Excellent, comrades. Let us proceed with all haste. Time is hardly on our side, so the sooner we start in earnest on the detail the better. We have been planning and developing the basic transportation technology for a long time. It is high time this sense of urgency was transferred to the development of suitable crews and internal fittings. Looking at my compad, I see it is time I moved on, so I call this meeting to a halt."

Boklung holds up a forelimb. "One more thing, if I may? The best potential male yeng soldiers for this expedition will be found amongst the gladiators. I seek permission to approach the Gantri's management to try negotiating the release to me of time-served warriors. We don't know what other civilisations we will have to subjugate. But whatever happens, sentient creatures fight far more flexibly than predictable unfeeling robot soldiers."

Clanten nods. "When the time comes, I will do what I need to do to ensure that you may select a few of the best gladiators, but in the interest of maintaining public support, let us not deprive the population of its best yeng champions just yet.

And this really will cost a lot of money and political good will. I will start putting some thought to this. If the powerful families that control the Gantri defy me, then we may be forced to use special methods. An accidental breakout that provides only one clear escape path, right into the bowels of the Arcraft is always possible, wouldn't you say? Yes, that would keep the cost down, and as a bonus I might be able to manipulate the aftermath to ensure that uncooperative directors of the Gantri are removed. Yes, I am excited by that prospect. Hargg; you never heard this, Boklung, but I already have a couple of my best yeng inside the Gantri Amphitheatre, as I believe you do. One in particular, a yeng overseer, and his side-kick—a Choochin—may be helpful. Yeng already hide in the sewers, don't they?"

"I never heard a word, Zir!" Boklung says. "Hypothetically, I know just exactly which yeng might be most suitable to lead such an unfortunate rebellion. Hggh, yes; I can see some great ideas brewing. One in particular isn't in the Gantri just yet, but I have a feeling he will be."

"Might that be the very individual that caused all your recent embarrassment in the first place, Boklung?"

"That could be the case, my Honourable Councillor, thank you so much to both of you for your time."

Sinanna, that wasn't good for my nerves. I could have been arrested if Clanten hadn't seen the common sense in my views. So after all, Ngu Clanten isn't just a useless apparatchik that would do anything to get to power; well, not unless ze sees me as zis meal ticket which is totally nonsensical. Ze has proved to be far more open minded and in tune with the needs of the Arcraft than I expected. Ze seemed to be so wedded to the State and yet ze has proved to be as cooperative as the Admiral. With Clanten's support, and zis executive influence, I'm sure we can ameliorate the power of the Council. The challenge of getting the majority of the executive to agree to everything I want was always going to be too great, but with the Speaker of the Council as my ally, things seem far less daunting.

Then there's Lebl as well, Clanten's handsome offspring. Yes, I have designs on one Clanten in particular. I have long fancied sweet Lebl. Perhaps my alliance in crime with Clanten makes such an official union less improbable. My fortunes, both in business and romance have taken a sudden turn for the better. For now, it seems that I did right to risk all.

"Before you go, Admiral. Thank you so much for the subtle playing of our friend, Ngu Clanten. You should be in politics, Zir."

"Yes, fun, wasn't it?"

12

ATHALIE WATCHES

After her escape from the hunt, Athalie has been surviving in the hills, never far from the Esterpharn Caves. Recently, she became preoccupied by something other than every rustle and every desperately needed morsel of food; she spied another human in this wilderness.

Jack spends his days around his settlement with no idea just how close he actually is to another refugee from 'spiderdom'. In contrast, Athalie is very aware of, and totally preoccupied by, her close neighbour. She has been struggling with a desperate need for company while fearing its consequences. Having been brought up on a breeding farm isolated from social connectivity of the city, she hadn't known that there were people living independently in the wilds. So as much as the presence of a living person attracts her, his strange existence raises fears. Her first assumption was that he must be a creature working directly for the spider; perhaps even there to ensure that the likes of her are tracked down and destroyed.

Athalie becomes even more concerned when she sees that the man isn't alone; rather strangely, a suvaran often follows him. Never before has she seen such a companionship, and she struggles to understand the concept of a man treating a suvaran more like a friend than a potential meal.

Athalie has faced many cruel trustees empowered by the spiders and often liable to take any number of violent liberties on any other human that causes them the slightest interest. Most of the trustees are castrated males that promise loyalty to their spider bosses as the only way of avoiding their own dispatch to the butchers. Athalie has had enough terrible experiences under the hands of these often-vicious creatures to make her wary of revealing herself to this man. That doesn't mean she isn't attracted to him, or seduced by his masculine strength and his seemingly arrogant confidence in his surroundings. She watches the mouth of his cave, ever eager to see him and ever terrified of been seen.

More than once, Athalie is convinced that some movement or unintended noise has given her away, but nothing prepares her for what eventually happens.

Athalie is contentedly switching her time between dozing in the sunshine and watching over the mouth of the cave, when, half-asleep, she feels a sudden chill down her spine. Convinced that he has discovered her, she slowly moves her hands towards the heavy stick she's been using as a club. Then slowly she turns her head to find herself staring into the eyes of a ... of a suvaran. Why would such a normally fearful creature be stalking her unless she was already a cadaver that promised only dinner? She is even more surprised that the creature doesn't back away when faced down by her stare. Eventually, she realises that the creature is so tame it can only be the man's best friend.

Thinking more rationally now, she does what she has seen the man do and offers the creature her hand so it can sniff it. Slowly, she rubs the scaled neck of the animal. Then, with a careless trust, the creature squats down beside her and stares back towards the cave. Athalie is suddenly aware that she has made a friend; a friend that she prays won't give her away.

In the next few periods the creature visits Athalie often. It lies beside her and demands her attention. When the creature responds to a call from the cave, she even learns its name, Pugwash. She feels almost guilty for the attention, as though she's stealing something away. That doesn't stop her wanting to intrude even more into that other human's life. To Athalie, exploring the cave becomes just a naturally intended progression of her survival planning. She could gather some possibly vital information.

When Jack and Pugwash depart, after having made preparations that suggest a long trip, Athalie creeps down and sneaks into the cave. Seeing how Jack lives, his bed, his stack of spare weapons and tools, even the water in the hollowed out block of wood that had been pressed into service as Pugwash's water bowl, all serve to strengthen the connection Athalie feels with her nameless man. Strong, until recently unknown, feelings have already taken on a familiarity that allows her to imagine him standing close, muscle toned, happy and smiling down at her. She imagines him pulling her close and lifting her chin, so that he can gaze deep into her begging eyes.

Before she leaves his home, Athalie can't resist the idea of quickly trying out the bed. She finds the experience both comfortable and somehow strangely comforting. Indeed, she might well have drifted into a dream-filled doze if she wasn't suddenly aware of the slithering approach of a nagwad. That sends her scurrying back out into the light and up to her usual spot amongst the rocks.

Later, it isn't the expected insistent nudge of Pugwash that stirs her but the sound of several human voices and the surprising appearance of a hunting party in front of the cave ... Once more, Athalie fears for her life and now also for that of her imagination's new lover.

13

A GIANT FREIGHTER IS BUILT

Time moves on, and after a couple of near-disastrous setbacks, Boklung is put in overall charge of all aspects of the Arcraft Project. Admiral Bagfung is relieved of zis day to day duties, only too pleased to escape with zis reputation intact. The Admiral also knows that ze may actually be able to do more to help Boklung's plans from the safety of a little political distance. Boklung's increased responsibility can be seen as a poisoned chalice, as was certainly the intention of most of the creatures on the Council in authorising it. Boklung certainly sees this further appointment as coming at yet greater private expense. However, as the new Director of New Frontier, ze is determined to make seniority work in zis favour, both in terms of influence and long-term wealth. Just the logistics of the project would be enough to tax most Aranian, let alone dealing with all the technical and politically charged issues that come as baggage.

An exceptionally large hangar is needed to contain the huge juggernaut during its final assembly. The size of the thing, and more importantly its overall weight, will vastly surpass that of any ship previously launched into space from this star system. The monster isn't going to be launched from terra firma. Rather, it is to be pulled into a geostationary orbit by tug craft and accelerated from there. The whole project has been put together at low cost, including the engineering specifications. By design the thrust engines are too underpowered to enable a launch with a full payload from a terrestrial space port. The warp engines that kick in at approaching light speed are only a little less compromised.

The freight capacity has been maximised by leaving out many standard fixtures, and the draught load has been minimised by keeping the build weight, and in some respects quality, as low as possible. There are no luxuries aboard, and safety and functional flexibility have been severely compromised. Many of the cost-saving techniques employed have been learnt from the slave trade. Boklung prays that saving money hasn't completely undermined the project's ambitious goal.

Engine performance wise, all that is deemed necessary is that the craft be able to accelerate through warp speeds, even if it takes an Ungolian day to get it there. Once sufficient velocity has been achieved, Alcubierre's Principles start working. At that stage, a close wrap of space-time will move with the craft and the outside forces on its structure will be reduced to almost nothing. At warp speeds the shields provided by the inevitably created space-time bubbles keep all space debris away from spacecraft. However, the outer skins have to protect against rock strikes until warp conditions are achieved. So the relatively weak structure of the Arcraft will be at most risk whilst building up to warp one, the speed of light. Due to its painfully slow acceleration, Arcraft One will be in danger from debris strikes for a considerably longer period of time than most space engineers would consider expedient.

The most dangerous time of all will be when the tugs are withdrawn. They must escape some distance from the Arcraft before it reaches 'Warp One', or else they will become trapped in the space-time bubble around the giant ship. Trying to breakaway at anything over the speed of light distorts local space and destroys everything inside any bubble. This means that the Arcraft has to make the very last acceleration to the speed of light completely under its own steam.

Most of the engineers are of the opinion that, from a standing start and without the pull of the tugs, the engines would probably explode well before even 'Mach One' speed could be achieved, even taking full account of the launch being from a high orbit. As most intelligent thinkers can't help but quickly work out, there's actually a deeper motivation for the substandard power specification than keeping down structural weight and costs. The last thing the Aranian want to risk creating is a fully autonomous spacecraft with the capability of being turned and used against Ungoliantis when it has potentially dangerous yeng aboard. The Council only voted in the project under assurance that the craft would only ever be capable of an outward journey, and this was when everyone believed that the yeng would be controlled by ambulatory Aranians amongst the crew. Everyone except Boklung, that is.

Many wonder whether the Council had sanctioned the building of a class of sure-fire death traps. But at least this created a shift in attitudes beneficial to Boklung and zis 'conspirators'. It is perhaps no wonder that many of the initially most insistent calls for an Aranian crew have started to become less strident, if not yet disappear.

Boklung has come to terms with the heavy burden of costs landed on zis back especially as ze is sure that many expenses can be recuperated in one way or another. As we have already seen, Boklung also knows that ze shouldn't cut costs by reducing yeng quality. The paranoid concerns of the Council have already reduced the technological flexibility of systems to an absolute minimum. A less than physically top-notch crew would only add to that weakness.

Any omnipresent being can't help but see that for the immediate future, the long-term existence of two, if not three, of the Multiverse's most interesting species has been made the responsibility of just one head and four pairs of 'legs'.

Boklung hopes that if ze succeeds there isn't going to be any nasty rebound coming from those councillors jealous of zis success. After all, those that wanted zim severely punished are now faced with the possibility of seeing that they've, at least temporarily, only cemented zis greater power and prestige. Boklung has no trouble imagining how bitter and just plain foolish some of zis political and personal enemies might feel. Aranian have the capacity to be every bit as jealous of a peer's success as any yeng. Inevitably, power corrupts and especially when the marginally less powerful carry grievances.

Luckily for all the creatures in this story, Boklung has a far more 'enlightened' vision of zimself than being merely a powerful business Aranian of zis generation. Boklung is a complex creature and something of a visionary, who for many reasons is beginning to look upon yeng as far more than simply useful livestock. In fact, not unlike the occasional yeng that comes 'to like animals rather more than people' Boklung is coming around to the idea that in many ways ze prefers yeng to zis own kind. This attitude is certainly contributing to Boklung's determined belief in zis vision about what is required for the Arcraft project.

A higher ideal, namely the future balance of influence between advanced species, rather than the nuts and bolts of the expedition, starts to dominate Boklung's thinking. We have seen some of this already in zis determination to bring Clanten on side even at great personal risk. With this shift has grown zis belief in zimself as a vital ingredient of the future's construction. Perhaps, after all, Boklung is no exception to the rule that a personal growth in power can push one towards megalomania. Fortunately, zis vision is generally about being seen as the great benefactor of sentient life, rather than about being a selfish demi-god. But ze is no saint either! With the help of a bit of special egg selection, the planned Aranian colonisation of distant space will now benefit the descendants of Boklung far more than those of any other dynasties. Indeed, Boklung's bias, zis personal ambition, is starting to make the Arcraft project one of balance between zis own genetic legacy and that of zis yeng, to the exclusion of most others. Though one other, zis Cheetan business partner will also be a big beneficiary provided ze continues to play loyal cards. Perhaps it is fair to say that actually ze is taking megalomania to such an extent that ze sees zimself as having a bigger vision, a bigger role in the future, than any other sentient creature in known history.

***

Um ... yes, you must see my influence. Boklung is almost thinking like a sort of mortal, flesh and blood, time-lord. Actually, I'm less and less sure how in control I really am. It seems that something far more profound, something far closer to the Creator than me, has smoothed the path of such a revolutionary thinker. Moment by moment, I feel every thought is my invention, but really, deep down, I feel that a far greater presence than Orlando Oversight has a stake in this unfolding story. I direct Richard, but who directs me? As for turning Ngu Clanten, sure, I was hoping to influence zim, but I can't be in all the players' heads at once.

***

Long before Boklung's first official meetings with the engineers and designers, ze had come to the realisation that the Yeng will actually need a huge amount of physical space. The key requirements are, obviously, space for food production, waste management systems, oxygenated air producing machinery and exercising areas. As we have already seen, Boklung is a clever enough political operator to know that zis vision is only going to be achieved by carefully orchestrated degrees. Boklung has to steadily pull the other players with zim as ze redirects or purposely overlooks the demands of the Council.

Boklung already had zis own personal choice of individuals running the design team. Chief Engineer Ushkeenz, an Aranian that ze trusts more than any other, has often worked with Boklung in the past, both in an official capacity and on private business concerns. Boklung actually likes Ushkeenz because of zis willingness to question those senior to zim, which isn't often a strong Aranian trait. One day ze enters Boklung's office and draws zis attention to something that is obvious even though it is completely the reverse of Boklung's vision.

143

"Can't we reconsider the idea of sending yeng at all?" Ushkeenz asks as ze takes a seat opposite Boklung. "We could make good use of the payload saved by not doing so."

Boklung is prepared for this question to regularly be bounced at zim, especially from the likes of Ushkeenz. "No! That cannot be a consideration, even if we Aranian were up to the demands of the voyage. Don't forget that the hatchlings will require fresh meat. Yeng can serve the role of nutrition providers for a considerable time before our natural prey species can be produced and fattened from frozen genetic material. Yeng will provide sustenance through the first bleak period of colonisation. Most importantly, if we weren't sending them we would have to provide nearly the same amount of room for other equally resource greedy livestock species. We can't guarantee any new world providing us with an instant source of anything edible, let alone palatable. As to a robot only crew, that's a non-starter for a mission of this complexity."

Ushkeenz interrupts, but with a bit less conviction in zis voice. "Yes! But the cost in terms of the available freight area is massive. We could take so much other useful equipment."

"Yes and no. It is true that we will need a lot of space for ambient life sustenance on-board, but don't forget that if we didn't have that equipment assembled from the start, there would be a need to build all or most of it on arrival. In order to support our first generation of new-born Aranian, we will need to source almost exactly the same equipment as is needed for yeng maintenance. We just don't know what the target planet will naturally provide for us. Sure enough, we are selecting targets that have parameters as close as possible to Ungoliantis, but we won't know the subtleties of the environment on any future host planet until the mission actually touches down. Suppose landing brought on an immediate crisis because no transferable life support was up and functioning."

"Okay. I see where you are coming from, Zir. There's more to this than the basic mathematical logistics of flight that fill my head."

"The most important point about making use of a yeng crew is their adaptability. When things cease to run smoothly, and you as an engineer know they will, then the flexibility of the yeng will come into its own. Remember also, while you're trying to weigh the balance, that yeng are much more psychologically 'resilient'. Just think what the cost might be to send out an Aranian crew with all its massive needs and expectations. Making the craft into a good environment for us would use up immense amounts of physical space as well. Then there would be the political fallout to deal with should a wholly Aranian crew be lost."

"So with what you told me in confidence earlier, we really are working on plans that at times are at loggerheads with the demands of the Council. I am beginning to get it, Zir. You really are saying that if we must send Aranian then they should only be travelling as frozen goods."

"Yes, Chief, that is exactly right." Boklung, satisfied that ze has made zis case well, rests zis back against the cushions on zis seat.

Ushkeenz, however, maintains zis stiff posture. "My loyalty to you, Zir, should never be doubted. I was just getting things clear in my own head. Another issue, Zir, is the reluctance of Uskistan, the Chief Exec of Norsbo, to hire out to our project the Norsboklin hangar. It is the only one large enough within ten thousand kilometres of here, and certainly the only one that Cirithia controls."

Boklung gives the Aranian equivalent of a sigh. "The Admiral is going to need sanctioning if ze doesn't give way. If ze takes the issue to the Council, we may fail to get a satisfactory judgment this side of never."

"So what is it you would like me to do to make the problem disappear?"

"Nothing, Chief, don't you go worrying yourself about that. I will find a less valuable agent to take the risk of dissolving the problem should that really prove necessary. A knife across zis throat would do the job, but that's not me, and I'm sure a less bloodthirsty solution is still possible. A tasty scandal could sufficiently serve our purpose. We must avoid raising any fears of conspiracy. Possibly the greater good will demand ze be bled, but I'll do what I can to find a less brutal solution. If you discover any particular vulnerability that Uskistan might have, then talk to Borstave about it."

Ushkeenz nods, appearing somewhat relieved.

"I will be meeting with the Executive Committee of the Council before long," Boklung continues, "and it would be useful to find something to help me undermine zis standing with them. As far as I know, only one member of the Council is strongly influenced by Strin Uskistan. And I'm sure that this friend is controllable. Posheenian is very powerful even amongst the higher echelons, but ze is also a known substance abuser. I believe I know how to handle zim, with the help of a few free herbs from the Spakron Gardens followed up with a touch of extortion."

Tiny tremors in Ushkeenz's eyestalks give away zis lack of conviction that extortion is wise. However relieved ze is to not have blood on zis limbs, ze is a believer in force rather than persuasion.

"We have always had to be prepared to get limbs dirty, Chief," Boklung reminds zim, "and now seems to be no different. The Arcraft project has to succeed whatever the collateral damage. So if I come to doubt the loyalty of anyone, then sanction will be swift and harsh. I know you think I'm taking a political risk when there is a direct and guaranteed solution, but try to trust my judgement on this."

"I'm ten legs loyal, Zir. I do trust you. I'm just saying."

***

Later, Boklung calls zis Head Gardener into zis office. The Gardener, a muscular individual whose eyestalks sit closely together, stands and awaits zis orders.

"Borstave," Boklung says, "I have a sensitive job for you. I want all the dirt you can get on Chief Executive Strin Uskistan. You may offer a bribe to any corruptible soul in zis employ. Also put one of our best yeng trustees onto getting information from

146

Norsbro slaves. Have you got any contacts you can vouch for anywhere close to zis command?"

The Gardener nods. "I will have private words with my mercenary friends in the Guards."

"Good. I know that your sympathies have long been with elements that would like the city to be run ... Hggh, rather differently. We may also need a permanent solution. I have put Ushkeenz in the picture on that. However, the Chief is critical to the project, so zis legs must be kept clean. The two of you might want to consider using a group of yeng to do any necessary wet work. But only if my more civilised efforts fail."

"We will study various options." Ze turns to leave but stops and turns back when Boklung continues.

"And another thing; make sure that Meskulan Posheenian gets a particularly large delivery of the strongest line of augmented zoongrass we have. Enough to knock out a herd of Dodarks. Controlling Posheenian might well be the key."

***

Two old Urtain transporters had long been acquired and stripped back to their fuselages. The plan was for each one to be outfitted separately prior to the two being bolted and welded together. The late scheduled assembly of the two halves of the fuselage means that there was little initial urgency about getting the use of the hangar. Already the old command module of what will make up the rear unit has been removed. In the original design, with yeng confined to the rear section, the two halves were to have been separated by secure bulkheads on either side of a four metre wide void compartment. This void was to have been as free of atmosphere as empty space through which the spacecraft might travel. The 'bots were to be programmed to kill any yeng that managed to cross the near vacuum between the bulkheads. Not that that would ever have been likely. This early design, which Boklung never intended to follow, was forwarded simply to get around the paranoia of the Council raised by the prospect of giving yeng any freedom whatsoever. Boklung's plan from day one had been to get the project up and running, and adjust build details later.

So as to not present the Council with too much ground on which to object, the double bulkhead is to remain. The atmosphere-free zone between the two halves of the ship could be useful should a sentient creature need removing, whether aliens, rebellious yeng, or even frozen eight-legged payload.

14

THE MINE

Osterphelia's team is assembled and fully briefed. The day of departure has arrived. She has three of the people she particularly wanted: Koolsverne, Scunthorpe, and even Peter Finch. The rest of the team consists of three females, Estellathree, Cantonia, and Joy Reed. Boklung insisted on choosing the last two.

Phelia is naturally concerned about the inclusion of two likely spies, but neither is short of useful skills. Cantonia is a highly skilled tracker, and Joy Reed has ostensibly been selected because she arrived in the same batch of imported cargo as Jack. Having been so spatially close for so long, she believes that she will recognise him. In reality, despite the closeness of their paths, they have never been much more than vague acquaintances. Phelia feels that she should be able to pick Jack out herself, especially if she was to see him in the familiar surroundings of The Gardens, but just possibly not against the backdrop of the wilds. Cantonia naturally drifts to her accustomed place at the head of any column, even though this early on her tracking skills aren't needed. As soon as they move beyond the confines of the city, Cantonia takes the lead from Osterphelia.

Phelia is glad to have gained the services of Estella. She is expected to be useful as she grabs the attention of most men, let alone the assumed-to-be-female-deprived Jack. She is also a useful herbalist. Phelia's only regret about the inclusion of this

149

girl is that this is sure to rule out any outside chance that Jack might be interested in herself.

Boklung had earlier passed on the unproven theory that Jack was the killer of the Aranian hunter and given Phelia the map reference of the pit. Ze instructed the team to begin their search in earnest from there.

They have also taken other reports into consideration, including a note about a human with a pet suvaran that had escaped hunters deep in the Esterpharn cave system. Phelia feels that finding the runaway won't be a problem, but capturing him most likely will be.

Each member of the team has a firearm similar to shotguns used on the Earth in that they shoot a cartridge of pellets over a short range. These weapons are capable of killing a human, though they might only sting larger and tougher skinned creatures into aggressive action.

****

Jack, meanwhile, is much further west than he has ever been before—a period of hard-paced walking away from the caves, which is the best part of twelve earth-hours. For some time now the rumblings of what sounds like heavy industrial activity has drawn Jack's attention. He sits, with Pugwash beside him, on the edge of a steep escarpment looking onto what initially appear to be ant-sized creatures far below. Jack realises that he is staring into the depths of a vast opencast mine.

Chained lines of humans work the terrain with pickaxes and shovels, filling large hoppers on bogies set on rail tracks. The loud industrial rumble that first grabbed Jack's attention comes from the grinding metal of these hopper-wagons as they are manhandled by humans along the spiralling rails up the sides of the massive pit. A scattering of spiders and human 'trustees' sit in groups watching the toiling slaves. Jack is well used to the wretched lives of some of the unfortunate slaves in the city factories. But what is before his eyes is far grimmer than anything he has seen before.

Far too many humans toil down there for them all to have been set to this labour as punishment for some perceived crime.

He reckons that thousands labour in the hellhole, and that's just in the half-slice of the mine visible from where he sits.

Jack talks through his thoughts to the always attentive Pugwash. "Those creatures have drawn a poor lottery ticket even by the normal standards of slavery. I wonder if they're all first generation slaves, Pugwash, or if they are born and die in this place?"

If they're born to this—which is likely—there might be a breeding camp not far away. The depth of this mine must've taken more than one generation of lives. In comparison, we domestic and farm slaves are fortunate.

Jack stares at the scene, shocked by the visual scale of the works. To judge the depth, he looks at the relative size of people near the bottom.

It must be a kilometre deep, and maybe twice as wide. Hard to tell. It might even have been here as long as man's been on this planet. Perhaps the need for cheap labour first drove Aranian to harvest mankind. No, that's rubbish, isn't it? Stupid economics. If a species can cross space, it can far more easily build machines to dig the dirt. There was probably already mining here and all of a sudden up popped free labour. It's harsh economics; humans bred at minimum cost to labour until they die. I need to see this close up. But what to do with Pugwash?

"Pugwash, here boy! I need to tie you here, I'll be back soon."

Pugwash looks up, perhaps bewildered to be abandoned anywhere but in the caves. Jack slips the knot to loosen his companion's collar just a little. Once, when a pack of hazzarmanders found their way into the cave system, Pugwash had been forced to free himself and flee deep into narrowing passages. Jack can only hope that if he doesn't return, Pugwash will be able to pull enough to slip his collar again.

Seeing no sign of any buildings from his position, either in the vast quarry or around what he can see of the rim, Jack concludes that the humans are probably housed somewhere on the far-side from his present location. He can't see even a trace of smoke or the glint of any bright object to provide a clue as to possible location. He strains to see the detail across the other side. There are chains of people all over the almost sheer-looking slopes.

"I'm going, Pugwash, but I promise to be back before dull-light."

I'll circle to the north and see how far I can get. It might be possible to go all the way around. But it's a long way. Better get a move on. If I don't start, I won't finish. On second thoughts, I can't really leave Pugwash that long.

"Change of plan, Pugsy, you're coming with me. But you'll need to stay on your lead most of the way ... Come on, mate, let's go."

I'm glad Pugwash doesn't bark like a dog. Safety in silence! Anything's better than being caught. Even if I survived their interview technique, I don't fancy being set to work this pit.

Jack made good progress along the outside of the rim and soon found himself in the midst of a wide carpet of sweet berries. He ate some, stuffed more in his pockets, and gave Pugwash most of his ration of jerky. He couldn't find any water to stock his water-skin, though.

What'll I do when I get close? Just watch, I guess. I've never thought about humans working so far from the city, but why wouldn't the spiders use us like that? There might be all sorts of communities in the bush I've never heard of. We're really the work-horses of this world.

Spartacus failed against the Roman Legions in the end, but I bet his rag-tag army felt their couple of years of freedom was worth all the suffering. Any days of freedom are worth the risk of death after such slavery.

Jack creeps back to the rim to see what is happening. Spiders and human overseers meander between the snaking lines of workers, keeping their charges moving. The crack of whips echoes off the massive quarry walls. He watches in horror as a presumably dead, or over-old, human is tossed far out and tumbles to the quarry floor. The brutality strikes to Jack's heart, but also makes him wonder if he could really claim any moral high ground.

His memory flashes back to childhood and his nasty boyhood behaviour. He remembers pulling the legs off crane flies and burning spiders with magnifying glasses. Jack mentally kills wasps by the thousand and even kicks the life out of cornered rats. For a while he sits holding Pugwash close. Whether this is to guard the suvaran or reassure himself is unclear.

I'm little better than those killers, or at least I wasn't. A right little bastard at times, that I was! I showed no more respect for life than these sadistic spiders. Who am I to judge them?

Savage youth aside, at least I had some education. Not like the poor sods born here. And fewer are coming from Earth these days. What'll happen when Earth-trained humans are no longer arriving to give courage, hope and an understanding of freedom to the slaves bred here? Our species is too valuable to be lost, but we may survive only as a very inferior intellectual animal, like those Type-Two stupid mule-like humans the spiders are keen on breeding. And there's the drugged feed, though not in The Gardens. Thank God Boklung treats zis slaves better than most.

Jack looks back at the scene below him, and anger rises at the cruel treatment the slaves are receiving at the hands of their masters.

If a change in the balance of power is ever going to happen, it'll have to be soon, before they've dumbed most of mankind down into farm animals. At least spiders like Boklung seem to value our intelligence, though many don't.

Only Earth-born humans know how to be independent and have the desire to achieve it. Man did inherit the Earth, but only after thousands of years of struggle, and without having to face the might of an intellectually stronger species. That's all changed now.

One thing's for sure. If we're going to stand a chance there'll have to be one heck of a lot more 'free' people. Isolated individuals can't achieve much more than keeping themselves alive.

"You're not bothered whether suvaran are the pets of men or of spiders are you, Pugwash? So long as you aren't on the dinner menu and are well cared for you'll be happy. Unfortunately for you, pets are not really a spider thing."

Much as I love you, Pugwash, I wish you looked more like a dog. Maybe we could liberate the Earth animals from the Spider's zoos and turn this planet into something similar to the Earth. The geology and flora and fauna isn't so different. We just need to fill it with our own creatures. Okay,

Jack suddenly realises that Pugwash, uncharacteristically, has wandered off while he daydreamed.

Hell. I should have kept zim close. I wonder if ze's found a suvaran friend? There ze is, and looking very sheepish, if that's possible.

"Pugwash, come here ... Now you really must go on the lead, as I promised. Where have you been? Stay here, Pugsy. Keep me company. I worry when you go off."

Jack leashes his pet and, persuaded by the changing lines of sight, chooses a path further back from the rim.

They are walking through high scrub when, suddenly, Pugwash dashes ahead straining zis lead, then ze abruptly stops pulling altogether. The suvaran holds its snout high and sniffs the air. The whiff of some creature, somewhere ahead, has raised its concern. Jack soon smells a strong odour and something crashes through the undergrowth towards them. Jack assumes a yargord is rapidly closing on them.

These, the biggest creatures on Ungoliantis, are vast bipeds, with a massive elephantine trunk. Whilst being mostly vegetarian, they don't mind what creatures they kill. Anything that gets in their way, including spiders, is likely to perish. It's a wonder the spiders haven't driven the yargord to extinction because of the creature's habitually aggressive behaviour. Jack suspects the yargord's existence has only been tolerated because it's considered good sport for the arenas. Dozens of humans are regularly pitted against the giant beasts, and almost invariably they lose.

The noise of crunching undergrowth and heavy feet gets louder. Jack and Pugwash quietly retreat behind an outcrop of rock. The five metre high creature passes, sniffing the air. It's surely aware of their closeness but, feeling unthreatened, moves on. As it passes it smashes its thick crocodile-like tail against the solid face of the rock they're hiding behind. Jack suspects that's just to let them know they've been smelt as well.

As the huge biped rumbles away, Jack ponders the idea that if mankind could fight behind units of yargord then the spiders might have something to fear. He can't help but think of the great generals like Hannibal who marched into battle with their then nearly invincible elephants.

Jack only briefly lets his mind drift before grounding his focus again. The shock of coming so close to what could easily have been a fatal encounter, one which he may have stumbled into if it hadn't been for Pugwash, needs a moment of recovery. Poise restored, Jack moves on.

Close relief, undulating terrain and tall vegetation rapidly reduce the view. Jack tracks closer to the rim, using the denser cover. But when they traverse closer to toiling humanity the chance of suddenly walking into real trouble grows. The sound of whips cracking echoes around the mine. The sound raises unpleasant memories of chasing hunters and punishment regimes.

Soon the buzz of activity sounds close by. They're following a discernible path, and Jack feels it's time to go on alone. He moves back into the undergrowth, hoping to secure Pugwash well out of danger. He ties his pet with an extra length of rope—always carried for the purpose. This time, there'll be no last minute change of plan.

"Stay, Pugwash ... Don't pull, settle down."

Jack moves on, leaving his long spear despite it being his best defence against spiders. A shaft of wood nearly three metres long is nothing but a hindrance to a stealthy approach. With just his machete in hand, he heads towards where he believes an encampment might be. The second sun is overhead by the time Jack gets his first glimpse of a spider.

15

THE HUNTING PARTY

Jack holds his breath and slowly slides behind the thick trunk of what looks like a massive Earth bamboo. His level of alertness rises as the fetid smells of unwashed human and perspiring spider invade his nostrils.

The noise of activity and the vocal commands of spiders echo off the thick trunks of the mature vegetation. The mixed voices of the dominant species sound rather like the roar of a wind-blown fire spreading through dry undergrowth. Moving ever slower, tree by tree, stepping over twigs and exposed roots, Jack glides towards the noise. One second his view contains nothing but green and blue stalks and leaves, and the next he suddenly spots the raised forelimb of an Aranian overseer, and a fast whip that strikes out like a venomous snake.

Jack becomes snake-like, snake quiet, undulating towards a steadily clearing view. Soon he sees lashed humans as they stagger up the last steps of the long climb onto the rim of the mine.

Every other slave that emerges, staggering as though to free themselves from the very earth, receives a mindless lash. The filthy, mostly naked beings, stagger away like a column of exhausted mules, pushing their skips towards a mountain of already excavated coal. Those yeng that aren't naturally dark skinned are stained to greys and blacks by the jet black coal they carry. The lash is clearly half-hearted, like some traditional ritual that no one is prepared to risk ending, but even without venom in its crack, there's no lack of pain if it strikes flesh. Obviously accustomed to the swish of the whip, the slaves do no more than turn a shoulder or half-lift an arm to protect their faces. The gesture is more in the nature of a 'just-in-case', as more often than not the whip merely cracks the air.

For a wild moment, Jack wonders whether a sudden and heavy charge could launch the spider into space, to an unavoidable death a kilometre down. Good sense intervenes to block such a suicidal thought. Even if successful he would only gain a pyric victory, as it would be followed by his own no doubt far more prolonged and painful death. Besides, he thinks, this overseer isn't behaving any worse than many 'human' jailers of men. Jack wonders if he can do anything positive, anything more than watch these people suffer? Probably not; nevertheless, he hangs around to get a stronger sense of what might be.

After he has 'milked' the immediate scene for information, he moves steadily away and begins a tour around the edges of the active zone. A high wire fence appears, and in the distance, long squat grey buildings. The view arouses clipped images of various detention centres from human history. He remembers photographs of concentration camps from the American Civil War, the Boer War, the Gulags, and a myriad of other infamous subjugations. This could be any one of a billion examples of human to human cruelty, except that here the inmates are marshalled by spiders.

At least the majority of the slaves seem to be in reasonably good health, in that they have clearly been fed sufficiently well to keep up their strength. Obviously, the spiders understand that like all 'machines', slaves need fuel and general maintenance. Abusive usage of any useful tool is counterproductive.

Jack almost respects the eight-legged beings when he sees a pen of children, apparently being allowed to grow unworked until old enough to have some chance. He reflects on the engineering principle that engines run longer and better if well run-in when new. He measures this against his view of a worker being cast out into space off the mine's wall. Good and bad is found in all known intelligent species.

Moving quietly on, Jack passes kitchens, a transport terminal outside the wire where coal is being loaded, vegetable fields, workshops and then spider housing. His passage around the periphery of the small mining town takes him close to the massive air-skirts of one of the hover-trailers used to convey the coal. The idea of hitching a ride is very tempting, even though the destination is sure to be a spider city with the probability of being returned to slavery.

Soon enough, Jack sees real animal brutality and it doesn't come from the generally half-hearted lashes of the spiders. While skirting the wire, Jack finds himself approaching some sort of work detail. A spider, relaxed and looking half asleep, suns itself perhaps twenty metres up the path, and much closer, only five metres or so beyond him, a naked child is pinned face-down, legs forced apart, about to be violated by a brutish looking 'man'. The rapist, armed as he is with a clearly displayed knife, must be some kind of trustee. Other slaves huddle some way off, staring timidly into various corners of the sky. No help will be forthcoming from them. It appears that such abuse is a regular occurrence. Jack's mind races to find resolution.

He keeps an eye on the spider just long enough to be satisfied that it's so close to sleep that it's unlikely to notice anything. Jack quietly rises from the undergrowth. Human eyes swivel towards him. He steps rapidly towards the preoccupied bestial and strikes its head with the flat of his machete. Jack grabs the rapist's arm and drags the unconscious weight off the victim, a young boy.

The wide-eyed child tries to scamper away from Jack, in case he offers worse. The spider raises its head and glances vaguely towards the huddled slaves. The boy and Jack duck down into the grass. Then, like a tide, the band of slaves moves across in front of the spider's field of vision.

Insistent hands signal Jack to melt away into the bush. The boy hesitates, then surprises those watching by suddenly stepping back, pulling the knife from rapist's belt and driving it into its still-unconscious owner's throat. The spider, apparently sensing something unusual happening, moves towards the crowd.

"Allez vite, prenez le corps, vous deux. Vite!" someone whispers.

Jack grabs the body by the shoulders and pulls him towards thick vegetation, his eyes demanding the boy's compliance. Meanwhile, the slaves form up two by two as slowly as they dare. Jack pulls the bloody corpse away into the undergrowth with the boy making a half successful attempt at lifting its legs.

***

Twenty kilometres away, Phelia's party finds the pit where the spider was slaughtered, then heads in the rough direction of the caves. Cantonia wishes to make quite sure that any reward offered by Boklung is forthcoming. Despite the passing of time and the difficulty of tracking across rocky terrain, she feels confident. She isn't alone in taking the task seriously, with the only indifference amongst the posse being confined to the mind of Peter Finch. The intent to succeed may well have been less if they weren't all so very aware that their tagging chips were sure to be monitored by the most powerful of locators. Bribery and fear of retribution alone may well have done enough to stop any attempt to go native, but being monitored so closely by the spiders surely undermined any lingering thoughts of rebellion.

Phelia feels the weight of leadership as she tries to envisage the likely outcome of meeting their prey. *It's time to make best use of Estella's abilities, and I'm not thinking medical. Sex is always on bucks' minds, and Jack's no exception. None of us except Koolsverne has anything like the physical strength or aggressiveness of Jack, so a honey-trap seems the best option. We can spring that without getting too close. There are seven of us and we have good weapons. Estrella can make the first move. He won't be able to keep his eyes off her. Hell, I can hardly tear my eyes away, and I've never been tempted that way even though male lovers are as rare as gold dust.*

The even terrain allows her thoughts to proliferate as they walk.

The group dynamics are difficult, but for now they all seem to respect me as leader. Peter Finch is more than ordinarily interested in Cantonia's lithe frame, and he's old enough to be her grandfather, the dirty old man. He obviously goes for the athletic, powerful type. I hadn't thought about him in that sort of way, though why not when real men are so rare. Finch is old but not decrepit. He reminds me of the oldest joke on the planet: 'There are plenty of good sports, but not enough good balls.'

Then there's Joy Reed. Talk about butch. She may know Jack, but I doubt she has any sexual interest in him—or any man—and does she know him well enough to be able to identify him? I doubt it. I suspect her loyalties are purely to Boklung, so though I'm the one suffering her roving eyes, I'd best not make my prejudice known until I've pricked her loyalty. I wouldn't be surprised if she wasn't physically number two to Koolsverne.

What none of them know is that if Phelia thought she had half a chance, she'd be joining Jack.

I'm told he played a cunning hand, outwardly loyal until he got the chance to slip away. The man is practically a legend around The Gardens; a legend I've been sent out to capture alive; a legend I wish I was brave enough to emulate.

Phelia squints at the hill high above them. She thinks she sees the mouth of a cave.

If he's there he's sure to have seen us coming. It's a good defensive position for a hideout, at least from this direction. There's no chance of a stealthy approach and no need to split into groups. I'm certain the quarry can count to seven however we do this.

Cantonia stops and stares up at the cave. The rest of the team stop behind her. She turns to Phelia. "This isn't easy, boss. I've seen no sign of anyone passing that's less than several days old. He may have not come this way lately, but I'm also wondering if he's up there at all."

"I understand that," Phelia says, "but we'd better assume he's at home. Look up there: could any other position give such a commanding view? That's where I'd set up home. Spread out in a line. Reed, Estrella, move to the left of Cantonia, twenty metres apart; you other two on my right, and you Estrella, I want you to be in obvious view. We can't make a stealthy approach, so why try. Remember that we get paid more for a live capture; I'm sure Boklung would like to make an example of Jack. Okay, Estrella, move it. Keep your guards up, all of you. Reed, Estrella doesn't need your helping hands, move out wider."

Minutes later, they bunch up in front of the cave.

"Cantonia, is this the right place?" Phelia asks.

"Well, someone's been living here, that's for sure. We can all see that."

"Finch, Scunthorpe, stay wide. Guard our backs—the rest of you follow me inside. Scunthorpe, you have the torches; pass them around."

They take the torches and enter the cave. Phelia calls ahead. "If you're in there, Jack, give yourself up now, or risk death."

They file in with Koolsverne leading. Seconds later, they give the magneto-charged capacitors of their torches a few turns and the cave floods with light. Creatures slither and scamper away into the shadows. Sound, amplified by the rock walls, bounces around the group. They spread out, split up and head down different tunnels two by two. Phelia moves in Reed's footsteps.

Cantonia stays back, studying the detail, before finally settling for her theory that the occupant has been absent for a day or two. She heads back towards daylight, speaking loudly. "It's a waste of time looking here. I'm going to look for a trail."

A short while later they all return to the mouth of the cave.

"We'll use this cave for the next retreat," Phelia says. "I'm going to have a further look down that large tunnel to the left. It seems to be the most promising. Reed, come with me. Finch, go and find Cantonia. Watch her back! Just watch. Got it?"

A short while later, deep in the tunnel, Phelia gets the feeling that she's in greater danger from her companion than from anything hidden. This is confirmed when she suddenly finds herself jammed head first into a squeeze from an overhang and feels a hand that is more inclined to stroke her rear than push. When Reed squeezes through after Phelia, she suddenly finds her chin being forced up and angry eyes staring into hers.

"This is not the time or place, and even if it was, young lady, I'd rather lie with a spider than a woman. Do I make myself clear?"

"I'm sorry, I thought . . ."

"Do you ever think about anything other than sex? Shit girl, you make most bucks look timid. Real men might be rare, but that doesn't mean that every woman is secretly attracted to a good looking dyke. Just because I'm friendly towards you doesn't mean I'm interested in, you know. And, of course, it doesn't mean I'm not flattered that you can't resist my arse." Phelia drops her voice to a whisper. "You're here because I want us to get to know each other better, and I don't mean in the way you're thinking. Boklung insisted that you be part of the team, which makes me suspicious about your loyalties. Let's get finished so we can get out of this damp squeeze."

"Yes Boss, I'm sorry."

"Would you really know Jack if you had to pick him out of a crowd, or are you just Boklung's ears and eyes?"

"I have to report on you, and the others. But actually it's Finch that Boklung trusts the least. He's getting old, but you know."

"And Jack?"

"I don't know. I should recognise him, but ... I would've said anything for a chance to get out of the city."

"So you'd run if you though that gave you any chance, is that it?"

Reed shrugs sheepishly.

"That's okay; I think the answer to that question is the same for all of us. And Cantonia, is she working independently as a spy, or is she just a good friend of yours?"

"Boklung selected her. I hadn't seen her until we stood together in Boklung's office. I think she's been a favourite of zis for a long time. She's even worked as a tracker for the Hunt."

"Then she isn't a particular friend of yours."

"Definitely not, she thinks 'you know' is a disease!" Reed is still on all fours with her chin held in Phelia's palm. She feels the back of her head being pushed into the rock roof above her and closes her eyes. Then suddenly she feels Phelia's lips roughly caressing hers. Her eyes open wide, stunned.

Phelia releases her and turns away, saying, "While we're here you work for me, sweetheart. Remember that. You report what I want reported."

After a short rest, Phelia's posse gathers around her outside the entrance. "So, Cantonia, did you and Finch find out anything useful?"

Cantonia glances at Finch and then back at Phelia, before she uncharacteristically drops her gaze, only then does she find a reply. "We followed a path that a suvaran had made, and found some disturbed undergrowth. I think another human, one familiar with the suvaran, has been hiding and watching Jack."

"That's interesting. What else can you tell us?"

"The other's female. She hasn't been out here long, judging by her lack of bush craft. It looks as though she followed Jack, but she might be watching us for all I know."

"But you're sure it's a woman?"

"Unless a man squats to piss!"

"Okay, let's move out. And you two, I'm not stupid, Peter 'bad boy' Finch, you can watch our rear, rather than Cantonia's. I don't want our guide any more distracted. You're really not too old are you?"

Finch grins, and as they set off, Phelia reflects on the sexual shenanigans that have infected her team's minds.

What is it about a bit of relative freedom that gets everyone's hormones buzzing? Even Scunthorpe seems to be eyeing up the girls and I always thought of him as a eunuch's eunuch. I haven't seen him show any interest in sex in all the time I've known him.

16

CONFRONTATION

The boy, having escaped Jack's grasp, runs for all he's worth. He crashes through the undergrowth with Jack in pursuit. The boy may well get them both caught if he can't be stopped. The gap between them slowly narrows. Jack grabs the kid's shoulder, scrambles to get a hand over his mouth in case he screams. He pulls him in tight, and supresses his breathing and flailing limbs.

"Shuush! I'm on your side. Do you speak English? ... No, I guess not. Restez tranquille!"

They hear a spider passing close by and hold their breath.

"Shuush. Allons-y! Suivre-moi." Jack racks his brain for more French. Failing, he talks in English in the hope that it'll be enough to give reassurance. "Don't be afraid of me, fear the spiders. If you wish to go you can, but shooshh … go quietly, or you'll get us both killed."

The Boy stops struggling, but Jack thinks he's just waiting for an opportunity to break free. At least his breathing seems a little calmer. "Quel nom avez-vous?"

No response.

"I'm Jack. Jack." He keeps pressure on the boy's arms waiting for a response.

"Anton."

Jack takes a moment to compose a sentence or two of once-good schoolboy French that's now rarely used. "Reste si tu veux. Je pars. Garder le silence ou suivre tranquillement. Je suis libre. Pas un esclave d'araignées. Vous choisissez."

Jack lets the boy go, then scrambles back and moves away, crouching low. He looks back after a few seconds. Anton follows cautiously.

***

A soupçon of French seems useful to remind us all of the language difficulties that exist between all populations and species. Everywhere, a lack of a common language causes misunderstanding and sometimes murderous division. Nothing divides populations of man against each other as deeply as language. Above all other factors, even religion, ethnicity or greed, it is language that most often generates an initial lack of trust. It certainly helps limit cooperative attempts to fight the Aranian.

Most species do all they can to communicate in a standardised way, but not so the human. By stark comparison, even though they are different species originating from different planets, the Cheetan and the Aranian strive for shared vocabulary. They both see language difference as a common enemy to be overcome at all costs.

Anyway, most of you probably think that this book is mere fiction and so mixing languages only adds unnecessary complication. Certainly the second clause of the above sentence has some justification.

Later, Jack and Anton are just coming into sight of the patiently waiting Pugwash.

***

The suvaran is pleased to see Jack return, but observing the new human, remains subdued. Pugwash can't help but be a little wary, confused, and perhaps already concerned about zis status in a growing pack.

Jack suddenly realises that the human is almost as worried as the creature. "Anton, this is my pet, my friend, Pugwash. He's not dangerous. Talk to him and let him come to you when he's ready. Have you ever seen animals as friends?"

165

"I have a loutre."

"I don't know what you mean, but I guess you understand what I'm talking about. Come on, we'd better keep going in case we're being followed."

They hurry back the way Jack came, with the sound of possible pursuit quickly fading behind them. They do their best to talk, and with a mix of French, Aran and emphatic English, get on well enough. It seems that Anton decided to follow Jack because his mother had long instilled in him the notion that if he ever got the chance to run he must. At least that's what Jack gathers from their stilted conversation.

Anyway, Jack's quite sure she wouldn't want her son hanging around to be slaughtered by a vengeful associate of the dead overseer. Fear for what he's done and the novelty of freedom no doubt helps reinforce his mother's words. Jack expects Anton to turn with the first real difficulty, but for a time he has the human company he has so long craved.

The boy seems to understand what's going on; considering everything, he's doing well. He isn't a Type-Two, but to Jack he seems a little slow at times. Jack figures that it's probably just shock or the effect of 'medicated' food, and he hopes that if it's chemical it'll wear off quickly. He's a tough cookie, though, and sharp witted enough to bleed his attacker with a very deliberate and well-aimed stroke of the knife. There was nothing slow about that. Jack had better watch his back, at least until he feels Anton trusts him.

Will the cave still be safe? The risks of discovery will be far greater now with three creatures hiding together. Jack's sure the time has come to move further from the spiders, but he still can't decide in which direction. Towards the mine can hardly be counted as a clear move towards safety.

***

With the bounty hunters and the free heading towards each other, a collision looks increasingly likely. Jack feels relatively sure of himself, certain that he's following his own tracks home and relieved to have escaped the environ of the mine. On the other team, Cantonia's tracking is unlikely to let her down now that she's picked up Jack's recent trail.

Cantonia hears a couple of breaking twigs echoing in the still air. She raises her hand, then waves to the team to spread out behind her. At the same time, three hundred metres away through the trees, Pugwash sniffs suspiciously, trying to place a distant scent. The creature stops, only to feel the harsh pull of its lead.

"Come on, Pugwash, we need to be home."

The suvaran resists but only for a moment, trusting to the instincts of zis master. As it happens, even as ze stopped it was probably too late to prevent a meeting. Only a couple of minutes of walking later ...

Jack is suddenly aware of a half-naked beauty walking towards him. His mind cartwheels, and before he can really even register that what he sees is real, a sharp command stops him dead in his tracks.

"Stop, Jack!"

Surprise is complete.

"Drop your weapons. I am Osterphelia, head of this party. We are here to take you back to face Boss Boklung. You are Jack Baker, escaped property of Cingwin Boklung. You are a first generation breeding male." She turns to Reed. "This is the man, isn't it?"

Reed nods.

"If you resist capture," Phelia continues, "we are to return with just your head."

Anton turns to run, but Kools has got behind them and blocks his path. Jack is in shock; the overwhelming surprise of the meeting temporarily takes away his capacity for action. After a moment of reflection, he manages to open his mouth.

"I agree to cooperate if you let Anton go. Let him return to his mother. She's in bondage to the owners of a nearby mine. Let him go with my suvaran. I'm sure you'll get a bigger bounty if I let you take me alive. The boy's no danger to you."

"I'm sure we can take good care of him."

Koolsverne butts in. "The animal will make a good dinner."

Jack tenses. "If Pugwash dies, so do you."

Phelia senses that she has to quickly stamp her authority. "I believe in compromise; all three of you live for now, and all three are for trade. I think we can find someone to pay well for the amusement of owning a pet suvaran. We heard rumours that you'd befriended one. I've never seen the likes of it. Is it just a disguised earth-dog?"

"In a manner of speaking, yes, Pugwash is my dog."

"Enough of this crap," Koolsverne shouts, walking towards the prisoner, "let's stick the creature and head out of this God forsaken land." He drives his spear towards Pugwash.

The tip of the spear is still short of the creature when there's a blur of motion from Jack and the assailant falls forward clutching at his throat, blood already pumping from a severed carotid artery. He gurgles and makes a half-made hand movement towards his neck, but death is only a second away. Immediately, Jack is felled by a blow from Scunthorpe. A bloodied flint-stone blade falls from between his fingers as he drops to his knees.

Jack slowly comes around to swirling vision, a throbbing pulse bouncing through his skull and the awareness of being unable to move his cramping arms from behind him. Pugwash nuzzles his face and utters a cattish whine. Jack smells roasting meat and is relieved that it isn't a suvaran on the spit. Well, possibly it is, but at least it isn't Pugwash. To his right, Jack sees two men digging and realises they're constructing a grave. He manages to roll into a sitting position and wriggles along the ground until he's resting his back against a rock.

Phelia walks over, stoops down beside Jack, and glares into his eyes. "It wasn't necessary to kill Kools, you bastard!"

"It wasn't necessary for him to threaten my animal."

"You're a fucking head-case, and you're lucky Boklung wants to have a chat with you. We're here to do a job, and I'll do my best to make sure we manage it. I guarantee we'll keep your circus suvaran alive for now, but I'm less bothered about you. I have a soft spot for friendly animals, but not for cold-blooded killers. You'll be kept bound, and every time you so much as blink I'll cut a slice out of that creature, or your young boyfriend. The man you killed was a friend of mine and our best soldier. Understand that!"

Jack sets his jaw and stares back without flinching. "Then you should choose your friends better. If you treat Anton and Pugwash right, I'll accept my fate, at least until you're relieved of responsibility for me. Otherwise ..."

"I don't believe this." Phelia stands and puts her hands on her hips. "You're in no position to threaten me ... But ..." She narrows her eyes. "You have a deal, and as long as I'm this band's leader it'll be honoured. Finch may look past it, but he's no less the cunning survivor than you are, and I'm assigning him to keeping you prisoner. Reed, amongst others, has taken a shine to the creature, and I've told Scunthorpe to keep a special eye on the boy. He speaks the boy's language. But you'll do as we say, or else."

Despite his weak position, Jack still tries to gain a little influence. "Don't you wish to be free? You don't have to return to work for spiders. I know freedom, first on Earth, now here. Have you ever been free? Have you any idea how hard I would fight for that chance again?"

"I think we've seen that, Jack, and I've no wish to see you kill again. You'll remain bound at all times until we stand together before Boklung; me to see reward, you to ... to surely die one way or another."

"Even Spartacus died, but note well what he achieved first. He nearly brought an empire to its knees."

Phelia snorted. "I haven't a clue what you're fucking talking about. Now get up and walk. The only thing that stops me bleeding you out is that Kools was as much of a bastard as you."

17

MARCH TO THE CITY

Jack, nursing a sore head, stumbles along lashed to Anton with a short rope. The suvaran happily trots along on a choker lead held by Reed. While they walk, Jack ponders his capture.

That was stupid. I was so worried about what might be following us that I forgot about what might be in front. Now I'm captured and doomed to face Boklung again. I'd love to meet zim as a freeman, even if only for the few seconds it'd take the Aranian soldiers to strike me down.

How's ze going to handle a recaptured escapee that ze might've worked out is the likely killer of an Aranian tracker? I don't suppose they could prove it, but they don't need to. Being a lowly slave, and one of another species, they won't feel the slightest compunction to prove anything. My best hope is that Boklung values me as part of zis stud herd enough to keep me alive. Some hope! My balls aren't that valuable. I guess, at best, I'll get a job as a gladiator facing monsters in their bloody arena. Long live Spartacus! I wish. Most likely I'll be publicly executed as an example to the rest of The Gardens.

Phelia glances back from her place at the head of the band and frowns.

Has this female leader got an interest in me, a passion for freedom, or merely an interest in obeying Boklung? Jack wonders. *By the confusion in her eyes, a mix of all three. She was shocked by the death of the thug, but in some strange way it may have deepened her interest in me. Curiosity mixed with revulsion maybe; primate instincts overriding rationality. Of course, she may just want to keep me alive for the kudos of presenting me to the spiders, though her dancing eyes suggest I've got to her on a more basic level. She sure reminds me of what I've missed in the wild.*

And then there's that devastating distraction. Pphhh! I fell for that one, as my father would have said, 'hook, line and sinker'. It must be the oldest trick in the book, walking bait ahead of the hunt. It only takes an instant of distraction, and I was certainly distracted. Actually, she's too beautiful. So perfect, she makes me nervous ... Not a feeling I'm familiar with. Does she make me feel inadequate? Maybe; perhaps there's a lesson here.

My chances of getting freed are limited so long as I'm bound. I sort of promised to behave, but bollocks to that. My eyes got me caught, so now they can find me a way out.

"So Peter, Peter Finch," Jack says to his grey-haired companion as they trudge towards the city, "that's your name, right? I remember you, and I remember that woman over there as well. She was in the same transporter as me on the way from Earth. Actually, I've seen most of you before, haven't I? What are you doing with this band of rogues? You're a bit long in the tooth to be scampering around in the bush."

"We do what we must, and anyway, like you, I feel the urge to stretch my legs."

"So you're not keen to return to the city?"

"I'm keen to live as long as I can, and part of my strategy for doing that is doing exactly what people require of me, which, for now, means being out here in this wonderful countryside. I'm old enough to live in constant fear of being culled, but I don't plan on ending up in some Aranian's meat-pie just yet."

"I've been free for a long time now and only got captured because of bad luck and a view of too much female flesh. I had a reasonably comfortable existence out here and I've blown it."

"I envy you, Jack. I'm sure it was tough at times, but freedom, getting back a little of what we used to have . . ."

"Where are you from?"

Peter sighs and pushes the strap of his shotgun higher up his shoulder. "I was born in Burlington Vermont, on a street overlooking Lake Champlain, but I've been here since I was twelve years old. Jesus, I practically belong here now. I was fairly lucky; my folks and even some of my friends from the neighbourhood came with me. Back then, the spiders weren't so keen on mixing up populations. They kept my extended family together, but my parents died soon after we arrived. Three or four of us from the same shipment are still alive, working in and around Spakron. Unfortunately, all those close to me have gone now."

"Yeah, well, if you decide to hightail it, let me know."

Phelia, who has been half-listening, decides she's heard enough. Perhaps she fears liking her prisoner too much.

"Hey, shut your prisoner up back there, Finch!"

"Yes, Dear Leader!"

They stop to eat and soon move on again.

Jack senses eyes watching them. "I think we're being followed," he whispers to Peter, "maybe even from before the Esterpharn caves. It didn't worry me enough to mention it, but if it's more than my imagination, then I think it's one of us, not a zombie, or a spider, but I can't be certain. It might seem stupid, but I don't sense danger."

Peter tilts his head and listens. "My ears aren't what they were. Just one, do you reckon?"

"Yep. Light footed, but not an experienced hunter. Do we tell our esteemed leader?"

"No. Why scare it away; let's see what happens. I trust your instincts. Unless we sense aggression, stalking rather than following, then we'll keep this to ourselves. Knowledge is power. Actually, the stalker may be a lady, one that's had an eye on you, Jack. Cantonia picked up earlier that another person was hiding out here."

Jack glances at his companion with a frown. "Now you have me really confused."

"Don't worry about it. I'll tell you later; Phelia is giving me dagger eyes."

They march on. Jack's thoughts flick through recent events, looking for reason in Finch's words, but the thought of escape soon reinvades his consciousness. He risks annoying Phelia by talking to Finch again.

"What's changed in Cirithia, then?"

"How long is it?"

"A few Aranian months; I don't know, five years possibly."

Peter nods. "Not a lot at first, as you might expect, but recently that's all changed ... It's probably just idle chatter, but possibly something big is going down. The word is that Boklung is having a couple of old space freighters welded together, and there's been some strange experiments on slaves in a brand new factory unit in The Gardens. I even hear talk of a one way expedition across the Milky. Apparently, this crazy great ship is going to be crewed by at least some humans, rather than bleeding spiders. Would you believe it? In addition, I understand that selected slaves are being sent to Trogaffin. I don't know whether that's related, or if any of it's true."

"There's never smoke without fire. Some of the rumour will be solid enough. ... Wait, I just heard something; I think whoever's following us is getting bolder."

"Hey, Scuny, drop back and keep an eye on our prisoner here," Peter calls. "I need to stop for a call of nature." He steps away towards nearby undergrowth.

"It'll be my pleasure." Scunthorpe waits for Jack to pass, then gives him a hefty shove as he does so.

Jack glares at the man, but chooses not to pick a fight.

"There's no need to push," Peter says. "Jack's perfectly cooperative." He drops back, crouches down and waits. Soon after, a barefoot young woman appears, doing a very bad job of stalking the party. Finch rises as quietly as a hunting lion and steps towards the girl, who's only an arm's reach away. She stands transfixed like a doe in the glare of sudden lights.

Peter gives one short *"wheet"* of a whistle, and the hunting party turns.

"That'll be Peter Finch," Jack says. "We were being followed."

A few seconds later, they see Peter guiding the girl towards the gathered group.

"Wow," Scunthorpe says, "followed by an angel! No wonder that stupid old fart was whist—"

"Shut it, you idiot!" Phelia says. "Estrella, find the girl something to wear before we have trouble."

Estrella takes off her pack and searches inside for an extra garment.

"Do you speak English, girl?" Phelia asks, walking to meet her.

"Yes."

"Why were you following? Are you on your own?"

"I'm hungry and alone. I ran from the hunt; they're all dead, my sister . . ." Tears glisten in Athalie's eyes.

"How long ago was that?"

She wipes the tears away with a grimy hand. ". . . Long time!"

"Well, there might be an extra reward for bringing you in, half-starved skeleton though you are. We'll stop for a few minutes. Estrella, clothe her, then feed her, then, Scunthorpe, bind her to the other prisoners. We're getting quite a collection."

Pugwash wanders over, rubs against the girl's calves and purrs like a cat. Jack realises that she and the suvaran must be previously acquainted. Common sense tries to find a way of dismissing such a possibility, but logic and the acquired information leaves little doubt about anything except the details.

"Surely you can let her go," Jack says. "You'll not get much bounty for her."

Phelia turns and glares at him. "Maybe, Buck Jack, but just how long do you think she'll survive out here alone? ..." She raises her eyebrows in a challenge, but Jack doesn't respond. "I've had enough of lippy prisoners. I don't want any more delays. We march until we reach the city. No breaks even at low-light. Cantonia! Get ready to lead us out by the shortest route, just as soon as our latest guest has been fed and watered. We travel straight and quickly, however hard the terrain is."

As soon as Athalie is clothed, fed and tied to the other prisoners, they march on. Bound like a chain-gang, the prisoners struggle to keep the pace.

Jack, a buck used to having women available to him then long deprived, now finds himself surrounded by women that he's unlikely to ever get a chance to do more than stare at, even should they be similarly interested in him. He not only has eyes for the natural grace and confidence of a still very attractive older woman, Phelia, and for the unsettling beauty of young Estella, but also the newcomer who has long had her eyes on him, if not for him. Actually, there's no contest. Jack has been completely overwhelmed by the new prisoner. This is more than the usual quotient of sexual interest; this time, the spell of something far more devastating has been cast: love at first sight. Pugwash's friend may not have either the devastating beauty of Estella, or the deep spirited allure of Phelia's self-assurance, but for Jack she promises a deeper connection than he has ever felt before. Despite all the flattering attention of women that has always massaged his ego, this is the first time in his life that truly instantaneous infatuation has caught him in its web. Many people never experience real love at first sight, but those that do understand how strong its chains can be.

So long I'm alone, not a girl in sight, and now I'm surrounded by them. What's happened to me? Stupid enough to get caught, overwhelmed by beauty I'd fear to touch, murdering bastard, and now what ... I can't think straight for Christ's sake.

Sorry, ladies, you and me, that was just sex talking. My stalker's an angel I must've been born to meet.

Athalie is so close to Jack that her hair almost brushes his face and yet she's too far away. Overwhelmed by her presence, he feels as though he's been looking for this woman all his life. "What's your name?" he whispers.

"Athalie ... I've been hiding near your cave."

"I thought you must've been. So you've seen me before?"

"Many times, you and Pugwash."

"I don't know why I never saw you. But it does explain why I've felt, um, less than well hidden lately. But what about Pugwash, why didn't ze warn me you were about?"

"Because Pugwash and I have been friends since the first day he came to snuffle me awake. I fed him with meat I'd stolen from you. He must have followed the scent back to where I was hiding."

"Ah. I though it was Pugwash that was stealing from me. Why didn't you show yourself? I wouldn't have hurt you."

"I didn't dare, and then you were gone. When I saw these hunters, I thought we were both doomed. I wanted to warn you, but I had no idea which way you'd gone, so I followed them."

Phelia glanced back. That and the lazy flick of Scunthorpe's recently acquired stick stopped further chatter, but it couldn't cut the rapidly growing bond between the two prisoners.

18

LOOMING AMPHITHEATRE

While Phelia hurried her group back towards the city, the high tiered stalls of the giant Gantri filled with circular row upon circular row of stomping spiders. In the middle of the concrete floored arena stood sixteen humans selected to fight against a creature the gladiators usually called a triffid.

The Aranian name for this creature is a phonic interpretation of the sound they make as they hunt for food. This noise is not unlike a bit of cardboard on a rotating spindle rapidly tapping against a solid bar. The thus-named wertutututa is a huge leguminous-looking creature capable for scaring its prey half to death not just with its hunting tunes but with a great variety of other haunting noises. The wide range of its vocalisations are all interpretable as differently timed and variously gusting winds blowing across a great variety of different paddled boards. Most prey species and even the mighty yargord are easily spooked by the sounds. Humans fare no better.

These creatures feed by impaling prey on barbed, rope-like filaments, which shoot out of their anal-looking mouths in the blink of an eye and reach as far as twenty metres to penetrate and still their victims. The creature then draws the tendrils back inside with prey impaled.

The roughly two metres wide and six metres long tube-shaped bodies of these 'triffids' usually appear standing upright,

177

but are occasionally seen recumbent. When lying down, the creatures move along the ground by lifting at the front and pushing forward, then pulling from the front to move the lifted back. The movement is seen as waves of contraction and expansion of muscle rings running along the body, rather like a gigantic stunted maggot from the Earth. When upright, they move by contracting their height by a half and then springing forwards roughly a meter above the ground. They can travel like this at the speed of a human jogger for an almost indefinite period of time. The jumping movement, in some ways rather like that of a kangaroo, looks comical from a distance, but certainly isn't when one is prey.

The triffid hops across the arena as the gladiators that have been cast as its adversary start to organise their defence. Fortunately for the humans, three of their number are seasoned veterans. They soon have them all organised into three units of four. Each team is led by a veteran. Two groups head for opposite sides of the arena, whilst the last group moves towards the triffid, bashing swords and shouting defiantly. The triffid soon plays to the plan by jumping towards the noise. The humans, a mixed bag of men, women, young and old are armed with shields, short javelin spears, and a wide variety of cleavers and swords.

Now that they have the triffid's attention, the noisy team start walking slowly backwards so that they are still facing danger. This confuses the triffid's sense of perception, whilst it is still being drawn on into the middle of the arena. The other two groups are quietly advancing. On the signal from the veteran in the first group, all of them charge, shouting at the now confused vegetable. Only one doesn't join the attack. One timid man hangs back then retreats towards the arena wall. He doesn't live long as an aranian soldier on the high first tier stabs down a spear to skewer him from his collar and through his insides with an exit between his legs.

The other eleven are soon in range of the tendrils of the suddenly concerned bouncing legume. The creature belches out a low vibrato wail of what might be distress before it lashes out its half-dozen tendrils in three directions. One young gladiator crashes down onto her back as her impaled head is propelled from her shoulders by the sheer force of the tendril slicing through her neck. A man hacks weakly at the sharp point of another 'tongue' that runs through his chest. The tendril lifts and with a whipping motion sends the now corpse crashing into the last still-tight group of four.

As individuals, the humans have no chance, but the attack has been well coordinated, so that now those still standing are close enough to start hacking at the creature's body. Victory is now in the humans' grasp, though not all those left will live to see it. Two gladiators get right in under the triffid's guard and slice their way through the fibrous yellow-skinned flesh. Soon, dark yellow, sticky gunge is flowing in growing rivulets to add vivid colour to the heavily stained concrete of the arena floor. Three more perish before the battle finally turns; the last to fall, the brave veteran who had orchestrated the pincer movement.

The triffid topples, right over the still-hacking men. The movement of the tendrils becomes more erratic, and then finally stops; one still wrapped around the severed leg of the expired leader. Those cut deeply in the skirmish will die slowly from toxins. Only four could ever live to fight another day, and one of these is about to play 'dead'.

A booming echo reverberates around the tiered stands, raised by thousands of spider voices. The audience show a deep appreciation of the cunning of the yeng fighters, as the remnants of the brave band sink exhausted to their knees. The survivors will be allowed to start making their way back to the holding pens.

Jesus Sanz, one of the two that literally hacked their way into the creature's tissues, is on all fours, apparently uninjured but wheezing away like an express train as he struggles to catch his breath. Jesus, who is one of three veterans, has already survived many bouts in the arena but knows that the any day now will be his last. Jesus made the decision to try and escape whatever the risk almost as soon as the Aranian who owned him condemned him to the Gantri for spitting in that spider's food.

For many weeks, he has been waiting, hanging on to life, to be one of those selected for the last bout of the day when the fight will be against a venomous creature. Today it has happened. He gazes up to see that the stands are already emptying.

As this was the last entertainment, cleaning teams will soon be coming in. Jesus crawls in a bee-line for the poisonous tip of the nearest tendril. Then quietly, slowly, he lifts the tip and slashes the razor sharp, poisoned nail across his belly. He scratches just deep enough to draw blood. Within a moment his vision is going, as the poison is drawn around by his strong heart. The last thing he does before he blacks out is to feel with his tongue the sharp slither of pottery concealed in his cheek.

Jesus is well aware of the fate of most victims. As we already know, human meats are utilized by Aranian food industries; however, this doesn't apply to the cadavers from the arenas where venomous creatures have been fighting. If there's the slightest chance of a toxin from the meat entering an Aranian food processing plant, the doubtful supply is incinerated. Jesus has learned from surviving gladiators that a small enough scratch from a wertutututua may not be fatal.

To all intents and purposes, Jesus appears to be stone dead. This is just as well, because if any blow from an Aranian elicits even a twitch from a gladiator then their head is sliced straight off. One gives a harsh kick to his rib cage. It should have been enough to cause a groan, but the poison has worked deep enough. The Aranian, satisfied that Jesus has left this life, bags him, then flings him onto the incinerator truck.

The spiders use the previously closest cadaver to Jesus for a bit of gratuitous 'football' practice. They soon reduce her to a state closer to that of mince than a carcass of fresh meat.

Jesus has gambled correctly on the truck's departure being too late to make the trip to the incinerator today. It's already low-light, which is the time when the spiders normally down tools. The clean-up crew park the truck in the works department of the Gantri where it will remain for the equivalent of two Earth-days. If the poison hasn't already killed him; if there's still a trace pulse, and if Jesus's system can maintain this trace of life until the toxins decay, he has a chance.

***

The cityscape of Cirithia slowly grows to dominate the forward vision of the hunting party, and the harsh vistas quieten them.

Jack, totally depressed, stares at the still-distant huge outer wall of the Gantri Amphitheatre. The dark shadows of the concrete city give it a severe grandeur, as great as any powerful architecture ever built on Earth. As with all the Aranian's overpowering edifices, it's crudely functional, not designed with any frivolous architectural reliefs. The view reminds Jack of his father, an art historian, regularly attacking 'modern' bleak architecture.

Jack would never forget all his father taught him about design and ideas, then beyond his young years. He could still see him saying, 'This minimalism, the functionality of form, so lacking in art, in beauty'.

I know what father would now say if he was here. 'The cities of Ungoliantis could have been modelled on the worst raw concrete structures on the Earth, often looking more like massive dam walls and power-station cooling towers than businesses and homes.' Something like that, anyway!

The tops of these monstrous concrete structures break into parapets and recurves as seen on giant seawalls. Here, these overhangs are built not to repel the power of waves, but rather to help stop Aranian simply walking up and over buildings that need to be secure. Some buildings, which need particularly good security, have balconies or other vicious overhangs on every floor, resting on a wide variety of square and flared returns.

I guess the spiders feel differently about such minimalist functionality. After all, they don't build cities to satisfy the human spirit any more than humans built houses to satisfy fish.

Jack wondered what sort of harsh reception he could expect. Logic told him that Boklung would wish to make an example of him, make it clear that the consequences of future attempted escapes would not be pretty.

181

Ze's a benevolent owner when compared to most Aranian, but I'm still just a poorly disciplined farm animal as far as ze is concerned.

Jack knew that the best he could hope for was to be sent to the Gantri, rather than just be strung up to rot as an example to the other slaves. To cope, he knew he had to focus on the best outcome and plan for a long future. He must prevent fear from overtaking hope. If he didn't, he was already dead.

I have to learn how to use the spiders' technologies against them—their guns, for a start. They chip us and probably chip themselves. Maybe that's how they control the guns. That means we'd have to cut the chips from their owners when we seize their guns. Of course, they can probably trace any tag taken from a spider right to whoever has it. Even if we could get around that little detail, they probably record physiological status too, which might explain why I couldn't fire the gun even when I was in the pit leaning against the still-warm spider.

Where would they put it? It's hardly practical to dissect every bit of flesh to find out! But there must be a way. Even if we find the chips and implant them in ourselves, our physiology might be so different that the new data stream would block the gun. If that happens, it's probably easier to completely reengineer the mechanisms rather than try to get around the block.

Jack turns and gets his face as close to Finch's ear as he can. "Peter, listen up! Have you any inkling as to how the Aranian arm their guns? I've played about with one, but couldn't make it fire. Can you think of anything?"

Peter shakes his head. "I've never really hung around to stare down a barrel."

"Have you ever heard of anyone managing to fire one? Or any engineers that've tinkered with them?"

"Now that you mention it, I've heard that this ex-car mechanic, Jesus somebody, or some 'spanishy' sounding name, said he found a way to fire the things."

Jack grins. "Great. Where would I find him?"

"In a butcher's shop; he went to the Gantri a while ago."

Phelia turns and glares at them again.

Jack mimes zipping his lip and gives her a wink. She curls her lip at him in disgust.

If by some fluke this Jesus is still alive, I might just get a chance to see him. I'll be sent to the arena if I'm lucky enough to avoid immediate slaughter. Unless they know I killed that spider. I'm dead, straight up, if they do.

Here's hoping Boklung still has a soft spot for zis stud. Though ze'll have had me replaced. There's nothing special about me. Mind you, why has ze gone to so much effort to capture me? Maybe I'm a political embarrassment. As a member of the City Council, ze's supposed to set a good example. Losing a human, especially a stud male, can hardly have enhanced zis political status. Yeah, that'll be it. I've shown the spider up. Ze's sure to be planning painful revenge. No wonder ze wants me alive.

Athalie suddenly trips, and Jack ploughs into the back of her. Somehow he manages to twist to the side as they both fall, but being roped together with Anton, all three of them end up in an ungainly heap.

"Sorry," Athalie says from the bottom of the pile. "I tripped on a root or something."

"No worries," Jack says. "Are you okay? No twisted ankle or anything?"

"I'm fine."

"Keep your wits about you," Jack whispers to Athalie as they scramble back to their feet. "You never know when an opportunity will come to run."

Scunthorpe's stick cracks across Jack's back. "Shut it, Jack," he bellows. "Save your breath for the spiders."

Jack grits his teeth and glares daggers at the man. "Do you want me for an enemy, Scuny, old mate? I'd lay off with the stick if I was you."

"I'm only doing my job."

"That's what they all say."

Another blow didn't come.

Before long, they're walking past outlying homesteads. A public hover-bus pulls over, and after Phelia has talked to the Aranian driver, they all clamber aboard. The prisoners' hearts beat ever faster as they get closer and closer to The Gardens. Jack regularly looks up to take in as much as he can of the route. As the long, wide view slowly disappears into cramped short streets, the shoulders of both hunters and captives start to sag. It's as though restricted vision isn't just reminding them of the growing confinement of the physical body, but also of the enslavement of their souls.

Jack forces himself to study the profile of the Gantri Amphitheatre once more; its massive walls now dominate every raised glance. A noisy space-shuttle passes overhead, dropping towards the airport. As the roar of the craft fades, Jack's mind transposes the din to that of noisy spiders watching gladiatorial slaughter. He imagines himself standing on the blood-covered stadium's floor with a mass of dead and dying creatures at his feet. The question crosses his mind as to whether this is a vision of him as the last honourable survivor, or as a cold executioner, the very bringer of mayhem and death. Does the picture conjure a simple hope for freedom, or him as an instrument of ritualised murder? He decides that there can only be honour in staying alive if he eventually uses it to fight against the enslavement of all creatures.

Over the Gantri a row of huge flags are flapping and billowing, each with its own differing independent rhythm. Jack imagines the flags in communication with each other, as they constantly buffet like free spirits chatting across the parapets of the imprisoning walls. From this latter thought he takes some comfort, for it reminds him that even the spiders haven't yet managed to supress nature.

The spiders can enclose me in their walls and direct my limbs, but not my mind. Whilst I breathe, I have hope. If I can stand strong in the fresh air, in the swirling breeze of the arena, then anything is possible. There's always hope while there's life. I'll find the brave spirit of Spartacus. I'll stand below the jeering multitude of eight-limbed creatures, and only fear a death over which I have no say. I could be executed or bound on some scaffold, but if given the freedom to die defending myself with a sword, I'll relish every combat, and not surrender my mind to the crush of hopelessness until the very moment some butcher's blade bleeds me out. If I get to the arena, then rather than dwell on each slaughter, I'll see battle as growing me, making me strong enough to rip through the flesh of a whole empire of spiders, just as Spartacus ripped into the entrails of Rome.

19

RETURNED TO DIE AND DEAD

The transporter turns into The Gardens. Boklung waits in front of the main office block before a packed assembly. It looks to Jack as though every member of staff and common slave has been assembled for his return.

The prisoners and their hunters disembark. Phelia sidles up to Jack and whispers, "We'll look after your suvaran; we've become quite attached to the creature."

"Thanks. Sometimes it answers to its name, Pugwash. I'll be grateful if you can keep him alive."

"One of us will find a way. Good luck, Jack. In a different life we would've been on the same team."

"Perhaps we still will be in this one. If Anton's freed, can you look out for him as well?"

"Don't worry about anything but your own survival. I had to return you. I'm sorry. But you didn't need to kill Kools. Mind you, if our roles were reversed …"

"People need to believe in heroes. I'm not saying I am one, but keep alive the myth of the yeng that defied the spiders. If I live, I will be Spartacus, and even if I die today I'll be defiant Buck Jack. I'll forgive my capture if you just make sure of that. As for Kools, I'm sorry because he was your friend, but not for what I did."

A couple of hulking spiders separate them. They herd Jack, Anton and Athalie into a corral, while several others relieve the posse of their never-needed shotguns and other weapons, and send them to stand in the crowd.

Boklung prepares to speak. Ze'd been eagerly tracking the group, and immediately the transporter picked them up ze'd ordered all to the assembly point to witness the return of Jack with a rope around his neck.

Boklung would really like to keep Jack alive, while knowing full well that all the normal punishments for escape require his death. Ze has very ambitious plans for Jack as a figurehead leader of the yeng detail assigned to the first Arcraft. The very cunning that has made Jack such a problem slave also makes him an obvious choice for leadership on a trip into the unknown. Boklung has already decided that the best ze can do to keep Jack alive whilst still demonstrating to zis political foes and other slaves that the buck is being properly punished is to dispatch him to the arena. It's the least bad of bad choices. Even though few yeng survive for long in that place, Boklung hopes to eventually be able to buy Jack back, or else enable his escape from the Gantri. At least selling Jack as a gladiator is undeniably an appropriate punishment.

Boklung begins a stridently delivered speech. Jack ignores zim to talk quietly but firmly to his fellow prisoners. "Hey, Anton, Athalie, listen. Let me do the talking."

He puts his arms around his companions, and the three of them stand together, staring up at Boklung. Jack gets the impression that they are all in for a very long speech. Boklung is known by all and sundry to love zis own voice.

After listening for a moment to the initial indictment, Jack whispers again: "Athalie, your owner sold you to the hunt, do you know why?"

"I was imported from the Earth with my sister, and then sold to a yeng breeder in Krassus. A dozen of us were imports, the rest were born here. My sister and I were later rejected from the breeding house. I never became pregnant, and Hannah never went to term. We were shipped out as quarry for the hunt."

"What skills do you have? Any training here or from the Earth?"

"None. Those of us marked for the hunt were only taught how to run."

"Okay; keep quiet about all that ... Try for a decent job. If they believe you were bred purely as hunt fodder, you'll be sent back. If they don't assign you to the hunt, they might send you off for fattening, or worse. Do you like animals?"

Athalie nods.

"Pigs?"

She shrugs.

"Well, you do now! You're a pig handler. There's a herd in The Gardens. If you can get yourself assigned to the farm, talk to a woman called Kayla; say I asked her to teach you in a hurry. You worked in a pig unit in Krassus, but became surplus to requirements and so were sold to the local hunt. Whatever happens, say you're skilled."

"I will," Athalie says, but she doesn't look confident.

Jack turns to the boy. "Anton, are you listening? Just tell the truth about where you came from, but add that you've done farm work."

Anton nods.

Having finished addressing the crowd, Boklung moves to stand in front of the corralled prisoners. "Stand apart and stand straight!" ze shouts. "Yeng Jack, you caused me a lot of embarrassment by running. Protocols suggest that I have you put to death in front of your kind, but I won't let you go so easily. You have proved your cunning, and your ability to survive. Now you must prove yourself in combat. You are fortunate that I'm not vindictive. Many would have you tortured. I still have to face the inquisition of the Council because of you; however, the longer you survive, the more of my money that I can get back. As an incentive to you to live, I may yet have a future plan for you."

"If I may speak, Zir," Jack says boldly. "I was wrong to run, especially after the trust you showed in me. Well treated slaves should never run. As your rightful property, I accept whatever punishment you think is fit. I regret the annoyance and problems I've caused. Though I have no right to be heard, I beg that you don't punish these other two. The boy, Anton, is a hard working coalminer and has done farm labouring. I took him prisoner and forced him into helping me. I enslaved him. And this girl, Athalie, is an expert with pigs. She was raised in Krassus to work with those animals."

Boklung looks the other two prisoners over. "I'm a soft touch, Jack. If I wasn't so, you may have never been given a chance to escape. And since I take some pride in being magnanimous, they will be assigned to work here for now. In return, you will never surrender to another's sword. I am putting a heavy wager on you. I expect to get back some of what I've already lost in government fines. But first, as is the minimum demanded by law, you will be flogged to make an example of you in front of all my yeng ... Tie him to the whipping post."

A guard holding a chip scanner steps forward from behind the prisoners. "Zir, it is my duty to report on the yeng data. I can't read any of the prisoners' tags properly. The buck yeng doesn't even seem to contain one, so I can't confirm that he is the slave we take him to be. And the female's is working but I can't read it. It hasn't got a Cirithian code. The young one's tag only gives me industrial data; it is a model that is only used in rural mines."

"Don't worry, soldier, do you think I don't know my breeding yeng?"

"Of course, Zir," the soldier says and steps back.

Boklung turns to Jack. "But tell me, yeng, how do you creatures get rid of your tags?"

"I cut it out of my gut," Jack lied. "I knew where it was; I remembered it being fired into me." *And it's still there, spreading toxins into my blood, I shouldn't wonder.* Actually, he risked death by electrocution, frying it by shorting the Garden's generators before he left, but he wasn't going to tell a spider that yeng have learnt to do that.

Boklung's eyestalks draw closer together. "How am I meant to believe that you simply cut it out?"

"Ask your soldier."

"The scanner finds no trace of any sort, Zir," the soldier says.

"Enough." Boklung waves a limb. "I guessed as much already. To the flogging post with him! And you, soldier, send word to the yeng registrars that yeng Jack only escaped because his chip was inserted too shallowly."

Jack prepares himself mentally while two spiders tie him to the flogging post.

He plans to distract himself from the pain by focussing on how stupid he's been to end up back in the city. If that fails, he'll focus on Athalie.

I could suffer almost any pain if she's my prize for stoicism.

People circle past him in silence, except for their very quiet whispers of encouragement. If Jack weakens and begs for mercy, he'll lose what influence he gained as the heroic buck that defied the system for so long. He decides to pretend contempt and hopes to be able to stop himself screaming so he can gain even more support. That may be important one day.

The vague and distant promise of being bought back by Boklung gives him a little hope. But is it just some crude and false promise to encourage him to fight, to make Boklung money, or is there really a chance of being saved?

I wonder if humans are really being sent into space. Gads, I hope Finch is onto something. How would a flight like that work? What role would slaves have?

Even the vaguest hope gives Jack more reason to survive, but he wonders why Boklung would even raise the possibility of his return. By the time the trustee comes with the whip, Jack feels as if he's been tied to the post for hours.

Shit ... Here comes trouble. It's that bloody spider-licking trustee, Isaac Harper. That pervert won't spare the lash. I hope I faint quickly.

Time stands still ...

Jack hears the air splitting ...

Ffffwack ...

"Hey, you piece of shit, Isaac, can't you even crack a whip?"

FfffWACK ...

***

Meanwhile, not more than a few kilometres away, as one brave yeng succumbs to the oblivion of unconsciousness, another stirs.

Jesus slowly becomes aware that he's alive and fights his way back from the sleep of the dead. He hears the roar of engines. Memory gradually returns, and after a while, he recalls the arena and the aftermath of the fight. Then suddenly, two things happen in unison, a vicious headache stabs through his forehead and he comprehends that he might be recovering too late to save himself. Already he imagines he can smell the putrid smoke of the city's incinerators. Jesus tries to move his limbs but fails. The toxin of the wertutututua hasn't yet completely decayed.

Blind terror grabs at his already over-challenged mind. Jesus is close to screaming, until his tongue brushes the slither of pottery still in the pocket of his cheek. Reminded that he has the means to escape the suffocating heat of the body bag, he struggles to force movement into his frozen limbs. He feels the hover-truck stop. A cold sweat grips him, and he imagines just how bad it will feel to be burnt alive. Then, even as despair nearly wins, his arm muscles twitch and the faintest glimmer of hope returns.

The truck's body begins to lift. Jesus feels himself sliding, then tumbling down a steep slope. He realises that the whole load has been tipped into the furnace hopper. Luckily for Jesus, the hopper isn't quite empty this morning, which will give him a few minutes to save himself—if he can direct his muscles; if he isn't killed, or worse, left crushed but alive on the chute; if he can cut his way out and find some grip to stop his inevitable

slide into the flames, then just possibly he has a chance.

He takes the pottery in his still-stiff fingers and slashes at the fibres of the body-bag ...

190

20

KILL OR BE KILLED

Jack wakes to agony. He has inadvertently turned in his troubled sleep onto a lash-torn shoulder. He tries to blink away the pitch dark, but fails. Real dark is so rare in his life that for one terrifying moment he fears he is blind, until with much relief, he sees a glimmer of light high above his head. Then, disorientated, he wonders if he may for some reason be deep in his familiar caves.

Jack stretches out his hands; one touches a rough wall and the other takes in the cold concrete of a floor too smooth to be in any cave. His shuffling feet confirm that he's been sleeping on a cold, flat slab. Slowly, he realises that the grey blur of light is the high window of a cell in which he's incarcerated. Agitated thoughts beg to work beyond the physical agony that at first dominated all else. He feels as though he's been flailed until every nerve is fully exposed and constantly firing.

Bugger ... Is there any water in this hellhole? That bastard, Harper, obviously overfed his sadism, as I can't remember anything after the first couple of lashes. I should be grateful for that. At least the crowd didn't have to hear my screams. I'd hate them to think me weak. But Harper and his collaborating band of deviants will be totally pissed off that I lost consciousness so quickly.

Jack tries to sit but the movement opens his wounds. He groans and lies on his front with his head on his hands.

191

Bang!

Geez, the light.

"Wake up, vermin, you are off to work in entertainment. You sorry specimen, I can't see you living long. But first, this yeng has been sent to clean your wounds. I guess the Gantri doesn't want over-damaged goods."

The door slams shut, but the light stays on. Jack can't believe who he sees. "Athalie! Am I pleased to see you." He moves his arms beneath him, intending to push onto them in another attempt to sit. "Aagh ..."

Concern quickly replaces Athalie's smile. "Stay still, let me see to you." She lays a basket beside him and withdraws a cloth and a bottle of what Jack assumes to be disinfectant.

Jack relaxes and waits for her touch. When it comes, though gentle, it still stings. "Aagh ..." He smiles up at her. "I'm getting better already. I feel as though an angel has come to ease my pain."

"Oh, I'm no angel, and believe you me, I wouldn't want to be. I couldn't believe it when Phelia told me to visit you. She could have sent anyone ... Actually, I think Boss Spider was behind it. Phelia said I was a living message from Boklung, an encouragement for you to stay alive. I'm sure some decent food would have been more encouragement, but still, here I am."

"This is beyond any dream. Except, I'd feel even better if it'd been your choice to come ..."

Athalie stops dabbing at his wounds and gazes into his eyes. "Jack, I'm so pleased to be here! I didn't think for a minute that I'd ever be lucky enough to see you again." She resumes her administrations.

"You make it sound as though you wanted to come as much as I wanted to see you."

She smiles but keeps her eyes on her work. "Probably not; probably much more! Remember, I've been watching you for quite some time."

"I feel as though I've known you forever."

"Ssssh! No more daft talk. We have no time for that. And I'm sure I'm hardly the first to hear your smooth words." Athalie leans down and kisses Jack's neck. "Thanks for looking out for me. Kayla asked me to give you a kiss from her. The rest are all mine …"

***

Later, two spiders march Jack through the streets from the Zanin Barracks to the Gantri. Jack's aware that many slaves and other herded creatures have walked this way, never to return. He's glad it isn't far, because his legs have never felt weaker.

When did I last eat? I really don't remember.

They pass slaves going about their daily business, and nearly every one of them finds a gesture, a flick of the hand, even a risky smile for him.

Athalie had insisted on giving him a token, a pendant. He's never received a more treasured gift in all his life, and though he'd never forget Athalie anyway, the token, some sort of amber he thinks, makes him feel even closer to her. He doesn't know how he'll keep it safe in the arena, but he's determined to try. He hopes it stays well hidden under the tattered vest she gave him.

Jack's heard that the gladiators are mostly kept in cages under the floor of the arena. He assumes the varied species must be separated into different pens, so he has some hope of having the company of other humans, even though they may sometimes be called upon to fight one another. Jack's been alone too long, as recent events have reminded him. Most humans need company, and he's no different.

Athalie, what beauty, I can't believe that I found her so very late. She makes me feel I'm almost walking on air, even though I trudge towards my death.

The towering walls of the Gantri crush Jack's spirit. He can think of nothing uglier than the brutal concrete of this monstrosity—the ugliest building in an ugly city. He misses not just his freedom, but the natural beauty of the wilds.

It isn't fair to say that the spiders are devoid of artistic feelings, but they certainly are when it comes to architecture. I guess that apart from the brute cost of artistic design, simplicity is needed for structures that slaves can easily be whipped into producing. The poor gloot, squashed alive into forms and then desiccated.

Jack recalls the very plump guinea pig his sister had on Earth—in ways similar looking to a gloot. The poor silica-based creatures are kept alive for as long into the process as possible, so as to make good quality bricks. If they die quickly, they dry out very fast, which makes the subsequent brick brittle and flaky. Jack imagines them still screaming in agony as he passes the bleak architectural monstrosities.

Luckily, painful death doesn't leave a permanent marker, though some say they can sense places that have witnessed too many cruel endings. Imagine this place, or the Earth for that matter, if the screams of the departed never faded, but just built on each other, generation after generation.

"Faster, yeng," one of his spider overseers says. "You probably won't die any later because of the few minutes you spend in dawdling."

A whip cracks close to Jack's ear, causing it to sing. Temporarily deafened, he fails to hear the next hissed command, but it isn't hard to guess its meaning. He speeds up. Bystanders give him sympathetic stares and part as water did before Moses. No one wants to risk drawing the attention of the Aranian soldier. Fear alone would be enough to peel away any crowd even if the spider's whip wasn't so randomly flicked. But then, against the natural flow of the crowd, one women steps across the road so close to Jack that it seems they might even collide. She pushes a biscuit into his hand and immediately glides on into the melee on the other side of the road, disappearing before the spider has even had time to hiss a threat.

Jack hasn't realised how hungry he is until he holds that biscuit, hidden between his tightly tied wrists. The fact that someone has just risked so much to give him a little food can't help but buoy him up. At the same time, this human kindness makes him feel slightly uncomfortable. What a ridiculous risk to take to just possibly give a doomed man a little sustenance.

Some images from an old film Jack saw as a child flash through his mind. He remembers a procession through the streets of ancient Rome, of slaves on their way to be fed to lions. How similar, apart from the complete absence of spiders, the scene was to his present surroundings. Pictures of slaves heading towards an equally huge, though far more decoratively designed, arena fills his mind. Then, to keep his mind off his impending doom, he ruminates on the differences and similarities between the two races.

The Romans were always on the hunt for exotic creatures to entertain them, and the spiders are no different. Ungoliantis is a strange place, yet in many ways similar to Earth. The spiders are both completely different and also so like humans. They can travel across vast tracts of space, but have economies still dependent on hard physical work. Though capable of great art and science, they entertain themselves with blood sports. They have hugely longer lives than man, yet still complain that life is too short. They, like humans, believe they're God's chosen. As with men, their own kind are sometimes enemies. They even mourn their dead and build shrines to their ancestors whilst at the same time denying the needs of the living.

They favour the spear, though they have the most advanced of weapons; they have communicators that are just as clever as any once-common device on Earth and yet they do nearly everything 'by word of mouth'. They can produce incredible spacecraft, yet use land-based transport systems sparingly. They use any number of slaves rather than simple machines. Jack recognises that spider and man are never going to see any environment through similar eyes, but some things seem to make very little sense.

Perhaps simple ergonomics, the way a creature physically interacts with the world, can explain a lot of this. After all, the physical form of spiders and humans is as different as that between a spaceship and an agricultural tractor.

Ungol art and entertainment nearly all revolves around the drama of the arena and the hunting of wild creatures. They do play intellectual 'games', especially chess, which they've embraced with something amounting to an obsession. Strangely, the spiders don't seem to have found much in human culture that they find quite as interesting as the sixty-four squares of the chessboard. The more frivolous games played by humans, especially children, are absent from Aranian culture.

Aranian are fond of athletic 'sport', though that's more to do with military training than with recreational interest. They like sophisticated foods and the mental escape of intoxication, but have no interest in song or dance.

Different, yes, but when all's said and done they're just flesh and blood beings that love and hate, live and die, eat and drink. If they just had two sexes and a lot less limbs they'd seem much less strange.

Spiders are not immune to the bug of war, but it seems that their conflicts are far less about slaughter and far more about scoring points. They fight wars more like how gentlemen once duelled, rather than as bitter struggles that end with pillage, rape and a loss of civilisation. Engagements are limited, controlled and contained. Aranian wars are restricted to combatants and are structured more as contests of strength than fights to the death. They're like gladiatorial contests where to kill is less honourable than to cause an opponent to yield. More like Chess, in fact, where the best victories are achieved taking a minimum of pieces and with flamboyant speed. Cirithia is at war at this very time, but no one would easily know it. Their unwritten rules on the 'sport' of war even hold to varying degrees when they fight other species.

While Jack continues to trudge through the streets, he wonders if having an equally advanced species on a neighbouring planet has strengthened both their regard for their own and their respect for some other creatures. Is it possible that another equal sentience could have changed human evolution if one had appeared earlier in history?

And yet, contrary to all their apparently superior standards of behaviour, spiders are only too happy to see different species fighting to the death, as the existence of the arenas proves.

Man is worse; only we can enjoy the slaughter of our own quite so much. That's what any alien species would note about humans first. For thousands of years, until the spiders landed, man was mankind's only truly intelligent enemy.

Jack is hardly a true believer in any religious heritage, yet he sees some hope, not for him the individual, but for the universal future, in the fact that the spiders' religion is similar to those of humans. The holy book of Eruvatar has much in common with many sacred texts from the Earth, and Jack's pretty sure that spiders and man worship the same God. It helps him to believe that the Almighty has compatible plans for both species, and that the success of one doesn't depend on the annihilation of the other. He doesn't think humans could live in the same universe if their God wasn't one and the same.

Haha—fine thoughts!

To be honest though, he doesn't think belief in God, or the possibility or not of an afterlife, has much to do with how determined humans are to survive. He chooses to live in order to spite the eight-legged monsters, to see Athalie again, to be free, not because he fears that God may require he doesn't waste the gift of life. While he breathes he prefers to trust in life lived, not in what may follow death.

Like most of us, I'm probably driven by cowardice rather than bravery. The Romans once would've said dying well is the truest courage. I've no interest in such grand gestures, though.

Jack and his accompanying soldiers arrive under the deep shadow of the Gantri's hellish doors. In his mind, Jack hears the cries of a thousand pained creatures and one or two evil bellows that are just too appalling to be of any sentient world. He knows that the dungeons hold powerful 'dragons' from diverse worlds; hundreds of different creatures that he'll have to slaughter regularly if he's to stay alive. The only religion that matters here is the worship of the sharpest, strongest, best balanced blade.

Holy shit, my legs are shaking so much I'm scared I might collapse. Oach! There's no need to prod me that hard. I'm moving fast enough.

Jack is yanked to a sudden stop in front of a particularly foul-smelling Aranian soldier.

"Haashhh! More meat! Hand over his papers, comrade."

"He is an ex-breeding buck named Jack Baker of Spakron Gardens. He spent almost a cycle in the wild; this is a dangerous creature," Jack's companion says while the Gantri soldier reviews the papers.

"It had better be dangerous if it intends to live. Yes, these papers are in order. You may leave him, comrade."

By the time Jack's fear subsides enough that he can thaw his frozen mind, he is being herded away into the bowels of the Gantri. A myriad of creatures hoot and holler from their cages as Jack passes by. The vast majority are humans, but there's no shortage of what are to Jack still strange, even unknown, exotic creatures.

He passes cages of giant cat-like zyfose from the planet Asgormia, native biped yargord with their huge elephantine trunks, and wertutututua, the triffid-like creatures with venom that kills Aranian and human alike. The smaller creatures are not necessarily less dangerous. Amongst them are hazzarmander with scaled armour like armadillos, and screebur, which look like solidly built hyenas. Both these last two are dangerous when in packs. He passes giant birds, turvult, looking not unlike pterodactyls, with wings clipped so as to keep them confined to the arena, and many crates of small creatures that are bred to provide food for the larger ones. These include drabbets and suvaran. Some larger herbivorous, bred-for-food creatures, like the dodark, are used as sideshows in the 'entertainments'.

Overwhelmed by this mesmerizing menagerie, Jack feels he needs a knife to cut through the fetid stink and almost solid wall of noise. He finds himself being pushed deep into the middle of the massively arched basement of the Gantri, until he is suddenly slammed up against the side of a cage full of his own kind. One glance is enough to let Jack know that this enclosure is unlikely to provide an even half-tolerable confinement.

Old fashioned keys unlock the cage, and one of the spider soldiers shoves Jack inside. The metal clangs behind him, leaving him staring into the eyes of a huge monster of a man. The nature of the challenge is clear, bow to the wishes of this self-appointed leader or fight. Some battles are worth fighting, but this isn't one of them. Not for now, at least. The spiders disappear back the way they came, leaving Jack standing before a mass of haunted eyes, all staring at him.

This gorilla's breath stinks. Hell, I could gag. "I'm Jack, pleased to meet you. I guess you're the boss in this cage."

The creature nods. "Bruno. And don't think to cross me. You take old Tucker's space, close to the crapping hole."

"He's dead then."

"That's right and not from entertaining. I shut him down for not showing me respect."

"I get the point. Listening to you is obviously in my best interest."

"You no touch unless I give permission! All the arse is mine. You're mine."

Great! Not only is this reject in control, he's also a bleeding bi-sexual rapist. Well, if you touch me, you bugger, that'll mean trouble. No wonder the fifty or so souls in here look so totally subdued. They're hardly the best material to work into a spirited unit.

Jack sits quietly in his spot for a while, then tries to whisper to the man next to him.

"Quiet," the beast shouts.

The man turns away.

Bloody wonderful, not even a chance of a decent conversation!

Jack leans back against the wall and manages to have a long doze. He awakes to murmurs and movement when a sort of gruel is slid under the bars into the cage by one of the oddest creatures he's ever seen. This 'trustee' is a three metre tall, bright-blue creature with a covering of feather-like scales. It walks on two of three limbs, dragging the third leg of what could be interpreted as a tripod, astern. When not moving, the creature rests on this tale-end limb, seemingly balancing without any difficulty.

That's weird enough, but its arms are even more bizarre. None of the three upper body limbs looks alike, or even seems to be attached to the same section of the body. Each arm appears to have four or five joints, which aren't always located in the same place. They seem to free-float along the creature's arms. Jack finds himself staring until it fixes its three large eyes on him. When Jack looks away, the blue 'alien' saunters off towards a gaggle of overseers talking in front of what must be a large well.

I thought I'd seen all the strange creatures there are to see, but clearly not. "What's the name of our blue friend?" Jack asks no one in particular.

An awkward silence stretches out before anyone replies.

"He's a Choochin, mister, with a venomous bite," says a young girl from the far side of the cage.

Before Jack could reply, the ogre who considers himself the boss of the cage takes a stride towards the child with his fist raised.

Jack stands. "If you strike the kid, you'll answer to me. I asked the question, so I take responsibility for whoever's brave enough to answer."

Bruno swings at the girl, who somehow manages to duck out of the way. Then he turns and walks towards Jack, without a care as to whom he tramples. Jack is ready for him, and aware enough to know that if it comes to a wrestling match he'll stand no chance of prevailing.

The bulk rolls into a charge. Jack side-steps and uses the man's momentum to propel him into the bars of the cage. Jack grabs the man's straggly mane of hair at the last minute and pulls back so that the flat of his face takes the full force, making the impact more devastating. Bruno slides heavily to the ground, while trying to turn. This exposes his windpipe, which collapses under Jack's rapidly delivered fist. The cage has a new boss.

The activity brings down a posse of angry overseers.

"Which of you yeng is responsible for killing this champion?" the duty spider asks.

"Me, but he isn't actually dead yet."

The spider grabs the felled man's head and rips it straight through the bars, crushing his skull as though a watermelon. "You think not, yeng! You will fight in his place tomorrow, since you obviously know a bit about combat. And you had better give a good account of yourself. What is your name?"

Jack stands tall. "Jack Baker, formerly the property of Cingwin Boklung."

"Guards, note well that this Jack fights tomorrow in place of Bruno."

"He's not had his basic training for the arena," one of the human trustees points out.

"Well that didn't seem to help Bruno, did it. Haaaagh."

Shit! That was dumb, but I'd do it again. I have to face the arena some time, so what's lost but a short period of relative safety in this stinking dungeon. Let tomorrow come. The sooner the better, because a long wait will mean I haven't slept.

Jack turns to his fellow inmates. *Time to develop some rapport with this lot.* "I've rid this cage of a tyrant, and I'll try to be less of one. If any of you have any tips that might help me stay alive up there, please help me now. Then try to keep as quiet as this existence will allow, so I can sleep. Those of you assigned to lie close to the latrine, move with me to take up Bruno's overly large space."

An older looking man from the back corner of the cage speaks up. "I thank you, Jack Baker, for protecting the child. As to helping you, I wish we could. None known to us except that bastard Bruno have survived long. Only the zyfose and yargord from these near cages regularly return. I'm sure we will all pray for you, Jack."

"Thank you. I'll need all the help the Almighty can give. If I survive I might even believe in Him more. Can we spare a little water so someone can bathe the welts on my back? I don't want infection getting in."

"The death of Bruno will free up half our daily ration," a man replies from beside Jack. "We have more than enough for your back, and that bastard's tent of a shirt will make good bandages."

"Thanks. Have any of you been up there and come back even once?"

"I have. My tactic hasn't been honourable though. I survived two combats by hiding behind the brave."

"No shame in that. Intelligence is as honourable a weapon as brawn. Shame comes from not helping others when you can. Since you've the intelligence to let the warriors do the fighting, you'll teach them how to move as ghosts. We need co-operation, pool our skills for the survival of all. We need the one who can hide and stab from the shadows, the one that can run, exhausting the enemy, the one that can think fast enough to spring a trap and the one that can wield the sword. What's your name?"

"Amos."

"Well, Amos. First, teach the child that dared speak your art of invisibility, then perhaps she can teach you a lesson or two about how to speak out boldly when others' voices fail." Jack turns to the assembled yeng and addresses them all. "If I win, then call me Spartacus, and shout my name at the spiders. If I fail, then another of you must carry that name. Let the spiders see that slaves can be masters. Let them come to respect the name of the most powerful slave from our history, Spartacus of Thrace, even if a thousand of us need to take turns carrying that name. Now, who else thinks they're fighting tomorrow?"

The inmates look around at one another but no one speaks.

"That's a pity. But from now on we all help each other, at least until the moment one of us is pitched against another, and even then if you're brave enough."

***

Jack stands between two gates, the one behind him barred, preventing his escape back into the comparative safety of the Gantri's bowels. From beyond the other door comes a deafening wall of noise, the rhythmic stamping of feet backed by the hissing voices of thousands. The Aranian certainly enjoy their bloodthirsty entertainment.

Jack has already been invited to select his weapons, though he has no idea what he's to face, or what weapons any possible companions may be carrying. A javelin had tempted him, to kill at a distance, but using one he'd never tested the balance of seemed over-risky. In the end he'd taken a short heavy sword and a shield. The spiders only allowed each gladiator two items.

"Enter the arena before I spear you, yeng," says a hissing voice from above him.

Knees trembling, Jack pushes on the door and steps into the glaring sunlight. He shields his eyes with his hand and the hilt of the sword. Then, realising his vulnerability, he starts to move around the wall of the arena, hoping to avoid offering himself as a target before his eyes have adjusted enough to let him get a measure of his enemy. Slowly, the ground before him comes into focus. Way out in the middle of the arena is a small group of humans of such small stature that they look like children. Their rapid and rather irregular movements only seem to confirm that conjecture. Soon, Jack is left in no doubt that he has to be a leader, as his fellow combatants' high-pitched, frightened wailing finally confirms their young age.

I've been sent out here to fight with children! Well, in God's name I pray that even spiders wouldn't stoop so low as to try and make me fight them.

Is this terrible circumstance designed to draw Jack into sacrificing himself through trying to protect the children? Or is it just for amusement without any reasoned rationale? Whatever, he has no choice but to do his best to defend them. He couldn't live with himself if he didn't try. They may be young, but that doesn't alter the fact that they need to fight. A flock of lambs and one old ram, to fight a pack of what? Wolves! Obviously, some mentally sick Aranians are behind the decision to make sport out of the death of kids.

Jack notices two packs of screebur waiting in pens along the walls. *The key will be killing the pack leaders, or somehow setting the packs at each other's throats. The children all have long spears and shields. Their best tactic is obvious.*

"Do we want to live?" Jack asks when he joins the children.

No one replies.

"Speak up, I can't hear you, do you speak English?"

A few weak replies add to the background din.

"Yes."

"I don't want to die."

"I'm frightened."

"Gather around me in a circle looking out," Jack says in a commanding voice, "so that each of you can just touch me with an arm out behind you. Quickly! Those of you that understand, show those that don't. The tallest of you, that's you and you, and you two, put shorter friends on either side. Move. That's it.

"Now push the base of your spears into the floor just behind you. Good; now hold the points up and squat behind your shields. Brace your shields with one knee and place your other knee at right angles to the ground. You girl, that's good, you others copy her. Get as much of your body behind the shields as you can.

"Now stay as quiet as mice until I tell you to scream, and however frightened you are, don't move from your spot. If the creatures run onto your spears, thrust out and sharply back to release the animal, then plant the butt in the floor again. Be brave! We'll win. Are we ready? Yes, we are. All together now: Are we ready? ... Yes, we are. All of you, are we ready?"

"YES WE ARE."

"LOUDER! Are we ready?"

"YES WE ARE."

"Good. Don't try to spear them, just keep formation, and let me slice anything that climbs up our shields. Here comes the first pack. See, we have them worried. They're used to yeng splitting and running. You'll live if you do as I say. Soon the starving ones will start to feed on those we slaughter. When that happens we still stay in formation. Not one of you moves, even if we're still here when low-light comes."

Is this the best we can do? I think so. Is it enough? "Hold still, that screebur edging closer is going to charge. Don't move, just scream as it runs at us ..."

The children scream. Jack reaches over the defences and cleaves the beast's head in two.

That's one skull split. "When they come again, it'll be a whole pack. The same applies. Block your shields, hold your spears tight. Here they come ..."

Jack slices two before the pack pulls back. One shield has to be picked up again, the young boy who lost it being helped by the older boy next to him. Now the screebur are wary, and as Jack predicted, their interest starts to centre on the dead and wounded members of their own packs.

"The spiders are hissing already. They're going to hate this. We're spoiling their sport. But none of you moves even if we have to stay like this for a huis. Starting with you and you, take turns to sit on the floor and stretch your legs, but the instant the beasts look like they might charge, you squat and brace your shields. When I say change, the person to your right rests. When we move it'll be in this formation, and we only have to do that if they set different animals on us. Each of us is weak, but together we are invincible. Those that understand, do what you can to explain to those that can't."

Many creatures were sent into the arena that day, including other humans, but apart from Jack himself, the band never moved. They let other fighting groups die around them, never breaking formation until the suns were low. When the entertainment ended, they retreated together towards a gate, accompanied by a slow stomp of frustrated spider feet. Other days would never turn out quite as well as this, but Jack now had the respect of every yeng that heard the story of his invincible army of children. Within a short time, every creature in Cirithia had heard the name Spartacus.

In the next three Earth-years, Jack never felt stronger than he did immediately after he saved those dozen children from that high-light's slaughter. Those years were just the length of one season on Ungoliantis, just the length of one winter. By the time the sunlight grew stronger, the first Arcraft was already nearing its launch date.

21

ATHALIE'S MISSION

Though Athalie and Jack have had very little time together, and almost no opportunity for a private word, a spark of mutual interest has become a flame. As is so often the way, infatuation needs little logic or persuasion, and often positively benefits from a lack of time for considered formation. Athalie, when she isn't remembering the terrible death of her sister, or worrying about surviving the next five minutes, has found herself thinking ever more about Jack. Certainly the mutual interest has more to do with personal need and powerful biology than with any real depth of understanding. That's the nature of infatuation, whether or not it runs even to the foothills of true romance. Athalie takes comfort from Jack's survival in the harsh environment of the Gantri. His perceived strengths work as a much needed counterbalance to her felt vulnerabilities. Even less logically, she can't help but hold to the idea that his thoughts have found as much time for her.

Word regularly gets back to The Gardens that Spartacus still lives, raising the spirits of all. Now all seem to remember him, and either something he said, or some deed he did. The fact that many of these memories are obviously fictitious doesn't seem to matter one iota. Legends tend to generate history with few anchors in real past events, but history never the less.

Athalie's daydreams drag her mind through a sea of fear and pain back to her all too brief childhood, to her bedroom in a suburb of the then still-intact city of Ely. In its flat, open and then-safe lands, one could feel that nothing more dangerous had ever walked on eight-legs than a Daddy Long-Legs spider perched in the corner of a living room.

She remembers the diary she kept under her bed, and a boy, her teen crush that she wrote about so much, but never had the nerve to talk to. That life seems so far away now, like a film on decaying celluloid stock. Desperate to give her life more meaning, she resolves to see if there's some way of getting close to the arena without becoming its fodder. For now, she's grateful to be alive and to have work with pigs. In terms of life in Cirithia she has a secure existence; one that Jack effectively secured.

We listen in on Athalie's thoughts while she mucks out the pig pen.

These creatures are a load of work but I mustn't complain. If I wasn't sent to the hunt it would likely have been to the arena, and then I might be dinner for these very animals.

She stops shovelling. Her eyes light up with an idea.

Kayla collects the pig food from the Gantri. Could I persuade her to send me instead? I'm sure she'll let me, especially if I do a little more to help her out while her back's playing up. I could be a little bit braver about shifting the boars. She needs to believe I'm strong enough to get any job with the pigs done and feel she hasn't got to be my nursemaid any longer. She has to see I'm no longer hysterical or sobbing my eyes out every time she asks me to slaughter my charges or grind human cadavers for the pig meal.

One Ungolian day later, Kayla, in need of a rest, has been persuaded to forgo her next trip to the arena. She'd seen a new hardness in Athalie's eyes, enabling her to trust that the girl would cope. After a stream of repeated warnings about how to conduct herself and which trustees to avoid, she allowed Athalie to push the handcart onto the public road and through the busy streets away from The Gardens. Athalie's mind is whirling with a mix of excited anticipation and fear.

I must be mad doing this. Jesus, these roads are scary, especially after I've been isolated in the piggery for so long. It seems a lifetime since I was in a street with my sister, both of us already sold as what ... as breeding machines being marched out of Krassus. Then Annah ripped apart by screebur and nearly me as well. Gads, I mustn't be thinking about that now. Pull yourself together, girl.

Kayla was right to be worried about letting me out, especially on a trip to the Gantri. Hell! It's bad enough pushing this heavy old cart without having all those eyes fixed on me. Look at them all, the slaves' stares seem even more dangerous than the spiders'. What's so bloody interesting about me? Perhaps I'm being paranoid. Surely the most they're wondering is where Kayla is. I'll just keep my eyes down and get on with it. I can hardly go the wrong way, can I? Who could miss that monstrous mountain of concrete, or is it 'glootcrete'?

Anyway, they're probably only giving me the eye because I'm staring at them. I am, aren't I? I've never seen so many slaves going about their daily business unsupervised. This city would fall apart if one day we humans just downed tools. No chance of that. Oh God, supposing I don't even recognise him. Ha, him me, more like! Why would he remember me from any of a thousand other women with a crush? I'm stark raving bonkers to be doing this. Just get the meat and hurry home.

Ugh! Athalie shivers. *It isn't just meat for Christ's sake. It's someone's father, someone's child. God help my soul. I pray it isn't Jack's bruised remains I have to wheel back to the pigs.*

Before long, Athalie stands at the workers' door to the Gantri and speaks to the guard. "I've come for feed for the Spakron Gardens piggery. Kayla has sent me."

"Hissss." The spider eyes her with obvious distaste. "What are you going to do for me if I let you in? You know how that yeng looks after me?"

"Kayla wishes you well. She sent me with a packet for you; some herbs for your aches and pains."

"Gooood! On the way in, you drop it in the waste bin by the door. Discreet like, drop it with this entry chit I give you. If you get caught, I'll gut you myself. Do we understand each other? Now move along, straight down the main isle when I open the door. Some advice, so that you will live long enough to bring me more herbs! Don't stop to dawdle, or else some yeng overseer will insist on handling you in more ways than you can imagine.

You think we be cruel. You haven't seen a thing until you've witnessed their deviant recreations. Now get out of my sight!"

"Yes, Zir."

Gads, just the creek of the door is enough to put the wind up me. This place makes the piggery smell like a rose garden, and brurr, the damp. How do people survive down here?

Athalie walks past cage after cage of not just humans, but hundreds of weird creatures, even more stunned by the scene than Jack was his first time. She wonders how much misery is contained in this huge dungeon.

What was the name of the trustee that looks out for Kayla? Um— Castus, I must remember to ask for him if I'm threatened. But how can I find Jack amongst so many? Searching all the faces in a single cage would take too long.

"Athalie ... Athalie, over here, behind you."

She swings around. "Jack." *He remembered me.* "Where are you?"

"Look left, stop. I'm in the middle of the cage. It's so good to see you ... Is Kayla okay?"

"Yes. I asked to be sent. I thought I might see you. Oh! I mean, you saved my life, I think. The piggery, you helped me ... I wanted to say ..."

"Stop! Quiet. I'm happy to see you. Now walk on, an overseer looked this way. When you come back, talk, but just keep walking. Go ... Whatever horror you see, don't flinch, don't draw attention to yourself."

He's alive. He remembers me. Calm! Focus on that, not on this horrible place.

As she approaches the sweating mound of flesh at the collection point, Athalie tries to focus on the remains of exotic species, rather than on the human corpses. A group of overseers moves in around her like a pack of circling wolves. The lighting is dim, but what the eyes can't see the nose makes up for.

After this I'll never complain about the smell of pigs again.

"Look boys, a fresh young whore," one of the overseers says. "Where're you from, girl?"

"Spakron Gardens ... Kayla sent me."

"Well, you're eye-candy compared to that old whore. Come, give us a kiss."

Kayla slaps a hand away. "Get off me. I'm here for work, not as your fancy. Oach, get your hands off, else I'll scream 'til spiders come."

"Oh! You will, will you?"

"Let her be, Christoph," another human overseer says. "That Spartacus is watching. He doesn't look too happy. In case I don't kill you, he will."

"Fuck you, and fuck that lucky bastard! He doesn't scare me."

"Don't piss me off. And just remember your bravery if the spiders send you to face him in the arena. Don't cross either of us, if you know what's good for you."

"You're dead, Castus," Christoph spits out between gritted teeth, but he does back up.

"Back to your work, all of you," Castus says, "and pig-girl, get loaded, and get out before these vermin grow bold. If you come back another day, shout for me. If I haven't been murdered in my sleep, I'll keep these scum off."

"Thank you, Castus."

"Any friend of Kayla's is a friend of mine."

Athalie sets about trying to lift the nearest detached animal leg into the cart.

"Here, girl, use the hook, like this, and the cleaver to cut bits you can't lift. I'll help you this time. You'll soon get the hang of it. Don't pull your back like Kayla did. An injury like that could be the end of you."

"Argh! It's heavy."

"And you're not built as sturdily as Kayla. Take your time, breathe deep ... See you tomorrow, perhaps."

This place is every bit as terrible as Kayla told me it was. I'll never push the cart. Argh, use your effing brain, pull it, that's better ... Once I get it rolling faster ... That bloody head-case is staring at me. Just keep moving ...

Soon, she passes Jack's cage again. This time he's pressing up tight to the bars. "Castus just saved my bacon, back there."

"So I saw. Give my best to Kayla; now keep moving. Don't look back."

She does as he says, her thoughts jubilant, though she pulls a gruesome load through a hellish dungeon. *I've seen him, and he's just as I remembered. Despite this place I feel quite light-headed. Oh, Jack, stay safe. Somehow, while you're alive, I feel there's hope for us all.*

She wonders what happened to the boy, Anton, after Boklung sent him to the fields. Perhaps seeing if he's safe should be her next mission. And what about Pugwash? What harm could there be in asking around?

22

YENG SOLD TO THE CHEETAN

Parallel to all the activity around the Arcraft, Boklung and Huigark Hosk's plans for yeng breeding units on Trogaffin proceed apace. The first shipment of equipment has already been dispatched. The High Council of Ungoliantis has agreed to a limited exploratory trade agreement between the city of Cirithia and the city Troskiatin on Trogaffin. Boklung is starting to plan the transport of breeding yeng. Most of the exports will be from amongst a shipment of newly imported yeng, which have been confined in the new science research facility of The Gardens. These new slaves are to be augmented with a few 'old-timers'. The experienced slaves are to be, theoretically at least, on loan. Boklung has argued for their inclusion on the grounds of helping the new arrivals learn to cope with the overwhelming stress; to help them realise that even the nightmare that is now their life can become tolerable.

Boklung has a more private reason for the inclusion of experienced slaves. Ze has charged the chosen few to cooperate in maintaining secret contacts with Cirithia. Boklung has picked out these old hands from amongst zis most trusted in order to find suitable 'spies', which puts further pressure on zis business. One of those trustees is to be none other than the current yeng

212

in charge of zis piggery, Kayla. A consequence of this will be Athalie's inevitable promotion.

Boklung personally delivers the news of Kayla's exportation, an indication of zis respect for her. Ze summons her up to zis private house and receives her in zis office, as ze does with all but very superior Aranian. Ze really wants business data, but as an aside, ze will be able to check that the slaves are being maintained in good condition.

"Kayla, I am lending you to a project on Trogaffin. Athalie and Storm will run the pig unit until I get you back. You are being relocated with a nucleus drove of pigs. As a trustee, and a particularly valuable one, I have made it clear to the Cheetan that you are only lent to their business, and that you are not to be treated like a common slave. You will have a special tagging chip under your skin, which will store and transmit additional data. I need to be privately kept up to date about exactly how the Cheetan treat their new slaves, so that we can intervene if necessary. This is our secret. With it goes my promise to do what I can to reclaim you as soon as is expedient and give you as much freedom as we are allowed to give yeng."

Kayla fights to keep her expression neutral while her heart races in fear.

"We have no intention of letting on to the Cheetan that their performance is being monitored. If you are suffering badly, I will be able to pick up the information from the chip, or at least Aranian agents on Trogaffin will. You are needed there in order to try and build hope into the lives of the yeng. If they lose the spirit to live, then they will become the ghostlike shells that any despondent creature can become. If that happens, then the Cheetan will lose interest in their welfare and the business will fail. I am sure you understand that if yeng don't make good livestock then your species won't get a chance to build a real foothold on Trogaffin. Slavery is better than being fattened as food, and the long-term prospects for life on that planet are actually far better than here. The planet is larger, and suffers far less from population pressures. While you exist as a species and have a foothold in diverse systems, any future is still possible."

Kayla nods and manages to find her voice. "I'll cooperate with whatever plan you see necessary, Boss. I would be lying if I didn't tell you that the idea of being dispatched to that planet frightens me, but I'll draw personal strength from the fact that I'll remain your property. Yes, the survival of my species comes first, and the further we spread, the greater our chances of dispossessing others."

"Hggghh. A bold response with an obvious but cleverly deniable stab at Aranian superiority. You are lucky to be the property of an Aranian with the ability to appreciate defiant wit. As I get older, I'm growing wiser. Perhaps I shouldn't say this to a yeng, but I will; I feel a new power in me, even possibly a superior presence acting through me. When I was young, I was like every other Aranian, believing in the absolute superiority of my race. I now truly believe that not just Cheetan but yeng as well are in many respects our equal. I can foresee a time when yeng are no longer our slaves, and certainly no longer fundamental to our diet.

"Anyway, however much my views change, for now we both have to accept the real world we live in. You will be departing on a transporter tomorrow. Pick thirty healthy sows and two boars to be freighted with you. Take the next couple of periods off, and enjoy our beautiful fresh air. It will be the last you get for some time. The atmosphere on Trogaffin is too thin for your species, except for very short periods of time, so you will be housed in sealed units. Can I trust you to keep your special chipping secret? In return I will do all I can to ensure your safe return to the better climes on Ungoliantis sooner rather than later. A medic will visit you to insert your new chip. And the Arcraft Project, I am sure you know about that. It is my promise to you that with the cooperation of trustees like you, I can ensure that yeng once again have better days, even if not in the Lush System. Do you understand me?"

"Yes, Zir. I have seen many times that we mean more to you than machines. You're proof to me that Aranians are creatures of the same God. You can be sure that I'll keep quiet.

Only a fool would fail to keep a secret that is so clearly in all our best interest. I have been your spy before, Zir."

"Yes, Kayla, I remember very well. To me it was not long ago at all, even though you were little more than a child."

Boklung is just about to leave when, remembering something else, ze turns. "Oh! I nearly forgot, you are to be inseminated before you go. We have you booked to be put to a stud during your next sleep cycle. Understand that I have thought this through. Your pregnancy will give me perfect grounds on which to demand your very early return, Kayla."

Even if Kayla had felt bold enough to respond to this more than significant news, Boklung was gone well before the enormity of the words set in. When they did, she didn't know if she regretted every collaborative word, or thanked Boklung for giving her an outside chance of having a child she so craves, despite a life condemned to slavery.

Just like Phelia, Kayla had never come to terms with the guilt she felt for wanting a child when her existence was so tenuous and hard. On another level though, she could see the animal in herself, could recognise the selfish drive of biology. Deep down, Kayla wanted a child more than anything else in the Lush System. If only the father could be Castus. If only. But how the heck could Boklung just drop that news in at the end of the conspiratorial chat they'd had? An answer to that question comes when she considers that laying eggs is less of a life-changing event than carrying a human foetus to term.

I'm not sure I understand zis logic; why pregnant now, when so late to be a mother? Perhaps there isn't any. Well, possibly ze tells the truth as ze sees it, believing it empowers zis chances of getting me back, but I doubt that's the reason. No, there's a more straight forward reason, something to do with zis wider collaborations with the Cheetans. Maybe ze is just running out of yeng as ze has so many projects running.

***

"Sinanna wept! I still feel quite faint," Kayla says when she returns to the piggery.

215

Athalie takes Kayla in her arms and hugs her tight. "Sit, sit down here." They drop down together against the piggery wall. "Don't worry so. You'll be all right."

"Me: a mother! Bringing new life into this servitude! And what about the bleeding pain. Holy-shit, it's worse than that, isn't it. Forced to bring a baby into a world where it isn't even safe to step outside, or possibly where I won't even find suitable foods. What's more, me, who has long tried to convince myself that bringing a child into this tough life is wrong."

"Don't fret so. You'll be a good mother when the time comes. As my mother used to say, 'nature comes naturally enough'."

Kayla buries her face in her hands. "Which 'hog' am I to be poked by?" she mutters. "Whoever it is, better treat me right." She looks up with moist eyes. "Will you let Castus know? Tell him not to worry about me, that I'll still be Boklung's property. The Cheetans won't harm me or my child so long as we're Boklung's special concern."

"Of course I will. Don't you worry about a thing."

Kayla manages a half smile. "Castus and I go way back, friends ever since we met on the slaver that grabbed us both from Earth. If you get the chance, give him a little of the same zoonherb you take for the spiders on the doors. And ... um ... to get more herb you need to be real friendly to Storvarn in the hot-house. I'm sure you can guess what our relationship has been. He may be a castrate, but he's also very much still a man. I'm sorry if that makes things difficult. I'll see him once more, and try and make it clear that he shouldn't expect the same of you."

"Don't worry; if life demands that you have to be impregnated and then exported to God knows where, then I'm sure I can find a way to handle Storvarn's needs."

"I'm to be tagged to give secret data. I found I had a natural ability for spying when Boklung used me years ago to inform on a family of spiders from the city of Krisk. Boklung looked after me then and I'm sure ze'll do the same now."

"Well, you must be stealthy, as I can't bear the thought of anything happening to you. Just make sure the data you get on the Cheetan is critical enough that our Boss insists on your return and while your child is still in you.”

Kayla nods but doesn't look too hopeful.

“On another topic,” Athalie says, “who do I talk to about getting some help tracking down an individual working on the outer farms? When Osterphelia brought us in, Jack had been captured along with a young boy, maybe ten-Earth-years old. He didn't even speak English; the two of them spoke in French. He may have a pet suvaran with him. If he does, that should make him easy enough to trace.”

“If they're here, finding them should be easy enough. I mean, a pet anything is hardly usual, and a suvaran, unique, I imagine. A drabbet, yes, but a suvaran? You need to talk to Rex. He's the housing manager of farm block D. He's an old chap that always wears an ancient old hat that he managed to keep his hands on all through capture, transportation and assignment to the farms. He knows more about the arable lands than anyone else. If the boy is anywhere on Spakron land, he'll know about it.”

“Great. Thanks.”

“Go before next sleep time, before curfew, while I'm still here to keep an eye on things. As soon as you get back, I'll go and see Storvarn. They won't come for me until the suns are low. Then I'll be put in a shed with whatever stud they choose to match me.”

“Are you sure you don't want me to stay with you? I mean, you have a lot to come to terms with.”

“No, that's all right, sweet-pea. But later, when I've entertained that buck, then I'll need your company.”

Later, as planned, Athalie finds her way to the farm settlement and into Rex's barrack. “Kayla suggested that I have a word with you, Rex,” she says. “I'm Athalie, recently assigned to the piggery under Kayla.”

“I know you. Brought in with Jack—Spartacus as they call him now. I was there when the boss made a spectacle of you all, especially Spartacus.”

"Yeah. I'm looking for the boy, Anton, who was with us. He might still have a pet suvaran with him. If they're safe, I'd like to let Jack know. I collect, umm, feed, from the arena, so I get a chance to see the gladiators."

"That's okay, luv, there's no need for reticence here. We know exactly how the pigs are fed. We all end up as fertilizer one way or another. Of course I know the boy, not many would risk life and limb for a suvaran. It would've made a dinner if that boy hadn't protected it. He wasn't able to keep the creature with him, but I rather think that Osterphelia has it safe, under the floor of her hut. Anton visits there whenever he can. I'll track him down and tell him you were asking after him."

"Thank you, Sir. Remind him that I'm the one that Osterphelia's party caught trailing them. Let him know that I'll get word to Jack that he's safe."

"Sure, I'll let him know."

Athalie digs into the pouch hanging off a belt at her waist and pulls out a small package. "Here, some zoongrass Kayla sent over, for your trouble."

"And Kayla, what of her?"

"She's being sent to Trogaffin. It seems they want to breed both our kind and pigs on that Godforsaken planet. She's being put to a stud before they send her, tonight. Actually, Boklung says that she's only on loan, so it's all very confusing."

"She'll be put with that muscle-bound idiot Ushan. I'll send word that he has to treat her just right if he wants to keep his nuts."

"Thank you. ... Um, can you tell me, Rex, since you seem to know so much, why is everyone so keen to call Jack, Spartacus? I never got around to asking him."

"Aye, there's a story! ... The name Spartacus is a signal to all men that Jack will fight, if necessary to the death, in order to win his freedom. Freedoms won by the sword of the ancient gladiator named Spartacus are both truth and legend rolled into one, and, for once, the truth is at least as big as the legend. He led an army of slaves against the mighty city of Rome, nearly bringing the Roman Empire to its knees. That was over 3000

Earth-years ago. I'll tell you more, there's talk that a giant spaceship is to be run by robots and humans, and you won't hear many rumours just now that don't somehow mention Boklung and Spartacus in the same breath."

"Yeah, I know about the Arcraft project. Are you suggesting Jack might become a part of it?"

"That's right, girl. Don't get too excited, though; a gladiator escaping that life is as rare as a chicken with teeth. But then, I'm sure Boklung can breed chickens with the finest of gnashers."

23

ATHALIE IN CHARGE

Athalie watches from the doors of the pig shed as Kayla guides her herd towards a transporter. She hangs well back, just in case a vindictive spider is looking for more slaves to add to the chain. Saying goodbye had been a sad affair, since Kayla is hardly going to a better place; not in this life anyway. To be in a sealed building on that harsh planet, under the whip of a species even more terrifying than the Aranian, sounds like a life in Hell itself.

Kayla has only ever seen a few Cheetan—those ten-legged dragons. What she remembers most is them smelling like flesh rotten with gangrene. The one she saw up close was the personal guest of Boklung. It actually stayed in Boklung's house.

I should've offered to take a load of pig slurry to fumigate the building when the Cheetan left. Aranian pong, but Cheetan, yuck! Those creatures make the spiders look positively beautiful.

Kayla glances back and gives a little wave before she enters the transporter after the pigs. Athalie tries to give a reassuring smile, but wonders how thin Kayla's chances really are of ever seeing this planet again.

She really seems to trust that spider. I'm not sure I ever could. Anyway, I have to brave it; I'm the boss of the Garden's pig unit now. It's up to me to make it work. I hope she hasn't forgotten to pass on any vital information.

Though she feels wretched admitting it, she realises that there's an upside to Kayla's misfortune. She'll be able to see Jack whenever she can find an excuse to collect more feed. But before she can visit the Gantri she has to attend Boklung's meeting for overseers and team leaders.

That'll be something new. I'm officially a member of The Gardens' cadre, a junior one to be sure, but one with those dubious privileges nevertheless. Little old me, has taken another step away from the status of quarry for the hunt's screebur. At this rate I'll be the Queen of Sheba before I'm through.

***

The slaves stand in three straight lines in front of Boklung and Borstave. Athalie finds herself in the back row standing between Grace and Osterphelia.

"So then, Athalie," Osterphelia whispers. "You've done well for yourself, but what of poor Kayla?"

"She's been sent to Trogaffin with a herd of pigs, supposedly short term."

"That's sad news. I'll pray for her."

"And Boss had her impregnated before she left."

"Hmm. Boklung seems to be trying to get every female ze owns pregnant … Have you heard about the Arcraft being built to transport humans to start a new colony on some distant planet?"

Athalie nods as Phelia goes on talking.

"Strange events in our strange world! Everyone's asking, why send us rather than go themselves? I suspect it's to establish a base so the Aranian have a settlement and a source of meat when they arrive. Whatever, it's a chance to escape this slavery. Expect to have a child to carry if you go."

Athalie's eyes suddenly widen. "Jesus, I feel quite faint; I just realised that I've missed my period. Um …"

Phelia smiles. "You've no reason to worry unless you've been with a buck."

"True. Anyway, I've heard the rumours about the spaceship."

221

"Apparently, Boklung has to find the crew zimself. So it could be us."

Athalie's eyes light up. "It's really happening, then?"

"It seems so. You might get word to Jack. Let him know that he really has something to stay alive for."

"Rex, a farm foreman, said Jack's name is already linked with the project." Boklung and Borstave stop talking to each other and turn to the slaves. Athalie lowers her voice further. "I don't know whether I believe him. Or perhaps I can't afford to believe, in case he's wrong."

"Silence, yeng." Borstave's rasp booms out. "Listen to our leader. Any more whispers and I'll have you all flogged."

Utter quiet sweeps over the lines of slaves. Boklung's equally commanding but less strident voice takes over.

"Now then, my yeng amongst yeng, I have news of great changes. It is time to set the rumours to rights. Some of you are to be selected for a voyage to distant stars. Those selected will never arrive themselves, but your grandchildren should. Cirithia is sending yeng, not Aranian, initially at least. I'm sure the brightest amongst you will find enough reasons why. What little I know of yeng history includes the knowledge that yeng once sent less advanced creatures than yourselves into space. Sent to test the air, one might say. Those dispatched will enjoy an unprecedented amount of freedom, granted that it will be in the long-term confinement of a spacecraft. We are putting considerable resources into providing a healthy environment, after all, the crew's survival might be vital to a successful mission. Those chosen for this first flight should feel privileged. Other flights will follow.

"We need yeng of high intelligence. We will have to trust to the genetics of inheritance that enough of your children and children's children will be bright as well. The course of the 'Arcraft', as this new fleet of space vehicles are being called, will be pre-set, as will nearly all systems. However, we must assume that the wit of sentient beings, rather than 'bots and machines, will be needed when there are the inevitable unforeseen crises. I have been personally charged by the Council to find the largest part of the yeng crew. I feel a certain duty to the greater good to select some of my best. Those are, despite your obvious limitations, you lot of scruffy individuals.

"Over the next days we have a new consignment of yeng coming here to replace those I lose. These will need extensive and fast training. I require you all to identify and instruct replacements for yourselves in case you are to be amongst my 'pioneers'. I have also stepped up all breeding operations. Now go and prepare yourselves for this opportunity. Any of you that make life difficult will instead be put on the next flight to Trogaffin. I'm sure I don't have to point out the relative disadvantages of that. You are all dismissed."

"So it is true," Phelia murmurs to herself as they walk away.

Athalie scrambles to walk beside her. "It's truly amazing, isn't it? Well, it's good for our species, surely, but good for those sent? I don't know. But if Jack's going then so, damn it, am I."

"Boklung has said enough to suggest I'm going," Phelia said. "If I have any influence, I'll do my best to fix it that you go as well. I bet the project needs a pig farmer."

"Thanks, that's kind. Another thing, inconsequential, but then perhaps not so much now? Do you know where Jack's suvaran is? It's been suggested to me that you do."

Phelia smiles. "Funny you should ask. I have this strange idea that if I really do get a ticket for the trip that Pugwash might just hide in my luggage."

"That'd be wonderful."

"Keep in touch, Athalie. We may be busy."

"I can get word to Jack. Meat collection, you know."

"Excellent! Let him know we all need him alive."

***

After the next rest time, Athalie rushes to get back amongst the holding pens below the Gantri. She pushes her cart as slowly as she feels she can without drawing attention to herself. She begins talking as soon as she nears the pen in which she's been accustomed to seeing Jack. After half-a-dozen more paces, a man with hair longer and more scraggly than most manages to convey the news that Jack isn't there. Immediately, imagination leaps to the worst of scenarios, and she feels a chill deep inside her.

"Where is Jack. Is he …?"

"He's fighting. Up there now. Listen, you can hear the spider's stomping feet."

Athalie cocks her head. She catches the sound of the roaring crowd, and her heart speeds up.

"Don't worry, girl. If anyone is to return it will be him."

"He needs to stay alive. His old boss may be planning to buy him back."

"Keep going, girl, and tell us more when you return. A bloody overseer is looking interested."

The overseer marches over before she can move on. "So, it's the pig woman again, and her beau is away on business. Do you think I'm too stupid to know of your particular interest? What are you going to do for me, to keep me quiet, like? A special service, or I'll have you put in a cage and it won't be this one."

Athalie bites back a retort. "I'm sorry, Sir. I'll get on now."

"Yes, you will. On your knees!" He lifts the flap of hide that covers his crotch. "You know what to do …"

Athalie swallows back bile, but determined to keep out of trouble, she sets to the vile task. Better to taste his festering tissue than be raped.

"That's it, now use that sexy mouth … ah … ah."

While she does his bidding, a burly slave in the cage beckons Athalie to push her abuser closer to the bars. Athalie pushes slowly whilst she works her distracting magic on the foul-smelling privates of the guard. With a climatic grunt the guard takes one too many little backward shuffles, a large arm wraps around his throat and squeezes, then rips the guard's head violently around, snapping his neck. The slave gently lowers the corpse to the ground.

"Go, girl, before any other bastard gets suspicious. On the way back, accidently tip the cart. He's going in it."

Athalie, stunned for a moment, manages to get her act together. She quickly moves on towards the 'meat' stack at the far end of the prisoners' cages. Even though she's sure her demeanour must be telegraphing her fear, no one pays the slightest attention. A cage of humans tangential to and some distance from the murder has responded to events by starting an apparent all in fight. The distraction has worked a treat, drawing the attention of other overseers. Whilst this is going on, the corpse is pulled as close to the dark shadows of the cage's raised floor as is possible. Eager hands rip away the overseer's clothes as he's tugged up against the bars and into sewage that's heaped thickly under every cage. Athalie leaves her cart as empty as she dares to provide room for a complete corpse. When she gets back she's relieved to see that groping hands have somehow managed to render the guard almost naked.

Athalie feigns a stagger, spilling her load. Then as the clamour from the other cages grows, the unrest having quickly spread, she sets about struggling to pull and push the heavy man into the bottom of her now empty cart. As she works, she talks.

"Humans are being sent into space, as guinea-pigs for landings on new planets. Jack is wanted. All of you, this is an opportunity, even if not for yourselves, for our kind. Huff, ugh … And if Jack is to be reclaimed from this hell, then why not also other proven survivors, those that are strong enough to pioneer a new start? Even the thin chances in space have to be better than those of a gladiator."

Other 'cages' join in the general clamour as she wheels the overflowing cart away. The overseer will be temporarily missed but grieved by none. What is one more death amongst such a brutal existence?

As Athalie pulls the cart back towards the piggery, her fears of being caught slowly subside, only to be replaced by a growing fear for Jack's survival. Jack may have been a gladiator for a long time, but any bout could be his last. She also contemplates the fact that she's much in love with a wild killer she hardly knows, a man with whom she has only once been alone and then only for a short time. A short time, but time enough to change lives! She considers that what she feels is no deeper than infatuation, a dependence on a messianic myth carved out of her physical attraction to the rebel. Athalie knows there's a lack of common sense behind her desperate, irrational faith, but she can't help believing that Jack, who seems to be able to defy overwhelming odds, will put her before all others.

Athalie is sharply aware that her belief in Jack is already too important to her personal will to survive to be doubted. She knows, deep down, that her heart will be irreparably shattered if she can't maintain her dream. Athalie is one of life's long-time survivors, a skill that is perhaps dependent on holding fast to a belief in the improbable. Many would have found life all too easy to give up even before watching the cruel death of a sibling. She fortifies her determination by drawing on the tide of anger embedded in her horrific memories.

How much stronger still could Athalie be if she knew her love is as deeply matched, that she is also helping to keep her hero alive.

***

Fortified by his determination to see her, Jack prepares for the charge of yet another yargord. While she wheels her cart away from the terrors of the arena, Jack struggles to find enough guile to kill his adversary, weakened as he is by a fresh and deep wound to his side. Even if he wins the bout, the wound might still kill. Injuries when the victim is living in dire straits and with no serious possibility of medical intervention are far more likely to be fatal.

Back in the security of the piggery's store shed, Athalie has an unaccustomed task to perform. Usually the meat is cut enough to be fed straight into the grinder, but a whole cadaver is just too big even if she could lift it. The thought makes her feel giddy and raises bile into her throat, but she won't be safe until the overseer is reduced to mince. The dead eyes stare up at her, the cheeks hollow as muscles start to tighten, the death grin drained of life's colour. Even hardened as she is by a brutal life, that's too much horror to deal with. She leans down, grabs a cold arm and tugs until the corpse rolls onto its front. Then, grabbing the hair at the back of the head, she turns its neck so that the face is flat against the floor.

She lifts a machete, and with tears moistening her eyes, chops down as hard as she can. A second blow succeeds in severing the head, which she needs both hands to lift and fling into the grinder's trough. She turns away, feeling faint; her back scrapes down the heavy machine until she is sitting, legs tight up against her chest. For a few minutes Athalie's eyes squeeze shut, sending streams of salty tears down her face.

Her mind drifts away from the piggery and out across space, back to the vaguely remembered streets of Ely. She sees the faces of those she once loved and who once loved her, until the grind of metal against bone drives her back to the present. She starts to rise from the floor, but the sickly-sweet odour of slowly thickening blood overwhelms her, and she vomits long and deeply between still-bent legs.

Come on, girl! You can do this. He's nothing more than meat, just like all the rest you grind to meal every day. I'm not the corpse. What else matters ... does even that?

***

In the bowels of the Gantri, Jack grimaces with pain as a couple of his most loyal supporters use a little valuable drinking water and a rag that is hopefully not too many stains beyond clean on his wound. Even hard cases can only take so much agony. Now his life will depend on being given long enough to heal with a sufficient absence of infection. In such a filthy dungeon, where most lives can be measured in Earth-days, this is not likely. He takes comfort in the small victory of Athalie and his fellow residents over the apparently unmissed overseer. This brings a determined thought. *Next time, we strangle one with keys. Then we find a spaceship.*

24

BOKLUNG CONTEMPLATES

Not surprisingly, Boklung is, as is often now the case, fretting about the full implications of the State's demands on zis finances, and the insistence that ze finds the bulk of the yeng for the mission.

Though ze's increased production anyway in anticipation of the trade with the Cheetan, ze still needs to step up zis breeding programmes even more. Many of those best adapted to conditions on Trogaffin must be dispatched there. If that trade fails, ze'll end up in unquenchable debt. That the same yeng can also be the best suited for the Arcraft is a real complication.

So what are my priorities? Are they mainly in our local inter-planetary trade, or in the long-term future of sentient races? As for what yeng will be left to run The Gardens; Sinanna, give me strength!

Actually, the genetic priorities are a little different. When it comes to the Arcraft, wide genetic diversity will most benefit the yeng colony, as well as present physical condition and psychological suitability. Going into the unknown, a wide genetic potential may be vital. The stock for Trogaffin, on the other hand, needs to be geared to survival in a very specific environment.

Boklung will face a lot of short-term financial pain, but ze's determined to turn it all into eventual profits.

I need to test the strength of my business partnership with Hosk, and see if ze is willing to put more money where zis mouth is. Ze is wealthy in zis own right, and as ambassador can no doubt commandeer funds from all kinds of hidden sources.

Pinardos's report is very interesting. Hosk is certainly playing one government against another, and my new knowledge about zis divergence of trade taxes into zis own off-planet accounts gives me a hold over zim should I need one. Just letting zim know that I know will give backbone to our 'friendship'. It seems that Hosk believes my indebtedness will give zim financial leverage over me. I must be very careful not to rely too heavily on zim as my banker.

When Boklung boils down what ze'd like to achieve in zis life, what ze'd like to be remembered for, it's furthering the ambitions of zis species. But more than that, it's helping to advance sentient life in general, yeng included. Though the yeng are zis slaves, ze's extremely fond of them. In fact, all living creatures excite zim. Ze knows ze's not typical, since Aranian's are not known for showing great concern for other life-forms. It seems to be a consistent truth of species close to the Aranian level of development, that they see themselves as being so special to their 'God' that they can be blind to the importance of all Creation.

What arrogant beings we all are. Nevertheless, I'm sure that we Aranian will always lead the way, and hopefully without ever having to do real harm to other intelligent creatures.

Hggh ... At least that is a benevolent arrogance, rather than savage indifference!

If I can really get Jack back alive, and if he is still as sharp as he was, he will provide an excellent catalyst to build the Arcraft crew around. No way will I let the Council send a doomed-to-failure expedition into space. I'm going to do my damnedest to make sure the venture succeeds, and that means having an intelligent and determined crew. Aranian alone might conquer the Universe, but Aranian, Cheetan and yeng working cooperatively, then how much better the odds will be.

What's important is to instil a culture of co-operation. The on-board 'society' will be closed to the outside world, including the norms of Ungoliantis. What matters is pursuing every possibility of success, and not worrying about which species is immediately at the top of the next tree.

Yes, I must be so very arrogant that I trust in the natural superiority of my own race's innate potential to float to the top of any barrel.

Is it just chance that has put zim, a believer in sentience rather than selfish genes in command of Aranian and yeng future? Sinanna works in mysterious ways. Perhaps, ze should think in terms of calling God 'Creation', rather than Sinanna? Sinanna is, after all, only the name for the Almighty that the Aranian use.

I will invite Hosk over, under the pretence of being social, for 'a drink and a game of chess'. We need to talk, but I don't want zim coming with zis guard too high.

Boklung's financial security may depend on drawing out freely given Cheetan money without incurring strong financial penalties. Ze also needs to find a way of getting on the right side of more Councillors with direct interest in the Gantri. Perhaps ze can kill two drabbets with one stone, by inviting the right individual over with the ambassador, so massaging both their egos.

Yes, a name comes to mind, Dunkuin, that's the one. I'll get my staff to check zim out. As I recall, that creature would play with anyone's privates to gain a little political advantage. I need the psychological and political profiles of all the governors of the Gantri, Dunkuin in particular.

Boklung writes a quick note. "Grace. Take a message to the administration office." Grace rushes in from her post at the door. "Don't lose it; here, let me put my stamp on it."

"Yes, Zir." She does a quick curtsy and hurries out.

With the slave gone, Boklung fixes on an issue that has been at the back of zis mind for some time. Ze thinks seriously about getting zis own eggs on-board the Arcraft.

And who should ze cross-fertilise with? Zis choice shouldn't necessarily be about whom ze fancies, but it could be. Robust good health, strength and intelligence must be zis criteria.

The younger zis chosen happens to be the better, and ze must be from well proven stock.

Lebl couldn't be more perfect. Ngu Clanten has chosen the lovely Lebl as heir apparent to zis private fortune. My love is as bright as a button and a very independent thinker. I certainly love tangling my parts with that handsome creature, more than any other I've ever known.

Boklung contemplates the facts that ze's already expressed zis interest and that such a union fits well with zis need to keep zis influence with Ngu. Their bonding might almost be at the instigation of Sinanna, as it coincides so perfectly with the broad goals of the Arcraft Project. Assuming that God supports the intended journey.

"Grace." *Hggh … oh yes, already on an errand.* "Maxine, come here."

"Zir!"

"I wish you to send flowers and an invite to dinner, to Lebl Clanten. Ze is in my office address book."

I've so much to think about. The question of our presence or not on the Arcraft is rapidly coming to a head. The next vote should settle things. Having the theoretical ability to re-establish direct physical control by thawing out Aranian soldiers is bound to be popular as a way to allay fears. I have my hearing spiracles close enough to the ground, to know that those that are thinking along such lines are already in the ascendancy.

But a thawed and inevitable partially damaged group of Aranian running amok in this vast experiment is the very last thing the Arcraft will actually need. I may have to ensure a failure of the cryogenic system, so that yeng can be left in peace to believe that they are masters of their own destinies. I'm glad that Ngu Clanten seems to have accepted so much of my unorthodox thinking, but ze won't accept murder. That needs a special arrangement.

Who would ever have thought that I would one day conspire against my own race? Certainly not I! But then, I don't really believe I will be. No, my treachery will only be against our misguided Council, not a detriment to our long-term future.

Are yeng any less likely to end up as basket cases, living for generations on that ship? I have plenty of reasons to think so, not least of them being the way that most cope so well with being harvested from the Waterball. Now the yeng are to be escaping from slavery. Their dreams are being re-invented. As for succeeding generations, they will only know life on-board. They will be naturally adjusted to different expectations. Whereas, adult Aranian, that have seen the good life, who have enjoyed the pleasures of living on our diverse planet, when deprived of so much, would be certain to end up as head-bangers. Yeng, for all their sentimentalities and fears are psychologically robust creatures.

I seem to be turning into the strongest of advocates for yeng. How strange are the paths of life? Me, though one of the biggest slave owners on the planet, turning out to be one of the strongest supporters of their freedom. Yes, and especially important to me is the life of one in particular, no less than the very one that has caused me more embarrassment than has any other creature, ever. It is perhaps almost unbelievable that he has survived, but that has only increased my affection for the animal. One thing is for sure: many will struggle with my call to have Jack released into my care. Alternative paths to the same goal need to be explored, just in case legal avenues prove to be blocked.

***

As it happens, very much to Boklung's relief, the vote goes zis way only a short time later. The argument that few Councillors would be prepared to see their own offspring living in a tin-can in space for such a long period, especially on a mission with so little hope, was strong enough to carry the motion in favour of a non-Aranian crew. However, the vote in favour of the cryogenic unit was overwhelmingly carried, as ze'd thought it would be. Knowing that however bad things got in any eventual colonies, that no creatures would be able to return, eased the Council's concerns over giving yeng so much theoretical independence. In other words, both sides of the argument on safety pushed towards the same decision. The first, that the craft won't be safe enough for Aranians, and the second, that the craft won't be robust enough to be a credible threat even with an independent and belligerent yeng crew. Interestingly, having shifted opinion so far, one of the biggest debates ended up being about the quality of the 'defrosting' equipment.

At finish, the craft will be six thousand five hundred metres long, by six hundred and twenty metres wide, on the octal counting system. The structure will be mostly cylindrical, so as

232

to maximise its strength with the least possible weight of material. This is seen as vital as the specifications demand that the shell is kept as light as possible, consistent with being able to withstand small asteroid strikes and provide sufficient radiation protection to the payload, both living and inert. Even the 'bots can be destroyed by enough of the penetrating sub-atomic particles found in deep space.

Most of the craft is to be pressurized to seventeen atmospheres, as the yeng's biology is best suited to that level. The main yeng module is still to be the rear section. The craft will have lighting with a spectrum similar to that which penetrates to the surface of Waterball. All this exactitude would be less necessary if there wasn't the need to maintain yeng health through at least three generations. The expedition is designed to last for about six Ungolian-years, which is the best part of one hundred Earth-years. In this time the Arcraft is expected to travel forty five thousand billion kilometres.

A period after the vote, Boklung receives a personal visit from the Council's Speaker, Ngu Clanten. Clanten doesn't even exchange pleasantries before launching into zis obviously prepared speech. Ze is clearly delighted to deliver the news that the cryogenic decision had gone through. Obviously ze doesn't know that Boklung's spies have kept zim abreast of every word. And ze certainly doesn't know that Boklung isn't even prepared to accept this level of Aranian dominion.

"The Council has made the decision to demand that at least an octate of mature Aranian is to be on-board, in cryogenic suspension," said a contented looking Ngu Clanten. "This has been decided because it is a majority view that we should not rely on programmed 'bots to raise our youngsters. Of course, nurture by 'bots will still be programmed, as the healthy survival of the frozen adults isn't certain. The cryogenic unit will be housed deep in the bowels of the craft, ostensibly out of the way, but really in an attempt to keep it safe from yeng interference. We are going to discreetly ask for volunteers from amongst elite families rather than draw attention with a public call. Conscription would be a last resort.

"I worked tirelessly to undermine the call for a full Aranian crew, strongly pointing out how stupid and naïve such a policy would be. I am pleased that you have managed to explain so much to me, Cingwin. When I think how naïve my own thinking was until so recently. I have been having these dreams; ones that have made me see things so differently. Eye opening, one might say. It has been almost as though someone, or something, has been advising me while I slept.

"Of course, we won't be able to keep the cryogenic unit secret, so perhaps we had better seal the unit off from the rest of the ship."

Boklung replies, "I just hope the worst can't by some fluke happen. Imagine a planet ruled by Aranian mentally damaged by cycles in cryogenic suspension. You know how badly experiments have often gone using yeng as our model for freezing. We have thawed out so very strangely altered creatures. Indeed, that is where our model for producing cannibalistic yeng first came from."

"Yes, we know, but our best cryogenicists maintain that recent results have been far more satisfactory. The Council has considered the balance of probable risks, as outlined by the best of our specialists. I have no choice other than to insist that you carry out the policy. That is what I want anyway."

Boklung knows ze has to pretend to like the way the vote on cryogenics went. Rather than risk saying something to make Clanten wonder about zis thinking, ze tries drawing the conversation onto another topic. "Can I offer you a drink, Councillor?"

"That would be most welcome!"

"Excuse me a minute, whilst I order some tea ... Grace, a choice of herbal infusions, bring them out to us. We will be at a table on the terrace."

Boklung continues after ze and Clanten have settled outdoors. "We are free to chat out here, Councillor, away from the hearing lobes of all species. Just to emphasise the direction we are both going in, we need to indoctrinate the yeng to the idea that this expedition is their show, but making it as clear as we can that they are the protectors of all the sentient species involved. They will perform best if they feel the weight of responsibility, feel that they are being trusted. Obviously, they are not going to believe for one minute that we are doing this purely for their good alone, as some sort of altruistic benefactors, but we can at least instil the idea that they are truly pioneers for all our species. Further, we can make out that they are only subservient to the pre-programming of the 'bots for the duration of the flight. That requirement can be explained away easily enough on the grounds of technical safety. I believe we should say that, provided they don't do anything to harm the interests of Aranian and Cheetan, they will continue in freedom once the craft has landed. We don't need to be sincere, just convincing.

"We will say that the 'bots are in overall strategic control as only they have the capacity to compute all the codes and navigational procedures. There is little doubt that the 'bots are needed to ensure that the craft reaches the required coordinates and lands safely on a suitable new world."

Clanten, despite the distance zis thinking has moved, feels a bit uneasy with the direction of the conversation, as signalled by the odour rising from zis sweating abdomen. However, presumably because Boklung has already so substantially altered what Clanten previously thought to be zis firm opinions, it has become relatively easy for zim to trust that further reservations will soon be eroded as well.

"You seem to be saying that we should treat this slave species as almost more than equals. I think you must be careful not to go too far, Boklung. I certainly won't put the detail of your intentions back before the Council. They would have a fit if they knew that the head of the project was advocating such an independent spirit amongst the yeng."

"I fully agree. However, if I can convince you, will you at least do what you can to turn the Council's focus away from fine detail? This is all about smoke and mirrors. It is in the nature of yeng that they will try to find ways to win control over the 'bots. Rest assured of that. So we have to make sure that when they are in the ascendancy they don't try to redirect or destroy the robots basic programming. Navigation is vital, and just too important to be allowed to fall under yeng influence. Just imagine them trying to fly off and hide their colony in space, or back on Earth. That could be a disaster, especially if they succeeded.

"We can't pretend that our relationship has been anything like equal so far, they are slaves with little more rights than the pigs they rear. However, the yeng must be made to believe that they really are independent now and that they will remain so. I need to draw on strong individuals that I have already indoctrinated, and even on some already assigned to the arena."

Indoctrinated, that's a good one, but Clanten will like the sound of it. I need Jack. He most certainly isn't my puppet, but giving Clanten the impression that he now is may be vital.

Clanten replies: "But how are you going to ensure that they ultimately serve only our interests? What is there to actually prevent them altering the algorithms on which the robots function?"

"They have to truly believe that our interests are compatible." *I am going to have to risk telling Ngu more than I intended.* "Let me talk in complete confidence. Perhaps we can use those frozen adult Aranian to make the yeng believe they have uncovered our intentions. Perhaps we need to give them a victory, in order to hide our deeper plans. The secret that we must guard at all costs is simply that yeng will be carrying our future as eggs. My view is that we have no serious choices between two extremes.

"Either the yeng assume their independence and fight to save themselves and so the mission, or else we send a full Aranian crew. The latter won't ever happen for all sorts of reasons, which leaves us with reliance on the independent spirit of yeng. If they believe that they have already won the war they are unlikely to see any advantage in fiddling with the navigation. They will be less likely to see a reason for risking their own future by going as far as altering the programmed course the 'bots are following. After all, the target is a rare, hard to find, and safe landing site on a suitable planet."

Clanten scratches zis eye-stems unconsciously as ze thinks through zis reply. Ze is now so unsure of zimself, has moved so far, that ze has more or less become resigned to just lapping up everything that Boklung says. Of course, if Boklung pushes too far, so that Clanten feels threatened, there could be a violent reaction.

"I do get your point and yes, I have to admit that I can't see any flaw in your logic. You have my unofficial permission to build their independent spirit, and to construct the ship that you want. I will try to distract the Council from interference. However, I'm only prepared to go so far. If things go wrong, I will see you hang rather than risk my station. And I want to know nothing whatsoever about substantive changes of plan. If I know, I have to react. Do we understand each other? I'll turn blind eyes and deaf ears, and in return you will do nothing to compromise my position as Speaker of the Council. I disassociate myself entirely from the merest suspicions of intent to murder, however convincing your arguments.

"What I do insist on is that the robots are given the power to destroy the yeng if our Aranian future seems threatened. I go only so far as accepting the loss of short-term power if our long-term dominion is ensured. The real goal of the mission must not be compromised whatever diversions happen in its implementation. Remember, Boklung, only one ultimate goal matters: the establishment of successful Aranian colonies. The survival of all other species, however useful, is subordinate to that.

"As I have already touched on, I do feel that it isn't just you influencing me, Boklung. Some other force or forces seemed to be aboard in my mind. Another voice is giving weight to your clever persuasions. At times, I find myself agreeing with you, Boklung, almost against my free will, and certainly against so much that I previously believed."

"I feel a calling as well, Ngu. And fair enough, I won't embarrass you. I can do plenty to ensure that yeng kneel on the same prayer mat. For a start, as you know, I'm already forwarding plans based on the Admiral's thinking to ensure the yeng are taught to worship Sinanna. If we can get them to not just bow at our insistence to The Great Creator, but for them to really believe that Aranian are truly the race born in the image of God, then our natural supremacy will be better guarded.

"When we arrived on Waterball, we were seen almost as demi-gods, which certainly helped subdue yeng independence and reduced their trust in being the chosen of 'God'. Many yeng already attend our churches, especially where our priests have done what they can to emphasise the natural bridges to yeng traditional spiritual beliefs.

"There are many less subtle, more overt, policies to pursue. We can make available all sorts of invented cultural histories between Aranian and yeng. Our technological capability to alter instinctive behaviour stemming from epigenetic programming is new and only partially developed, but we have it. It is already being used to instil protective feelings towards Aranian. Actually, strictly speaking it is Cheetan technology.

"This touches on the reasons why I have insisted on keeping my Cheetan contacts up to date with developments. For long-term trust and cooperation with our neighbours it is vital that they feel involved in our colonial plans. We must take note of their concerns and buy into their expertise. The last thing we want is direct competition and, inevitably, war between our races, deep in our future space frontiers. We will face challenges aplenty without fighting each other. To this end we are also carrying a small number of Cheetan eggs. The science work is already been backed up by the inclusion of doctored histories in the ship's information libraries. There will be plenty of stories about past cooperation and friendships between Lush species and yeng."

Clanten nods thoughtfully.

Boklung feels that it is time to cement Clanten's 'enlightenment' towards high ideals with more base instincts. With this in mind, ze introduces a bit of crude bribery.

"As for our personal futures, Ngu Clanten, I would very much like you to join with me in developing the yeng business on Trogaffin. A great deal of money is to be made. I believe you are already fairly well acquainted with my close business partner, Cheetan Ambassador Hosk. I can assure you that the three of us have a great deal of mutually compatible interests."

"Haggh … Now we are starting to see the star system the same way, Cingwin. We must ensure that the right things are quietly done whatever others are demanding. Let's rub legs on our alliance. I'm beginning to understand you much better. If I may paraphrase, what matters is that we have functioning colonies to travel to, to invade if necessary, so that we can spread across space. After all, we seized control of Waterball at will and nothing will be much different in the newly established colonies. Once we have safe satellites to fly our armies to, there will be no stopping us. The long view is all that matters."

"Exactly! Hggh ... I need one favour immediately. As I said earlier, I need certain gladiators from the arena. May I now use your good offices to help me retrieve them? In return, I will ensure that future Clantens are well represented, if you get the drift of what I'm saying. Hggh ... I mean as eggs, not as frozen lumps of meat! As for me, I have personal interests in your chosen heir. Hggh ... Will you grant me official congenital rights with Lebl, if ze is content with such a bonding."

"Hggggggh! Most interesting, my, haagh, family friend, but first things first.

"Yes, I support the release of gladiators, but don't move too swiftly. Let's have the excitement of an expedition ready to set forth before we manipulate the cherished sport, the drug of the masses, over much. The withdrawing from combat of gladiatorial champions, and that is, I'm sure, what you are talking about, has never been done before. Timing the release of, shall we say for the sake of argument, the one they call Spartacus, may well be crucial. Perhaps the easiest thing would be engineering a late mass-breakout, close to the Arcraft's launch date? If your chosen can get aboard without either of us declaring for them, then we are both politically safer.

"As to the joining of our families, I am flattered by your interest in my prodigy. Yes, of course I am happy with that. Your descendants' brains will be a big bonus to the Clanten clan, and my offspring's beauty to yours. Hagggh, hagggh."

The two Aranian vigorously rub forelimbs.

"You make me feel quite overwhelmed," Boklung says. "Let us enjoy a shared hippotion to celebrate our shared goals and mutual trust. I think our little meeting has gone exceedingly well. Better indeed than either of us had any right to hope. To the best of hatchings!"

"To the best of hatchings."

25

STILL-LIVING-LEGEND

The suns are high in the sky as the two Gladiators meet in the arena. The Aranian audience hiss ever louder from the Gantri's stands, excited in anticipation of the seemingly inevitable sacrifice of a champion. Jack, hand to his wounded side, watches the steady approach of the massive yargord. The huge biped with an elephant-like prehensile trunk is far from the most intelligent creature Jack has faced, but that's relative. Yargord are clever enough to be trainable in basic skills, and this one has been trained. If measurable, the yargord's intelligence quotient might be equal to the human toddler or a monkey. In raw strength even a dozen adults are hardly its equal. Its crocodile-like tail, balancing the weight of its extended trunk, swishes back and forth through the dirt. Adding to its intrinsic fighting ability, this one has been trained to use gladiatorial weapons.

On its back it carries a 'quiver' of throwing darts, each the length of the javelins that the yeng gladiators use, but its main weapon is a huge axe. These are employed with great dexterity by the prehensile trunk extending from the top of its bulky body. Eyes ring the appendage, giving the creature all-round vision. Jack has only his usual octagonal brass shield and a sharp sword.

The two creatures track back and forth across the blood-stained concrete, both looking for a weak spot in their opponent's stance. Either way, this has the promise of being the last of Jack's many bouts. His old boss hopes that ze has a watertight deal whereby, after this one last fight, Jack will be quietly traded. However, one lone man, even Jack in perfect health, could never be fairly matched against this creature.

Perhaps not all is lost. While for the yargord concerns could never be highly cerebral, it has been comparatively distracted. The creature has mislaid its favourite toy, the soft fleece stripped off a Waterball sheep. A warden sympathetic to Jack's cause took the comforter when the yargord was sleeping the night before. He knew only too well how deeply the creature treasures the fleece. In addition, the creature may well suffer a small handicap from underrating its adversary. Having defeated up to a dozen humans at a time, it will not be expecting the skills of one alone to be a challenge.

The yargord seems to suddenly sense that the atmosphere in the arena is not the same as usual. The quiet that has fallen is certainly not an everyday occurrence. Now, the yargord, though unaccustomed to hanging back, is unsure enough to do so. The quiet has left room for the aggravating loss of its pacifier to surface. For one life-threatening second, Jack also loses focus as his normally comforting pendant, gifted by Athalie, bounces against his sternum.

One gladiator is without the security of its toy and one is deeply aware that, but for the seemingly impossible odds of this fight, he might have some hope for the future. The rules of combat don't allow draws, except in shared death.

All the restless night before, Jack had pondered the question of whether death is actually better than a one-way trip to some distant and godforsaken planet. Might a swift and suicidal charge be preferable? But then, if Athalie has been selected for the trip, they could soon be together. He hopes so.

The creature suddenly advances. Jack shakes his head and resets himself.

Focus, Jack! All you have to do is kill just one more monstrous creature.

The yargord hurls a continuous stream of spears, but from too far out to realistically hope to skewer one so skilled.

Jack crouches and lets the projectiles ping off the bevelled edges of his shield. Despite the fact that no missile penetrated flesh, Jack screams and topples under his shield. Now the creature is totally confused. It circles ever closer, sniffing the air with its trunk. Then it frees its axe, ready for a killing strike. Jack seems to be lying like a gifted slab of fresh meat, without the slightest sign of movement. The monster's trunk sniffs close and then rolls the body over. Satisfied its prey has lost consciousness, it moves nearer to commence its butchery. Suddenly, the lump of meat rolls between webbed feet, and a sharp blade penetrates the massive, exposed underbelly. It is too pained or too stunned to respond.

"Engulf my sword, a final offering; it's yours. I have travel plans and perhaps the hope of love."

The yargord falls, crushing down on its killer. The crowd hisses and stomps.

Now, if my wound doesn't kill me, then next, the stars. That's Jack's last thought as he loses consciousness under the weight of the toppled giant.

He wakes later to a crippling headache and the lingering stink of yargord offal.

Where am I? ... What's ... ?

"Calm yourself, Spartacus. You're alive, and with God's grace and my help, on the mend. You've been here through two work retreats since you slaughtered that yargord. Do you know that you're one of the very first to kill one single-handed?"

Jack just blinks and the voice continues.

"Anyway, you must have the luck of the Devil himself, because the spiders decided to give you special care. That must be a first as well. You're in a cell under the stands. I've been charged to keep you alive, on pain of my own demise."

Jack squints up at the owner of the voice—a muscular man with head shaved clean. "I remember you. Stanislav, warden and trainer ... you're the bastard that's so fond of cutting the throats of those that can't fight ..."

"So what! They just die easier under my blade. Calm yourself, my bark is much worse than my bite, unless the spiders are watching, that is. We all do what we can to stay alive, don't we, Spartacus? How many men have you slaughtered? Those that I see off to their maker are all-but-dead already, I just end their misery. My sharp knives work in their best interest as well as mine."

Jack manages to sit up. He frowns and rubs his temples.

"We've all heard rumours about the Arc," Stanislav says. "The chosen will have a chance to escape this life, and possibly even live. I'm sure you've got a ticket; nothing else explains your treatment. If you're to live, then I'll demand one as well. I expect you're here until they find an excuse to trade you that won't risk a riot from the public. But you might not live that long."

Jack narrows his eyes. "Are you threatening me?"

The brute curls his lip in a sneer. "I wouldn't see it like that. Rather, I may, for sake of our new partnership, be able to try harder to keep you alive. You blood's poisoned from the wound. I've seen the decline from where you are many times. But I can get my hands on certain medicines. Wardens have many privileges unavailable to mere gladiators. Of course, I have to have good reason to take the risk of 'borrowing' from the spiders."

"Ha, why should spider medicine work on us?"

"Why indeed, but trials and a few deaths have found us one that does. There's a rumour that it may even be penicillin. Not that the spiders would call it that."

"Looks like, whatever goes, without you I'm already dead."

"So it seems."

"If the spiders want to keep me alive, why don't they look after me? Why are you my nurse maid?"

"I'm not much good at reading spider minds, but I guess the spiders that matter don't want to be seen helping a yeng gladiator. Something like that! Better you die than some spiders are seen as open to bribes. Just in case they don't find a way to get you out, they'd rather you died in my hands. That way they can hide any conspiracy."

Jack stares at the man for a moment. "I could call your bluff. My guess is that you already have the medicine, voluntarily given. What's more, I figure that if I die, you'll take my place to fight the next yargord. But mutual cooperation is sensible. If you do the best you can for me, then I'll do my best for you. Are you my enemy, Stanislav the overseer, or my future comrade, Stanislav, voyager to the stars?"

"You self-confident prick. You have a deal. And I no more go back on my word than the famous Spartacus does."

***

A huis has passed since Jesus Sanz cut himself from the body bag and clung to the incinerator hopper's steep chute. Muscles slowly recovering from the poison, he'd pulled himself over descending bodies. All day he'd watched and helped on their way the cadavers that had followed him onto the slide. Eventually, low-light has arrived, and to Jesus's relief, the spiders disappear. He pulls himself over the side of the slide and falls the three or four metres to the ground. With a sore back and a further bruise on his head, he staggers off into the city, where he hides in the market and picks up on the street-talk about the Arcraft.

After many days of to-ing and fro-ing and having gleaned information from one of the hardest and most obstinate women he's likely to ever meet, Cantonia, he finds his way first to the hangar and then, eventually, inside its lofty space.

When the yeng workers and Aranian engineers have departed, and the lingering fumes of the yengicide used to ensure the craft is empty have dispersed, he slips aboard. He finds a void to hide in, below what he guesses to be a slatted-floor for some sort of farm animal. There he remains, sneaking out only when desperate for food and drink and for technological paraphernalia to satisfy his creative mind.

Jesus explores his new home, becoming something of expert on the architecture of the ship. He has to avoid the growing numbers of robot soldiers and the occasional parties of engineers, but generally avoiding trouble proves easy. An eye

245

needs keeping on the growing number of active cameras, at least when the bridge is occupied.

Later, Jesus liberates a gun from a soldier 'bot, which he strips down and modifies. Now he's the best armed yeng on Ungoliantis.

26

ATHALIE SWIMS

Athalie thinks of little other than Jack. Ever since she heard he'd been badly wounded, she's been unable to eat, and cries so much that she suspects she could drown on her pillow.

She knows that even if he's on the mend, he's likely to be called to fight again long before he's recovered. He's got to get out of there, but how? What can she do? She's already been back to the arena twice in this planet's interminably long day, and another visit so soon will be sure to raise suspicions. Her pigs don't eat that fast.

He hadn't been returned to the cage, and she wonders if that means he's already dead. None of the gladiators knew anything except that he'd won his bout and was dragged still-alive from the arena. Another had already taken his place as cage leader.

That bastard Capolla sure stepped into Jack's shoes as soon as Jack failed to return. But if not him, it would have been someone else.

I wonder if I can break in so that no one knows I'm there, get in without my cart. Possibly; after all, the guards are only looking for breakouts. Who but an idiot would try and get into that place? Has anyone ever? I know one way that just might work: the Well.

Water for the prisoners comes from a well in the basement. Athalie has seen water being drawn up often enough and it's only about twenty metres from where the cadavers are stacked. She knows the water is drawn from a tunnel that connects the sump of the well with the River Induna, and one thing that sets her apart from many yeng and all spiders is that she can swim. She used to swim across the Ouse, near home, for a dare when she was still tiny.

Her parents would've had kittens if they'd known. But she's sure they would've thanked God that her familiarity with water had given her the courage to hide from the spiders in that filthy pond.

Oh sis, I do so miss you ...

If anyone can swim through to the well sump it's her, but whether she can climb up into the basement of the Gantri and remain undetected is another matter. She plans to go the next low-light, before she can worry her way out of such recklessness.

What'll I do if I make it? Who gives a shit? Do I really want to feed pigs for the rest of my life?

***

Later, she slips into the wide, fast-flowing river full of creatures that would happily eat her. By the time she gets across, if she does, she'll be a long way downstream from her entry point. But she can't work her way down the far bank because all the bridges into the city are closed and guarded at this quiet hour. A boat would be safer, but too easily seen even in this gloom, so she has to swim it, and before her nerve completely goes.

If I set off from just below the Droftsma Bridge, by the time I cross I won't, hopefully, be that far from the Gantri. Come on, let's do it! As Mum used to say, 'If you don't start you won't finish'. Jesus! What was that that plopped into the water? Forget it. This is just the Ely's River Ouse and Dad won't find out if I'm not seen.

She swims with and across the current, not fighting it over much. But will there be a grill to stop river debris, and will it stop her? Almost certainly yes, and absolutely no!

Some critter nibbles her stomach. *Argh.* But she keeps going, imagining she's still on Earth, doing a dare to win a bar of chocolate or something. The light seems to dim for her as she nears the Gantri, but it must be her imagination, because its shadow is cast away from the water. The structure seems to lean out over her, and possibly the flared top does.

At halfway across, she reminds herself to guard her energies. She'd burn too many calories trying to make the bank before the conduit. As she passes the arena, she sees a heavy grill that looks like it has a bit of a gap at its top. She might just squeeze her way over.

Flip! A bloody spider's fishing just where I'm likely to reach the bank. What the hell do I do now? I'll have to drift past zim under water. Here goes.

This is creepy, and I daren't open my eyes. I dread to think what might be in the water. The river is moving swiftly enough that I should be way past zim before I need to surface. Let the air go gently, just another ten seconds, as I mustn't start gasping and splashing when I surface. Now . . .

"Uuuuuhh."

Good, I've got past without it stirring. Now, to quietly make the bank.

Athalie slides over the river's concrete retaining wall, onto the footpath that runs along the side of the stadium.

Now, how do I get back past the spider? I've nowhere to go that doesn't leave me exposed. I see no alternative to creeping behind the creature. Why creep though? Walk boldly, as if going about a legitimate errand. Still, I'll move silently, not giving the spider too long to be aware of my approach. Come on, move, ... heart in mouth, hardly daring to breath. Will the creature question that I'm dripping with water? Will it wonder that a slave is about after curfew? This is mad. I can smell the creature. I mustn't run. It has sensed me, and is turning.

"What're you doing out at this time, slave, and dripping wet?"

"I fell in the river, Zir, losing my master's papers. I'm late from trying to recover them."

"Then I'm taking you in. Sit whilst I put a halter on your neck ... Or then again, perhaps if you give some relief to my organ, then perhaps I let you go."

Athalie supresses a sigh. "Yes, Zir. I can pleasure you." *Like hell, I'd rather die! Mind you, our species is as perverted as his. But at least this one, unlike that human trustee, probably washes.*

She takes up a submissive position before the standing Aranian and reaches towards engorged flesh. "Let me stroke you. What a big hole you have, Zir."

Athalie suddenly springs up as hard as she can and throws all her weight into the engorged nether region of the creature towering over her. She lets all her bottled anger explode in this single act of violence. The creature slowly overbalances and falls with a splash onto its back, into the fast-flowing river. Before the safety rope can pull tight, Athalie yanks it free of the heavy metal ring to which it's fixed. Now the spider has no chance. None of them can even float well, let alone swim.

Athalie's legs collapse, forcing her down to squat like a trembling heap of jelly. The spider is swiftly born away with just the tops of its still-twitching hind legs showing above the surface.

I don't believe it. Little old me has just killed a fully mature spider. That's one for the home team, Sis.

Now for my next challenge: the grate! I need to be back in the water, but I should walk well past it first so that I don't have to fight the flow. I feel so weird, what with an emotional high in killing a spider and cold fear that my crime won't have gone unnoticed.

She turns slowly, staring into the gloom, looking for the slightest evidence that she has been seen.

Shit, cameras! I never thought … But then, the spiders don't generally use electronic surveillance, so why here?

She stares up at the towering arena walls, seeing nothing that looks like a lens.

Hell; I'll probably be dead soon anyway. Stop fretting about things that probably don't matter and get on with it.

Athalie again slides into the water and lets it carry her downstream until she can grab the grate. The badly corroded, heavy mesh provides plenty of easy handholds. She stares at the gap at the top, which actually does look large enough for her to get over, but it also appears to be edged by sharp teeth of corroded metal. Athalie clambers up to take a closer look. She decides that risking squeezing herself over the top is a last resort.

Next, Athalie pokes about with her feet below the surface and, after gulping air, 'walks' her way down with her arms, but she finds no gaps. She lets the water lift her, then climbs clear of the water to the top again. Gingerly, she pushes her shoulders and then her tummy over the rusty spikes, then tries to lift one leg over. Rotten metal snaps, and one hand-hold gives way. Gravity wins and she plunges back towards the water. A spike rips at her second knee as it follows on over the top.

Oach! That hurts.

I just know that I'm bleeding badly. Quickly now, push away from the grill and swim for life. My blood is sure to draw predatory fish. At least the grate should stop anything big, but already I feel creatures nibbling at me. Jesus, I'm scared. I want to scream. I'm so frightened. This is silly, why didn't I rest against the grate before I started swimming? I have never swum so fast, or been so desperate for breath. There's no going back now. I'll let myself spin onto my back again, and float up to the roof of the pipe. There will be air. Hell, no. The top of the culvert—there's no air space. My lungs will burst. Hand over sore hand along the pipe, kick, kick; I'm getting slow. Drowning. The pain ... So this is what? ... Is that a patch of light? ...

27

JACK IS TRADED

Boklung makes a rare journey to the Gantri, though not with any plan to see an entertainment. Having heard about the injury to Jack, ze feels that, close though a deal is, ze could lose the yeng if ze doesn't more directly intervene.

Stanislav stands before zim in a stark interview room and replies to Boklung's question. "Yes, Spartacus is injured, but he's recovering. Zir, you're not the first that wishes for an audience with him. Many in here would see him dead, and I'm striving hard to keep him alive. He's slaughtered so many that he's built an army of enemies. I'll guard him whatever the cost to me, though this would be easier if I knew you'd buy me out as well. My own life is in some danger through my actions."

"Yeng; are you trying to tell me what to do?"

"No Zir, I'm the humble servant of all Aranian and honoured to be in the presence of one so esteemed. It's just that life has given us compatible interests. Mine are merely about survival and yours about the management of the great project we hear about."

"When I have seen Spartacus and talked again to the Director, I will exercise my judgement. Now, you have delayed me quite enough, yeng. Show me to my slave then make yourself scarce."

"Thank you, Zir. This way, if you wouldn't mind following one so humble?" He leads Boklung from the room and down a long corridor.

***

After seeing for zimself that Jack is alive, Boklung visits Clamfusk, the managing director of the Nuzkarflux Amphitheatre. Ze sits in zis office in front of the gristly old Aranian's desk.

"This is highly irregular, and not only that," Clamfusk says, "Spartacus is my top attraction. But taking into account that your project requires him so badly, and the overtures that others have made to me, I have tentatively agreed to your offer, Boklung. However, on reflection, I have to say I find the amounts you have mentioned to be somewhat derisory, personally speaking . . ."

"How about in addition to a cash payment, I guarantee to provide your office with a supply of zoongrass? The gladiator is wounded anyway, and with the sort of care that the Gantri customarily gives, he might never fight again."

Clamfusk draws zis eyestalks together. "I'm less ambivalent, but still the offer is on the low side. You really don't seem to appreciate how much we depend on gladiators like Spartacus to bring in the money. I can make what you offer on a single day's betting."

Boklung's mouth tightens. "Okay, my final augmentation then! You will be my personal guest of honour at the next hunt meeting and receive a season's free membership. I will also allow you to bring a guest to each meet. As a tiny recompense, I require just one additional thing, the overseer, Stanislav, who so well steered Jack back to something approaching health. He needs to be suitably honoured. He looks like a strong fighter; one that could do justice to the role of Spartacus. Let the creature fight."

"Ha. Like all my overseers, he is merely a coward that would inflict any cruelty to save himself. He deserves nothing, but if you insist, then please give him whatever honour you like. Let us rub forelegs on our deal."

The spiders stand and meet at the side of the desk. "Deal," Boklung says as they rub limbs. "Honouring this overseer is important to me, and to you, Clamfusk, for financial reasons. I wish him disguised to look as much like Spartacus as possible and to have him armed with the weapons Spartacus uses. Then send him into the arena to fight a yargord single-handed. Advertise that Spartacus fights again, of course. I wish to lay a heavy bet on him losing, as I'm sure you will also. I know you have ways of tightening the odds sufficiently to achieve the most lucrative of outcomes."

Clamfusk chuckles. "That will make for an excellent entertainment, Boklung. What a pleasure to do business with you. Money all around; I'm sure we will both profit well from the fight."

"Don't thank me too much. The entertainment was the idea of my once, and future, slave Spartacus. We had a little chat when I was taken to check my goods. I was delighted to agree, after having witnessed the arrogant manners of that overseer's tongue."

28

SCIENTIFIC COOPERATION

The cooperation between Boklung and Hosk has been so successful that they've been able to access the help of many of the best astrophysicists and engineers from both systems. To cement the cooperative venture, they've gathered most of those involved in the conference room of the Interplanetary Council in the city of Arknala.

Boklung addresses the delegates. "We have instigated this interplanetary conference to allow the free flow of ideas and cooperation between us. I am very grateful to my friend Huigark Hosk, the Cheetan Ambassador to my city-state of Cirithia, for helping me to persuade you all to find the time to be here. I am grateful to the Interplanetary Council for making its good offices available so that we can meet on truly neutral territory.

"As you all now know, we Cirithians, with the help of many others from both our races, have put together the Arcraft Project in order to advance the process of setting up permanent break-away colonies from our resource limited star system. This conference is designed to help ensure that we have complete transparency and a common goal in mutual development of our Cheetan and Aranian futures. Before we go further, let me address the issue of comparative advantage in this project for our two races. Initially, we are mainly only going to risk the lives of yeng. Later when systems have been proved, I will personally guarantee that Cheetan will be well represented as crew members and eventual colonists; at least they will be while I have anything to do with the process.

"Old balance of power issues within our star system must not be allowed to raise their ugly head. Space has no known boundaries, so provides limitless room for all of our independent and cooperative ambitions. Space is probably as big as all sentient creatures can imagine it to be and then a billion times larger. Irrespectively, we are already aware of so much space that it is inconceivable that we will ever need to be standing on the same patch unless we wish to do so. However, I believe we will want to stand together, united against common enemies that are too big for us to tackle alone. In reality, we probably need each other and even other sentient species, and that includes yeng, if we are going to colonise even a tiny part of this galaxy.

"Hopefully, having raised the prospect of collective benefit, we will be able to start our debate with a really broad theoretical subject and start talking serious science rather than politics.

"We both have many great scientists, but Cheetan have more theoretical mathematicians than we have yeng slaves. It also goes without saying that we can only benefit if Cheetan engineers check every aspect of our project and especially our navigation systems.

"One of the things we must consider is communication. Both our races have been able to build warp speed spacecraft for a couple of generations. We know well that we can only communicate efficiently by sending back messages at increasingly rapid warp speeds as distance grows, and these speeds have to be highly accurate for messages to arrive in the correct relative order and without scrambling distortion caused by variable signal compression.

"Communication can seem impossibly difficult, and as you know, we have to time-code each message relative to others just in case a space-time anomaly causes them to arrive non-sequentially. We Aranian have had problems simply keeping in anything like real time contact with slave-ships around even the relatively close Waterball. We are humble enough to know that we need Cheetan communication technologies and expertise, just as you currently need some of our environment maintenance and manufacturing skills for various domestic projects.

"Far longer journeys across our Galaxy will only compound time-related problems. We have never before sent a mission into space with a live crew that is intended to never return. As we all know, while they travel in the Arcraft's warp bubbles, both physiological time and perceived time will appear to operate just as they do in our period-to-period lives. They will age at their normal biological speed, as will we, but they will have travelled into a different space-time. This will have all sorts of unforeseen physiological and psychological impacts.

"Many theories and contradictory mathematical models of time distortion have resulted from the slowing of time with velocity, and the speeding up of time with gravity. But what does real experience tell us? We see that the time shift can be both a lot smaller and a lot greater than our old mathematical models predicted. Can we factor in the effect of every black hole, hot sun, and inter-star void that any chosen route will pass? ...

"That is enough from me for now. I open the discussion to the floor. And to get you started, I pose some questions. Relative to us, how will the Arcraft crews age? When they arrive at a destination, where will they be in their age line relative to us? What generation of Aranian colonists will we be communicating with in, say, a hundred cycles from now?"

***

Later, the debate shifts to the topic of dependency. Boklung again commands the floor.

"Your attention, please! Some of you have been questioning our dependence on yeng, even at times fearing it. Of course, we are not really leaving everything to the chance behaviour of an unruly race, though for psychological reasons we want them to believe we are. We Aranian, and hopefully some Cheetan, will be travelling as fertilised, frozen eggs.

"Yeng are both psychologically robust and expendable. As we must acknowledge, both our races are less than suited to the mental stress of one-way missions into the unknown. Being in a spacecraft with a low chance of ever even arriving at target, let alone of finding survivable conditions when there, would certainly cause extreme stress.

"The yeng are required to suffer on our behalf. They will try harder to survive if they believe that they are on a journey that takes them out of slavery into a new promised land.

"Now we will have a short recess for the assigned working groups to get to know each other, and to further debate some of the issues that have been raised. For any who haven't yet seen which group they have been allocated to, please see the board in the Assembly Room. When we return at suns-high, Ambassador Hosk, who is an infinitely better mathematician than I am, will lead the discussion.

"You may be interested to know that yeng scientists on Waterball discussed and mathematically modelled many of these issues, and crude though their understanding was, we must all recognise this species as having their own advanced sciences. Remember that yeng have split atoms, travelled space and explored, on some level or another, all the same complex problems that we have. I remind you all of this to help you understand that we really believe that the yeng are suitable as pioneers.

"Anyway, practicalities allow us to seriously consider only crews of yeng, or robots, or both. The Arcraft will have mixed crews of yeng and independently acting 'bots, for now at least. Purely to remind us all of yeng achievements, I've included in your briefing documents a short summary of the work of one particular yeng visionary, Albert Einstein. Some of his basic principles contain distortions or were poorly applied, but he did have a gift for understanding cosmic forces. Our knowledge is far greater and deeper but rarely contradicts his work.

"Just one more note before we disassemble. Of course, there will be Aranians on-board as guarantors of my government's plans. A small group of cryogenically stored adult Aranian will play a key role, when they are restored after a safe landing at destination. After long debate in Council, the establishment of a cryogenically stored force was overwhelmingly supported. We are happy to consider including a contingent of Cheetan in this unit. You may wish to debate the pros and cons of this.

"Enough from me, or else I'll still be talking when the Arcraft departs …"

***

Much later, Boklung returns to The Gardens, and Jack is delivered to zis office.

"Now then, Captain Jack," ze says as ze circles zis buck, looking him over, "you seemed to be recovering well." Ze stops before Jack and gestures to the cushioned lounging boards in the corner of the room.

Jack takes a seat, and Boklung settles at right angles to him.

"I am going to talk to you as an equal and in confidence," ze says.

Jack's eyes widen slightly, but he says nothing.

"I'm sure this will be a surprise to you, especially with our history of broken trust. However, I have to believe in you and that you'll be, outwardly at least, loyal to my vision for our species even if never directly to me.

"You know why I chose to buy you back from the Gantri. If there's any yeng that your kind will listen to, it is you. The Arcraft is all but built, and the composition of the crew is decided. You fly within a few days. I have given the impression of considerable time still being needed, while secretly bringing the launch date well forward. I can't risk a late loss of nerves from our inconsistent and soft-headed Council. Indeed, the conference I have just stepped from was organised more to help me muddle and disguise our imminent launch than for its claimed goal of encouraging broad support.

"I wish that, at the very least, Launch One goes my way. I am not naive enough to believe that I will necessarily have so much control in the future. This time, the steep learning curve and unwillingness of others to get their limbs stuck in have played to my advantage."

Jack nods. "I understand the purpose of the mission, but I don't quite understand why Aranian, um, why you, are going to give we yeng quite so much control … or do I?"

"I'm sure you do. Your intelligence is one of the reasons for your selection. I won't insult you by claiming anything other than that we consider the mission too dangerous for Aranian. However, I think that if I was in your legs I would see this as an opportunity. If the mission is a success then yeng will be its first benefactors. You could even live through a few generations before yeng ever feel the presence of Aranian again."

Jack frowns. "You're putting a lot of trust in your slave species."

"Not so much in your species as in you! If the mission is a success, then other Arcraft will be arriving on your new doorstep and not just to your new outpost of civilisation, but to thousands of other settlements in widely dispersed star systems as well. Your mission is pioneering for all our sentient species. Isn't survival the vital goal for all? We are both valuable creatures deserving of a permanent place in evolution. Millions of species have become extinct, just counting those we have accidentally or deliberately killed off between ourselves. We don't want to be going the same way, do we? As I've often said, 'Isn't even life for a slave generally more tolerable than no life at all?'"

"Sure, I see that, and, at least, being your property, Zir, is better than death. Much better even. Though, as I'm sure you'll agree, slaves are often far less well treated."

Boklung puffs out zis thorax. "Thank you for that, Jack! I try to ensure that excessive cruelty is avoided whatever the species, and I'm sure it is to the advantage of yeng to cooperate. I need a leader capable of bringing yeng onside; a yeng that can see that we both worship the One True God. I need a leader with the vision to see that this universe has room for all and probably needs all our sentient species."

Jack smiles. "I'm your man. Unlike many of us, I don't hate Aranian. Though I do hate slavery, I can separate the two. Your species is no more destructive of other life-forms than is ours, and possibly less so. You can be certain I'll cooperate, provided that at all points I feel that we really are a part of your vision for the future. Even so, I'm not so naive as to believe that we're more than a secondary concern to the survival of your race."

Boklung stretches zis lower limbs before zim and raises zis eyestalks in a challenge. "I'll not consider the possibility that you or an equally cunning member of your crew might have theoretically cut-short the life of one of us. If I knew that you had, that would be the end, but I won't ever know, will I?"

Jack supresses a smile. "Hypothetically speaking, I understand. What race would think differently? I'm fortunate in having such a wise boss, one that understands the subtleties of my language as well as I do. If I'd been killed, you would've lost a popular leader of yeng and not just an arguably lucky hunter. That would not have been in either race's interest. And if I did unjustly kill, Zir, I would only be damaging all our hopes."

"Exactly! Now, I demand that all yeng on the Arcraft go through the motions of worshipping Sinanna. I really believe we worship the same God, under different names. If yeng can accept that Aranian are created in the image of God, then a proper understanding can be forever established between our species. I'm sure that I don't care how many legs God has, but I, as do you, need to be pragmatic. We need a common doctrine that suggests God is seen as having no legs or variable numbers to suit Zis whim. The robot systems on-board will have little control over much other than navigation. But two things they will be programmed to control are any obvious sign of serious religious divergence, and activity that look to be to the disadvantage of Lush System species. I've no idea how a robot can be programmed to understand such subtleties, but I'm assured it will be done."

"Well, I'm hardly a pious believer, but I've no objection to God having ten, or as yeng count, eight legs. I agree it's important that we all believe in the One God, and after all, apart from our individual belief in our own importance to God, our doctrines are very similar. So all you're really asking is for us to take seriously a single doctrine that's based on common sense.

"The truth be known, Zir, many of us have long accepted that the One God can take any form Ze wishes. The simple fact of discovering that we're less than unique as an advanced species, and not the most powerful, has already changed yeng views of the Almighty. Only a fool of a yeng still holds to the idea that God must look like man, or in truth, even like Aranian. We all worship the One God, and that's all the critical information that matters beyond our survival."

Boklung's eyes sparkle, pleased that Jack is fulfilling zis expectations. "Yes, and it isn't the number of legs that defines God, whatever the shape of our religious icons. Our philosophers acknowledge that we have no clearer vision of the Creator than have you, however we chose to represent Zim. All we know for sure is that we can't fathom a Multiverse without a Creator."

Jack nods again, and Boklung continues. "Do you also understand that we are close to having exhausted this planet, just as you sucked so much out of Waterball?"

"Yes, Zir, yeng are aware of such things. We learn, as do your young, from Aranian books. We learn your language and history, just as some of your scholars learn a little of ours."

"Yes. I have long understood how much beyond what is necessary to a slave is absorbed by yeng, though it is perhaps best that most Aranian are blind to your species' depth of understanding. If the true equality of things were widely known, then sending out a mission dominated by such an animal as you might never be passed by the Council. The politicians need to maintain their arrogant belief in our absolute and broad superiority. In public, I actively encourage this view while encouraging you to select yeng that are well educated as well as physiologically robust."

Jack grimaces. "Personally, I'd rather not be the only arbiter of selection. I could generate enemies by not picking family, for example. Enemies which as future leader I'm unlikely to be able to afford.

Though I see the sense in me choosing at least some of the crew, the job's best shared. I guarantee to do my best to weld all those chosen, whether by you, me or others, into a strong team.

"Both physical and mental robustness should be our first consideration; however, there are one or two individuals I'd like to choose that might in some way fall short of general standards."

"You do a good job for me, Spartacus, then I won't interfere with your selections."

Jack smiles. "I could never have hoped to be owned by such a great Aranian as you, Zir."

29

SUBVERSION AND REVOLT

Athalie is aware of three things in the same moment: a pounding headache, an irregular knocking and a swinging shadow above her. Next, as her eyes focus, she sees a bucket, swishing from side to side. Then she starts to feel numbing cold.

Athalie struggles to move from under the path of the now descending bucket. She fights the water, hands splashing, and brings herself up against the wall of what she's now relieved to recognise as the base of the well. She hauls herself up onto a narrow shelf at the foot of a wooden ladder and stares up at a circle of dull light high above. A deep shiver runs through her, brought on by the twin grips of fear and cold.

Slowly, Athalie's higher mind regains control over her brain's instinctive reactions and turns her initial perception of the shine of a cloud-obscured sun into that of artificial light from the top of the well.

I must have blacked out, but I got here. That's the easy bit done ... Do I wait, or do I climb now? Now. It'd be a pity to get so far only to die of cold.

After rubbing her hands and feet to restore circulation, Athalie gingerly starts to climb the ladder. The structure is at first precarious, half-rotted; however, it becomes more solid as she continues upwards. The bucket speeds past her, dripping water into her eyes. Her biggest problem is pain from her injured knee.

What do I do when I get to the top? Wait 'til everything's quiet then try to slip out unnoticed? I could hide in the shadows on the far side of the well. I pray they're dark enough to hide me.

Has whoever hauled up the bucket moved away? Perhaps the overseers are mostly asleep. I'll risk a peek. Yes, all looks quiet, except I need to exit on the side away from this ladder. How do I do that? If I climb out here, I am going to be in full sight of all the cages. Someone is sure to holler out on seeing me. I have to work my way around the rim. Well, it's feasible. Perhaps I can use the rope? ... No, I can't reach it. There's nothing for it. I'm not scared of heights, just of falling! Come on, be brave, let go of the ladder, now shuffle, shuffle. Oh shit! Something's coming.

A loud squeak heralds the bucket's descent yet again.

This'd better be quick. I can't hang on here forever. Damn knee's giving in; come on, fight it. Just a bit further; that ledge looks better.

While the creek of the winding gear muffles her movements, she makes herself safe, then waits for all to be quiet again.

What happens if I'm caught ... before my death? I'm more scared of the process of dying than death itself. I love Jack so much I feel that a part of me is already a part of him. What remains of me is meaningless without the whole, the whole—us together. But it is more than that, isn't it. We've only been together once, a few stolen moments in a damp cell, yet I know I'm carrying his child. Is it wrong to risk the life inside me? Am I selfish? No. All I know is that love drives me, gives me no choice.

All becomes quiet.

Time to go. Aagh—shit—that's all I need; my knee hurts like ... Come on, you can do it.

Eyes averted so as not to signal her presence with their whites, she silently drops to the ground and scampers away like a mouse, looking for one of the wraps that most of the Gantri yeng wear. She looks close to the stacked cadavers, which often have clothing stripped from them. She badly needs to get some warmth into her limbs.

Athalie hears someone panting, peeks around a corner, then jolts back, stifling a gasp. An oversexed overseer is pleasuring himself with a corpse, and Athalie's pretty sure it's that of a child.

I'm going to vomit ... No, I'll find a knife to open his throat. What then. Flaming hell, he is going to die, and this brick will have to suffice. He is coming to climax; no, never.

Whack.

Now, stove in his temple before he revives

DUMPppph.

That was more satisfying than killing even a spider. What is more, this bastard has a set of keys. First, let me close the poor child's eyes.

Fuck—I've been seen. Well, then what better can I do than run to Jack's cage?

"Hey, stop that prisoner. A prisoner is out. Stop her!"

Shit, the floor's slippery; run.

"After her."

"Ouch!" *I'll run past the cage, leaving the keys in the nearest hand. Come on.*

"Hide them well," she says, then scans the cage's occupants. "Where's Jack? Jack! I can't see you."

"Run, girl; he isn't here," the man says.

"Is he dead?"

"Run!"

Her mind's in a spin, but she runs. Heavy footfalls draw ever closer. She slips again as a guard lashes out with a chain.

Fuck! My knee!

Athalie takes the force of a heavy chain across her neck and back. It slams her, unconscious, into the concrete floor.

Her assailant catches up, puts his hands on his knees, panting, then makes a point of kicking the head of the slumped girl. Other overseers gather around. "The bitch killed Thomo," he says to everyone and no one.

"Where the hell did she come from?" another overseer asks.

A third voice replies, "I reckon I saw a shadow come out the well, like some bleeding water nymph. I just didn't believe my eyes."

A fourth overseer laughs and lifts his 'toga'. "I've never had a water-nymph."

"Nymphomaniac," the first man says, and they all laugh.

Even as she lies unconscious, Athalie plays a vital distracting role, a part which the overseers see past far too late. Already, Jack's old cage is empty and the keys are being worked on the next. The first skirmish is brief, as a heavy tide of slaves head towards the main gates. In the second wave, strong arms lift Athalie from amongst the corpses of the guards. The flow of ragged slaves breaks out into the streets, causing panic among spiders and yeng alike.

Castus knows where he should be going. He feels fortunate that the breakout happened without him having to risk instigating it. He isn't sure he could've made it happen, even with the help of Clanten's other agents.

He follows the escape route already planned, shouting for his friends to follow, and holding Athalie like a sack across one shoulder. While the melee charges down the street towards the centre of the city, half a dozen gladiators keep tight against the arena's wall until they find a sewer grate. Now Castus has to work out how to get aboard the spacecraft with his secret loyalty to Clanten guarded; at least until he learns which way the wind blows.

30

YENG SELECTION

While Athalie is climbing the walls of the well, Jack is a couple of kilometres away in The Gardens talking to Osterphelia, whom Boklung has already selected to help with training. Jack is heavily bandaged but manages to get around without help. The pair have already caught up with each other's recent history.

"Okay then," Jack says, "helping Boklung find a good crew is easy. But what are we going to do about all our friends, and about the limited numbers we can select?"

"We do the best we can for as many as we can," Phelia replies. She tilts her head and peers at him. "You've got a bit of a grimace on your face; how's your wound, Jack? Would you like me to look at it?"

Jack winks. "No, its fine, really. Maybe later, if we get a little privacy!"

Phelia rolls her eyes. "Do you ever think of anything but sex? You're just addicted to having every other female you see ... I know you toy with me. Anyway, Jack, even if I was tempted, I'm not playing second fiddle to anyone, especially Athalie. Which reminds me. When Boklung said ze was bringing you in, ze actually suggested that I was free to 'use' you as I wished. Haha. My own stud on a lead, ... I wish!"

"Haaah! How could I have refused? Athalie to cuddle and you for a bit of fun. Seriously, have you heard anything? I

268

thought you might have some information. I haven't seen her since Boklung allowed me to have a 'medical' visitor to my prison cell. I'm really worried. I never thanked you enough for being so kind as to choose to send her, by the way."

"Don't be worried. No one has seen her recently, but she won't be far away. My guess is that Boklung has her working with an isolated group of pigs in the new experimental unit."

"Well, I hope I see her soon. She means a lot to me."

"It's only been two retreats since you returned. Be patient. I bet you she'll be with you before long."

"Hmm. I hear we have no chance of securing my friend Kayla for the Arcraft."

"I'm afraid not, Jack. Um ... That reminds me, I didn't want to tell you, but actually Storm hasn't seen Athalie either."

Jacks eyebrows knit together. "Now I really am worried. He works with her, right?"

"Don't fret. We have no reason to believe anything bad has happened to her. I only told you about Storm to save you the wasted time of chasing him up. Do you know the final fitting out of the Arcraft has begun? A giant hangar suddenly became available when an industrialist was found dead. There are rumours that ze was poisoned with contaminated meats. I'd be very surprised if zis sudden demise had nothing to do with events. I've been told that the craft will be undergoing pressure and electrical systems trials within a few periods. It seems unbelievable, but Boklung has indicated to me that the launch is far more imminent than most Aranian think. It's as though Boklung is trying to take everyone by surprise."

Jack and Phelia stop their conversation and turn in the direction of many voices shouting and the rat tat tat of guns.

"What the heck's all that racket?" Jack says. "Sounds like it's coming from the stadium."

Phelia's eyes grow wide. "Is that gunfire?"

Jack nods. "Sounds like a riot by the gladiators. What else could it be? Maybe we should go."

"No, it's not our fight! We have work to do here, work that might give mankind some real freedom. The spiders will supress any uprising soon enough, and our sacrifice for that cause won't help anyone."

Jack stares towards the Gantri and shakes his head. "But I should go."

"Oh no you don't!" Her voice takes on a commanding tone anyone would find hard to disobey. "This is where you're needed, selecting the best crew you can, and then possibly trying to get some of the slaves on-board that are sure to be lined up for punishment when whatever's happening is over. There can only be one ending to any rebellion by yeng in this city, Jack, and well you know it. We gather the largest contingent we dare under the noses of the Aranian, including our friends. We have to assume that the best chance of a future is for those that go, right?"

"Yes, but what do you know of the legend of Spartacus? Many believe I can make a difference, and perhaps with the help of that legacy I really can. Maybe by joining the rebels now, I can inspire them to victory."

"My mother told me a little, and what I know of Spartacus is that he ultimately failed and was crucified by the Romans. Need I say more? Come now, Jack, we have work to do and not a lot of time. Save the legend for when it can bring permanent results. Let's choose a crew capable not of the impossible task of taking a city, but rather of keeping a spacecraft from the control of its builders."

Jack grimaces and turns back towards the ruckus.

Phelia grabs his arm. He turns back, and she looks at him with steely eyes. "We have to understand what this is about; it's the survival of our kind as an independent race, not as slaves forever in this God-forsaken solar system. We mustn't lose focus on selecting those with skills that'll help us survive. Hell, life is bearable here, under some slave owners at least, but freedom is everything. The Arcraft represents new opportunity even if it doesn't immediately offer the sort of freedom we all wish for."

Jack sighs. "Yeah, I guess you're right, Phelia. But there's something I won't be diverted from; I have to go and see if

Athalie's returned to the pig unit. She may have come back since you spoke to Storm."

"Fine, I can't stop you! But I'm coming too. We can discuss the selection on the way, and I'll make sure you stay in The Gardens. We need to be back in the office before curfew."

"Come on then. If I have to have a chaperone she may as well be one I fancy."

"Cut the crap! You bloody sex maniac."

They arrive at the piggery a short time later.

"Storm," Jack asks, "is she here?"

The tired-looking young man shakes his head. "I wish. I've had to do everything on my own."

"Okay. When you see her, tell her I called, and ask her to report to the main assembly area as soon as she can. And you, if you want a chance of being on the Arcraft, then go with her."

"Not me! I'm keeping both feet on the ground, but I'll tell her. Good luck, Mr Spartacus, Phelia."

Phelia replies for them both, "Thanks, and when you see Kayla again, give her a hug from us both. We need to get back. Whatever happens, make sure Athalie finds us as soon as possible; got it?"

"Got it ... but, um ... this selection ... is it really as simple as me telling her to go to the assembly ground?"

"Athalie will be an animal expert on-board," Jack replies. "And you'll presumably be promoted by being given your own help."

***

Phelia has no intention of leaving behind any more of her and Jack's friends than they're forced to. She's already spent a lot of her free moments tracking down individuals and persuading them to try and find a way to board the Arcraft. A group has gathered in Phelia's hut, and are keeping a low profile while they try to devise a way of getting into the spacecraft immediately prior to launch. Pretty soon this group has grown to nearly twenty, including Cantonia, Scunthorpe, Estrellathree and Peter Finch. After more searching, Phelia manages to bring in Anton. A now mature and somewhat heavier Pugwash, who had made zis home below the hut floor boards a long while ago, is an honorary addition to the team. The hut smells like a farmyard, what with the number of people crammed within its walls, especially with Pugwash under the floor.

Cantonia arrives at the hut with the news that a party of escapes are hiding in the sewers. Phelia challenges Cantonia on her past cooperation with Boklung. She admits spying for zim but promises her loyalty to the group. Cantonia also passes on other information her spying skills have brought her. She reports that not only are Boklung and Clanten in a sort of alliance, but that Castus, a leader of the band in the sewers, is one of Clanten's spies from the arena. Later, Phelia sends Cantonia with Anton and Pugwash to try to establish contact with the hiding gladiators.

In idle moments, Jack becomes increasingly amazed about the way so many different 'happenings' seem to be so closely connected. Everything from his remarkable survival to the growing commonality of purpose between him and Phelia, to the tight dovetailing of events between diverse slaves and spiders, seems to be working together towards an inevitable destiny. He prays that Athalie is following the self-same path. He looks to the sky, wondering who exactly is orchestrating events. He can't help thinking that, at least, some half-important angel must be involved. He thinks of some corny book in which suddenly every disconnected fact is made to fit with logic cast to the wind.

31

THE GATHERING OF CREW

A couple of sleep cycles later, Osterphelia and Jack are back in Boklung's office while their master is engaged elsewhere. Jack looks miserable and distant, which makes Phelia worry about the weight of responsibilities and the more private concerns he's carrying.

"Come on now, Jack. We need you at your best, not contemplating your navel. We have a lot of work to get through. We've had it confirmed that a few gladiators are hidden in the sewers, and Cantonia is doing her best to re-new contact with them."

"Do we know how many there are?"

"Cantonia said there were about thirty of them."

Jack snorts. "Who's thirty?"

"Good question. But remember, however they're counted, they may not all be human. Apparently, many cages were opened before the spiders got back in control. Another group's assembling in my quarters in The Gardens, and you'll be pleased to hear that I have both Anton and Pugwash. Actually, smelly old Pugwash has been living under the floor of my hut for most of the time you've been a guest of the Gantri."

That brings a smile to Jack's face. "That's fantastic, you mean Anton and even Pugwash may be able to get aboard?"

273

"I hope so. I've sent them off with Cantonia to establish proper contact with Castus's group."

"Great news! What about the other survivors? What else haven't you yet told me?"

"Um, well; you know most of what I do ... but there is one other thing I wasn't sure whether to tell you."

"Well?"

"Apparently, the outbreak was started by a woman who broke into the Gantri. Castus said she went in to free you."

"You mean ... Athalie? ... Is it possible?"

"I can't say. But it's another reason not to give up hope of seeing her again."

"I can't believe it. I don't know whether to laugh or cry. Just the idea that someone broke in is incredible."

"Not just broke in. Broke in and started a rebellion."

Jack grins. "And I thought I was a high achiever! If Castus is involved in all this, she might be one of the thirty. He was one of very few guards respectful of us prisoners. What's more, I actually told Athalie that Castus was one she could trust. We have lots to do, Phelia. Let's get moving. If any Gantri trustees were accepted by the rebels as one of them, it'll be him and possibly his blue three-legged friend."

Phelia's eyes sparkle. "That's more like the Spartacus of legend. Come on, Jack. Whatever's happened to Athalie, she wouldn't want you moping about her."

"Will Castus try to get his group on the ship? He might have other plans?"

"I think he'd see it as a must-try. It never occurred to me that he wouldn't, but I could be wrong; I never even considered that any yeng wouldn't want to go. Two things, though; if Athalie's with him, she'll convince him, I'm sure. The other I'm not sure about, but I think our fates are linked somehow, Castus, you, me and Athalie. I can't explain. It's just a feeling; don't think me mad. But Castus was a gladiator before an overseer; fate must have already conspired to keep him alive."

"If you're mad, so am I, because I feel much the same way. I've trusted Castus from the start. I don't know why. I've never even talked to him—talk between gladiator and overseer is never easy—but I respect him and know he respects me. We had a natural bond in the Gantri; two advocates for the prisoners. That was a brave stance for him to take amongst the deviant horde of trustees—friends in high places or not."

***

Boklung walks into the arena with Borstave, Jack and Osterphelia. There, prisoners from the rebellion are being held in a temporary cage under unshielded suns. Clearly, many inmates are rapidly succumbing to the conditions, adding to a growing pile of those that have died from old wounds or new fighting.

All the yeng prisoners have chains connecting necks and both ankles. There are at least a couple of hundred fit yeng in the vast cage, plus as many in the group of dying and corpses. All those still alive are yeng. There is even a dead yargord in the middle of the cage. It appears that yengkind hadn't been prepared to share their accommodation.

The representative of the Gantri delegated to negotiate with Boklung is no other then Dunkuin, one of the creatures Boklung has been trying to influence. Ze waits for them with a couple of Aranian soldiers and shakes with what appears to be genuine fear when ze sees Boklung approach. Boklung has learnt enough about Dunkuin's unsavoury sadomasochistic perversions to mean that ze is certain to agree to any demands. Boklung exchanges greetings with the governor, followed by a whispered private conversation as they stroll towards the pen.

Boklung has convinced officials that the Arcraft mission means almost certain death for the yeng, but simply by another means. With that assurance, permission to select from the cages of rebels and escapees recaptured from the wilds has been granted. Anyway, Clamfusk, the Gantri's chief, is holding to zis secret agreement to handing some rebels over to Boklung in return for a very large shipment of the strongest zoongrass.

Boklung and Dunkuin stop at the door of the cage. The two soldiers join them, followed by Borstave, Jack and Osterphelia.

Boklung turns to the chief guard and holds out a slip of paper. "Officer, here is my permission to take a number of prisoners. The number is discretionary, isn't it, Dunkuin?"

Dunkuin nods.

"My yeng slaves will select most of them. I struggle to identify one from another."

"They all look the same to me as well, Zir," the guard replies. "Stand back from the bars, yeng, or else none of you get out. Only move forward when you are pointed out. Those selected will be allowed through the gate one at a time."

Jack walks around the cage. A middle-aged man stoops to lift a body then steps to the bars so that Jack can see them both more clearly.

"I'm Thomas Griffiths, Sir ... um ... this is selection for the Arc, right?"

"Yes, and you, Thomas, what skill?"

"I'm a farmer, both here and on Earth. And this girl in my arms, she ... ah … um ..."

"Is one we can do nothing for," Jack says quietly. "If you can leave her, you may approach the gate."

Boklung interrupts: "Osterphelia, you choose one, then Jack. You need to explain your reasoning if you take any that I think look too old, fragile or badly injured."

"We need medics," Phelia says, "especially any with real Earth training."

A middle-aged gladiator steps forward. "I was a paramedic; Western Australia."

"Who can vouch for you?"

"I can," a man replies. "He saved my life when I was poisoned by a triffid."

"What's your name?" Jack asks. "And what skills do you have?"

"Stefan. Nothing much other than being a gladiator, but I have a knack for sniffing out those that lie to save their skins."

Jack raises an eyebrow. "Sorry, I can't select you, but I'd appreciate your help judging those who volunteer."

"That'll be an honour, Spartacus."

"A space mission needs many skills," Phelia says, "We need people trained as scientists and technologists."

"I'm a physicist," one man says. He points to the man beside him. "And this man helped me stay alive; he's Jamanuran, a mathematician."

Jack looks at Stefan. He nods.

"You two can go," Phelia says.

They continue in this fashion until they've creamed the cage of its most skilled. Then Jack turns, saying, "Stefan, you will be my staff sergeant. Step forward."

The man's grin reaches from ear to ear. "Thank you, Sir."

"Right then," Boklung says, "let's hurry away before our fortune changes with some petty official finding fault with procedures. Borstave, Phelia, take these slaves straight to the hangar. Get them fed and watered and start training as soon as possible. As for you, Captain Jack, follow me. We have a lot to do between now and the launch."

***

In the sewers under the Nuzkarflux suburb, the depleted band of rebel gladiators plan their future. Most are in favour of trying to get aboard the Arcraft, whilst a few plan to head for the bush and a life trying to keep one step in front of Aranian hunters.

Castus has reported his meetings with Cantonia from The Gardens and introduced Anton and his pet to the group. Timing seems to be the key to likely success. What they need most now is to find a contact that has access to the hangar and who can keep them supplied with progress reports.

The slowly recovering Athalie has already renewed her friendship with Pugwash. She strokes zim as she talks. "I plan to use this low-light to get back to The Gardens. I need to see for myself that Jack's alive, and we need to make contact with those there that can help co-ordinate our moves. I'd like one of you to go with me."

"I'll be happy to, Athalie," Castus says. "But are you fit enough?"

"I'm fine. And the group needs you here, Castus." She turns to a solidly-built man with a deeply lined face. "Capolla, if you stay here you'll only quarrel with Castus and probably try to eat Pugwash. So could you help me? You're our best soldier, not to mention our strongest. And besides, you're one of the few that've earned the respect of Spartacus."

Castus's eyes narrow. "How do you know you can trust me?"

"We'll all fail if we can't trust each other. Anyway, I do know that despite your own influence you were loyal to Spartacus while he led your cage. I trust you'll keep that loyalty. And Jack would've chosen you take command of the cage if he could've been there to say."

"Why do you say that?"

"He can see quality, just as I can." *Gads, I can talk some crap.*

"Hell, woman, this is just female guile, but I won't take orders from any trustee, ex or not, not now, not ever, so I might as well go with you."

"Good, that's settled."

"Good luck, Capolla," Castus says. "We may never be friends, but we need not be enemies."

"I'll accept that, for now. I can kill you later."

Athalie heads off through the sewers with Capolla following reluctantly. She stops when she feels they must be somewhere close to The Gardens, and locates a hatch in the sewer ceiling. "Here, help me lift this storm cover." She climbs a few steps up a ladder on the wall and reaches up.

"I don't like this," Capolla says. "There'll be spiders up there."

"If you don't like it, I can't stop you turning back, but I need you to help get this lid open."

Capolla looks further down the sewer.

"Are you going to help me or what?"

"Shit, I smell gas, and not from what we're covered in. We need to go back and fast. It'll kill us."

"I'm not going; help me budge the cover, then go."

Capolla reaches up and gives the hatch a shove. It lifts enough to let in a glimmer of light. Athalie smiles and helps push it open. "Now run; warn the others."

"Here, take this." He hands her a metal bar. "I can run faster without it. And who knows, you might even break a spider's toenail before you die."

"Go, damn you; run!"

Capolla takes off back in the direction from which they came, while Athalie gulps air from as far into the open air as she can stretch. Then, coughing, she clambers up, only to catch the strip of cloth tied around her hips on the half-rusted edge of the rim. A cloud of green gas spirals around her as she yanks on the cloth. After a couple of tries, the fabric finally rips free and, leaving part of it still impaled, she staggers away and falls to her knees, retching bile.

When her stomach stops heaving, she looks around to get her bearings and makes out some of The Gardens' accommodation huts. She also sees a couple of spiders, luckily distracted and hampered by gas masks, pouring liquid into a culvert two hundred metres along the line of the sewer. She looks back to The Gardens, and through streaming eyes, manages to make out what she prays is Osterphelia's hut away in the distance across a potato field. With her vision failing, she staggers across the muddy ridged-up ground.

***

Meanwhile Capolla runs for his life. For such a heavy man he does very well, but the natural ventilation of the sewer draws the gas ever closer. He knows he may have made a fatal decision.

The bloody spiders must have tracked us to the sewers. Fucking chips!

He trips once, then lifts himself, face covered in faeces, and charges on again. Every metre seems to be getting longer as he heads towards the other gladiators. He falls again, grasping his aching arm, even as he glimpses the others. He manages a choking scream: "Gas! Castu ..." As he blacks out he thinks it strange that he took the trouble to warn Castus.

Castus sucks in all the air he can and belts up the sewer closely followed by the Choochin. Together, they grab and lift Capolla, and drag the heavy man towards the others, who've disappeared down the recently identified side passage that runs roughly in the direction of the spaceport. When they make the junction, other hands help them through. By good fortune, the air in the side pipe draws towards the rapidly thickening cloud of yengicide. The whole party is following Anton and his fiercely guarded suvaran as they hurry up the pipe against the flow of effluents. The Choochin, seemingly almost unaffected by the chemical fog, helps the coughing and vomiting Castus and unconscious Capolla away to safety.

A couple of kilometres away Athalie knocks on the door of the hut and collapses. As unconsciousness drifts over her she prays that the baby inside her is unharmed.

Scunthorpe opens the door and, hoping that no spider turns, drags her inside.

32

THE LAUNCH

Only a huis has passed since the final structural assembly was completed, but that has been enough time to get the Arcraft prepared. So, just four Earth-months after Athalie had heaved the corpse of the strangled guard out of the Gantri under the very noses of the spiders, she has led those hiding in Phelia's hut through the sewers to join up with Castus.

Much earlier, Cantonia, whilst out scavenging food for the hut, had met an old aquaintance, Jesus Sanz, who was ensconced in a 'den' at the back of a market shed, busy stripping down a tag scanner. Knowing, as she immediately had, how valuable his skills might turn out to be, she would be delighted if she knew that Jesus had followed her advice to head for the hangar.

Boklung, Hosk, and just about every other important mover and shaker from the city, and many dignitaries from other states, gather to witness the suddenly rescheduled launch of Arcraft One. The official yeng crew have long been aboard, and the space tugs are being organised to begin the long haul of pulling the giant craft into the beyond. Launch control begins the final countdown.

Athalie has yet to be reunited with Jack, because he hasn't been allowed off the Arcraft since the day they selected what rebels they could from the cage in the Arena. Boklung is determined to keep zis controversial Captain out of the public gaze. Jack doesn't even know for sure that Athalie is alive and well, having to trust the honesty of third-party reports. And only Athalie knows that, all being well, Jack is a father.

If those Aranian and Cheetan dignitaries standing with Boklung knew that Jack Baker captained the Arcraft, they would almost certainly have a collective fit. As far as the vast majority of dignitaries are concerned, the Arcraft is still being operated entirely by carefully programmed 'bots.

Celebrations are proceeding apace. To witnesses such a seminal event in the history of the Lush System is seen as a privilege. Boklung is trying to remain upbeat, whilst fearing that the yeng could yet doom the project if they should decide travelling isn't in their best interest. None of the dignitaries, not even Boklung and Hosk, know that a band of feral yeng, including hardened gladiators, are planning to fight their way aboard at the last minute, when the countdown becomes irreversible. Boklung has had no good reason to doubt the Gantri owner's claim that all the rebels from the original outbreak have been accounted for. Phelia has used all her guile to kept her crowded hut a secret even from most other slaves, and certainly from certain trustees and the spiders.

Boklung and Jack skirted around, secretly adding to the yeng crew. Without ever authorising stowaways, Boklung had, however, left Jack in no doubt that ze would turn a blind eye. Ze had also quite deliberately told Jack and Phelia that the Aranian guards would be withdrawn for their safety a while before the launch countdown started. Ze expects some late additions, even though ze has no idea who they might be. However, Boklung would never consider a battle charge, to get on-board, tolerable.

The robots are programmed to suppress any yeng that show signs of aggression. Sudden extra numbers could send 'bot alarm bells ringing. Fighting would be a likely outcome. Any activity that threatens the launch is sure to give Boklung the deepest concern and puts zis authority into question.

Ze was already taut with tension before the launch countdown started. Now the pressure mounts. The whole mission may hang on a single thread, and a yeng one at that. Spartacus, as now even Boklung is inclined to call him, may just be the only glue that can hold the plan together.

Boklung turns to zis friend Hosk, and whispers, "If all this goes wrong, will you be willing to give me sanctuary on Trogaffin?"

"Of course. But it won't. You forget that all our sentient species have much to gain from this process. Even if the worst happens, if your worst fears are realised, a chance remains of our eggs being delivered safely, by automated systems, to another world. That would mean maintaining control from here, but we could get the Arcraft out of this sun system and establish a flight path before we lost total control. Remember, Boklung, that even if all those currently living on the craft die, that the craft is still programmed to deliver Aranian eggs. It is almost irrelevant who is aboard, provided the launch goes ahead."

"Yes, I know you are theoretically correct, my friend; it is just my nerves. Anyway, there will be other missions. But I hope that Spartacus doesn't lose control. That yeng has been a complete revelation to me. He has independently come to see things much as I do. One of the last things he said to me at our last strategy meeting was, 'We will all eventually fail in taming this universe working against each other. Progress needs all our skills, all our genetic diversity, all our sentient powers, working together. Even that may not be enough.' Supposing they found our eggs without Spartacus being there. They would understand the depth of our duplicity without his wisdom to ameliorate their deepened concerns."

"Spartacus will live," Hosk reassures zim. "We must believe that. Anyway, the only other yeng that know anything of the uniquely constructed components containing the seeds of our futures are now on a transporter destined for my planet. What is more, the construction teams are going to be split up between several separate self-contained factory units. There is no way that word can get back and spread to yeng on this planet, let alone to billions of kilometres out in space to the Arcraft. Finding the eggs without knowing of their existence and then actively looking for them is extremely unlikely."

"You are certain none of the builders remained aboard?"

"I'm certain. Or rather, I am certain that if any remained, they are no longer alive. Remember, Boklung, that Cheetan engineers had the craft fumigated with yengicide before the crew was allowed on, and the hangar has been extremely well guarded."

"Yes, I must be positive. As uneasy as I was with your harsh decision to cleanse the craft, I do see that it might have been necessary. The new colony will be established. We must have faith. How could Sinanna, sentients' Ceator, not want all sentient species, all Zis children, working towards the future? How could the Creator wish to lose any of Zis intelligent inventions?"

"Do I point out to the obstinate royal dictators that run my planet that a small future Cheetan population may escape their hegemony? Hggaaaah … my friend, I think not."

"Haarg, haarg. And do I tell my race that the Cheetan built into the Arcraft more than just some of their advanced technological systems?"

"Hasss, Hssss, my friend. Not a bit of it. You were clever indeed to programme only cooperative history between our two planets into the robotic computer systems. We keep our secrets from our home planets. They should remain ignorant for now of what we have potentially achieved. The racists of both our systems will roll in their graves, knowing that we, between us, have potentially created a racial equality that may last for all time. A harmony that hopefully survives long after our Lush System has been reduced to cosmic dust."

"And for the yeng?" Boklung asks.

"The future of the yeng may rest in the hands of Spartacus. I hope they follow a suitable path. I feel a growing affection for that funny species, an affection only paralleled by their love of what they call dogs."

"Oh, yes." Boklung nods. "I have never known a more loyal and lovable creature on four limbs. I slipped some aboard along with more familiarly useful Waterball species."

"Hagggggh." The Cheetan's mouth widens slightly. "I'm pleased to hear that. Have you seen my cage of spaniels, Boklung? You really must. If only we could engineer them to live more than half a cycle."

"I haven't seen yours," Boklung says, "but I am familiar with the species. You Cheetans are softer creatures than I ever would have believed. Keeping pets. Has your regimented planet become as soft as ours?"

"Hggh! Not yet, just me and a few fringe individuals for now. I fear I've lived here too long … Keep calm Boklung—look, the monitors suggest that so far disaster has been averted."

"Yes … Thanks for distracting me, my friend. It is difficult being totally dependent on other's fates. Look, the tugs are starting to move into position, a new chapter in the history of the Lush System has really begun. We must assume success." Boklung picks up a glass of bubbling liquid and hands another to Hosk. "To Aranian, to Cheetan, to yeng, to dodarks and dogs; let us drink to our future."

"To our species!" The creatures take a swig of their drinks. "This is a fine hippotian, Boklung; from which regions did you source it?"

"Waterball, my friend. It is just a little inebriating. A most popular concoction amongst yeng. They call it champagne."

Suddenly, a controller runs from the control room onto the balcony where the dignitaries are assembled.

"Boss Boklung. Boss! There's trouble in the hangar. Yeng fighters are trying to get aboard."

Now Boklung really panicked.

33

YENG MASTERS

A debate has been raging in the sewers for days between disparate groups of rebels. Castus eventually persuaded those that wished to stay on Ungoliantis to move off and find their own hiding place. Phelia had managed to sneak back to her hut before being constrained as completely as Jack from leaving the Arcraft. There, she found Cantonia alone, having remained behind to guard the others' backs when they headed down into the sewers. Phelia passed on information, directly from Boklung, that the launch was planned for just sixteen periods' time.

She also passed on details about security movements planned prior to the launch and the incredible news that Boklung and Jack were actually allied in deception, though Cantonia took some convincing. When Cantonia eventually accepted everything that Phelia had to say, she felt relieved that her loyalty to Boklung wasn't being compromised by her recent support for the rebels. She especially reflected on the fact that she had come within a whisker of shooting Jack dead after he felled Koolsverne only a few Ungolian months before. The real reason for her reticence and regular estrangement from the yeng rebels was now nullified. She looked forward in the hope of re-establishing her relationship with Peter Finch. Cantonia laughed to herself, remembering all her sneaking backwards and forwards between Boklung and various groups of yeng.

Once Phelia has left, Cantonia leaves the hut, shutting the door carefully behind her, and sets off to her now true allies.

***

Underground, near a culvert that sits inside the hangar, sit a group of yeng, including Castus, Capolla, Phelia and the recently arrived Cantonia.

Capolla frowns in reaction to Phelia's words. "So you maintain that Boklung has given a sort of tacit approval to extra yeng getting aboard, and that Jack and Boklung have actually planned for this, together."

She nods. The other yeng's faces indicate various states of confusion mixed with hope and suspicion.

"Hell," Capolla continues, "we've been arguing about this for two full-lights. I struggle with some of it, but I guess it's time to trust, even though I never do."

"I find it hard to believe as well, and I'm the bleeding messenger. But the time to act is now. I've heard that spider soldiers will be withdrawn just before the final countdown, and now there's proof." She points up through the grate. "See for yourselves. The place has been milling with spiders, but where are they all now?"

Capolla stands and squints through the metal. "I can't really see much through this."

Cantonia stands beside him. "Yeah, but their numbers are definitely down. We have to go now or the ship'll be sealed before we can get on-board."

"Why should we trust you?"

Cantonia raises her voice in frustration. "I don't really give a shit; I'm going and so are my group. Anton, Estrella, and Athalie are with me; sod the rest of you. Let's go."

"Well, we can't live in this luxury forever," Castus says. "And it's time for me to come clean. I'm a spy for the Aranain Councillor Clanten, and ze told me to gather rebels down here.

287

We were meant to be invited aboard, but that isn't going to happen. Maybe Boklung and Clanten don't quite see eye to eye. Anyway, believe it or not, Clanten encouraged my breakout from the Gantri. I don't know why, but it all makes a sort of crazy sense. We have to trust fate. I'm following Cantonia and Athalie. Everyone has to decide for themselves. Come on, Capolla, if you come, most of these reprobates will too."

Scunthorpe pipes up, "Okay, let's do it."

Capolla glares at Castus. "You bastard, Castus, I knew you were a two faced son of a bitch. Working for the spiders; gads. Boklung, Clanten, Spartacus, Phelia, fuck it, perhaps even Sinanna's in on this. How the fuck can we fail? It's like some crazy future has been ordained. Half the nutters on the planet in some secret alliance, the whole Galaxy has gone bleeding mad, and you, Castus, now I understand how such a creep stays alive. Let's get on-board that crazy ship."

Cantonia's eyes moisten with what would be called tears in any other woman's eyes. "Thank you, Capolla, now we're together, let's do it. And for the record, Castus isn't the only one giving up a secret. All along, my only master has been Boklung."

***

A group of yeng emerge one by one from the 'spiderhole' cover and charge towards the still-ajar cargo doors of the Arcraft. But not all the spiders have been stood down. Two spiders stand in their way, already raising their guns. Scunthope drops like a stone, and Anton staggers as a bullet rakes across the top of his head. The yeng retreat. It seems that the planned breakout has failed before it started. For a couple of minutes, Cantonia, Estrella, Finch, Reed and a wounded Anton hold the spiders' attention. They duck and dive behind heavy crates and machinery some distance from the ship and escape back into the sewers. Things seem increasingly hopeless. Reed is nearly cut in half by gunfire.

At this point of despair, Jesus Sanz arrives. He lies on the loading ramp, panting, and slowly calms his breathing. He lifts his rebuilt gun and fires. His first couple of shots go wide, but he is getting the measure of the gun. His third shot hits one of the spiders in the middle of its thorax.

The return of gunfire spurs the rest of the yeng into action. Castus and Capolla reach the spiders and drive at them with metal stakes. Soon, the wounded spider is slaughtered, and the second flees down the hangar, panicked by facing returned gunfire.

Sanz is suddenly aware that the cargo door is closing. He tries to jam one side with the gun. It disintegrates fast.

"Quick," he shouts, "all of you; anything you have to block the cargo door. Hurry."

Castus shoves a metal bar in, and several others follow suit. The hydraulic rams start to strain. First inside, Cantonia hits buttons that she prays will override the door system. She succeeds with the second bank of controls. The door begins to descend again.

Now a different race in time begins; spiders burst in a hundred metres down the hangar. Anton returns from the sewer, dragging Pugwash with him. The doors are being lifted again, as Finch drags Anton and the suvaran over the lip. Bullets ping off the metal.

"Down flat, all of you!" Athalie screams.

Castus shouts into a communicator on the wall. "This is Castus; can anybody hear me? This is Castus; a group of us are in the unpressurized cargo hold."

Jack picks up on the call. "Castus, it's good to have you on-board. We heard gunfire. Who else is with you?"

The ship rumbles and shakes as the preprogammed launch countdown reaches a key point.

"Can you hear me? Who's with you?"

"Oh, just a few old friends and this mad woman called Athalie."

"Athalie is here! Thank God. Hold on ..."

"Jack!" Athalie cries into the communicator.

"Athalie, I'm so glad you made it. How are—"

"I'm fine, Jack, we just need someone to come down and release an airlock for us. Um .... right at the back by the cargo doors. I can't wait to see you, Jack; I have some special news. I'm so excited. I'd better go; we aren't safe yet ... Sorry, I can't breathe ..."

"Athalie!"

She coughs, lets go of the phone and collapses at the same time. Finch grabs the communicator.

"Finch speaking. Don't worry, Jack. She's fine. Just send someone down to let us out before we suffocate or freeze to death."

"We're already on it. See you later."

Up in the control room, Jack turns to Stefan, "That's right, isn't it?"

"Yeah, a group's heading down to get them, and I've got some more technical minds coming up here. The 'bots are starting to get confused. If we aren't careful we'll be fighting an army of them."

"Take over, Phelia; I'm going to find Athalie." Jack pushes past Jamanuran as he steps through the door, then disappears.

Stefan beckons the mathmatician over. "The 'bots are getting agitated. How do we deal with them? They'll fight us if we don't do something."

"They're probably struggling with mathematical logic," Jamanuran replies. "They count too many of us, and we're behaving aggressively. I'll tackle the robot communications mainframe, but I need time. Expect them to start shooting. You need to think of ways of hiding people immediately." He races off.

Phelia speaks, her eyes sparkling with an idea: "What about the rear compartment above the Warp engines. Make a false floor out of storage crates, with steep steps up to it. Robots can't climb steps. Well, most of them."

"I'm on it." Stefan turns to the people nearest and shouts, "You and you, follow me."

"Finsbury," Phelia calls to a woman sitting in front of a console of dials, "you go up front with Jamu. Help him with the the robot logic problem, but first send some reassuring messages back to mission control. We have to stop the spiders aborting the count. Try to make them believe that the rebels died in the hold, and that the 'bots are running the bridge."

Suddenly, those on the bridge hear firing coming from the bowels of the ship, and seconds later the Choochin comes screaming in, shouting high-pitched gibberish and pointing back the way ze came. No one needs to understand the words to get the message.

Further down the corridor, a brass-coloured robot with blinking lights works its way forward, shooting at any human that moves. It has already killed two or three and done some damage to the ship. Halfway to the stowaways in the cargo hold, Jack finds himself blocked by the out of control 'bot.

He flicks on his wrist communicator to speak to Phelia. "I'm blocked by a 'bot soldier. I'm going to deal with it."

"No, Jack," Phelia shouts back into the communicator, "leave that to others. We're all relying on you."

"No time; concentrate on keeping the ship moving; if the countdown stops, we've had it. I'll deal with this tin-can."

"No! Jack!"

Jack drops the communicator and yanks himself around the shielding wall to the airlock he has been crouched behind. He sees a couple of dead yeng and the soldier 'bot beyond. The 'bot sees him and raises its gun. Jack is charging.

Jack is sure of covering the ground before the 'bot can level the gun on him. By the time he realises how much his still-mending wound has slowed him, it is far too late. There's a burst of fire and the 'bot walks on past Jack's prone and still body. Entering the next corridor, two more 'bots join the rampage, and the gunless humans flee before the onslaught. Somehow the Choochin remains standing unseen, tight against the wall, as the robots pass. They seem to be totally oblivious to zis existence.

Meanwhile, the great survivor, Jesus Sanz, and the other rebels now released from the hold, start closing on the fighting robots from behind. They pass other 'bots standing confused, and no doubt even more baffled by the unregistered humans now rushing past them. It is only too clear to Jesus what he needs to do. He turns towards what he knows to be a hydroponic plant-growing area, close to where Jack fell.

I must be quick, but this place is ideal. I need sulphur, lighting tubes, flash capacitors, then five minutes with my penknife and some tape. DIY EMP, and a lot of luck! What can go wrong? Geez, that guy lying there was brave charging like that. What was he hoping to achieve? Hang on, I recognise him ... Spartacus! Come on man, stop staring, move it!

Athalie, who had stayed back to help the collapsed Anton, now catches up to see the prone form of Jack. The Choochin is leaning over him, apparently trying to administer first aid.

Down the passageway, the yeng are trying to sort out a defence. Stefan has diverted a group to help him build a platform and barriers to impede robot progress. Capolla has found a couple of heavy fire axes, which he is using to disable 'bots that look to be on the point of getting over their confusion. Meanwhile, Jesus, in amongst horticultural lighting, rips components out and tapes them up in a new configuration.

Castus now takes command of those fighting, dispatching some to source weapons, and others he allocates into teams to tackle the 'bots separately. Weaker individuals are dispatched to find sheets and clothing to cover the 'bots' eyes and auditory sensors. The defence is holding for now, with various boxes piled across the passageways.

***

Meanwhile, back on the launch-viewing platforms, pandemonium spreads as word of the fighting on the Arcraft filters back. Boklung is desperately trying to keep the situation calm.

"Listen up! We don't know what is going on, but there's no need to panic. If by some fluke, dangerous parties get control of the craft, we can shoot it out of the skies at will. For now, let's keep calm. There's absolutely no threat to us at the moment. Even if the worst happens, the Arcraft has no weapons systems that can't be easily overwhelmed. We have a squadron of Zip Ten fighters standing by to destroy the craft if need be."

Ngu Clanten steps forward. "You are in command for now, Boklung, but don't try our patience. In the meantime, all none essential forces are requested to clear the area immediately. Porza, get a unit of Guarda on a transporter at once, boarding gear ready."

Boklung is guiltily hoping that zis trust in yeng hasn't blinded zis judgement.

What made me think that the yeng escapees would be able to just walk aboard? Why did I allow a battle to ensue at such a moment?

Ze looks to the sky above the spaceport, mumbling to zimself. "Sinanna, what have I done? What possessed me? I must do all I can to progress the launch. Let not my sacrifices be in vain."

Then ze raises zis voice for all to hear. "Everything will soon be under control. Who dares defy me? The launch will proceed. Let the risk be on my head."

Tarp smirks. "Don't fret so, Cingwin Boklung. My guards were very surprised to find the launch site deserted so early. I had to send in a couple of my soldiers to guard the craft."

"I withdrew the soldiers for their safety, you fool."

"Well, we'll have to see how the courts judge that, won't we?"

"You stupid interfering idiot, Tarp, you don't know what you've done."

"I have ordered your arrest, Boklung. If the yeng win control, you'll be taken straight into custody."

***

Jesus Sanz is moving through the passageways with a heavy bag of equipment. He is doing his best to close on the 'bots without being seen. Once he has gotten as close as he dares, he stands, raises both hands and, pushing the bag high over his head, walks towards the robots.

"I surrender. I surrender. I love robots. I surrender."

From the other side of the barrier, the defenders look on, spellbound, as Jesus walks right into the group of 'bots before dropping his bag. There's a small explosion, and a blinding flash of light.

"With any luck the guns are locked, gentlemen," Jesus says. "Would some of you care to come and disable these stupid machines?"

Castus speaks up: "What makes you say that, um ... comrade?"

"I am Jesus Sanz, electronics engineer, once gladiator, and now stowaway. That, gentlemen, was the timely release of an electro-magnetic pulse. Um ... I hope no vital equipment is close, because if it is it will be fried along with the guns and the robots' central processors. They are, for now at least, scrap metal."

To demonstrate the point, Jesus walks up to the nearest 'bot, and gives it a shove. It falls with an almighty crash. He then turns, a recent smile of satisfaction already dissipated. "One more thing, I'm sorry to report that Spartacus is dead."

"Never," Castus replies. "Surely not. What happened?"

In the sudden quiet after the 'bots' demise, an anguished wail is heard from further back down a parallel corridor.

From the flight deck of the Arcraft, Jamanuran watches the scene of Jesus's victory on the monitors, relieved to see that the immediate danger has passed. As instructed, a now compliant robot pilot is sending a hastily compiled message to the launch pad. Juma hopes that the Aranians at the launch control monitors don't see a penknife sticking out of the back of its partially dismantled head.

"Robots in control, repeat: robots in control. Rebellion suppressed. All is A-okay on-board Arcraft One. Goodbye, Ungoliantis, and hello to all futures. This is Chief CP45 SAM, from the bridge. Repeat, yeng rebels suppressed. Mission is go!"

Meanwhile, in a now deathly quiet passageway, the strange blue-skinned creature has two hands working inside Jack's chest cavity, as it quietly whistles a discordant melody. Is it praying, practising some strange form of resuscitation, or possibly developing its autopsy skills? Finch is holding Athalie so that she can't get in the Choochin's way.

Suddenly, the creature beckons to Finch, and as he eases forward, it grabs Athalie's hand and pulls her until she touches Jack's chest.

"Jack dying," it whispers. "I do best. He talk me, you speak him …"

"Athalie, I'm so happy to see you safe," Jack rasps. "I'm sorry I can't …"

"Jack, don't go, not now. I love you … I'm pregnant, Jack; we're having a child. Stay with us."

"That's the best news I've ever had. I love you. I think I'm dying, I see only shadows … love our young Spartacus … Spartacus lives …"

"No, don't go. You can't. I won't let you. Spartacus? Suppose it's a girl? No, you're right; Spartacus is a fine name."

"Kiss me …"

EPILOGUE: NOTES FROM ORLANDO

Yes, the narrative is over, but this story raises some important questions that I will now address.

We are clearly in a unique universe with its own periodic rhythms. However, even a time-lord can't say exactly where the Annun Universe sits in the framework of space. I can go anywhere, but can never construct more than crude diagrams of small bits of the Multiverse. Anyway, all correlations are subject to constant change. There is no known map of 'Everywhere in Time'. Such an overview is God stuff, way beyond the comprehension of any known sentient designs.

Would humans, themselves, ever treat a perceived to be less-intelligent life-form any better than the Aranian did in this 'time'? Almost certainly not. Humans might debate the ethics of sending a breeding family of chimpanzees on a vast journey across space, but if progress indicated any possible advantage in doing so, then it almost certainly would be done. I'm sure mankind would say, "Bye-bye chimps." Have Aranian or Cheetan ever enslaved their own in the way humans have? Never; only man can treat other men as beasts of burden, as animals, or even as objects.

I have a broad idea about what is 'presently' likely to happen in the future, although inevitably details change as time shifts. So I'm quite unable to make a truly authoritative prediction about what happens on the micro level to Arcraft One. There are always an infinity of futures to look through. I can only guess from what is currently likely.

Perhaps later I'll find 'time' to look, to see what becomes of Athalie and her Spartacus, but not now. I can't afford to be distracted from other important events in my present tense. What I can say with a high degree of certainty about the macro of the story is that the Aranian colonisation won't run exactly as even Boklung plans. As for the broad picture, I will go as far as to say that the destinies of Homo-sapiens and Aranian appear to be joined into the distant future, whatever scenarios I consider, in whatever time-worms I have visited.

I claim that Aranian really have no less, and may well have more, 'sentient morality' than humans. What about me, would I think or act so very differently if I was a member of a sentient population in this story? I doubt it. What real choices has a species got when a home planet gets too small, or polluted, or reaches the end of its physical timeline? What species would consider itself to be any less special? Eventually, one must quite simply colonise another world, or die. And what species would take such a broadminded view of sentience, unless through finding the fluky leadership of a visionary like Boklung? What choice did my once people have but to attempt abandoning Gallifrey? Why didn't my people just quietly accept the dominion of the near invincible Cyborgs? I will always regret that, more than anything else, it was arrogance, their self-important belief that they came first before God, that doomed my people. They really thought that God would guard His unique chosen, failing to grasp that they were far from unique and not even particularly useful.

I really want to believe that man is an important part of the mathematical order of the Multiverse, not just a temporary by-product of biological arithmetic in an isolated region of space. Mankind is hopefully always to be a player in 'The Everything' of God's Creation. Don't all higher creatures need to believe they will survive time? Isn't that the very core of religion, the ultimate hope behind prediction, the essence of science fiction? Um ... I can only see that my race weren't seen as crucial; well, except just possibly as source 'minds', 'souls' to create a few time-lords, um, 'dirtbugs'.

I would risk ultimately destroying myself if I tried to really intervene and permanently change any fundamental path. I alluded to this in the prologue. That is so because all creatures are connected through the great vortex of space-time. If I change your history in any fundamental way, then by some infinitesimal degree I may have altered my own. That tiny change could, theoretically and eventually, alter everything that will ever happen. I didn't for this reason intervene to save Jack, though I did, I admit, direct many of his moments. I also intervened in the thinking of Clanten and Hosk, Cantonia and even eventually Capolla. But actually, Boklung was almost entirely zis own Aranian.

Luckily, the flapping of a butterfly wing usually fails to move even the air around a grain of sand, let alone starting a chain reaction of movement that changes everything. But there's always a risk, and sometimes a need. If I had true control over the fundamentals of time, I would be as God. I'm not, I'm infinitely less. What is more, I would rather be the butterfly without a single conscious thought, than a time-lord that did lasting damage.

Of course, the only principle in this history that definitely had no real independence of thought was the writer. As I explained earlier, many writers spend a lot of time in a transient state. All I have done is give the author future fact while carefully maintaining his belief that he is writing fiction. This very tiny intervention is allowed only because it fails to upset the balance of time, or because a higher being actually directed me. Of course, I don't know which of these two hypotheses is true. We have returned to the impossibility of assessing any degree of free will.

All I know is that as sentients we need to feel we have at least some limited freedom, because what exactly would be the point of our conscious existence if everything was ordained? There wouldn't be any, would there? Life has to be about more than a sterile inevitability, more than painting by numbers. The alternative is that conscious existence is no more than a disease, an isolated carbuncle growing in the fabric of a mathematical Cosmos, which has a singular and calculable destiny. Ultimately, the disease would likely be overcome, rather than permanently change anything.

I can't accept that I am either a part in a running computer programme or worse, just a sentient virus, any more than you can. For all practical purposes, I see the future as being as fluid, as unpredictable as a properly shuffled pack of cards. If everything is just inevitable, totally predictable, perfectly balanced mathematics, then there is no point to thought. There need not then be even any belief in God. Gads, I hope there's some sort of free will.

I believe I can see constant changes that I have freely created. Despite everything I have said, perhaps the truth is totally the contrary. Perhaps absolutely nothing at all is inevitable. Not even your death or my continued existence. Perhaps, when we really get to the point when this book happens, then Jack will live beyond the story, even though he doesn't yet.

Above all, if you are human, I hope you are pleased to see that your species has a future brighter than many would have predicted from the battle-scarred tower blocks, the inequalities and cruelties of the twenty-first Christian century . . .

I, Orlando Oversight, say, "Nothing ever truly dies, nothing is ever truly lost, everything ever created is somewhere, waiting on this or some other time-worm in the infinity we call time."

Of course, that isn't all good, is it? Because, just as all 'good' is preserved, then so is all 'evil'. I, Orlando, deal with that by believing that the God is Good; that, ultimately, the greatest force in the Multiverse will always be Good. Jack isn't all good, in fact he is often little more than a particularly bloodthirsty killer. Even Athalie isn't all good, or else she would have been unable to abandon her sister, or kill another being. Likewise, none of the characters are purely evil, not one of them.

All we can say is that science fiction hopefully does what it is born to do: namely, change expectations. The written word, as does all communication, plays its part in the air around the butterfly's wing. Thanks for getting this far, even if you skipped all the way from the cover to here. Richard needs a coffee; it is time to free this biological dictating machine ...

COMPENDIUM OF FACTS

Aranian and yeng words.

Annun Universe— The universe we live in.
Arckraft— Spacecraft made for distant missions.
Bluur Valley— Valley of the Bluur River.
Cantonia— Expert tracker. One of the posse chosen by Boklung
Capolla— Gladiator that led the cage after Jack was wounded.
Cheetan— The 10-legged species that has a civilisation on the planet Trogaffin.
Choochin— Blue-skinned creature with three arms and three legs.
Cingwin Boklung— Owner of Spakron Gardens.
Cirithia— Aranian capital.
Clamfusk— Managing director of Gantri Amphitheatre.
Crinklow— The planet gloot come from.
Cycle— One thousand Ungolian-days; sixteen Earth-years.
Dancharis— Satellite town to Cirithia. The next nearest town to Cirithia.
Dodark— Six-legged herbivorous species.
Doonlau— A band of forest east of Cirithia.
Drabbets— Rabbit/rat-like creatures.
Dunkuin— A governor of the Gantri Amphitheatre.
Eruvata— Holy book.
Esterpharn Caves— Caves where Jack lives.

Estellathree— Herbalist-Medical skills, beautiful. In the posse.
Finestorian Asteroid Cluster— A disputed asteroid belt.
Freedom Valley— What Jack calls the Bluur Valley.
Foulter— Guinea-pig-like scavenger.
Gallifrey— The home planet of several Time-Lords, (Dr Who,
TV series).
[I give full credit to all those creators of the TV series that have
given this planetary name to popular culture.]
Gantri Amphitheatre— Named for the Trigan Empire of Mike
Butterworth
Genscieu Institute— Bred the Type-Two yeng.
Gloot— Silicate life-form used in construction.
Godolinium— Rare mineral, not found on Ungoliantis.
Grace— Domestic slave of Boklung's.
Hazzarmanders— Pack animals, a bit like very fierce armadillos.
Hippotion— Intoxicating drug.
Hostagrifonta— Neighbouring city-state.
Huigark Hosk— Cheetan Ambassador.
Huis— Ungol month—Roughly.
Jack Baker— Spartacus.
Joy Reed— Acquaintance of Jack's from the slave ship. One of
the posse.
Induna River— Flows through Cirithia.
Kármán line— Boundary between planetary atmosphere and
outer-space.
Kasterborous Constellation— (Dr Who, TV series).
[I give full credit to all those creators of the TV series that have
given this name to popular culture.]
Koolsverne— Physically strong and intellectual. One of the
posse.
Kraccus— Small satellite town to Cirithia.
Krisk— Town in Hostagrifonta.
Lebl Clanten— Heir of Ngu Clanten. Chosen sexual partner of
Boklung.
Lush— The local solar-system.
Mollash— A spherical creature that can grow almost any number
of limbs.

Nagawads— Snake-like creatures.

Nuzkarflux Spaceport— The main port for the city of Cirithia.

Nin Tarp— Chief Prosecutor.

Ngu Clanten— Speaker of the Council of Cirithia.

Norsboklin Hangar— The biggest spacecraft hangar in the region.

Octad— An Ungolian 'week'. Roughly 46 Earth-days.

Octate— Eight of something.

Oktig— The octal counting system's equivalent of percentage.

Orflandis Hiygleest— Cheetan Trade Commissioner.

Orlando Oversight— Time-Lord, and this book's 'convener'.

Osterphelia— Foremaid of the Spakron Gardens.

Peter Finch— The old man of the posse.

Pinardos— Aranian electronics engineer.

Pontarii— Commander of the city Garda.

Posheenian— Senior Councillor and serious substance abuser.

Pretorienza Tree— Large willow-like blue flowered tree.

Prortung— Admiralty employee seconded to the state law courts.

Rapawaira Hills— Rolling 'grassy' hills—grazed by herds of Dodarks.

Retreat— Sleep period for humans

Salvius 7— Class of slave ship.

Scandium— A rare mineral not found on Ungoliantis.

Screebur— Four-legged hairless creatures similar to hyenas.

Scunthorpe— Good linguist. One of the posse

Shift— Work period; i.e. not 'retreat' for humans.

Sinanna— The shared God of Aranian and Cheetan.

Sliefnam— An artificial satellite space station. Banking services.

Solush and Ralush— The two suns.

Spakron Gardens— Boklung's business, on land zis family gifted to Cirithia.

Stanislav— Yeng guard in the arena.

Storvarn— Works in The Gardens' hot-houses.

Suvaran— Heavily built lizard-like creature. Pugwash.

TARDIS— The Dr Who has simply had such a vast influence on popular culture and particularly on me that I felt unable to avoid mention of Dr Who's mode of travel. I fully acknowledge the use of others' intellectual invention.

Timartaeafok— Earth in Aranian, written phonetically. Waterball, in translation.

Triffid— Creature influenced by John Wyndham. Real name, Wertutututua.

Tristian Marshes— To the south of the Forest of Doonlau.

Trogaffin— Another planet in the Lush system. The home of the Cheetan, Hosk.

Tragoranashmeed— An outer planet of the Lush System.

Troskiatin— A city on Trogaffin.

Turvult— Vulture-like flying beast.

Uccinipose Ulocinas— A Cheetan astrophysicist.

Ungoliantis— The Aranian home planet; acknowledgment to J.R. Tolkien.

Urtain Transporter— Huge cargo-carrying spacecraft.

Ushkeenz— Chief Engineer on the 'New Frontier' project, and assassin.

Uskistan— Chief Executive of Norsbo and owner of the Norsboklin Hangar.

Wertutututua— A 'triffid'-like creature. Venom that can kill yeng and Aranian.

Waterball— 'Translated' name for the Earth.

Wetbug— Fish-like creatures.

Yeng— Human.

Yargord— Huge biped creatures with elephant-like trunks.

Zoongrass— A stupefying herb. (Tribute to 'Fireball XL5'.)

Zanin— Paramilitary police.

Zyfose— Large four-legged cat-like creature. From Asgormia.

Octan Mathematics, Ungoliantis and Earth.

1000 Ungolian days=1 Ungolian cycle=16 years in Earth time. 16 (base 10) Earth-years is 20 (base 8) years.

1000 Ungolian days (base 8)=5736 Earth days. (base 10)

1Ungolian day=5.736 Earth days (base 10) 5.57 (base 8)

1 Ungolian day=20 Ungolian hours. (base 8) 16 (base 10)

1 Ungolian day=137.664 Earth hours. (base 10) 211.523 (base 8)

1 Earth year=365 days (base 10) 555 (base 8)

1 Earth day=30 Earth hours (base 8)

1 Earth day is just under 3.5 Ungolian hours.

Gravity is lower on Ungoliantis by roughly 10%. This means that the boiling point of water is 100, with an octal counting system on Ungoliantis, as it is at higher pressure on Earth, with a decimal counting system. 20 degrees on Ungoliantis can be reckoned as being 25 degrees Centigrade.

This story uses pure arithmetical counting rather than the linguistic style made popular by the USA of Earth's '20th Century'. Many humans, because of this cultural quirk, call a number followed by fifteen zeros a quadrillion, when mathematically it is only so many thousand billions. In their last centuries on Earth, many disasters resulted from confusion between different human populations as to how to logically count. It is probably just as well for mankind, at that stage, that they didn't also have to deal with the variances of octal and decimal counting systems.

A NOTE FROM THE SCRIBE

I thank you very much for reading this book, however you came upon my pages. A book that is never read is about as useful as a mot of fluff.

I'm a citizen of the United Kingdom and New Zealand, currently resident in Switzerland. My fortunate geographic locations and private circumstances have given me the time and space to throw out words like great bundles of confetti. Some must by chance fall well.

As this book goes to press, I have seven substantive books to my name, plus one gift-market book written with few words. That light tome was a collaborative invention compiled with two other authors. I've many short stories appearing in a number of anthologies. My novels are all speculative science fiction while my short pieces cover many genres. I've also written 'modern' English language versions of French neoclassical plays that spouted from some quite different region of my author personality.

Details on all my writing, including free stories and 'bloggins', plus my reviews of many other writers' works, can be found at:-

http://richardbunningbooksandreviews.com

If you have any questions, they can be posed directly to me through the contact form on that site. I'll do my best to welcome them all.

Kind regards, Richard Bunning.